ROMANNO BRIDGE

ROMANNO BRIDGE

Andrew Greig

Quercus

First published in Great Britain in 2008 by

Quercus
21 Bloomsbury Square
London
WC1A 2NS

A CIP catalogue record for this book is
available from the British Library

ISBN (HB) 978 1 84724 315 7
ISBN (TPB) 978 1 84724 316 4

10 9 8 7 6 5 4 3 2 1

Printed and bound in Great Britain by
Clays Ltd, St Ives Plc.

To Dibby Greig, for everything.

'There ain't no journey what don't change you some'

Huckleberry Finn

Closing

A man on a motorbike finally came to the end of the road.

He sat astride contemplating gate, padlock, chain. Once he would have felt compelled to do something about those. Instead he switched off, unstrapped his helmet and let sound in.

Eight miles into the Rothiemurchus Forest, towards the end of a short winter's day, the world was quiet. No human voices, no birdsong, just a hiss of water from melting snow, damp wind seeping through pines.

He got stiffly off the bike, clipped the helmet over the handle-bars, climbed the gate and walked up the snowy path through the dark wood. He wore camouflage trousers and jacket but did not look like a soldier – at least, not from a war that anyone had won. After a hundred yards he paused, tossed the ignition key into the undergrowth and trudged on.

When he knew himself truly lost, he stopped to unsling the old pack over his back. Fumbling with leather-encased hands, he pulled out a jiffy bag containing letters and photos he could keep no longer. He hesitated, turning the bag over and over, then dropped it into the peaty ooze under an uprooted tree.

He took a smaller path, then a smaller one off that. At a ghostly intersection he stood in the rapidly fading light, pulled off his gloves and hurled one after the other into the darkness under the trees.

A while later, he unstrapped his watch, dropped it without breaking stride. He had no further need of time.

The last days had been a matter of discarding, in order, the few

I

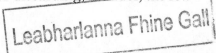

remaining things that mattered to him. There was little left now. The pack was empty so he hung it dark and drooping on a branch, like a shot crow left by gamekeepers.

In the end the trail just petered out. For a while he pushed and shouldered and stumbled his way on through the dense scraping pines, feeling the welts rise on his hands and cheeks, feeling something at least. The ground rose a little and tight-knit firs gave way to a stand of leafless birch. Somewhere far off a pheasant gargled into silence.

This was the place. He put his hand out and sank into the thick bank of dead leaves that had built up in the lee of a ruined wall from some long-disintegrated estate. The leaves were cool, wet, soft. His first memories had been of lying under trees, big old trees, a rough trunk trembling against his back as the wind blew.

Lying on his side he dug down to where the leaves were dry. When the hollow was deep enough, he rolled into it, lay on his back and with a vague swimming motion swept the leaves over himself till everything but his face was covered.

His numb right hand unzipped the breast pocket of his old leather jacket and felt inside. Working in the near-dark, he opened the little box, took out the pill. He wiped a fragment of leaf from his lower lip, felt the cool metal of the ring which had brought him to this, then swallowed.

He closed his eyes and swept dead leaves across his face.

PART ONE

I CAN HEAR THE WHISTLE, BUT I CAN'T SEE THE TRAIN

I

Kirsty Fowler woke with the premonition of a whisky hangover then stumbled to the bathroom. Dawn was cracking open, first light ran down over the slates and chimneypots then flowed onto the river to be carried westwards toward the sea. The world was silent, as yet unsullied, about to begin again.

Got so much loving locked up inside of me.

She shook her head – let me not turn into a love-wimp! – turned away from the window, swallowed paracetemol, made tea and went back to bed. Alone, in bedsocks, and nothing wrong with that.

In a few hours she must make a decision that would change her wayward life. One good man was dead already, and at thirty-one she was not yet too old to die young, so she had to get it right. *If he offered ten thousand, it must be worth a lot more.*

She propped herself up on pillows, drank tea and stared at the wall opposite, off-white and grainy as an old cinema screen, and sought guidance from the journey so far.

* * *

Maybe she had moved to Dumfries because she needed to lie low for a while after that business in the Highlands, and the douce, respectable town seemed the right place for it. On arrival she talked her way to the editor of the local paper, showed him some of her recent work. He glanced at them, the by-lines, the exclusives, the mastheads of the papers she'd placed the fake Macnab story with.

'You should be in London, lassie,' he said. 'Not wi the likes of us. This is a local paper, not a stepping stone.'

He stood up, interview over. She kept sitting, ignoring the file he was trying to hand back to her.

'All life is local,' she said. 'I'll do a couple of pieces on spec, and if you like them, give me the job. You know you want to.'

'Kirsty, nothing very much happens round here.'

She had to grin at that. She'd once said that herself, and it hadn't stayed true long.

'Suits me fine,' she said. 'I've only one condition.'

He raised his eyebrows at that. They were thick and near white, which made her wonder about his dark hair. A bit vain, then. And the way he looked at her gave her something to work on.

'You're a bit of a chancer, aren't you?' he said.

'Chance is a fine thing, if you give it a chance,' she replied. He looked at her enquiringly. 'Just something a friend of mine picked up in Nepal. My condition is you keep my name off any by-line. I've no desire to advertise myself.'

He sat back down and stared at her.

'I've heard it all now,' he said. 'I've been in this trade for thirty years and I've never heard someone ask *not* to have a by-line.'

His fingers strayed over her file. Outside the rain drifted onto the wide slow river. She thought of another river, another man, one who didn't dye his hair, who'd said he loved her, as though a game wasn't just a game. Not for her.

'I've read your stories long before today,' Willie Kincaid said slowly. 'About how the John Macnab caper was all just a security training exercise, and no deer was ever poached at Balmoral, and HRH had nothing to do with it. I'm sure I believe every word.'

His eyelid flickered, just a hint of a grin at the edge of his mouth, and she realized she'd probably underestimated him and that working here could have its moments. So she said nothing, just sat there in his office grinning back at him. His big hand spread and relaxed on her file. He swivelled his chair and looked out at the river as though there was something there other than time passing.

'You're a bit of a hooligan, aren't you?'

'Sometimes you've got to be a bit of a hooligan to get a seat at the window.'

He laughed and she knew she had him. He stood up and reached a battered trilby off the hat-stand.

'Spot of lunch and we'll talk about it,' he said.

His hat had a couple of fishing flies snecked in it, Blue Zulus, she thought. A brief memory flash of Lachlan, the ghillie with whom she'd passed the odd happy hour, as he showed her through his fly-box. So they walked by the river, crossed over the old bridge, talking all the while. By the time they reached his pub she'd got the job and had stopped thinking on the Highlands, that eventful summer and the pals she'd left. Which suited her just fine.

The secret to being free, she reminded herself as she walked home alone that night, is knowing when the party is at its height – then leaving.

Dumfries is a quiet and largely respectable market town. And Willie Kincaid was right, nothing too much happened there. Nothing wrong with that – just ten miles down the road was Lockerbie. Being hot news is not necessarily good.

So she rented a small flat near the river, found a decent eating place and a couple of charitable pubs, and made the beginnings of a life. She had the tweeds from last summer's adventures cleaned and repaired, and sent them back, without her address, to a man who didn't know when to leave the party. She tried to reform her hooligan ways. She missed her dog but it didn't seem fair to Shonagh or the hound to send for him now. A bit of loneliness is good for the character.

If anyone had asked, she'd have said she was cooling off. Hiding out, if you must. The moment Neil Lindores admitted he loved her, the panic had started in her blood. He didn't know what he was saying. Maybe he did, but he'd said it to the wrong person.

She had to forget that he'd touched her like he'd known her for ever. Like he wanted to know her more and more. Better to go down to the pub, see new friends, drink and laugh and flirt awhile, then go home alone by the river run. And she did. For months in that quiet town she was a reformed character.

And then Life, that remorseless hound, sniffed her out, as it usually does no matter where you hide, even in Dumfries.

She had been doing a feature about care homes in the county. Seemed like everyone wanted to come to Dumfriesshire to peg out. A human interest piece, strictly non-political, Kincaid had warned her. His paper didn't do politics. There was human interest there all right, though much of it was painful and she felt queasy about mining the sorrow of it.

Maybe that's why Kirsty went back to see Billy Mackie a second time, because he'd made her laugh. He'd been a stonemason in Glasgow, apprenticed there in the fifties after his National Service, had a fund of stories that were enough to let her forget awhile he was dying of emphysema from the dust (and a forty a day habit).

She went back to see him on a December evening with a bottle of Grouse in one hand and a tape recorder in the other. He seemed pleased enough to see her in the small pallid green room his world had shrunk to. They had a couple of drams and his eyes began to light up. They'd got to talking about fakes and frauds, both people and the things they made. About how easy it was to pass things off if one had the nerve and the punter was keen enough to believe.

He told her a story about a stuffed greyhound, and she came back to him with a version of how she'd once lured part of the British army and Deeside constabulary into taking her for a man in tweeds, and that a man who'd never existed in the first place. Of course, she'd promised never to tell, and signed official papers to that effect, but it was clear Billy Mackie wouldn't be around long enough to pass it on.

He liked it. As she enlarged on her story, he laughed till laughter turned into a choking cough that hurt as much in her chest as his. He gestured her back into her chair and took another drink once he'd stopped coughing. Then he went quiet and distant and she thought maybe it was time to leave.

He put his glass down on the table firmly, like he'd made up his mind.

'Are you a patriot, lass?'

'No, I'm a refugee,' she said, wondering what had brought this on.

'Whit?'

'I'm not really from anywhere. Dad in the army, Forces child-hood, all that. Aden, the Rock, West Germany.' Her standard answer, true in its way.

He looked at her sceptically. Old milky eyes, cataracts she sup-posed. Bit of mischief in them yet.

'Are ye a patriot?' he repeated.

She sighed. It was one of those 'Have you stopped beating your husband?' questions.

'My country is 5 ft 10 ins high and I'd die for its independence.'

'Quite right. Never had much time for patriotism myself. It was *Das Kapital* on my mind as a young man, not thistles. An inter-nationalist, right? Tear doun the borders and lets have the inter-national brotherhood of man! We got it in the end, except the global economy is not exactly whit we had in mind. History, eh?'

He stopped and coughed till her stomach turned and his eyes watered. She moved towards the oxygen cylinder by his chair but he waved her back.

At length he stuffed away his hankie and looked into his glass, sipped.

'I was no patriot then, but there were those who were. Like the master at the staneyard, Andrew Jamieson. Now Andrew was thick as thieves with a bunch of them, red hot for Independence, aye meeting and plotting. Maistly blethering and drinking, if the truth be told! Ye'd hae thought Scotland was Helen of Troy the way some folk sighed over her, but they were hot to trot and ripe for mischief. I thought it was just talk, just dreamers haivering. But I was wrong, it wasna all guff...'

He tailed off and looked over her shoulder at the wall. He was looking back down the years, and she was scarcely there. But she was listening all right, leaning forward, willing him to keep going, because she could smell it. There was a story here. Maybe not a big one, but a true one. Something that mattered enough to stay with a man all his life.

She was wrong. It wasn't so much a story that he'd kept buried for fifty years, more of an unexploded bomb from an old war, buried in some allotment and now as he was dying the worms were pushing it to the surface. As he looked up at her, she could see the glint of its shell casing in his eyes.

'Can I trust you, lassie? Can I trust ye?' he said urgently.

'You can trust me to pour whisky and keep my trap shut.'

He chuckled, pushed his glass towards her. She filled it till he extended his big flattened fingers and then she stopped. He picked up the glass and peered down into its gold-brown depths as he spoke, as much to it as her.

'I'm not asking for your silence, lass,' he said. 'I've never told this tae another living soul – except for my wife Alison and she's lang gone and I'll be joining her soon enough...'

There was nothing she could say to that. Couldn't tell him some bright polite lie. His death was there in that poky room, it was on the table between them. So she raised her glass to him.

'Whatever you have to tell me, Mr Mackie—'

'Bill,' he said. 'Billy.'

'You can trust me Billy to...' She hesitated. She'd always tried very hard not to make promises she couldn't be sure to keep. So she seldom made promises at all.

'...to do whatever it is you want done with whatever you have to tell me,' she finished lamely. 'Except maybe forget it or you. Cheers.'

Now he looked up at her, all bright-eyed, and for a moment she could see the young man he must have been, passionate and funny and honest, and almost envied Alison. There's not many of them about, the ones ready to put their whole heart on the line, and she'd left one. He smiled, a big slow smile spread across the pain of his dying.

'Christ you're a one,' he said. 'I'll trust you to know whit to do with what I'm about tae tell ye. God knows I never did.' A long pause then he raised his glass to her or to something, the past maybe, raised it high like a proper toast.

'The Moon Runners!' he cried. And then he drank, just a measuring sip. He wasn't pissed, it's important to know that. He knew what he was saying, and told it carefully as a bomb disposal expert scraping soil away from that big ticking secret found among the cabbages.

2

Billy Mackie's story

Andrew Jamieson was a master stonemason with his yard on the South bank of the Clyde. A decent, skilled, respected man, with a weakness only for whisky and nationalist politics. After a couple of approaches, the young apprentice William Mackie made it clear his allegiance lay elsewhere and it was left at that. The two never socialized; it wasn't done for master and apprentice.

So he was fair astonished when three days after Christmas in 1950, nine o'clock on a freezing night, his landlady knocked on his door and let in Andrew Jamieson. He had on a heavy coat and scarf and held his bunnet in his hands, turning it nervously as he approached the purpose of his call.

'I need your help, lad. It's a... difficult matter.'

Billy stared at him. Said sure he'd help, no bother.

Jamieson just stood there, turning his cap and smelling of whisky. Not drunk but he'd definitely had a couple.

'Are you a patriot, young Mackie?'

Seemed a daft question, so Billy just shrugged.

'I'm no friend of the State,' he said.

The older man looked at him steadily, then nodded. Billy had never seen him so agitated and uncertain. Then Jamieson came out with it.

'There's no one else I can trust who can work stane, and it has to be tonight.'

'Can it no wait till the morn?'

'Not this stane. It's like... borrowed. I'll pay ye double time – and you'd be doing your country a service.'

William Mackie stared at his master. And then he knew.

'Oh man, you havena got it?'

'I have that.'

William Mackie burst out laughing. He was still shaking his head and chuckling as he strapped his work boots on. His heart was beating faster, as a young man's should at the prospect of a bit of adventure. Though it hadn't quite been said yet, he knew Andrew Jamieson had only gone and got the Stone of Destiny, lately stolen from under the throne in Westminster, that all the polis in the country were after.

The stoneyard was bright with frost, the moon high and bone-white, casting stumpy shadows from the tombstones stacked along the wall. The blank ones gave the young man the willies, like one day he'd turn and see his name on one of them. The night was silent in the way cold nights are, even when there's a swish from the Clyde and a lone tyke barking. William Mackie shivered while the master fumbled with his keys, then they were through the gate and into the yard.

Jamieson hurried to the big shed, unlocked it, pushed Willie in and closed and padlocked the door behind them both. He shone his torch onto a pile of dustsheets.

'Right lad, cover the windows.'

Then he switched on the main light. In the centre of the work-shop on a pallet was a heavy green tarpaulin spread over a box-like shape. Jamieson looked at him with a smile that may have been apologetic or maybe embarrassed at his own excitement. Who can know, now they're all dust? But for certain he did smile, then with one big yank pulled the tarp away.

On a pallet sat a block of rough sandstone, with a rough cross on the upper. To Billy's eye it hadn't been finished off at all.

'So this is it? The Stone of Destiny? No awfy well done, is it?'

He thought the master might be offended, but he nodded and hunkered down by the stone, still in his overcoat.

'It's in far worse shape now, lad.'

The far corner of the Stone was broken off. A fair sized chunk lay apart from the body of it.

'He was aye a clumsy bauchle,' Jamieson grunted. 'It happened when they pulled it out frae under the English throne.'

'So you want me to mend it? Nae bother.'

Jamieson swivelled and looked at him. His eyes were in shadow and something in their hollows made Billy uneasy, and for the first time he realized that this caper could have serious consequences.

'What we're going to do tonight is make twa copies. Then we break them, like this wan here. But you leave the final mending to me, right?'

Copies, that's what the master mason said. Young Billy liked the ploy. With the whole country gone mad looking for the Stone, Billy could guess what he was up to. But even as they set about preparing two unformed sandstone blocks alongside the original, he had a notion Jamieson was keeping something from him. There was surely some juggling still to come before the night was out.

As young Billy worked through the night shaping up two rough copies of the stone, the master seemed more than nervous as he prowled up and down the workshop checking the length of the bronze mending rods, trimming them to size.

Twice Jamieson seemed about to say something, then closed his mouth and went back to his workbench. He was bent over a sheet of parchment, his forearm across the paper like a schoolboy hiding his working. Then he picked up the phone, dialled, waited. At that time of night?

'You got it safely hame? No, they havena a clue.' He listened, said 'Good enough', then abruptly put the phone down.

Billy bent over his work. He used the excuse of going back to the original stone to keep a closer eye. Jamieson spread the roll of parchment, Mason's ring on one hand, his old crescent-shaped one on the other. He took a sharp knife and cut the paper into three. Then he slipped the black fountain pen from his waistcoat pocket and wrote. It can't have been much, a line or two at most, but he wrote something on all the rolls. Something different on each one. Billy was sure about that. Forty-five years later he leant forward and wagged a big gnarly forefinger at Kirsty: 'All different. Mind that, lass.'

It was six in the morning by the time the three stones were lined up alongside each other, ready to reassemble. The bronze rods that would act as dowels were in place. The two men stood looking down at them in the lamp light. Billy was privately disappointed how small and poor the stones looked. That the ancient throne of Scotland? A man would look plain ridiculous sitting on yon, knees up about his ears.

Eventually Jamieson sighed and stirred. He seemed weary and troubled.

'I dinna trust them,' he muttered. 'It's jist a lark to some these days.'

He went over to the workbench and came back holding three rolled tubes of paper. One was to be hidden inside the Westminster Stone alongside the rods, to certify that it was indeed the one taken from the Abbey.

'So what's to happen to the right Stone?'

'Nivver you mind, laddie.'

'And the other yins?' Billy persisted. 'What do the papers say?'

'That the others are a copy. A fake, right?' Billy nodded, waited. Jamieson swung his troubled head and looked him straight on. 'But mair than that—'

The sound of a car engine in the silent night. It coughed and spluttered, slowed. Headlights stained the curtained windows. The car came into the yard. Stopped.

The master and the apprentice looked at each other. A muffled series of thumps on the locked door. Then again.

'A minute!' Jamieson cried. He thrust one paper at Billy.

'Fit it inside, laddie, then close up wi cement. Now!'

Billy slid his paper in the gap alongside the dowel, aware the master was feverishly doing the same with his stone. Then the third while the low thumping on the door began again.

'Out the back, son. Better you dinna see this.'

Billy nodded. Was picking up his jacket and cap as Jamieson opened the door. In the shadow of the back door at the far end of the shed, Billy looked back, saw two men in coats and hats, and behind them a smaller person, a woman perhaps. A murmur of voices, quite educated sounding. The last thing he saw were the three stones lined up on the trestles, and already he wasn't sure which was which. Then he was hurrying home through the streets with the first milk carts and workers heading for the shipyards, his mind birling with the final words old Jamieson had whispered to him in that rush before the door opened, like a man about to spew and unable hold back longer.

'The *real* Crowning Stone, Columba's Pillow, lad – these fools have forgotten it ever existed. I've sent it hame.'

3

On her half-day, Kirsty drove to Edinburgh to do some research in
the National Library, as though she were a real journalist not a
fraud. She spent a couple of hours speed-reading in the Reference
Room. She scribbled down references, names and possibilities,
most of them ending with ??, or exasperated !!. It seemed that
anything about the Stone of Scone that went beyond basic facts
moved in a world of wish fulfilment, self-delusion, and perhaps
deliberate misleading. She had personal experience of all these,
and it was a theme not without interest, but there was nothing
solid for her there.

She went into the newspaper section and hurried through old
editions of the *Scotsman*. The Westminster theft on Christmas
Eve 1950 was all there. What a fuss it had raised, how many
gleeful or condemnatory speeches, letters, rants and sermons! The
essence of it backed up Billie Mackie's story. Copies had been
made, possibly by a Glasgow stonemason and keen nationalist.
She found hints and suggestions that the recovered stone wasn't
the original one taken from Westminster Abbey, but nothing
more, no mention of another Stone that pre-dated them all.
Cross-referencing, she found various suggestions as to where the
original Westminster one might now be if not in the Abbey, and
noted them down with diminishing enthusiasm.

She wasn't cut out for research in libraries, wasting her eye-
sight on old paper and blurry microfiche. Out in the wide world,
that was where real things happened. Then she found a passing
reference to a much more recent work, which took her down
shelves dripping with dead wood, fingers moving along the

bound issues of *The Proceedings of the Society of Scottish Antiquarians*.

The light outside was already fading as she flicked through 'The Stone Behind the Stone', a recent scholarly article by one P.B. Sidlaw of Crieff. It argued for the existence of something else altogether, the *real* Crowning Stone, aka the Destiny Stone, aka Columba's Pillow or Jacob's Pillow. It was a far more ancient coronation stone, one that may have been a travelling altar of the earliest Christian missionaries. Her attention sharpened. Sidlaw's argument – based on measurements, representations on royal seals, descriptions of the time – seemed credible. The tone was rational, reasonable, and sounded like the work of a historian not a fantasist. For instance, he thought 'Jacob's Pillow' just sheer myth-making and textual confusion.

She was struck by the phrases: 'the *real* Crowning Stone', 'Columba's Pillow'. The same words Billy had given to Andrew Jamieson in his story of that freezing night, the mason's yard, the master shoving clues as to where the Westminster Stone was headed alongside brass dowels into the stones, and then turning to him at the last minute and saying, 'The *real* Columba's Pillow, lad – *I sent it hame.*'

Mackie said he'd no idea where *hame* might be. She'd believed him, yet she had the sense he was keeping something back. In any case, this Stone sounded far more significant, ancient, potent and valuable than the sandstone slab taken to Westminster by Edward I.

She sat in the Reference Room, one desk among many, with the sense of many minds pursuing their own obsessions. That's what we do when something hooks us from the daily bore. We become interested, then obsessed. Possibly a bit screwy. So many ways of getting lost in this life.

So many ways of getting life back! She took the article to the photocopying counter so she could read the rest of it later. To find and prove the existence of the Destiny Stone, now that would be something. But how, after nearly fifty years?

Coming from the library, too near the Law Courts, she saw an advocate and paralegal she knew from the old days. She hurried across the road, narrowly missed being flattened by a speeding 42 bus, and heard someone call the name she no longer went by. She found herself diving down Candlemaker Row, clutching her files. Which took her through the Grassmarket, taking the long way back round to her car, and up the gloomy West Port, and there she passed the secondhand bookshop, and on impulse she went in and asked if they had anything on the true Destiny Stone.

The man behind the counter, not looking up from his book, pointed towards the back of the shop, low down.

'Nothing there but fiction,' he murmured.

All she came out with was a distinctly greasy paperback novel from the seventies by one Alan B. Stewart, rejoicing in the title of *The Wondrous Stone*. The lurid cover featured a large carved purple rock that seemed to be steaming slightly in its crypt, with a group of cowled monks eyeing it uncertainly. Outside, on top of a hill, an improbable, inflated moon shone down on a woman with similar breasts; in the background towered an abbey with a strangely plastic-looking gold crown hovering over its implausible spires.

So much for research. She dropped the book and notes onto the back seat. Just one more lead to check out, then home. She started up and headed out of Edinburgh on the way to Dull.

The phone call came a week later. She'd just got back from the office after filing copy on a fresh round of local council cock-ups, plus a story about a pet rabbit that had been reported stolen but had later been anonymously returned, unharmed. News that week had indeed been thin on the ground, and she could only hope a few discerning readers would find the rabbit nonstory as pointless and sweet as she did.

She banged shut the door of her bolt hole and grabbed the phone. She'd given very few this number. A wheezy, breathless voice.

'Lass, I'd be grateful if you'd come see me.'

Billy Mackie. She felt a dirk of guilt dig in under her missing rib. She should have visited. She should have done more research. *The Wondrous Stone* still lay unread by her bedside all the nights she'd lain undiscovered in her bed.

'How about tomorrow evening, Mr Mackie?'

A pause, a hesitation at the other end of the line. Some warning stirred in her gut.

'Now would be better.'

She picked up her tape-recorder, notebook and a bottle, and was out the door. It had not been the casual request of a lonely man.

She buzzed the warden. Marnie Wilson, a big woman with sturdy sconemaking forearms, nodded as she let Kirsty in.

'Seems Billy is having a party this evening. A fella went up just five minutes back.'

Kirsty ran up the stairs, collected herself a moment then pressed the buzzer. Billy had sounded like a man trying to be calm. She called his name then buzzed again.

The door opened so suddenly she nearly fell into the man standing there. She recoiled. In an elongated, shaven head, his eyes were very pale and full of light, like holes had been punched through from some blaze inside. He wore a blue suit, wasn't tall, and she didn't like him.

'I've come to see Billy Mackie.'

'Mr Mackie doesn't want to see anyone.'

The man stood blocking the way in.

'I'm his niece, and he certainly wants to see me.'

He hesitated, his eyes flicked past her into the empty corridor.

'Come in, then.'

The voice was neutral, flat, and she couldn't place the accent. Angry men she could deal with, but control was more worrying. She went in.

Billy was sitting in his old armchair, his face grey, oxygen cylinder on its little gallows behind him.

'What's going on here?'

Her voice was nearly level. Now she was in the room, the man moved between her and the door.

'This mannie here – says he's called Adamson – wants to buy ma ring.' Billy held up his right hand, waggled his index. That odd crescent ring of his. 'I've tellt him it's no for sale.'

'Quite right too, Uncle Bill.'

The man's eyes turned full on her, his lean body bendy and tense as a whip.

'You know about the Runners? The Stone?'

'The what? I just meant if he doesn't want to sell the ring, that's his right.'

The man who called himself Adamson glared, then turned back to Bill Mackie. She winced, scorched by his disbelief and his indifference.

'This is just business for me. I'm authorized to go to ten thousand.'

Kirsty instinctively stepped towards Billy.

'That's far too much.'

The man who called himself Adamson almost smiled.

'I agree, but there it is.'

She drifted closer to the armchair and casually rested one foot on the blue pressure-mat that sounded a buzzer in the warden's room.

'I meant, it's too much to be right.'

Billy nodded, summoned up some last defiance. He really doesn't look well, she thought.

'Like I said, pal, it's no for sale. I'm ower near deid for money to mean anything.'

The man with the wrong eyes tilted his head forward.

'I'm not your pal, friend.' His right arm twitched inside his jacket. She glimpsed a leather sheath and then a ten-inch hunting knife flashed out. He twirled it gently, the hooked point sharp enough to sever one molecule from another. She'd seen Lachlan gralloch a stag with one of these. One firm pull and the belly had unzipped, right down to the bowels, blood pouring out down the groove.

'The offer has been withdrawn.'

For the first time there was some animation in his voice, and she understood that this, not business, was what he truly enjoyed. She'd heard of such people without quite believing.

'Give it to him, Uncle Bill.'

Billy sagged back in his chair. He stroked the ring as if saying goodbye, then began to twist and tug at it with the other hand.

'This hasna come off in years,' he muttered. 'See and get us some soap, Kirsty lass.'

She looked at Adamson. He nodded. The knife twitched under his thumb.

'Do as he says.'

The door buzzer sounded. Kirsty stopped, everybody stopped. The buzz again.

'Mr Mackie? Are you all right? Mr Mackie?'

Billy Mackie opened his mouth and began to cough. He coughed, heaved, gasped, motioned to the oxygen mask. Without thinking, she grabbed it, was just reaching for the On/Off valve when the warden came in, pass key in her hand, summoned by the pressure-mat.

Adamson hesitated a moment. Caught in the slow of adrenaline-time, Kirsty saw him take in the ring, the finger, the Warden, herself. She saw the option and the calculation as if it were her own. The knife twitched.

Then the blade was in its holster, the warden thrown back against the wall, and the man in the blue suit was gone.

She got home very late and not sober. First there'd been looking after Billy, then waiting for the police. A simple attempted burglary, Billy insisted. The man had got in claiming to be bringing a cheque from a magazine competition, then held him up with a knife. Called himself Adamson. There'd been no mention of the ring Billy twisted on his finger as he gave his story.

Kirsty had sat quietly, watching as Sergeant Todd took notes. She could still feel the chill of that knife. Handguns were unreal, existing only in movies, but that knife had been all too credible as it twitched towards her face. Watching Billy turn the crescent ring on his finger, she knew without doubt he was lucky to still have the ring and the finger.

Then Toddie had toddled off, muttering gravely about drug addicts, saying he'd circulate the description but not to worry because the criminal wouldn't be back. Eventually the warden too went off to bed, and Kirsty and Billy were left alone in the little sitting room with her half-full bottle and two glasses on the table. She looked at him and let the silence go on till he finally looked up at her.

'Lass, I've not been entirely frank with you.'

'Well I never.'

He spread his hands, silent apology accepted by her shrug.

'I could tell ye some mair things, but they might not be good for your health.'

She poured two big drams, passed him one.

'Nor is boredom,' she said. 'So tell me.'

And when Billy had done with his explanations, and finally persuaded her to slide his charge, the one that had come from the childless Andrew Jamieson's deathbed, onto her finger where it hung loose, together they drained the last of the bottle and waited for the people Kirsty had phoned to come by to escort her to the pub.

A quick hug and promise to come back next night to hear more, then she was off to The Droukit Dug with Ken and Isa. All the way she was keeping an eye out as they walked through the streets with the ring inside her sock rubbing at her shin, but there was no neat, quick man with wrong eyes, a blue suit and a hunting knife strapped at his chest. Likely he was long gone.

Then she'd had to sit through a couple more drinks among warm human jollity, smile and respond while her brain was in another place altogether, trying to figure the next move. And

finally – don't you have homes to go to and work to do tomorrow?
– she walked with the longtime happy couple Ken and Isa (apparently such do exist) down the High Street to the river, glinting
with broken moons swept into the night. No one lurking in the
darkness under the bridge. Why would there be? She was not the
target here.

Still, she double-locked her door and checked the windows were
snibbed. She took out the ring and looked at this talisman of
some fellowship that didn't really exist any more, guarding the
whereabouts of something whose whereabouts, meaning and very
existence had been largely forgotten.

Nice stone, an unusual pale yet intense green. Peridot, she
thought. The mount was crescent shaped and quite badly
scratched. So this was a Moon Runner ring. Romantic, sure, but
daft – even Billy Mackie had said so. Andrew Jamieson had gifted
it to him on his deathbed, along with what little he knew about
the other two rings that were out there somewhere. *Columba's
Pillow, I sent it hame.*

Daft or not, this ring was dangerous to possess. She could give
it to the Scottish Museum of Antiquities, then she'd be safe. Or…

Outside, the three quarter moon was riding high through
clouds. Night, moon, wind always stirred her blood. *The Moon
Runners*. She slipped the ring onto her finger then fell into bed.
Decide tomorrow. Her last thought was: that man with Billy, his
eyes weren't hollow. Hollow was the feeling she'd had inside when
he'd looked at her, emptying her of all meaning and courage.

* * *

Propped up on pillows with her whisky hangover receding, Kirsty
Fowler finished her tea and looked at the wall opposite and still
didn't know what to do. This ring… that knife…

So she did what most of us do when we don't know what to do:
got up, dressed and went to work.

No sinister assassins in blue suits – hadn't her father always
warned her that men in brown shoes or blue suits were invariably

cads? – lurked in the street outside. As she nodded and greeted and mumbled her way to the office, she wasn't sure if she'd even recognize the man who called himself Adamson, not if he dressed differently and put on a hat. He'd been nondescript, maybe in his forties, head shaved, slim and round-shouldered. Only close-up could you feel the difference. She wanted never to be close enough again.

By the metal footbridge near Burns' house she crossed the river, lovely old-new river always flowing without running dry. Never arriving, always arriving. If only one could live like that.

The morning was cold, bright, with snow forecast. She'd been very scared last night at Billy's, which didn't happen often, and it made her angry. She'd been frightened, and woken early with a hangover, had looked out and seen the world was beautiful and she was not and there was so much loving locked up inside.

She cursed, her hand closing on the ring in her jacket pocket. Even on her biggest finger, it was too loose. She really ought to give it to the museum, it should be safe there. She would be safe.

But she was angry and the glittering river offered beauty over sense, and so on impulse she dropped into Shotts the jeweller on her way to work, and that changed everything which came thereafter.

She was flirting idly with Kincaid, on automatic really, arguing about how she should report the attempted burglary at the old folks' home. She'd given him the sanitized version, but still he thought it dramatic enough to be worth writing up in full.

'Give our readers a wee safe thrill, Kirsty,' he advised. 'We all enjoy that. Detail the knife, how you noticed the runnel for the blood to come out along the blade. It's not often a reporter is involved in the crime – but you'll know all about that, eh?'

'I've no idea what you mean, Mr Kincaid,' she said and nibbled more shortbread, trying not to think about that knife, the hard light off its blade. 'But I'd rather just report it, a simple para and keep myself out. This is journalism, not an ego trip.'

'There's not that many know the difference,' he chuckled. 'And those who do, don't end up in Fleet Street.'

'Who said I wanted to end up anywhere?'

'But you're just passing through here?'

She licked the sugary crumbs off her fingertips.

'Ah, Willie, we're all passing through. It's just a question of how brightly.'

'Deep stuff, young Kirsty. But as your editor—'

The phone rang at Willie Kincaid's elbow. He grimaced, picked it up and as he cradled it to his shoulder added to her, 'Don't think we've finished with this.'

He listened. His smile disappeared, he handed her the receiver. 'For you. Marnie Wilson at the Home.'

4

A Highland policeman leaves his comfort zone

It wasn't Jim MacIver's territory, the Rothiemurchus Forest. He'd
been called in because the local force were 'a bittie short-handed'
as the chief constable had confided after the usual embarrassing
business with the handshakes. A Lewisman by birth, trees in such
unnecessary profusion made Jim MacIver feel constrained and
uneasy, and he didn't like not knowing what was really up when a
fellow Mason asked, without quite asking, for a favour.

So he was, by his standards, tense as he hurried along the darkening trail behind the RSPB laddie and big Fergie Cardrona. Jim
wanted to be back in his small Highland town, to amble to the
pub in the evenings, spend weekends gardening while making cal-
culations about his pension and wondering what he'd do with his
life in retirement. It was dismal and depressing, scraping through
this dank forest. It could make a man think on his former wife
remarried in Australia, his daughter Mhairi busy with her surf
school in Cornwall, a good and loving daughter who had to be left
to get on with her complicated life.

As another brittle branch whipped back into his face, Jim
MacIver nearly used strong language but restrained himself and
merely muttered '*Call ùine gu lèir*!' as he pushed on down the
ever-narrowing path. At the dismal end of a dismal day, contemplating the sorry shards of the story he was piecing together – the
abandoned motorbike, the gauntlets, map, backpack, the wrist-
watch, and then finally the man himself – it was hard not to take
that ever-narrowing path to heart.

As if a man came to a point where he had to discard his life, item by item. Went deeper and deeper into the darkness of the wood, further away from his own kind, to finally lie down in the shallow grave he'd fashioned for himself to be alone in. It wasn't to be thought on, such despair, in case of the contagion of it, the awakening of the sinful despair one might carry in oneself.

So he kept the familiar things around him, the daily faces, the bright, orderly garden front and back, the petty wrongdoings of the Highland town where he tried to keep some sort of balance – he thought of it as balance rather than order, for he knew that order was not sustainable in this world. Comfort zone, that's what they called it. That's what we try to fashion for ourselves, and fair enough. And yet Life, the bugger, has a way of plucking one from the impending pension and free bus pass.

As the pines thinned and the slope rose through birch to follow an old ruined wall, in his mind a face he'd nearly managed to forget turned and smiled at him. Ellen Stobo, now safely back in Canada, she had once pulled him from his comfort zone. Her wit, her warmth, her quick compassionate eyes looking on him through that daft Macnab summer while they tried to avert blood-shed, looking at him as he'd never expected to be looked on again, not at his age. Lips touching his as he'd never expected to be touched again. The skin, the body, may thicken and slow, but the heart does not. It just loses its nerve.

'*Eilidh, a ghaoil, b'e mo mhiann thu bhith an seo,*' he murmured foolishly, then remembering she had not the Gaelic, quietly said aloud before he joined the two men gathered round the great mound of leaves, 'Ellen, how I wish you here, my dear.'

'Here's the man himself,' Fergie Cardrona said ponderously. 'Made himself comfortable, hasn't he?'

Indeed he had. Jim stared down, taking in the scooped hollow, the body straight out on its back, the thin face, the hands crossed on the chest, the mouth open. A couple of crinkled birch leaves had drifted into it. Beside him, the RSPB laddie was recounting how he'd been tracking capercaillie through the woods, and the bird had come to roost right above this big bed of leaves and the wind had blown them aside and he'd stepped back as he peered up and felt something hard under his foot, looked down and seen a hand, then another...

Even as he crouched down carefully and took out his torch to see better in the dimness, Jim MacIver had one of those small, transient revelations that litter our lives like molehills on an uneventful lawn. This is the comfort zone. It means death.

He reached out and gently removed the rotting leaves from the man's mouth. *I will write to her. I'm no done yet.*

'Nae identification,' Fergie was repeating. 'But we'll get it through the bike. Nae sign of foul play, and the stuff chucked awa, and the peaceful way he's lying – well, reckon he came here to do hisel in. Must have been recent – he doesnae smell bad.'

Jim nodded. The whole scene was odd, but he'd known odder. A woman walked into Loch Ness with a money belt packed with stones; a man pitched his tent in the Lairig Gru, made a brew, half-finished it – the mug still there next day – then cut his own throat. The queer griefs and passions of folk.

'Check his hands,' the chief constable had murmured. 'You'll know what to do.'

Jim clicked on the torch. Left hand across the chest was bare. A faint band of paler skin around the third finger. Well. Though it was fifteen years back, he knew how that failure felt.

But when he looked at the right hand, he understood at last why he'd been sent here. The ring was chunky, the mount a half-moon, the stone glinted green as a weasel's eye.

It was very nearly identical to the one he had worn at his own father's funeral.

The torch light didn't waver. He pictured again the chief constable before he'd ever been that, just a fellow-Mason in attendance, how the man had touched his shoulder as they'd left the kirk, murmured a few words about the loss of Aonghas Dubh, Black Angus, a fine and faithful servant; how the man's eyes had flickered down as he spoke of the honour now passed down to him. When he'd got home and was alone at last, Jim had pulled off the ring that had been his father's, put it in the secret drawer in his desk and scarcely gave it another thought. It was a daft story, an empty title, the other bearers long lost to each other. His father himself had said as much. Keepers of a relic who knew neither what nor where it was, only that it mattered.

Now it had come to this. Jim MacIver and his Creator liked to keep each other at a respectful distance, but for the first time in a long time he called on some assistance – in Gaelic, of course.

He sighed as he stood up, feeling his knees creak.

'See I get all his effects after the post mortem, Fergie.'

'Aye, right, Jim.'

Then they stood and waited in the darkening wood till the men arrived with the torches, body bag and stretcher.

So it had come to this. Jim MacIver's comfort zone was as irrevocably deceased as the Moon Runner lying coffined in dead leaves at his feet.

5

Kirsty left the funeral feeling low. Not many find funerals cheery events, but it was extra saddening that such a decent, kind and characterful man as Billy Mackie should have had only the warden of his care home, an elderly union colleague, the minister and herself there to see him lowered. This is what happens if one has no mate or children. Was that the adventure she'd been avoiding? Probably. She had her reasons, mostly fear and fecklessness. Not such good reasons.

For the first time she, who had always claimed life a bit of a joke, felt it was maybe rather a sad one. And how must Neil have felt, seeing his wife being buried? She'd never taken his loss seriously enough, just viewed it as something that got in the way of him having fun and games. How she'd always been on at him to lighten up, put Helen behind him and move on. And it had felt good to bring a smile to his long face, see his eyes shine and pupils widen as he looked at her.

How could she have been so shallow? But feisty good time girl was what she did well. Our masks become us.

Now, walking back on the far side of the grey river, watching the sleet settle and vanish in it, words formed across her mind. *This is a grimmer game than I'd imagined.*

In the failing light, she mounted the steps onto the bridge. She'd never see Billy Mackie again, never hear more about the Moon Runners, never know how much he hadn't told her. Simple heart failure, the doctor had seen no reason to doubt it. No sign of struggle, just him dead in his armchair. But she had noticed, because she'd looked for it, that the plug for the pressure-mat was out of its socket.

'Ach, he was aye doing that,' Marnie Wilson had said. 'Catch it with his foot, ken.'

No reason to doubt it. She came down the far side of the bridge, passed behind the hedge, then a blur of movement.

'The ring, lady.'

His elbow under her throat, gloved hand over her mouth. She waved her hands as he dragged her back into the bushes.

'Haven't got it,' she gurgled. 'Look.'

A jerk so hard her head might come off. She gagged, choked as he threw her down. The knife was out, that blade twitching towards her eyes.

'Where is it?'

She could think of nothing brave or clever, just that twitching, hungry blade.

'At the jeweller's. It didn't fit.'

The man who called himself Adamson almost laughed.

'So let's go pick it up.' He pulled her to her feet, then hard up against him, the blade cold at her throat. 'One silly stunt and I'll gut you.'

She went with him, all fight gone, through the sleet hardening into snow, crossed the street towards the jeweller's shop. She had no cunning plan, no resistance. Might always wins, don't you watch the news? He had one hand inside his black wool coat and she wasn't about to argue. In any case, on the other side of the street two men, one runty and the other hefty, both with baseball caps – why do they halve the wearer's IQ? – and inadequate fleeces, at their master's nod followed them along.

She stopped outside Shotts. *Closed for lunch*.

'We'll wait,' he said.

So they stood there. She watched the snow settle like dandruff on his shoulders, sink into the dark wool. She heard familiar voices, looked up and along the pavement came her editor and his fishing crony Robbie Crawford. When they were a few feet away, she made herself look into Adamson's eyes.

'I'm just going for lunch with my friends,' she said loudly.

He hesitated, glanced at the approaching men, then recovered quickly. His gloved hand came out of his coat, shook hers like an acquaintance saying goodbye, but the final squeeze hurt.

'I'll see you back here inside the hour,' he said. Leaning in closer, he murmured, 'Call anyone, you're dead.'

'I'll be here.'

Then she was swept up with Kincaid and Crawford, off down the street. She proposed the County Inn. She looked back, saw Adamson settle into the doorway after nodding to the two baseball fans, who immediately set off shadowing her down the other side of the road. Her escort. This wasn't going to be easy.

Fine fug in the busy bar. Looked like most of the rugby lads were in after the match. Jammed shoulder-tight between Kincaid and Crawford in the corner table, she drank hot whisky and green ginger then got up and brushed past the goons at the next table, the big one with the shaved turnip head and the skinny, twitchy, malnourished one.

'Fags,' she muttered. 'OK?'

Without waiting for an answer, she went on by to the nicotine machine. At the table next to it sat Andy Shotts the jeweller with his sister, as per every lunchtime. There's something to be said for small-town predictability. While searching for change, she made her request, said it was important and she'd explain later.

Back in her corner, she sipped the whisky, had a chat with her editor and his drouthy crony, waited. Andy Shotts left. Her mobile phone buzzed in her pocket; she checked the sender's number. Well, well, she never expected to hear from *that* crowd again. Surely not a coincidence.

She didn't take the call. Too much to compute right now, think about it later.

When the jeweller returned ten minutes later, she went up to the bar to order another round and stood beside him. He dropped the ring into her coat pocket. 'Went in the back way like you suggested,' he said. 'Didni care for the look of your friend out front.'

Slightly dizzy, she came away from the bar holding two pints and the whisky. Stopped for a moment for a word with the rugby captain. Fortunately she'd always got on with the muddied oafs.

She put down the drinks at her table. Took a quick slug from hers.

'Catch you later, Willie. Bye.'

Then she pushed through the crowd, paused where her escorts glowered.

'Toilet,' she explained.

She went on past them, round the corner of the hall passage-way, took the back door onto the alley behind the hotel, then she was off and running.

Panting into the flat. Passport, sweater, filofax, cheque book, her notes on the Runners and the Stone, *The Wondrous Stone*, which had turned out to be interesting, socks, nightwear, knickers – she stuffed them into her shoulder bag then hurtled down the stairs. The rugby lads would have held up the heavies if they tried to leave, but it was only a matter of time before Adamson got suspicious.

As she grasped the chilly wheel and slid off into the sleet towards Moffat, the ring on her right index finger fitted perfectly.

6

Enter Leo Ngatara

Still, you're not entirely helpless, not merely an Antipodean hitch-hiker on the wrong side of the world. You can at least stick out a thumb with some energy, and bear something interesting on that destination board we carry about our person just by the way we stand and wait. That way, sooner or later, something does stop.

An old bottle-green Wolseley, for instance. He had been standing in slush at the Blyth Bridge junction for an hour, waiting for a bus that showed no sign of arriving, when the car went past on the Edinburgh road. He saw a woman's face as it slowed a little, felt himself looked over in the fading winter light. Being a large bloke with a kitbag, looking a bit the worse for wear – the match had been a doozy, a battle over a mud slide – he doubted if he would have stopped for himself. No woman driving alone would.

The brake lights came on, the car slewed into the snowy verge then turned across onto his road. The driver wound down the window and stared back the way she had come. Her coat collar was up, and over it thick hair spilled like liquid rust.

'Hey, Leo the lion!' she said.

In Dumfries, after an away match: a packed pub, bruises that hurt less because his team had won, a few drinks and a pushy, lively local reporter with uncontrollable red hair. They had sparred a bit, especially after she found out where he was living. Bit of a flash there between them, then she'd slipped off.

'Kirsty, how you going? You heading South?'

She hesitated, just a moment. Her eyes flickered past him.

'I could be,' she replied.

Once in a while a new life stops for you. You can only glimpse the driver. The only question now is: will you get in?

Leo Ngatara slung his kitbag in the back of the Wolseley, got in and they rocked off into the oncoming night.

She drove incisively, wheels flirting with the white line that separates challenge from needless risk-taking. The main road had been ploughed, but drifts of snow remained, and with the moon bright over the glimmering land he knew it had to be freezing hard. He tried not to wince every time she drifted into a corner and gunned the engine on the way out.

He was not good at being anyone's passenger. Still, her hands seemed strong and capable as she punched the heavy antique car through the night. A chunky silver ring glinted faintly on her finger, green spark from the stone.

She saw him looking.

'Present from a friend,' she said. 'Since I saw you last. Good night, that.'

'You disappeared suddenly.'

'It's a gift I have.'

The Borderlands were humped and secretive under snow, half-revealed by moonlight. Glimpses of sheep huddled by a dyke, a weasel's eyes sparking at the roadside, a pair of roe deer turning and bounding off across a blank field. His grandmother's winter-bound country. 'Bonnie' she would have called it. It mostly seemed small and cold to him. Recently he'd been feeling if nothing turned up soon he'd move on again. Someday he might even be ready to go home.

'So, outside centre, isn't it?'

'That's right,' he said, pleased she remembered.

'Big boy like you must be quick on your feet to play in the backs.'

He stretched his long aching legs into the foot well. It was warm in the car and he felt in no hurry to get out.

'Not as fleet as I was,' he said.

She looked at him again, that quick appraising glance, like a farmer checking a piece of livestock.

'Bet you run right through them.'

'I try to run round them,' he replied. 'Easier for everyone.'

'Good idea,' she nodded. Then added, 'But not always such fun.'

She was the kind of woman who needed to have the first word and the last. The first time they met in Dumfries she'd looked him up and down then said, 'My, you're tall.' He replied, 'You should see the other guys back home.' She'd arched her eyebrows. 'Must be loads of first-class protein in Kiwi-land.'

At least she hadn't assumed he was an Aussie. She was no midget herself and for him it made a nice change not having to look way down all the time. Flash to look into a new pair of eyes looking big at you. It had been a long time, but probably not long enough.

Now her fingers rattled on the big old-fashioned wheel.

'You're still staying at Samye Ling Monastery?' she said.

'Pretty much.'

She tilted her head, seemed amused. The corner of her long straight mouth tugged.

'Can't be many rugby-playing Tibetan Buddhists!'

'I'm just lending a hand till I rock off down the road.' Though in their way they were helping him out.

'Here – you're not celibate are you? Not a monk? Like the wee dreadlocks, by the way.'

'I'm just a chippie on their building extension,' he replied. Stick to the authorized version, the rest is done and gone. 'And celibacy is a crock of shit.'

She chuckled – the woman actually chuckled – adjusted her rearview mirror once again, then turned off abruptly at Innerleithen onto the minor road heading into Ettrick. In this weather? He looked at his driver's profile in the dashboard light: long straight nose, full lips quick to laugh or scorn. The secretive eyes in shadow. Yeah she was a doozy, no mistake.

She let her breath out, like she'd come to some decision.

'Could you put me up tonight, Leo? I wouldn't ask, but I need...'

He had wondered where she'd been heading for before she saw him, but now it was clear the real thorny was what she was heading away from.

'You need sanctuary?'

She glanced again in the mirror, not much more than a flick of the eyes, but he didn't miss it.

'Who doesn't?'

Samye Ling offered sanctuary of a sort. No questions asked, except for the really hard ones you end up asking yourself. When Leo first met Tim Lewis delivering sash windows to the building site in Carlisle, they'd got talking then Tim suggested he come and help out at this monastery he was connected to – they needed more skilled hands to help finish off. Board, lodging and some pocket money. The healing vibes and enlightening jokes came free. Tim Lewis had very open eyes that saw a great deal. He seemed a top bloke and Leo had agreed to a week.

Which became a month. Then he'd moved into a chalet by the river while its owner went on long retreat, and he liked it there. No one tried to corral or cajole him in any way, no problem going down to the pub of an evening. So he stayed another month. And another. It had helped, as much as anything could.

'In the days when I used to smoke,' Kirsty said abruptly, 'I seem to remember a dram went well with a fag.'

Leo tensed as she changed down, hit the bend then accelerated hard out of it, her hands drawing pale arcs through the dimness.

'Glove compartment,' she added. 'Help yourself.'

He opened it, felt inside. Among the gloves and tins of sweets was something cool and metallic. He smiled in the dark, unscrewed the cap and let the hard stuff trickle over his tongue, then the warmth going all the way down. Good as.

So they slithered and slid along the road slewing deeper into Tweeddale. The snow grew steadily deeper as the road climbed over the moors.

'Are you interested in Destiny?' she said at last.

He wasn't up for big questions at this hour.

'More in Chance,' he said.

'Chance,' she replied. 'Now that would be a fine thing. Still, it's a potent word, don't you think? Destiny.'

He grunted, had another taster at the flask, though he needed more resolution than it could ever contain. Something had shifted the day he overheard some bloke question Akong Rinpoche, the Samye Ling head man whom he had mistaken for the gardener, about reincarnation. *This is not very important. You must live now, all only now.* After that Leo entertained no more fantasies about seeing his child again. Or his wife, come to that, still estranged on the other side of the world. As for living now, he was working on it.

'Glenmorangie?'

'Not bad for a Kiwi,' she said. 'Now tell me – fifteen or twenty years old?'

'You afford more than ten on a reporter's salary?'

Her hand dropped onto his thigh. He tensed, used to impact but not to touch. She squeezed, patted, put her hand back on the wheel.

'Very good,' she said. 'Eight. Relax, I'll not eat you.'

'I should hope not,' he said. 'Not while driving.'

He got her giggle then. Then she turned towards him, her mouth suddenly serious as though she was about to say something that mattered.

She never got to say it. The headlights he had half-noticed growing behind them flared and they were being overtaken, pushed towards the snowy verge of the road. A big 4x4 drew alongside. Leo glanced across, saw two men in baseball caps and something about them was not right. The driver's gloved hands turned his wheel hard over, the nose lurched across and crunched the front wing.

The Wolseley spun into the snow bank at full speed. By Chance or Destiny it was hollow powder snow and they ploughed right through it, Kirsty still frantically turning the wheel. Leo saw the motor ahead then a dark shape ran onto the road in front of it. A thud and high squeal, the 4x4 swivelled and slewed off the road and down the embankment, the lights wildly skewering the darkness.

She got the car under control, pulled into the side, slumped forward on the wheel. They looked at each other, then as one looked back. The twin lights of the 4x4 blazed up into trees but weren't moving any more.

'Are we going back to see how those jokers are?' Leo asked.

'What do you think?'

It wasn't really a question. She was shaken, outraged maybe, but she wasn't altogether surprised. He thought of the 4x4 pulling alongside, then lurching hard across. Something far more deliberated than road rage.

She put the car into gear and they drove away from that place.

'You were expecting that,' Leo said at last.

She doffed her tweed cap, gave her head a good scratch.

'I didn't stop just for your brains or your beauty,' she admitted. 'But I really didn't think it would come to that. Sorry.'

He had a feeling it wasn't something she said often. Sorry. Useless, necessary word. Said over and over by himself and his wife till neither of them had any meaning left.

'Think I'll have a roll-up, Leo,' she said. 'Makings are in the glove compartment. I know something that's a lot worse for my health than smoking.'

He rolled and passed over, was glad to see her hand shaking too. She lit up, drew deeply, looked ahead a long moment. Then she seemed to make up her mind.

'Now I could tell you something that may be bad for *your* health. Want to hear it?'

He thought about it, he really did. Thought of his time since he'd left home to get as far away as possible. A year drifting through Europe, then the UK, gradually heading North from one building site to another, working into a stupor then blessed sleep. Work, eat, sleep, forget, that's all he asked. Then winding up at Samye Ling. Mostly semi-detached there, but something had been happening in those long weeks working in the roof of the meditation hall, the silence from below rising like incense.

He thought of the woman he had once loved and married, toughing it out in rehab in Christchurch. Above all, he thought of a four-year-old child so graceful, serious and self-contained but dead everywhere save in his own mind, lying in a churchyard above Milford Sound. Thought of the confident, gloating grin of the 4x4 driver just before he twisted the wheel and rammed them.

Leo reached again for her hip flask.

'So tell me,' he said.

7

'A real flash yarn,' he admitted. 'And I thought the Stone of Scone was a stale rock bun. But there must be more to it than a hunk of sandstone, to explain what happened back there.'

She glanced at him. Grinned that lop-sided grin, the turned-up corner of her mouth a hook that was beginning to lodge under his skin.

'You're not wrong,' she said. 'After Billy told me how he'd been involved in making copies, I did some research on the Destiny Stone and on the Westminster theft. The more I found out, the more interested I became. It's an odd story and I'm persistent.'

'I bet you are.'

'You want to hide a tree, stick it in a forest,' she continued. 'A forest of lies, rumours, myth-making and wishful thinking. In the *Scotsman* archives I found a letter from someone who had finally tracked down a Westminster stone…'

'And?'

'It was in a church in a place called Dull.' She took both hands off the wheel in a moment of exultation. 'Wonderful! Seems it had been moved there after being in Dundee for forty years in the care of a minister. Interestingly, he was a Scottish Templar as well as a nationalist. Bit of a problem, that.'

'Do Templars go round running people off roads in 4x4s?'

'Not as far as I'm aware. They mostly dress up and wave around big wooden swords sprayed silver. But Templars are pure smoke-and-mirrors paranoia territory. Before you know it you're chasing Joseph of Arimathea around Fast Castle, or damaging your mind in the manuscripts' room at the National Museum.'

She giggled, spun the wheel lightly. 'Boys' games, really. Not that I haven't enjoyed them in the past.'

He chose not to encourage her by asking.

'Dull?' he said.

'Right. Turns out this stone has been sitting in a disused, locked church in Dull, with a sign claiming it is the Real Westminster Stone Accept No Substitutes. Which almost certainly means it's bollocks – or a very audacious double-bluff – but I thought I'd better get over and take a look.'

'And?'

'And it's a fake fake! The crack in it isn't real, just a surface band of mortar. So it definitely wasn't one of Billy Mackie's. I put this to the warden who showed me round, and his reaction was odd. He didn't seem that bothered, like he knew something more. I've a feeling he was a Templar too, maybe even a Runner.'

Leo glanced at the green glowing clock. It was nearly midnight. The snow had got deeper and they were down to a cautious twenty miles an hour. He didn't ask about the Runner, wasn't even sure if he had heard her right. The grinding sound from the front right wheel arch concerned him more.

'I don't believe someone tried to total us over a copy of the stone pinched from Westminster.'

She said nothing, just grinned. Shrugged slightly.

'The real Westminster stone, then?' he persisted.

She inclined her head graciously. 'Getting warmer,' she said. 'The theft – you could call it re-appropriation – was an absolute sensation. Among other things, George V was dying and the coronation needed the Stone back under the throne. The police, press, politicians, security forces were all doing their hard little nuts in. Some saw it as a joke, but they took it seriously. But...'

She took her eye off the white slithering road for a moment and looked full at him. Her eyes were in shadow but still something hit like whisky down where he lived and breathed. The car slid and she turned back to let it slither round the bend, doing the right thing, which is sometimes very little.

'There was something said after the mending,' she said softly.

She paused for the longest while. He had forgotten how hearing a story, living an adventure, or falling in love can banish for a while sorrow and fearfulness. And as she drove on through the night, casually sliding over snow-bound roads with headlights vibrating into the dark like white tuning forks, he guessed this could be all of the above. Glancing at her profile as she drove, the long nose, hair thick and uncontrollable, the strong flirting mouth ripe for mocking and laughter, he knew he was in for it now.

'Yes,' she said at last. 'Believe me, this is anything but Dull.'

Then she told him.

The snow had become outrageous, thick heavy shreds of sky birling into the wipers and clogging. The grinding from up front was getting worse. They were never going to make Samye Ling that night. Kirsty pulled off the road and left the story hanging there as she bent over the map.

He sat there with his mouth open. His mother's family had muttered for years that Edward I had been palmed off with a fake when he'd sent a raiding party to Scone, but he had thought it was one of those stories the Scots tell themselves to feel better about their defeats.

'St Columba's personal travelling altar,' he murmured. 'That would be a total doozy, right enough.'

She glanced across, as if he might be taking the piss with the Kiwi malarky. Which he was. It gave him time to think.

'It probably came from Ireland with the Scotti in the eighth century. It might be marble, or a very large meteorite. This historian I've been reading reckons it was a missionary saint's altar – that's what they did, carry them from place to place. Possibly it had once been a Mithraic stone left by one of the Roman legions – the missionaries often adapted materials of the old religion. Whatever, it's one of the great mytho-historical objects.'

Like some people, he thought, the Stone seemed pretty much whatever you wanted it to be.

'The original Destiny Stone would be the Scottish Excalibur,' he said.

She nodded. 'Except that, unlike Excalibur, this definitely did exist! It was a crowning stone for hundreds of years, then it vanished. So...'

They looked at each other, shining faintly in the dark as if lit by their own excitement.

'So that was your mason's secret. He knows where the real Destiny Stone is.'

The light went out of her eyes.

'Billy's dead,' she said quietly. 'It's one of the regrets of my life I never went back to see him. I thought there'd be time.'

'Talking of which,' he said. 'We're not going to make Samye Ling tonight, are we?'

'Not with the wheel arch crushed. If we are where I think we are, there's a hotel a mile up the road.'

She put the car back in gear and after some slithers it began to edge forward into the drifting snow.

'But he told you where the Destiny Stone is?'

'He didn't tell me because he didn't know. But Billy left some pointers, and it may be something I can run with.'

She tapped her fingers on the wheel. He wondered if she was taking him for a ride. Even if she was, it could get him where he needed to go.

'And those nutters who tried to run us off the road, they're after the real Stone too?'

She nodded. 'It's an extraordinarily potent symbol to some, and a political headache to others. It's worth a hell of a lot to the State, to museums, or to private collectors.'

'Any idea how much?'

She glanced across at him. 'Enough to make life cheap.'

She might be a liar or a fantasist needing a life, but the homicidal baseball caps back up the road hadn't thought so. He couldn't leave her to face them on her own.

'Here's the hotel,' he said. 'Gatepost coming up on the right.'

She nodded and cautiously edged between the posts, past the snowclogged sign of the Cleaton House Hotel.

'Shelter from the storm!'

She parked in the driveway by the front door. A light was still on in the porch and another one inside. Looked like they were in luck.

She switched off the engine. In the silence they looked at each other, then at the hotel as the windscreen filled in white. He saw the tip of her tongue flick over her lips, then her throat moved.

'It's all right,' Leo said. 'I'm not after anything at all.'

There were two rooms left. His was a chilly, narrow cell, as if being single deserved further punishment. He put down his kitbag, stuffed with muddy rugby gear. Fortunately wash bag and towel were standard away-game kit.

He looked around the comfortless room then went down the corridor to knock on her door. It's only natural to want company after a shaking up.

She opened up, looked at him, mobile phone in her hand. Big, wide-set hazel eyes. A watchful person somewhere behind the flash show.

'Come on in,' she said. She seemed subdued and distracted.

He was unnervingly aware of her physical reality as she moved about her twin-bedded room. She flipped her tweed cap on the bedside table, scratched that flare of rust-red hair as if trying to clear her brain. How present she became to him in that moment: her solid hips in moleskin trousers, the crescent ring that was her sole jewellery, the good shapes she made taking off her coat, and the red cashmere sweater under it. She caught him looking, grinned a little awkwardly then looked away.

Quite right too. He had no business looking at this tall, cocky, joker woman just because they had shared a wintry car drive and missed being run off the road and had got each other excited about a hunk of old stone. They were grown-ups with histories, self-control and fears, so nothing needed to happen.

She had a small overnight case, and a brown leather bag she slung into the corner.

'Where were you heading when you picked me up, Kirsty?'

'I have a rather depressing mother lives near Dalmeny,' she said, then set about unpacking. 'She drinks. It's been a long time since we've been any use to each other.'

'Dad?'

'Was a big shot in the army. Don't get me started.'

She drew out a long flame-red nightdress and laid it on the nearest bed. She glanced apologetically at him, which affected him much more than her customary boldness. His hands ached as he hung up his damp fleece on the back of the door.

'I didn't set this up, you know,' she said.

'I know,' he said.

'Which bed would you choose if it were you?'

That was easy.

'The wall side,' he said. 'For security. I expect you always choose the outside one, in case you need a quick getaway.'

She dipped her head, a flicker of smile. Then she went through to the ensuite and left him alone in her bedroom.

He sat on the only chair and took off his shoes, then the damp socks. Even after the post-match shower, he still smelled of mud and linctus. His knees were aching and his ribs throbbed where the opposition back row had put in some big hits. Thirty was on its way, his quality playing days would soon be over.

He clasped the cold skin in his palms and tried to think what to do now. There was no way back to the good woman he had married, any more than there was to the good man he had once supposed himself to be. They had both died the afternoon they walked away from opposite sides of a slot in the ground. Yet the pump went on beating, and there were still scenes like this to be faced.

'Hey, big boy! Why so glum?'

She was at the bathroom door looking so alive, and he knew he wanted to and that it was too soon, and that his body would probably overrule him and that would be a pity.

He got up to tell her he was going back to his room when, passing him, she stumbled on her overnight case. He automatically grabbed her arm. She swung round, all big eyes and that quick mouth, and she made some little pant sound which might have meant anything as they grabbed each other and fell back onto the bed.

There was no stopping it. He didn't know about her, but it had been a long while for him.

She twisted and rolled on top, her hands moving all over him.

'Yes?' she said.

'Too right.'

The heat and swell of her, skin and smell and the feel so good. He was so big it hurt. The single bed creaked under their weight but nothing was going to stop this.

Except a jolly, pinging sound. On the bedside table her mobile phone was burbling. Her free hand, the one that wasn't gripping right where he lived, reached for it.

'I do have to get this,' she said.

She twisted, grabbed the phone, listened for a moment. Her hand slipped away.

'Saved by the bell,' she said. 'Sorry.'

He lay flummoxed as she went through to the bathroom with her phone. When she emerged she said nothing as she grabbed her coat, shoes, cap. She glanced down at her leather bag but didn't take it. She dropped the car keys on the bedside table.

'I've absolutely got to go to meet someone,' she said. 'Don't worry, it's not the bad guys. Take my car to Samye Ling in the morning and I'll find you there. There's some homework for you in my bag.'

He swung his legs off the bed, stood up and tucked in his shirt, feeling about seventeen again.

'Kirsty?'

She stopped at the door.

'Yes?'

'Maybe just as well.'

She looked, he thought, like that prop he'd wrong-footed before sliding over the line. Only much, much better looking.

'Maybe.'

From the window he saw her run across the snowy drive to a long and expensive-looking car with shaded windows. The rear door opened. She got in and it drove away.

He closed the curtains and was about as silently resigned as a wearer of the silver fern denied a legitimate try.

8

Even from behind there was something familiar about the silent driver skilfully flicking the snow-chained Daimler down the road. That bull neck, the pustules below the hairline, the good suit worn badly. That air of casually irresistible authority which she could not but resist. He must be in the Forces, she knew that look too long and too well from her father.

The man with the noble nose, floppy fair hair and killer cheekbones beside her on the back seat, now he was something else. Him she hadn't forgotten. That final scene in front of the castle, Neil and the gang, cuddly Sergeant Jim MacIver and that nice Canadian woman who looked like Judi Dench, and then him off at the side orchestrating everything, effortlessly elegant in a lightweight summer suit. She'd never caught his name, even when he'd briefed her later on the fictions she must write if they were all going to get out of this. She just thought of him as *the equerry*. Now six months later he'd turned up on her mobile to say they needed to speak about a Stone. Now. And she had broken off a jolly good thing...

He coughed gently. He smelled faintly of lemons.

'An interesting ring you have there, Kirsty. May I have a look?'

However courteous, it was not a request. She held out her hand. She'd expected his touch to be cool and soft, but the fingers that turned her wrist better into the light of his pencil torch were warm and strong. The torch light played on the silver mount, angled across to show up the scratches.

'Yes,' he murmured at last. 'Family heirloom, is it?'

'Present from a dead friend.'

'He must have liked you very much.'

'I didn't say he was a he.'

The equerry released her hand and sighed. The pale flick of notebook pages in the pencil torch light.

'William Mackie of Southside, Glasgow, former stonemason and political activist. Died in Dumfries last week. No traceable relatives. He must have trusted you.'

She looked out the window at the moonlit night. Nothing out there but snow and fields, trees and burns glittering in the throat of the shallow glens. Very bonnie country, as Neil would have said, but it wasn't in any meaningful sense hers. A loathing of being pushed around, that was hers.

'Bloody commie agitator,' the driver grunted. 'File thick as my thumb is long.'

And then she had him. There is a particular jolt one gets from being near a man at ease with violence, who moves in a world we hope not to stumble into. Who will, if necessary, see people killed and still sleep at night. Coarse, effective, and not stupid at all. Even if his existence is necessary and his cause is right, a bully is still a bully.

'A socialist, Colonel Mitchell,' she retorted. 'He left the Party after Hungary. Better update your paranoia files.'

'Mr Mackie was a concerned citizen, certainly,' the equerry conceded. 'But that cause is dead, and so unfortunately is he, so let us move on to more current issues.'

'I'm not very up on current affairs.'

'But you have recently become more interested in the past. One might almost say *in antiquity*.'

Colonel Mitchell turned onto a main road. She felt they were heading South. That Mitchell was doing his own driving implied something but she didn't know what. She tried to focus on his neck in the dimness, hold all three pustules in her gaze at the same time. *Multi point perception* – she'd read somewhere it calmed the mind, put it in a clear space.

'My friend Leo knows nothing about this,' she said. 'Will he be all right?'

'Bit late to worry about that, lady!' from up front.

She felt her companion's hand on her arm. He squeezed gently, sympathetically perhaps.

'For the time being,' the equerry said quietly. 'We've called down a couple of helpers in case your thuggish friends – I don't suppose you recognized them? – should get as far as the hotel. These are not very nice people.'

'They're bloody awful drivers, I'll say that.'

A muffled snort from up front. The car eased off the road, crunched down a gravel drive. In the headlights: an ivy-covered Georgian mansion. One light in the upper window. Outside sat a classic Aston Martin with shaded windows.

Sometimes you just get it.

'Have we come to see who I think we've come to see?'

The equerry slipped out of the car, went round to Kirsty's side and held the door open. She shivered at the cold. As she stepped down from the tasty Daimler, she felt his warm lemon-scented breath as he murmured in her ear.

'You won't be seeing him. Things are not as they were before. But he has requested I have a little private chat with you on his behalf.'

'Chat about what?' Kirsty said brightly. 'The travails of modern marriage?'

'About Destiny,' he replied. 'As in the Stone of. He has a certain interest in it.'

'I'll bet he does.'

She looked around the small, private sitting room. Apart from it being four in the morning and Colonel Mitchell pacing outside the door and the heir to the throne sleeping somewhere upstairs, it was a perfectly ordinary room with a nice fire in the grate and an ill at ease equerry for company.

'So, Kirsty. How have things been with you since... since we last met?'

'Oh, same old same old,' she replied. 'Lot of work, not enough fun, I suppose.'

He grimaced. 'I do know what you mean. Wait here,' he said, and left the room.

She sat and waited, mildly peeved she was not going to meet the boss. Must be something dodgy going on. Mitchell had seemed unimpressed, reluctant.

The equerry returned, bearing coffee. And some jolly nice macaroons. Hard to find a good macaroon these days, complete with rice paper and the glacé cherry on top. Her mum's stand-by, before vodka and divorce and unsuitable boyfriends took over.

Kirsty munched and sipped and waited. It was usually the best way to get people to talk. She found that on the whole people say what they have to in the end.

'The thing is, you see,' he said suddenly, 'if a certain person anticipates some day having to sit on a certain Coronation Stone, he wishes to know it is authentic. If one thought it was not, you see, one would not sit comfortably. Not *authentically*, you know.'

'Yes, I can see that,' Kirsty replied. 'I always try to sit authentically, but it isn't always easy.'

'No indeed!'

Another long pause. The coals shifted down. The equerry breathed, presumably. Outside the door, a faint creak as Colonel Mitchell paced. She wondered what he did in all these empty hours of waiting. Polished his gun, maybe.

'There has of late been a certain amount of activity concerning this Stone. It is a very small part of my brief to keep an eye on such developments.'

'Nice work if you can get it,' she agreed.

'Miss Fowler, we have reason to believe you might know something of where the real Westminster Stone is.'

'Yes,' she said. Then after a pause to enjoy his reaction, she added, 'Yes, I might.'

'You are presently trying to find it?' She nodded. 'And you think you will?'

'With luck and time and persistence, yes I think I will.'

Either the burning coals or the equerry gave a faint sigh. He leaned forward like a jockey entering his last lap.

'So, Kirsty, tell me where you think it is.'

Now it had come she wasn't sure how to respond. She thought of her old companion-in-crime Alasdair Sutherland, skimming over the estate fence on a hang-glider flown by his shortly-not-to-be-estranged wife, brandishing the two grouse Neil had poached hours earlier. It's the glee, she thought. The idiot glee. That's what I've been missing. I've been good since then – at least until the fumble interruptus with the hunky young Kiwi – but good just isn't enough.

'No,' she said firmly.

'No?'

'Yes.'

For the first time, a flush of anger on the well-bred face.

'One is not accustomed to being refused.'

But she had had this scene so often with her father, and there was no choice in how to play it.

'Perhaps one should get used to it.'

There was a long silence then. She wondered if she'd gone too far. But what could they do – lock her up in the Tower? Actually, there was quite a lot they could do. She put down her coffee.

'Don't wish to be rude or anything,' she said. 'But I can't tell you everything.'

'Might one ask why?'

'Yes.'

'And?'

She thought about it, still wondering which Stone they were really talking about. If he knew about Columba's Pillow, he wasn't saying.

'It's not about money,' she said at last. 'It's because if I tell you what I know, you'll cut me out and go find the Stone yourselves. And I'd so miss getting there myself, you see.'

The equerry nodded. His right hand tapped the polished arm of the chair.

'I imagine you'll have kept notes. And you have an Amstrad. If we go through everything, we'll probably know everything you know.'

'Possibly,' she admitted. 'But I have something – I am something – you cannot be, which is why without me I doubt very much you'll succeed. Because you'll not get the help I can.'

'And what is that?'

She relaxed back into the armchair. It had been a draining marathon of a day, but now she was entering the stadium out in front. She held up her right hand, waggled her index finger.

'By my estimate, I am the thirty-first Moon Runner to have worn this.'

'I'll need a free hand,' she said. 'And some of your resources. I take it this is all somewhat unofficial? Not approved by Central Office or Palace thingy?'

'This is a personal initiative. Only the most immediate staff know.'

'And his wife?'

'God, no!'

Kirsty nodded sympathetically. The equerry studied the fine carpet.

'All right, then,' she said. 'I need your help, you need mine. You want the proper Westminster Stone at the least. I want the story, suitably disguised, of course, and anything else that turns up along the way. I'll need paid for my time off the *Courier* – some of us have to make a living. And protection, if necessary.'

The equerry stood up, looking less weary now. He held out his hand.

'We'll sort out the details,' he murmured. 'Time for a very early breakfast?'

9

Leo does some homework

He was alone in the hotel room where they had never got to make love, have sex or however else you wish to name the sweet rumpus.

But you play well only when you accept it is what it is, not what you might wish it to be. So he locked the bedroom door and wedged a chair under the handle. He checked the bathroom window opened and that the drop out back was acceptable if he had to rack off in a hurry, then sat on the bed and reached inside her overnight bag.

Cool slick metal – her hip flask. A foolscap cardboard file. On the flap she'd scrawled 'The Protective Shadow'. At a glance, it looked hard going, her writing an exuberant scrawl. He pulled out a battered old book with a crock of shit cover. Still, it was print, so he propped himself up on pillows, opened the book and began to do some background reading.

A damp afternoon in early August when the wind dies in the Southern Highlands is similarly cursed now as in 1296. Crouched in the stand of trees behind Moot Hill, two hundred paces from the Monastery of Scone, Bishop Wishart cursed the plague that descended on his bushy eyebrows, nipping the tips of his ears, burrowing into the hair emerging from his nose. All living things were the Creator's, but surely He had made a mistake with midgies. Or maybe they were part of the Mystery, sent to try men's bodies, souls and patience. Perhaps a future sermon here?

But the midgies were tiny irritants compared to Longshanks and his seemingly-irresistible army. Bigger horses, bigger men, thicker armour and those terrible bows. Above all, that sense of implacable purpose, as though a man might be bent on slaughter as another would be on salvation.

First Berwick, where the latest news was that the corpses of every man, woman and bairn of the town still lay un-buried, by the English king's orders. Some twenty thousand souls, it was said, their discarded bodies stinking and swollen in the sun as the king sat by the High Altar, accept-ing without expression the fealty of the Scottish lords.

Then Dunbar, then East to Stirling. Another siege, another slaughter. Perth, Brechin, Montrose, Aberbrothock fell like drumbeats, like hooves of a terrible horse. At Stracathro, Abbot Smithson himself had seen the Great Seal of the Guardians of Scotland extracted from its niche behind the altar, smashed into a hundred pieces then thrown in the turpid river.

Bishop Wishart nipped more midgies off his eyebrows with as little regret as Longshanks himself disembowelling another group of rebellious lairds. He regretted now his decision to hold this meeting outwith the monastery, but that was no place for keeping secrets. And this had to be very secret and – now he'd made the fateful decision – very hurried. It had to be done tonight.

For there was no doubt in his mind Edward was bound this way. The first knights would be fording the river tomor-row, and grim Longshanks towering behind them, with one purpose in mind. The Scottish crown and sceptre were already on their way to London, the Seal broken, the ancient banners burned or cut to ribbons. All that remained now was the Crowning Stone, the altar of St Columba himself it was said, though the Bishop had reason to believe it much older and more terrible than that. The blessed saint was the only authority that had bound both Scotti and Picts. On that stone every king since MacAlpin had sat to be anointed and heralded.

Longshanks didn't want to defeat the Scottish kings. He'd had enough of hollow coats like Balliol. He was set on doing away with the Scottish kingship forever. There would be only one king of the entire island, and he would be crowned in Westminster. The invaders might break up the Stone, or take it to London as spoils, but one thing was certain: the Stone would not remain in Scotland.

Resistance was impossible, clearly. As it was, Edward might, on a whim, kill them all. His black mood had truly descended with his wife's death. Odd that love can take a man so. Subterfuge, the best friend of the weak (apart from prayer, which had somehow failed to save the twenty thousand souls at Berwick). When prayer fails, cunning must provide.

And here they were now, his chosen ones, pushing silently through the oak saplings. Three of them: the strong one, the loyal one, the clever one. Jarvis, Hogg and Halliday. It would take three to move and hide it, three to keep the secret of where. Even he himself must never know, for torture can make even a warrior-bishop talk. Halliday, the clever one, had assured him he had a hiding place in mind.

Always and only three. Let the Stone be moved tonight, by moonlight, moved safely down the secret lanes of the world until it could come home again. Perhaps when Edward died; perhaps next century; perhaps in some unimaginable future where the monastery itself was gone and such things mattered little.

He greeted the three men quietly, then as they all crouched tormented by midgies that late August afternoon behind Moot Hill, he told them what and why and how.

Leo put the book down, grinning. He liked the sound of burly

Bishop Wishart, probably a handy man in a fight, and they would all for sure have been tormented by midgies.

But judging by Kirsty's brief scrawls in the margins, the core of it was fact. Edward 'Longshanks' and his army did indeed turn up at Scone between the 8th and 10th of August 1296. Bishop Wishart and Abbot Henry knew for weeks in advance that he was coming. The troops did ransack the monastery, destroyed or removed anything of value. Most especially they removed what they believed to be the Destiny Stone. 'All public record – see Sidlaw p6', she'd written.

Leo opened her file, found a stapled photocopy. *The Stone Behind the Stone* by P.B. Sidlaw. He turned to page six and read. According to the Sidlaw bloke, the ransacked Stone had been transported to London. There Edward ordered an ornate bronze throne to be built to house the Stone for future coronations. The job went to 'Walter of Durham'. Here Kirsty had scrawled in the margin 'Royal Accounts. One hundred shillings – loadsa money!'

But something went wrong, something changed. Edward sent a troop of horsemen in great haste back up to Scone. This time they really went to town: broke down every door, every drawer, niche, recess. The Abbot's hands were thumbscrewed 'which gave him grate payn the rest of his days'. A local farmer, Thomas Jarvis, who proved unhelpful was quickly dispatched along with his wife and daughter, though his son, it seems, escaped. Kirsty had underlined that and scrawled in the margin, 'Jarvis, Hogg and Halliday – Billy said. Three Moon Runners. Where the others? Clues hidden in stones? What happened at Dunsinnan in 1819?'

So she hadn't given him exactly the full version of her evening with Billy Mackie. Considering what she'd got herself into, he couldn't blame her. He wondered where she was now, who were the people she had willingly gone with.

The horsemen did not find what they were looking for in Scone Monastery. Back in London, Edward abruptly cancelled his order for the great bronze chair and instead commissioned a cheaper wooden one to house the Stone, with explicit instructions it was *not* to be used as the coronation throne. 'Pretty conclusive,' Kirsty had noted. The king had realized he'd been duped, but couldn't publicly admit it. The irony was that the wooden chair was subsequently used for all future coronations: wrong chair, wrong Stone.

While musing over the general futility of human endeavour, and how in the case of people like Edward I this was no bad thing, Leo heard a faint thrumming outside. The night was very quiet; the sound grew louder.

He killed the bedside light and slipped to the side of the curtains. Very gently he opened a crack and looked down into the snow-glimmering yard. Two men were crouched behind Kirsty's car. He saw them clearly by the headlights that came slowly down the road, slowed and stopped, the engine still running. They were bare-headed, but the man who stepped down from the dented 4x4 was not. A long-peaked baseball cap shaded his face.

The men behind the Wolseley stood up, one called out. Baseball man turned, something dully glinting in his hand. Then after a moment's hesitation he jumped back into the battered 4x4 even as it began to roll. The two men looked at each other then ran off stage left and were gone.

Leo pushed open the window, gasped at the freezing air. The sound of the motor faded and then off to his left another engine turned over, revved then faded in turn.

Sweating and shivering both, he closed the window, pushed the catch across. *I know something worse for your health than smoking*, she had said. Now, like it or not, he knew an unhealthy amount too.

He thought of Edward's brutal henchmen working on Abbot Henry, casually gutting the farmer and his wife. Armour or baseball caps, horses or 4x4s, a honed broadsword or a long-barrelled handgun – only the details change.

He picked up the book again, drawn into the yarn. He used to tell tales to his daughter Kara, stories of where her people came from a long time ago, and to where, he sometimes let himself think, she had returned.

The moon was at its brightest that cloudless night, so there was no need for torches. Even in the nave there had been light enough to drag in the burdensome cess-pit cover and set it down by the altar steps. The three men looked down at it while they got their breath back: a chunky slab of unfinished sandstone with a rough cross where some novice mason had practised.

'Longshanks will never credit that for the Crowning Stone.'

'If he sat on yon, his damned knees would be up aboot his lugs!' Farmer Jarvis grunted.

But Halliday, the quiet clever one, had murmured, 'If he can't find anything else, he'll believe it. Or say that he does. There's few alive have seen the Stone since Balliol's crowning.'

Then they filed into the space behind the altar. From the recess Halliday took out the two sconces, murmured a prayer then dropped them into his bag and slung it over his shoulder.

'It's time,' he said.

Then Hogg pulled off the covering mantle and they stood silently looking at the gleaming marble of Columba's Stone. The moon outlined the knots and geometric whorls that chased each other down the corners. It flexed into life the carvings that covered the sides, the longships, waterhorses, the bull, blade, dogs, snakes, sun. Pagan images of course, but St Patrick himself had given them his blessing.

The monk crossed himself, the farmer flexed his muscles, the scribe noted the way broken swords of moonlight zigzagged down the altar steps. Then they fitted the poles through the handles, Jarvis took one either side of his great broad shoulders while Hogg and Halliday took one pole each. They lifted on count of three, and began to strain and stagger down the transverse towards the side door, out into the bright and silent night.

Leo could see them clearly, silhouetted as though imagination were moonlight, as they laboured down into the lane, staggering under their precious burden. The track would have been rough, uneven. Three men, two poles – the man in front must have taken both on his shoulders. From Kirsty's notes on the probable size of the Stone – much bigger, above all much higher than the cess-pit cover soon to be the Westminster Stone – that man up front must have been very strong indeed.

Even so, they could not have gone far in that one night. A few miles at most. In the margin of the historian's article, Kirsty had listed names: 'Cadseer Lane; Martins Hill; the Hallows; Hilton farm.' Then, underlined, 'Dunsinnan Hill – 1819 discovery? Home – where is it?'

He lay back on the bed, weary as a migrating hog, then picked up the book again, wanting to get to the chapter's end before sleep took over.

Through the hedgerow at Quilters Gap, skirting the bog then onto High Lane, they were moving slowly now. Twenty paces, puffing and blowing like oxen ploughing wet ground, then set the poles down again. And all the time waiting for men to come out of the night with swords drawn.

At one point Halliday, out on his feet, slumped down on the Stone itself.

'You'll never be King of Alban!' Hogg murmured.

'Why not? It's a small country.'

Jarvis grunted, looked up at the moon then at the long brae ahead. The place was up there, the one he'd found as a boy playing with Halliday on the upper slope, squeezing through gorse then under a slab and finding themselves awestruck in an empty chamber of masoned stone with faint drawings of animals in flight along one wall. That place was right old, older even than the Stone. Thomas Jarvis owned little in his life, but this secret between himself and Halliday was his most precious possession. Now he would have to share it.

'Come along, you lazy buggers. The moon sets in an hour.'

He squatted down, fitted a pole over each aching shoulder and waited, patient and hopeful to the last.

Leo Ngatara woke from troubling dreams of men in slow, cumbersome flight with some precious burden others must never find.

He was cold, lying on the bed, the bedside light still on, the book on his chest and Kirsty's pages scattered on the floor. His ribs ached when he sat up and crossed to the window.

Outside the snow had stopped falling. Her car looked like a slumbering polar bear. The moon set shadows on the tyre tracks of all the coming and going of the night. Where was she now? What had she got him into?

He thought of Kara, flopped asleep to his stories of grandfather's people and their adventures – mad stories, wild stories – dark hair across her unmarked cheek, the little chest rising and falling, and nearly smiled.

So the dead man in Rothiemurchus Forest was one Colin Weir. Jim MacIver drew the curtains against the early dark, poured himself a dram before settling down over the report.

They had a fingerprint match: Weir was a small-time chiseller, occasional dealer, busker, drifter, with his last known address in Norway. He'd had a couple of spells in some kind of hospital then seemed to have cleaned up and left the country. Nothing more was heard from him. The last known documentation was a street entertainer's licence in Oslo, made out to him and one Inga Johanssen.

So what had brought him to die alone in a Scottish wood with a Moon Runner ring on the wrong finger?

He reached out and picked up the ring, turned it thoughtfully, noticing the scratches round the mount. His own had quite similar ones. Randomly spaced, they were either damage marks or rough ornamentation. Jim's father hadn't even been sure if there were any other Runners still out there, only that the faith had to be kept. In any case, an oath was an oath; break that and nothing but greed and wayward desire were left.

He couldn't see this man as a Runner. The post mortem suggested the ring had not been worn for long. And on the little finger too, that was odd. The tradition had been the right index. So – what? He'd stolen it, or very recently been given it without time to have it fitted. A woman's index finger, now...

Well, why not?

Inga Johanssen. He reached for the phone and dialled International as fresh snow began to tickle on his windows. He wondered how deep it lay in Oslo. Or western Alberta, for that matter. Ellen Stobo must have got his letter by now, written and sent before the impulse had gone.

He groaned quietly. Putting himself forward like that.

'Sergeant MacIver from the Scottish Highland Constabulary. I need to talk to someone in the City Records Department.'

10

Colonel Mitchell dropped Kirsty at the Samye Ling Monastery gates next morning. She shouldered her bag and walked through the crimson arch into sanctuary – or, as the teachings would have it, the illusion of sanctuary. A few shaven-headed monks, some Tibetan, in saffron robes, moved across the courtyard or filed into the big hall with the gold and green eaves. Most of the other folk were Western civilians like herself. Perhaps refugees would be more like it, in flight from the madhouse.

But it's my madhouse, she thought, returning the nods that came her way. It's what I've chosen. The big bad joyful world as it is.

She spotted her car by a row of chalets near the river. There she asked a plump-faced Tibetan in old blue trousers who looked like the gardener where she might find Leo, and was directed with a smile like a stab of sunshine to the loft of the meditation hall where the extension work was being done.

She found him crouching inside the roof timbers, humming to himself as he bent over plans, one big hand clasped round the joist above him.

'Hi,' she said, feeling oddly shy. The hotel room, that brief carry-on interrupted. What had she done, dragging in this stranger? But then every lover was a stranger once.

He smiled, big easy smile on that strong brown face.

'So they let you go.'

'They gave me some nice biscuits and let me go. I'm afraid I said yes to something that might involve you.'

He folded the plan, put it aside and sat on the big beam. Down below in the main hall, a gong beat three times as he looked at her. Then a faint murmur of prayer, a rustle of settling. Then deep silence, rising.

Leo patted the beam beside him.

'So tell me,' he said. 'Quietly.'

She told him what she felt he needed to know. He looked at her steadily in the half-gloom of the roof space.

'No worries,' he said at last. 'Sling your gear in the back room and I'll see you at lunch. I'm afraid it's veggie.'

Then he picked up his pencil and spirit level and went back to work.

Now, two days later, she was looking out the window of Leo's chalet, up to the Meditation Hall. Weird and wonderful to see a Tibetan building here in the Borders, green and red and gold, the swooping upturned eaves, the paintings, carvings and statues that could be garish yet somehow were exuberant amidst the chilly austerity of Eskdalemuir.

The looping lines of prayer flags snapped and fluttered in the icy wind, sending streams of prayers out to the Divine. Such brave little scraps of colour, yellow, red, blue, green against the steely grey.

The encounters with Adamson had shaken her more than she wanted to admit. Inside Samye Ling she felt safe. Leo helped that illusion of safety, something about the sheer physical presence of him. Those shoulders! The muscle flexing along his forearm when he'd casually leaned over and picked up a chair, swung it over to her!

Yes, sanctuary, but she was still on edge whenever a car engine turned down the drive, or footsteps crossed the gravel around the chalet. Her face and complexion might not be flawless, but she didn't want anyone giving her free on-the-spot surgery.

For two nights now she and Leo had managed to keep their hands off each other. Something needed said soon, otherwise one of them would make that short, heart-thumping walk between the main bedroom and the little one, and the upshot would be lively. More gasping prayers, groans and squeals of human need and pleasure, rising up through the night from the world of Illusion.

The wonder was it hadn't happened yet. She must be getting cautious, or just sensible. Or maybe this laid-back young man with his big open face and short corkscrew dreadlocks just found her a bit plain outside the context of a snow-bound country hotel. No; he wanted her, no doubt about that. He was holding back for reasons of his own; a couple of times he'd seemed about to talk, really talk with her, then he'd looked away and come back friendly but distant.

Now it was time to venture out and take her chances. She'd agreed to find the Westminster Stone to get HRH off her back; she dreamed of finding the original Crowning Stone for Billy Mackie and just because. 'I've sent it hame', Andrew Jamieson had said. With Billy dead, no one else in the world knew of those words. All she had to do was work out where *hame* was.

A month or two back P.B. Sidlaw had published an obscure, dry and detailed article laying out the case for the existence of an original Stone of Scone. He had connected this Stone to a curious episode on Dunsinnan Hill near Scone in 1819, when an ornamental stone had been discovered in an underground chamber, announced in the press, then it had equally abruptly disappeared again.

There had been a couple of paragraphs about Sidlaw's article in the *Scotsman*. Then Billy Mackie, after a lifetime of keeping quiet, had suddenly confided in her. And a man with a knife had turned up with a couple of low-IQ helpers, wanting Billy's Moon Runner ring, which in turn related back to the Stone. All coincidence? Not bloody likely.

Time to stop sitting scared. An hour ago she'd phoned her editor Kincaid, who had reluctantly agreed to give her leave, following a request from much further up the food chain. He then went on to tell her, in a not entirely friendly voice, that after her sudden departure from the County Hotel, an unknown man had come into the jeweller's shop, inquired about a ring and on hearing it had gone had casually sliced a chunk off Andy Shott's counter and walked out again.

And she'd thought herself so smart. She hadn't considered for a minute what might happen to Andy.

After an awkward silence, she had to ask for another favour, a phone number. The call done, she sat and stared out of the chalet window, watching the looping strings of prayer flags snap their prayers for peace against the chill winds. *Too late to stop now.*

She picked up the phone and dialled the number Kincaid had provided.

'Yes? Who is this?'

The dry, precise voice sounded worried, hunted even. Maybe he was just the apprehensive type.

'Mr Sidlaw? My name is Kirsty Fowler. I was recently made a Moon Runner by William Mackie, who got his ring from a Glasgow stonemason called Andrew Jamieson? Mean anything to you?'

A minute later she put down the phone, grinning. Time to go back into the madhouse.

A thaw was on as they drove North on the long and winding road out of the deep Borders into the Central Belt. Snow still on the Cheviots' summits, walked over by elongated fingers of lemony sunlight prodding out of rents in the grey. Tired winter green was reappearing everywhere else, broken by clumps of drooping snowdrops. Heavily pregnant sheep drifted morosely round barns, a couple of swaddled women moving on horseback across the skyline, a kestrel hung over the Lyne Water then plummeted as they went by.

'You feel at home here now, Leo?' she asked.

He shrugged those shoulders, she felt one brush against hers, felt the quick squirm of lust. His long-fingered hand spread easy on his knee, inches away from hers on the gear stick.

'It's like this down the bottom end of South Island. Full of Scots too, only they ate better and got taller once they left home. Some even mated with the natives.'

His voice was flat and even. She glanced across at him.

'Thus your father?'

'Grandfather. My grandmother left Duns as a nurse after the Great War, met him at a tribal hospital. Guess they liked what they saw. It's not like in Oz, not such a big deal.'

'I'm glad to hear that,' she said, and that was all they ever said about it.

'You?'

'Me?'

'Where do you feel at home?'

'Home doesn't figure big with me, Leo. On good days it's wherever I happen to be.'

Again she felt his shoulder move against hers.

'And on bad ones?'

At that point she entered the roundabouts onto the Edinburgh City bypass, and for a while neither of them spoke. She drove, he looked out the window, the sun flicked on/off as they crossed the slender tensioned bow of the Forth Road Bridge. Snow-bright sepulchral domes of hills ranged along the Highland Line. What an improbably large small country, she thought. But home, what is that?

By the time the Lomond Hills rose up and sank behind, they were chatting about safe subjects and she'd stopped looking constantly in the rear-view mirror. It was as well she was smart enough to bring along Leo Ngatara when she went to Crieff that day. Pity that she wasn't quite smart enough to have asked herself how the homicidal 4x4 had managed to track her down from Dumfries into Tweeddale in the first place.

Kirsty rang at an unremarkable off-white door. She'd expected something historic or at least couthy, but P.B. Sidlaw seemed to live in a normal Fifties' pebbledash bungalow. Impatiently, she rang again and looked around the perfectly dull, empty crescent. Not a cat on the prowl, not even a net curtain twitching. In this little suburb, Life had gone out for a lunch-break and never bothered to come back.

'Perhaps he's away,' Leo said.

'I told him we'd be here.'

Now she knocked on the door. The light in the little spyhole seemed to change.

'Mr Sidlaw?' she called. 'It's Kirsty Fowler – I phoned you earlier.'

A muffled voice from the other side of the door.

'Who is with you?'

'His name is Leo Ngatara. A friend. He might not look it, but he's harmless.'

'Well, thank you,' Leo murmured.

A silence, then the door opened but only as far as its safety chain. She saw a tanned face, brown eyes blinking. She held up her right hand, let him get a good look at the ring she'd slipped from pocket to finger.

Clunk as a lock turned, then another, then the chain. The door opened.

Peter Bertrand Sidlaw was slight, brown and very dry, the kind of man who wore a tweed jacket and wool tie indoors. He had a neat, sharp face with a high and crinkled forehead; his glasses hung from a cord around his neck and swung as he re-fitted the security chain.

'I regret this performance,' he said. 'I'm not customarily a nervous man, but recently I had an unpleasant visitor.'

She liked him, she liked that 'customarily', given the full five syllables.

'Black coat over a blue suit, funny eyes – and I don't mean amusing – called himself Adamson?'

'He didn't give a name and he didn't have a coat. Just a suit, and brown leather gloves that he never took off, not even when I offered him tea. He seemed pleasant at first, but later when I wouldn't—'

Sidlaw looked nervously round the dim, book-lined sitting-room as if his visitor might still be lurking there, flexing his gloved hands.

'When you wouldn't what, Mr Sidlaw?'

'May I see that ring again, Miss?'

He clicked on a desk lamp, she put her right hand into the pool of white light. His head came down close; she turned the ring in the light as his eyes grazed over it. What he was quivering with now wasn't nervousness. He opened a drawer, took out a magnifying glass and had a good long look.

'Turn it this way... Yes. The mount has marks.'

'I thought of having it polished up.'

The little brown face whipped round.

'Oh I wouldn't do that, Miss.' He switched off the desk lamp and smiled for the first time. 'I didn't think I'd live to see one of these, certainly not this one.'

'So you know of another?' Leo said eagerly, and made them jump.

Peter B. Sidlaw looked at him, then at Kirsty, and moved slightly away from them both. Leo held up his hands as if surrendering.

'Look, no gloves,' he said. 'I'm one of the good guys and she's one of the good girls.'

'That's what you think,' Kirsty murmured.

'Anyway, she's one of these Moon Runners and this Adamson bloke is after us.'

'After me,' Kirsty corrected him.

'I'm sticking with you till this is sorted.'

'Did I ask you?'

'You gave me a lift on a snowy night,' he said. 'Where I come from, that means we're bound at the hip for eternity.'

She wasn't sure if he was entirely joking. Sidlaw had been looking from one to the other, looking very doubtful. Time to play another card. She took out *The Wondrous Stone*.

'You wrote this, I think,' she said. 'Alan Breck Stewart?'

Peter Sidlaw groaned, passed his hand across his forehead as if that would wipe out the memory.

'I was a young schoolmaster with romantic notions. I believed a story about twelfth century Scottish farming and ecclesiastical people would have widespread popular appeal, and perhaps let me give up my job. You can see what they did with it.'

'Well, we enjoyed it,' she said firmly. 'Didn't we, Leo?'

'Real flash read,' Leo agreed. 'I was right there humping the Stone with those blokes.'

Sidlaw looked suspiciously from one to the other. Then he chuckled.

'Don't tell too many people. It would be the end of whatever reputation I have.'

'No worries, Mr Sidlaw,' Leo said. 'It would be awesome if you'd sign it.'

Sidlaw held up his hand as if stopping traffic.

'That's going too far,' he said. He turned back to the desk and moved the desk lamp's pool of light over Kirsty's ring again. Then he turned abruptly to look up at them.

'I do know of another Moon Runner. Her name is Inga Johanssen. A few weeks ago, after seeing my article, she telephoned me from Oslo to ask about the original Stone of Scone.'

Kirsty felt the room slip. Billy had told her he had no knowledge of the other two Runners, even if they still existed. The Fellowship had decayed, lost touch with each other. Nothing human stayed unchanged over centuries, it was a fantasy that it could.

'I think we'd better all have a nice cup of tea,' she said firmly. 'We brought the shortbread.'

A useful few hours as the short day passed outside. The room was both sitting-room and study; the coal fire glowed and shifted, the dark rows of Antiquarian journals gleamed in their leather. Round and brown and bright-eyed as a vole, Peter Sidlaw talked quietly as he outlined the research that had begun with the Westminster Stones and taken him finally to the question of the real Crowning Stone and its whereabouts.

Kirsty was clear now this was where the fuss had started, with the obscure research paper in a specialist journal being picked up in a paragraph in the national press. That had led Adamson to this house, claiming to be an interested freelance journalist researching for a piece.

Apparently he'd listened patiently to the complex story of the stone Edward I had been palmed off with, and Sidlaw's evidence that this couldn't have been the real Stone. The material, the shape, the simple fact of its height, all wrong. From written accounts of earlier coronations, and the illustration on the King's Seal of him sitting on his Crowning Stone, it was quite clear that he had to be on a stone at least eighteen inches high. The stone taken to Westminster was just eleven inches high. Anyone sitting on that would look ridiculous, not kingly.

Adamson said he was convinced. He made notes of some extra details Sidlaw had unearthed about the 1950 theft and the copies made. He questioned him about rumours of clues left inside the stones as to the whereabouts of the real one. But what he'd kept coming back to was the question of the real Destiny Stone. Marble, or meteorite. White or black? Plain or heavily carved? Christian, pagan, Mithraic?

Above all, Adamson focused on the section of the article about the discovery of an ornamental stone in a hidden chamber in Dunsinnan Hill, and its subsequent disappearance. Did Sidlaw have any private theories, perhaps not ready to be published, about where the stone had gone after that? Who was most likely to have taken possession of it?

At this point Kirsty cut in. Was the stone found in Dunsinnan Hill really likely to have been the original Stone of Destiny? Off the record, in his personal opinion.

Peter B. Sidlaw rubbed the shortbread crumbs from his mouth and looked at her and Leo, leaning forward in their chairs.

'That's what Mr Adamson asked. I told him I have no axe to grind, I'm not a nationalist or a Templar. I'm just an independent historian looking at sources and evidence, and I'd say on balance...' he paused, looked around the brown book-lined room as if all his witnesses were marshalled there. 'It's highly likely. Dunsinnan Hill – incidentally, it's pronounced dun-sinnan, with the accent on the second syllable – is just five miles from Scone, the kind of distance you could move something the size of the stone in one night before a conquering army turns up hoping to take possession of it. Which, I think, is exactly what the first Moon Runners did: hid it in a basement chamber of the old fortifications near the top of Dunsinnan.'

'Done-sinning,' Kirsty murmured. 'Not bloody likely. And you told him that?'

Up to this point Sidlaw had taken Adamson's rising excitement for that of a fellow enthusiast. Perhaps he was indiscreet when he mentioned the legend of the Moon Runners, the supposed guardians of the Stone ever since they first moved it.

'So they aren't myths?' Adamson had asked eagerly. 'These Moon Runners?'

'I told him that in my opinion they were not active or significant – if they still existed at all – but that it wasn't really my area of expertise. It's possible they had some hand in moving the Stone away in 1819 when it disappeared again, though I'd be astonished if the fellowship really endured that long. I did say I was surprised when someone telephoned me recently from Norway enquiring about a Moon Runner ring which had been passed down to her.'

Kirsty rubbed her ring across her lips.

'What happened then?'

'My visitor seemed very excited, asked if I had this person's phone number or address. I said I did. He said he needed it. There was something about him... I gave her name, Inga Johanssen, but said I couldn't give out her number. That's when he stood up. He still hadn't taken off his gloves, and that made me anxious.'

'Did he threaten you?'

Sidlaw flinched and looked away.

'He didn't have to. He just said he must have her address or phone number. He didn't say anything specific, but there was something about him, you know...'

'I know,' Kirsty said quietly. 'One hell of a knife.'

'Knife?' Sidlaw looked faint.

'Inside his jacket,' Kirsty said. 'In some kind of holster. So you gave him Inga Johanssen's phone number?'

'I started to look through my desk. My hands were shaking so much I couldn't sort the papers. He stood right behind me, didn't say anything. I thought if I didn't give him what he wanted, he might... And if I did, he might anyway. Was that silly of me?'

'I doubt it.'

'And then the cavalry came,' Sidlaw almost laughed. 'If you can call cousin Eric, his wife Betsy and their alsatian Ernie the cavalry. They walked in for our bridge night, and there was nothing he could do about it. He stood right here, took his hand out from under his jacket – he seemed to think he was Napoleon – nodded and walked out.'

'And two days later turned up in Dumfries, wanting the Runner ring from Billy Mackie. This ring.'

'Mackie the apprentice of Andrew Jamieson? Who was involved in the Westminster theft?'

'The very same. He gave Billy the ring before he died. Then Billy gave it to me before—' She broke off, looked down into her teacup.

'He did ask about Jamieson, whether I thought he was a Runner. I said I thought he probably had been – at least, he hinted it often enough, but with drink taken, for Andrew the Truth was as soap in the bath – slippery, you know.'

When she thought about it later, she thought of that afternoon as *brown*. The warm, safe comforting brown of strong tea and mahogany shelves, Sidlaw's waistcoat and his lively, shy eyes. She had been happy in that room with the fire, the tea and shortbread, the deep soft old brown armchairs, all the books, and Leo sitting high and awkward in his chair opposite, keeping an eye on her and another on the silent street outside.

Peace and security and the promise of adventure, all in the one room. All illusions of course, but such good ones. She felt like taking up residence and never leaving, what with the wind getting up and the long dark road ahead.

But first Peter Sidlaw gave her the phone number and address of Inga Johanssen in Oslo. Then Kirsty asked about the third Moon Runner ring, where was it? He had no idea. There was a rumour it had gone into the Western Isles generations ago, possibly along with the Stone. She asked why had Adamson so wanted the rings – what was the use in them?

'I suggest you see Ailsa Traquair at the Museum of Antiquities. Say I sent you.'

She felt she owed him something in return, and gave a version of the story Billy Mackie had told her: about the Westminster Stone and the two copies and the scripts Andrew Jamieson had placed inside them. They talked about the various places those stones were rumoured to be.

'If I were looking for ceremonial stones, of which there is something of a proliferation,' Sidlaw remarked as he licked the last shortbread crumbs from his fingertips, 'I should start in Islay, or with the MacDonalds of Sleat.'

'How about the laird's house at Dunsinnnan?'

'The family sold it several generations back. I've been there and I'm satisfied the current owners know nothing of our Stone.'

Full of tea and shortbread and folk myths masquerading as rumours pretending to be history, it was time to leave Crieff. Kirsty and Leo waited until the evening bridge party finally arrived, complete with Ernie the unfeasibly large alsatian.

'By the way,' she asked casually in the porch, 'where would you say "home" was for the Stone?'

Sidlaw shrugged. 'The Jacob's Pillow story places it in the Holy Land. Then the Columba's portable altar theory, which is a little less fantastical, would have it originate in Antrim or Dal Riata. Maybe it came from Hadrian's Wall. Then there's Iona, and Scone itself. Why do you ask?'

'Just sentimental interest,' she replied. They shook hands with Sidlaw, then on impulse Kirsty kissed his cheek.

'Goodnight, Alan Breck Stewart, you old romantic.'

The front door closed and the two of them stood in the windy dark of the silent crescent. A ghost suburb, lacking even ghosts. Broken clouds above; the moon strained at the end of its invisible tether. Kirsty slipped the ring into the little front pocket of her jeans, unsure about everything.

Leo took her arm. 'Let's rock off home, Moon Runner.'

They crossed the street together to her car. He opened the passenger door, slid his bulk inside. She kept her hand on the ignition key but didn't turn it. It seemed important to get this straight.

'Leo, this could get complicated.'

'You gave me a lift when I needed it,' he said, entirely serious. 'Count me in.'

They looked at each other, what they could see of each other. She so nearly leaned in across the space.

'Thank you,' she said, and started up. Lights on, ready to roll. 'What with this woman in Oslo, the Westminster stones and the Destiny Stone, the Traquair woman at the museum, and Machete Man and his goons wandering about, I'm going to have to call in reinforcements. I'd like you to meet some old friends of mine.'

'No worries,' he replied.

She looked at him, laughed quietly then drove off. As they passed Perth, turned onto the M90 South for the Bridge, she said neutrally, 'So, care to tell me about what's been keeping you away from home so long?'

The following day, around noon in an obscure crescent in Crieff, a retired schoolmaster and antiquarian died messily of a severed carotid artery. His desk and study had been ransacked but as far as the police could see, nothing of value had been taken, except for the life and some researches of the dry, scrupulous Peter Bertrand Sidlaw. His one pseudonymous novel was not mentioned in the obituary, which would have relieved him.

His cousin Eric, once he was able to speak, told the police how on edge Peter had been this last week, and of the departing visitors they had met at the door, a red-haired woman and a powerfully built young man who sounded Australian. He had lots of those short curly dreadlocks and a brown skin, and though he'd been perfectly civil, Eric thought he looked a dangerous customer.

11

How hard we work to build and maintain a corner of the world we can call Home, thinks Ellen Stobo. In my case, early retirement from the Service to the family cabin with my horses and skis, books, photos and mementoes. Home is the place we navigate in the dark when we get up in the night, knowing without thinking the exact height of the door handle, where the landing step comes. Where we don't have to query too much.

Behind her, two men of business are settling into their familiar world, one so impenetrable she is almost interested.

'We're looking here for a system of product control liaison, someone to help Hans seek clients to design future contracts, reporting PDQ to the CEO.'

'Product capability intercept – we need to sell that to the people who are building the assembly centre franchises.'

'Phil,' the first speaker announces triumphantly, 'we're totally focused on sequencing the ready-built products that are driving the service sector!'

My God, does this mean anything? Did my twenty years in security make anyone secure? Does anything mean anything anymore?

Ellen hastily dons headphones, unsticks her thigh from the fat man beside her, pushes up the window blind and stares down at the few lights below. Must be somewhere over the mid-West, Calgary just a memory now, the little ranch near Pincher Creek snowed under. She'd been lucky to get out at all, accepting the lift to the main highway from Jake Pleasant in his big truck. Her wild cowboy neighbour, ageing now like herself, sincerely wayward, spontaneous, charmingly unreliable, the kind of man she'd dallied with much of her working life.

Home is more than a building, she concedes blurrily. It's family, friends, our job and pleasures. My work was mostly boring, occasionally violent and nasty, and I have been an independent woman who got the life she wanted. So why are you on this flight tonight, ya big palooka?

Because the opposite impulse lurks in us. It's what made a child who spent all one rainy afternoon building an entire pack into a card mansion, flick away just one foundation card to watch with gleeful sorrow the whole structure slide sideways, topple and slither down flat over the floor.

I am no bold, restless gypsy spirit. But I was the child who flicked the card, and the so-called adult who responds to a letter promising adventure from a man known only for three weeks last summer in the Scottish Highlands. I am that late middle-aged woman who left her home, horses and pastures in Jake Pleasant's care, to fly back across the world to meet a man whose shape can best be described as comfortable, who wears tweed jackets and has very shrewd blue eyes, who seemed to be offering a new mystery, one that starts with a dead man buried in leaves in a forest, and whose ending is unknown.

High in the no-place above Saskatchewan, Ellen shifts her knees away from the fat man, uncricks her neck, gazes out the window and lifts her free G&T in a salute to adventurers. Sometimes you have to grasp the horns by the bull, as Jake likes to say. She feels uncomfortable, uneasy, a little queasy, and very much alive, even as she hears the fervent voice behind her lift over the mid-range jazz on her phones.

'Paul, we're talking about *capability* here, capability in recent offload product management!'

* * *

A narrator notes

An ancient Sumerian tablet currently languishing in the British Museum records that the times are violent, chaotic and strange; that marriage is no longer honoured and young people do not speak properly; that the land is full of strangers, the gods not rightfully respected and the droughts are without precedent; drunkenness and sexual licence are widespread, and the whole kingdom may well be coming to an end.

Which tells us not so much that it was always thus, but that the inscription was made by an elderly person. The young are more concerned with living their time than comparing it unfavourably with others.

That is to say, as we sit invisibly in the green leather back seat of that old bottle-green Wolseley (soon enough to become rusted, then vapourized, returned to water, air and earth) as it surges through the Borders on the A701 in the last years of the twentieth century, carrying two nearly-young people towards Edinburgh to meet Ailsa Traquair, assistant curator at the Scottish Museum of Antiquities and expert in mediaeval jewellery, the previous night in the chalet at Samye Ling, Kirsty and Leo slept together.

Let us dispense with euphemism. They had sex. Being young and very healthy, they had little sleep. It was, as Kirsty murmured as she staggered with a glass of water back to bed, good stuff.

It was also unwise and a mite slag-worthy, for she knew she'd soon be contacting Neil Lindores, for whom her feelings were unresolved. And Leo Ngatara, before turning again to enjoy the full breasted, full-on hunger of this woman, knew that this was too soon, for he was still making comparisons with his whip-thin wife, and he still felt sick to be reminded of everything they had lost. He was too old to have sex for the sake of it and too young to resist.

She drank half the glass, passed it to Leo who drained the rest. Their eyes met, then their skins met and banished sense, scruples and doubt.

Which now return full force like the swollen burns as she drives without comment past the hotel where they had spent a small part of a snow-bound night. It was when I found out about his daughter, she thinks as she pushes on for Innerleithen with eyelids gritty from lack of sleep. That's what did it. What is it with me and men who have dead people they love?

I should just have choked her off, Leo thinks as he surveys the sleeping lion of Arthur's Seat sun-struck in the distance. Every time I tell it, I lose a bit. Kara's death is the only real thing I have left of her, and even that's becoming a story.

And as they wend across the ring road, he glances across at her, that fine straight nose, unruly fiery hair that like its owner can never quite be managed, and her lower lip still swollen from kissing, and wonders *Was that a sympathy fuck or what?*

'Nice day,' she says as the car runs down Liberton Brae towards the sunlit, wintering city.

'Awesome,' he replies.

They don't say more, but just sit there aching and loose-jointed till they find a parking place in Queen Street.

'Let's rack off down to the Hall of History.'

As I say: young, though neither of them knew or appreciated it then. It was just the condition in which we all lived then, the lethal, burning energy of being nearly-young before the fag-end of the 20th century was abruptly stubbed out.

Ailsa Traquair was tall, thin, angular, intense. Black jacket, long black skirt, long white fingers crusted with rings. Narrow eyes like little lapis lazuli chips stared from a white face. She was also, they realized, slightly plastered – it was the careful way she led Leo and Kirsty through to her office as though the dim corridor walls were bulging slightly. She stared at them across her desk, black hair pulled back in a knot so tight it hurt to look at.

She eagerly took Kirsty's ring, put it under her desk lamp, then brought out the magnifying glass, shaking slightly. She looked inside the band, at the pale green peridot stone, then she scrutinized the mount, tilting it this way and that. Her off-white little lower teeth gripped her lip. She seemed to be humming.

She switched off the lamp and put the ring down gently on an unmarked blotting pad.

'I thought this might be an original Moon Runner ring, but it is in fact a facsimile. Probably early nineteenth century, with a highly unusual additional feature. Yours?'

Kirsty could only nod.

'And Peter Sidlaw sent you?'

'Yes,' from Leo. 'He said you were the authority on Moon Runners.'

'How was he when you left him?'

Leo shrugged. 'Fine. A bit tired.'

Ailsa Traquair studied them through her invisible pane. She opened a drawer, and there was what sounded like a bottle rolling. But what she pulled out of it and placed on the blotting pad was not a bottle but five assorted silver rings.

'Too right I'm the authority on Fellowship rings,' she said. 'Not that it's brought me any advancement in this place. I suppose you'll want to know about the so-called Runners and their rings.'

'Yes please,' Kirsty said meekly.

Three rings and three Runners at any one time, the descendants or appointees of the first three men who moved Columba's altar stone from Scone in 1296: Jarvis, Hogg and Halliday. Its first hiding place was known only to them. Like Sidlaw, Ailsa Traquair thought a chamber in Dunsinnan Hill the most likely candidate. Also known as 'Macbeth's Castle', it had certainly been an Iron Age hill fort, and below that were suggestions of something much older. There had been a striking number of digs, amateur and professional, done on and around the summit, without any known major finds.

'Far more than makes sense,' Ailsa insisted, knocking back her coffee. 'Put it this way: some people have been looking very hard for something there for a long time. Excuse me.' She picked up their empty mugs and swayed into a back room, leaving Kirsty and Leo looking at each other.

'She's pissed. Why's she so nervous?'

'Something in the coffee,' Leo said. 'I can smell it from here.'

'Wasting their time, if you ask me!' Ailsa said brightly as she distributed the coffees. 'My guess is the Crowning Stone was moved elsewhere quite early on. It wouldn't be safe so near to Scone, not with English armies around.'

'The hiding place?' Kirsty asked. 'Is it specified by these rings?'

Ailsa Traquair nodded so hard her eyes wobbled. She pointed at the rings on her desk, picked one up.

'I've every reason to believe this is an original. It came from Sleat in Skye.' She picked up Kirsty's ring and held it alongside. Same mount, same pale green stone, same crescent moon curve. 'Yours is a good facsimile, probably copied from one of the originals, maybe this one. Can you see the difference?'

'My mount looks a bit more... worn.'

'You mean the inscription.'

'Excuse me – inscription?'

When Ailsa smiled, her upper lip slid off her teeth. She picked up a pencil and a ring, used its point to indicate the side of the mount.

'You must have noticed these marks on your ring?'

'I thought they were scratches.'

'You were meant to. But they're not. Not on your nelly.'

'So what are they?'

'You're sure Peter Sidlaw was well when you left him?'

'Yes. Is there something wrong with him now?'

Ailsa shook her head. The fluid bobbing motion reminded Kirsty of a nodding dog.

'People call them "Moon Runners",' Ailsa muttered, 'but they missed the joke.' She giggled. 'You see, it's not "runner" but "rune-er". Those aren't scratches, they're runes. Moon runes – you see? Medieval humour. Like their taste in punishment, pretty coarse.'

'Does anyone else know that?' Leo said quietly into the silence. 'About the runes being a message?'

Ailsa looked at him but failed to focus.

'I've never published my findings. Labouring in obscurity, that's me.'

Kirsty nodded, turning over her ring in her hand. Now she looked more closely, she could see the scratches were feathery marks, little twigs. They were spaced erratically around the rim of the mount, perhaps to disguise what they were.

'You said this was a late facsimile? What does that mean?'

'I'd say it meant the Stone had been moved again. If the real Stone was found after the landslip, someone cottoned on to what it was, put in that bit in the letter to *The Times* about it being "shipped South" and quickly moved it elsewhere. A new set of rings were made, with runes to specify where the Stone was now. Yours is one.'

Kirsty, scribbling notes, looked up.

'It was sent home?'

'You could say that.'

'Which is where?'

Ailsa got up quickly, bumping her hip off the side of the desk. She staggered slightly, then went over to the dusty little window, peered down at the dark Edinburgh alleyway below. A couple of lost visitors bent over a map. A lad huddled half-in his sleeping bag, hat pulled down over his ears, another hat in front of him. Bags of rubbish, one opened and being distributed by a cat. A Georgian back alley is still an alley.

She turned away from the window and looked at her visitors. The redhead's eyes were big, her shoulders strong. Attractive, if you like that sort. But she was probably at it with the big boy, they had that easy look about their hips.

The things we try to make fit, even when they don't. The science, the evidence, the puzzle. It's a life of sorts. Then just once in a while the living world comes in off the street, keen as a blade.

'If you give me your ring back, I'll give you a clue.'

More coffee. This time it seemed to focus her. Under the spotlight, she sketched the ring's runes on paper. Looked at them, frowning, pondering which order they should be read in, where to start. Pulled down a dictionary, then another.

'Gather round, my children,' she said at last. Felt Kirsty brush against her as she leant in. Softness of breast across her bicep. Concentrate. Science, evidence, clarity. People have died for less.

'The main runes read STAFR. It's a Norse word and just means "staff". Possibly as in an office-bearer. It may just signify that the wearer bears a position. He or she is – heh – staff.'

'You said "the main runes".'

'Yes, and this is the interesting part.' She leaned forward and poked the pencil tip at the mount. 'You see this one rune here, apart from the others? It's one letter: U. I've not seen anything like that before. It may or may not be significant.'

'That's all?'

'You need to find the other two rings,' she said. 'There is a tradition that suggests the rings give three co-ordinates. This extra rune, for instance, could be one. Do you know where any other rings may be?'

'No idea,' Kirsty said, looking her in the eye. 'Billy didn't either.'

Ailsa stood with her back to the window as Kirsty and Leo prepared to go.

'If I were looking for another interesting stone, I'd put my money, if I had any, on Finlaggan, in Islay. There have been rumours of something being moved before the recent archaelogical dig.'

'As a matter of interest,' Kirsty said as she slipped her ring back on, 'has anyone contacted you about the rings recently?'

Ailsa swayed slightly.

'Someone did phone a few weeks back. A woman. From Norway, I think. Said she was a busker trying to get into journalism and writing a feature article about guardianship cults. I didn't altogether believe her, though we seemed to get on. Said she'd come visit me soon, but she never has. The empty things people say...'

*

Outside in the street, they looked at each other. Kirsty breathed in the chill air, exhaled loudly. There'd been something odd and disturbed, almost tragic going on in that little backroom.

'It was like her granny had just died,' Kirsty said.

'Living always with the past must do something to you.'

She put her hand on his arm, for the first time that day their eyes met.

'You should know,' she said softly.

He moved his arm away, then tried to cover it as a shiver.

'So which way to your car?' he asked.

While Kirsty argued with the traffic warden, Leo stood in the street, watching the couples passing, happy or harassed, but all fully occupied pushing the future on small wheels.

He picked up an *Evening News* lying on the wall. He glanced at the back sports pages, checked on the cricket back home (lost again) and rugby (won again, but only just; the gap is closing). Mildly amused by the arguing voices, he went to the front page and there it was. '*Murder horror in Crieff!* A retired teacher and historian has been found…'

'Kirsty,' he said. 'Pay it and let's go.'

'Traquair must have known,' Kirsty said as she turned off the ring road and struck out across the moors. 'No wonder she was freaked out and pissed. Wish I'd never said that about her granny. Big mouth strikes again.'

Leo nodded. 'Some might call it on the generous side.'

'Didn't hear you complaining last night.'

'There you go.'

'There I go,' she agreed.

'Decent bloke is dead, Kirsty. Not really a time for joking.'

'Hey, I liked him too and it's just terrible. So what is it a time for?'

'Going to the police. Avoiding Mr Adamson. Finding Inga

Johanssen before he does. I'm worred she hasn't been answering her phone.'

She rattled her ring on the bakelite wheel. That old Bo Diddley rhythm. *I'm gonna tell you how it's gonna be/ You're gonna give your love to me...* Ah, bollocks.

'Right,' she said. 'Apart from the police bit. I'll phone and tell the equerry chap, Abernethy – he'll let the cops know what they need to, and keep us out of it.'

He nodded, still unsure what her relationship was with HRH and this equerry. It seemed to go back to the John Macnab caper, which she'd covered with a few jokes but seemed reluctant to talk more about. Alasdair, Murray and... Neil. Something in the way the voice changes over a name.

'So, we're going to Norway? Seems a good time to get out of the country.'

She laughed quietly, a little puff of amusement.

'I am going,' she said. 'With my friend Neil,' she added. 'You'll be going to meet my old gang in the Highlands.'

'Why take this Neil bloke?'

'Among other things, he speaks some Norwegian. He's a decent musician and he once busked around Norway. If Ingrid Johanssen is a street musician, his contacts could help us find her if she's gone on the run.'

Leo looked out the window again. A crow settled on the fence post and sat there, its grey head turning, turning, looking for easy prey to get through hard times.

'Anyway, I need you to be at the group meeting and fill everyone in with what's been going on. You know everything I do.'

'Really?' They drove on into the last of the day's blue, so pale, haunting and intense in the way brief things are.

* * *

Ailsa Traquair shivered though her little office was warm and the man who had entered had closed the door behind him. He sat in the chair where Kirsty had sat and waited, gloved hands calmly folded until Ailsa's hands had steadied enough to hand over the transcription of the runes. As he leaned across the table to take them, his suit jacket swung open and she could see the slim holster over where his heart should be.

STAFR plus U.

Now he looked up at her with a blaze of light in his pale eyes and told her exactly what happened next.

PART TWO

Deep inside my heart burns an inverted flame

12

How to go inside the mind and heart of the man who called himself Adamson? It would require some higher frequency of empathy, an imaginative equivalent of X-rays, to penetrate that singular being.

A capacity to kill a living being, close up and personal, when cold sober, and be indifferent yet also enjoy it – it is hard to find inside oneself.

His hired hands Bill and Ben are not so difficult to get. Vicious, starved and stunted Ben, product of generations of urban neglect, rejoicing in his brief power over others, knowing himself exploited and doomed – yes, one can feel how that would feel. And Bill the big man, bright enough bully, greedy and lazy – one can extrapolate. Hangers-on, thugs, the eternal mercenaries, caught up in someone else's schemes.

But Adamson was different. He would have offered no excuse, no justification, no regret. A genuine sociopath. Clever, reasoning, detached – piecing together how he worked and reasoned that winter, one has to admire his clarity. He was always one step ahead.

In his highly specialized profession of someone who would acquire what was not for sale, it seems he was rated as among the best. And the most honest. His expenses were exemplary and accounted; he never raised his fees once agreed; he never made off with the goods or blackmailed his clients.

The Destiny Stone job was his most public appearance. He must have regretted that. Bill and Ben craved attention, respect and fear, were essentially social beings. Adamson just wanted to do what he wanted. The rest was a matter of indifference.

The agile slight build, the oddly oval head, the blaze of light behind his eyes and the knife snug in its tan leather shoulder holster – as I write this, I see him again and still shiver at my ignorance, the indigestible fact of him in the world.

* * *

Leo Ngatara surfaced in the night and lay awake. Kirsty's face glimmered palely on the next pillow, turned away, mouth slightly open. So near, so far.

He pulled on sweater, jeans, shoes and went outside. The night was cold, very clear. He'll always remember the stars at Samye Ling, so many of them, wheeling through the night above the trees, and the river gurgling.

In his forestry years, back when he had his real job, Leo was happiest in the wide, high country, working up along the treeline. He had thought it would always be like that. Life is a cruise with the wind at your back for anyone fortunate enough to be born in New Zealand, land of space and long white clouds, set well away from the rest of the world's troubles. Wife, child, good life, no worries, an outdoor job worth doing well, the world's best rugby team – that's how it went. You're born here, you win. Even a part-Maori wins, if he respects who he is, and why shouldn't he?

Now wife, child, career in forestry – all gone. He had been a child, an amiable, fortunate child who had assumed the world was on his side. Now he was on the other side of the world, with a rowdy red-haired woman asleep in his bed and unknown trials up ahead.

He leaned over the chalet rail, watching Venus and Orion's Belt, all those unfamiliar stars. No Southern Cross, so many new constellations to get used to. For sure it is a threatening and uncertain world. Don't complain, mate – do something or get used to it: his dad's mantra. He didn't do metaphors, the old fella. He didn't beat around the bush.

His stray thoughts went out among the stars and got lost. One last look up at Venus, then he went back inside. She was still lying on her back but her eyes were half-open, looking at him sleepily as he got back into bed.

'Funny old world,' she murmured.

'You could say.'

Her long leg moving over his.

'God you're freezing.'

'You're hot.'

Her breath, little warm puffs in the hollow of his neck. It had been so long. Not so much the sex but this good feeling.

'Glad to hear that,' she muttered, then was asleep again.

He lay thinking of Orion the hunter, the glittering blade at his belt, the huge space between things, and the human breath warm and moist by his ear.

* * *

Alasdair Sutherland receives a summons

Point Blank on Ben Nevis is no longer the Final Challenge it had been in the late Sixties, but it's still a long hard gnarly route. Especially on the fourth pitch, already some three hundred feet up in that crack with spindrift whispering down into your eyes, the ice shattering like dinner plates, and a duff client below who doesn't keep the rope coming smoothly.

Alasdair Sutherland pushed his helmet back, peered up into the gloom. He didn't need to try the ice on the left to know it would fall apart at a tap, or that above was just a skim of verglas over black rock.

The crack, then. He shook fresh spindrift from his eyes, blinked then scraped the tip of his right axe into the little fissure. Pulled down. Twisted. Solid. He selected where his left axe would go, rehearsed the move in his mind. Twist, pull, step up, whack with the left into that good ice and Bob's your auntie. Whack and dangle...

Above the slither of snow and picking of wind, he became aware of a faint ringing in his ears. Tinnitus? All those years of Heavy Metal? He shook his head but it persisted. Too many pints of lager in the Clachaig last night? His right shoulder ached from the bad move last week on No. 4 Gully, his ankle had never been the same since that game of football – silly game, what's the point when there's no risk?

He realized the ringing was coming from the region of his heart. He grunted and made his move. Got the left axe in, then the right, clipped in and fumbled with his gloved mitt. This had better be good.

'Ally? Where are you?'

His dear wife Jane. She'd bought him one of these new mobile phones and insisted that he carried it when guiding. Usually he did but usually he kept it switched off.

'Oh, just hanging out on Point Blank.'

He glanced down, could just pick out the red helmet of his idiot client through the spindrift swirl.

'Kirsty's back, Al. She's in trouble, wants us all to meet at the old place.'

'Kirsty? That great mad bird!'

Alasdair held the sputtering mobile away while a descending cloud of spindrift smothered his face, clogged eyes and mouth. He shook it off, licked the melt. Definitely too many pints of lager last night. Definitely need some more tonight. Mortal fear of dehydration.

When he felt it was safe he put the phone back to his ear.

'So you want me to pluck the bacon from the fire? No problem. Bye.'

He flipped the mobile closed, stuffed it back in his breast pocket. Felt more cheerful. Guiding gets a bit flat by the end of the season. Time for some fun.

He pulled on the red rope to make sure it was running free, unclipped from his axe and proceeded to unlock Point Blank with his patient pickers and feelers. Alasdair Sutherland was sloppy and approximate about many things at ground level, but never when climbing.

He moved up steadily through mist and snow, humming 'Hey

Johnny Cope are ye wakin yet?' Just because he was feeling all of forty-two these days, he felt duty-bound not to act it. Grace under pressure, only thing he was good at. That's why he'd lived so long when too many pals had not.

Whack, dangle, kick, scrape, and all the time thinking, willing the future as he worked his way up through the short light on the wintering Ben.

* * *

Neil Lindores gets a fax

In his home office in a stubbornly unfashionable part of Edinburgh, a man in worn black jeans and lace-up shoes, with the grey biting deep in the dark hair he cut shorter as he got older, the lines well set in around his eyes and mouth, looked longingly out of the window onto the world outside. The mild spell had ended and now sleet was drifting down on the back garden shed. Up in the hills, in the Gorms say, or old Glencoe, it would be coming down as snow. On the Ben above two thousand feet, the ice would be in good nick.

He could be there with Al, getting scared into valuing life again on some wild route, instead of half-sleeping away his brief time on the planet. But needs must. Money must. Reality bites, then hangs on like a bulldog. The little private project that had filled the empty autumn months was lying in the bottom drawer until he could decide what to do with it. Perhaps one of his Queensferry Mafia drinking pals, in need of a good story and a few bob, could sort it out and put his name to it as fiction?

His eyes drifted, as they did too often, to the photo of four John Macnabs grinning guiltily but happily at the camera, the castle out of focus in the background, HRH at the window eternally shut out. So much sunshine, improbable laughter. That bracken-in-autumn hair she could never quite control, any more than she could being a bolter. Born to bolt...

'Dream on, Neil!'

His business partner and work-ethic conscience George Barns dropped the current files on the desk. Another glamorous day at the un-hip end of copywriting: some brochure work for industrial workware; a company report to be translated from management-speak into English.

'How's the Highland Hotels copy coming along?'

Neil Lindores sighed and pulled the sheet from the electric typewriter.

'Not the best, but it'll do. Only so much you can say.'

George scanned the copy then his copywriting partner.

'And how's the copywriter?'

Neil shrugged, looked away from the Macnab photo but found the one of Helen instead. His wife was laughing, slightly goofy and toothy – always such a joy when that calm face laughed. She was laughing and pointing away at something on her left, outside the photo. He could never work out what had so entertained her five years ago on a sunny afternoon in the last month of her life.

'Only so much you can say.'

George put his hand on Neil's shoulder.

'You've been working too hard, man. These short days get to us all. We're ahead of the game – you should take a long weekend, go climbing with your pals.'

'Yeah, winter blues.' His right hand shaped the chords on the desk top. Making music was another thing he didn't do much any more. Hadn't the heart to switch on the keyboard in an empty flat. Kirsty, now, she could sing, belt it out then break their hearts. *The Bolter Blues*, good title for a song.

'Oh, and this came in earlier,' George said, handing him a fax.

Further adventures of John Macnab? Romanno Bridge seventeen hundred hours. Public transport only. Bring passport, cash, change of clothes. Be there or be nowhere. Regards — Ross & Cromarty.

'Mean anything to you?'

Neil read it three times. A summons, then. Either Alasdair Sutherland was playing silly buggers – 'Ross & Cromarty' my arse! – or it was her.

'Life is a hippopotamus, George.'

'Come again?'

'It looks mean, ugly and improbable, and you don't want to get in its way.'

He looked outside to where the snow was blanking out the windows of his shed, and sort of smiled.

* * *

Murray Hamilton bails out

Stocky, bearded Murray Hamilton handed over his mobile phone, pulled on a Ronald Reagan face mask and stepped over the parapet of the summit chamber into freezing air. Standing on a tiny ledge on top of the Scott Monument on Princes Street, clipped in to a couple of old gargoyles, it was time to declare himself and do a bit of Green agitprop. It wouldn't alter the decisions of the obscenely powerful men holding their summit conferences insulated in their maximum security suites, but it would at least express his ideological contempt. In less political language: take the piss.

He edged along the tiny parapet with the banner in his gloved hands. Snow was falling steadily now, churned to slush under the cars inching along Princes Street. Wee white crowns forming on all those heads and brollies going by down below. Ten minutes since the call to the TV News; the vans should be arriving any time. Then the heads would turn and look up, to see what was going to be on TV that evening.

Were these urban stunts the last twitch of the powerless, or the leading edge of a new movement? Maybe the great causes were done, the struggle over, political anger and debate replaced by grumpiness and stunts like this. In his head, Murray was no longer convinced. His heart, though, remained unchanged.

Standing nervously inside the balustrade of the tower, Geordie Heriot secured his end of the banner and gave Murray the nod.

'Ready to go, wee man?'

'Aye. Just waitin for the vans tae come.'

He clipped the banner to his harness, waved around the spire to Edie McCready, a committed young anti-globalization campaigner and his companion in crime. Good pal, dead political. He saw her Dachstein mitt wave back behind the crumbling stonework. In the dreichness of the Nineties, some of these young ones gave him hope. They had the energy, the naivety to try to change things. Lately he'd been feeling as grizzled as his trim beard, and even that was less ginger than it had been.

Then the phone rang, its chimes tinny above the rumble of traffic two hundred feet below. Geordie answered, expecting it to be the TV people.

'It's your wife, Murray.'

Fuck's sake, it had better be important. Trish didn't phone him too often. Come to that, they didn't talk a whole lot these days.

'Whit's she wantin?'

Geordie held the phone to his ear, listened, nodded.

'Says someone called Kirsty is back and needs the old gang, urgent like. Says she's in trouble. Usual place.'

And there were the two white vans with aerials coming down Princes Street and stopping below. Behind them, the first police van. So the gallus doll is back. There'll be hi-jinks and trouble.

'Tell her I'll be there.'

With a last thumbs up to Edie he stepped backwards off the ledge.

* * *

A seat in the window

When Kirsty Fowler was but a wee bit girl, her grandmother told her if she wanted a good feed in a café, always take a seat by the window. They'll give you bigger portions, to encourage passers-by to come in off the street.

Alone in the chalet where she had been unwise but well entertained, Kirsty cleared the plates and coffee mugs, wrappers and bottles left from the last few days. In the past, she'd been accused – by Shonagh, among others – of leaving a mess behind her, but those days were gone.

Oh sure.

Rinsing the mugs, she became aware of her hands. She became aware of herself, standing at the sink in a strange chalet with snow swirling down in the grey-yellow light outside. What big red, freckled hands, she'd never liked them. Leo's of course were even bigger, which was nice.

She snorted and rinsed out the last mug, stacked it with the others on the draining board. She looked round the room, considered emptying the wastepaper basket and straightening the cushions, but that would just be neurotic. Like she had something to apologize for.

Neil, she had to think Neil. She'd been running from this for months. This complication with Leo was the last breakout of the silly old tart. Nervous, dead nervous, but she mustn't let it show. Need to look into his eyes, then she'd know. And if she didn't?

She brushed down her jeans, laced up her boots. On with the old orange jacket and tweed cap, overnight bag over her shoulder. One quick glance in the mirror – is make-up, however discreet, appropriate for adventurers? – a last look round the rooms where something good had happened, and out.

A Tibetan in monk's robes passed on her way to the car. His conker brown eyes on her seemed to see everything: the bravado, the fear, the necessary fake she was. Then he winked at her.

She turned left out of the entrance and headed for her rendezvous, still grinning, off to seek a seat in the window of the world.

13

The snow had stopped but the light was draining away as Neil Lindores stepped off the bus with his overnight bag and walked up the road to Romanno Bridge, wondering what he'd find there.

He'd phoned Al's wife Jane, who'd just laughed and said she'd no idea what her old man was up to, but he should just go and find out. Then he'd called Murray and Tricia, but all he got was the phone message of their daughter Eve (and his goddaughter, by way of consolation for the children he didn't have) singing 'Life is Just a Bowl of Cherries'.

So he had to go to find out. Kirsty's last words to him six months back: 'Great doing the gig with you.' Basically, so long and thanks for the fun. He'd thought she wasn't that shallow or scared. All he knew was she'd woken him up to the fact that his life was not over, then left. He owed her something.

There was no one at the bridge. The Lyne Water was grey with melted snow. He glanced down, saw cold currents.

The overnight bag over his shoulder, he walked slowly towards the green car parked in the lay-by beyond the old bridge, and the figure sitting motionless on the bonnet, hands in pockets of the familiar jacket and tweed cap perched on her thick hair.

'So what's the big adventure, Kirsty?'

She spread her arms wide.

'You're looking at it.'

Her eyes were wide and candid, but they always had been. Candour was not the issue.

'Is this another act? Another joke?'

Slowly, seriously, she shook her head.

'So,' he said, 'what's on offer?'

Her gloved hand on his arm, face inches from his in the half-light.

'Come with me and we'll take it from there. I'll jolly you up, and you can insist I try to be for real. No one's ever wanted that of me. So?'

He shrugged. Let her sweat a little. It wasn't just bruised ego on his part, though there was that too.

'How many times do I have to say I'm sorry?' she muttered.

'You could try once.'

She looked away. Her father never said it and her mother had all the time.

Then her chin came up.

'I think I need your help.'

Her hazel-flecked eyes were deep as the Lyne as she stared into him. He didn't know where the current would take them, only that it would be impossible to get back against it.

'Your place or mine?'

'Is that a yes?'

'Of course it's a bloody yes.'

'First things first, then.'

Her tentative lips were as chilly as his, but within their mouths there was warmth. Perhaps between them, enough warmth for a chilly world.

She stepped back and glanced at her watch.

'We'd better get a move on or we'll be late.'

'Late for what, Kirsty?'

She looked at him, hand to her mouth in parody of innocence.

'Gosh, didn't I tell you?'

'You did not.'

She got into the car, pushed open the passenger door.

'There really *is* a further adventure. A bit more serious this time. I'll fill you in on the way to the ferry.'

He slung his bag into the back and got in. She put the car into gear, made a wildly illegal turn across the white road and headed East into the gathering night.

* * *

The Arrival of Spartacus

Over the course of the evening, a number of new arrivals filtered into the Atholl Hotel, the beating, dilapidated heart of a small Highland town. On arrival they were met by Shonagh Harris, manager, bar-keeper, receptionist, reader of the fluid moral compass of the Atholl. She was in her late thirties, strong-built with short tight-curled fair hair, steady eyes and firm hands, and as well-balanced and as little lonely as it is possible for an honest single person to be.

Shonagh hugged Alasdair and Jane – both a little plumper since last summer but looking well on it.

'Glad to see you've lost the dodgy moustache,' she commented.

'It was a bit gay,' Alasdair agreed. 'Thought you'd be sorry.'

'Watch it, pal,' she warned, and sent them up to their room.

She watched them go, happily bickering, and reached up to pat the moth-eaten stag's head in the faded tartan lobby. Archie MacPherson's mouth was still locked open in eternal protest at its fate, perhaps its country's fate: stuffed and mounted, subject to preservation and slow decay by moth and cliché.

She remembered Kirsty reaching up and slipping a note for Neil into that stag's mouth. Shonagh had been a little hurt to have had nothing more than a postcard of Kirk Alloway with the scrawl 'Weel done, cutty sark!' from her in six months; she'd thought they meant more to each other. Then, yesterday morning, the phone call, a long one that left Shonagh distracted. And last night, another, with a last minute change in plans. Kirsty had sounded rattled.

Neil Lindores had been a more faithful friend. After that first long night sitting up together once Kirsty had fled, he'd called by several times. He'd looked baffled, hurt, and yet somehow lighter on his feet than the wounded, bereaved man she'd first met last summer, eagerly checking into her hotel under the name of MacGillivray with a long and suspiciously bulky fishing rod case.

'I'd thought better of her, *m'eudail*,' she'd told Neil. 'I don't think it was *your* need she was scared of.'

Things change, sometimes for the better, sometimes not. The lovely Pat had gone, of course, which made for some lonely nights with only Kirsty's dog Charlie for company. Lately he'd begun spending nights in her room, the only time she'd ever slept with a male for company.

The sincerely terrible Country and Western music of the Ceilidh Band was thumping through from the bar as wee Glaswegian Murray pushed in grinning through the door, followed by Tricia and their twelve-year-old daughter Eve, looking calmer and taller than ever. Must have left the wee boy at home. More hugs. Trish was smiling as she looked around, but it looked an effort. Perhaps Murray's curt beard was now more grey than gingery, his mouth more set. But still the russet brown sweater, with sleeves rolled up those Popeye forearms.

'Hey, is that a mobile phone in your pocket, *a charaid choir*, or are you just pleased to see me?'

'Aye pleased to see you, Shonagh,' Murray said as he pulled the phone out from his jeans with just a hint of a blush. 'Bane of ma life, this.'

'Dinni listen to him,' Tricia said. 'He's an auld moan.'

Shonagh closed up her office and went through with them to the bar. Alasdair and Jane were already deep into *craic* with Lachie and a couple of other ghillies. Any past hostilities between them seemed to have been dissolved in nostalgia and whisky, and the stories of the salmon, the brace of grouse, and finally the Balmoral stag, grew more vivid and even more improbable than they ever had been at the time.

Drink, laughter, tall tales and true to the background of Country and Western as the snow froze harder outside – with approval Shonagh witnessed another human evening broiling up in the Atholl as friends got close again. With Lachie and his pals there, the talk had to remain general. In any case, they couldn't start proper discussion without one more arrival, one she was curious about. Kirsty had been uncharacteristically non-committal when talking about him.

All that was missing from a classic Atholl evening – apart from love's young nightmare, Kirsty and Neil – was Jim MacIver dropping by in his best pullover for a couple of drams before closing time. He seemed to be lying low since that Canadian woman from last summer had returned – about time, Shonagh thought, that man stopped fiddling with his roses and engaged with a real challenge, like loving another human being.

Then again, who was she to urge such adventures upon people? There were times when she tired of being the cried-on shoulder, the wise adviser, the promoter of good sense. Seeing old friends again, so full of life and excitement at being called together again, Shonagh accepted the business with Pat had hurt more than she'd admitted. Three cigarettes in an ash-tray is always one too many, and she had been the one to withdraw… get stubbed out.

She became aware of Eve, sipping shandy and taking them all in with her calm, sceptical gaze. *Another generation is already watching. Lord knows what they really make of us.* She went over to find out.

'So how's life, *m'eudail*?'

Eve glanced towards her mum and dad then looked back at Shonagh.

'Life?' she said. 'It's like a Sherbet Fountain. It starts out all fizzy fun and then the liquorice tube gets blocked by your own spittle.'

Oh, my sweet Lord. Shonagh was searching for some words of comfort, wit or wisdom when Alasdair whispered in her ear, 'When's this flightless Kiwi gonna show?'

'The roads are bad. He'll be here.'

Then she reached for the TV remote behind the bar, and called for silence. They all watched the second-lead news item, the one where two figures abseiled down from the top of the Scott Monument, unveiling as they whizzed down a giant banner with the inscription BIG MAC EATS YOUR PLANET. Close-ups showed one in a Thatcher Mask, the other as Reagan. At the bottom they dropped into the assembled crowd of protestors, and with the police vainly trying to get through, vanished into the dusk of Princes Street Gardens.

Cheers and laughter through the bar.

'Who was that masked man, Murray?' Alasdair shouted.

'Ach, yon was Spartacus,' Murray replied, and tilted his glass. His wife Trish shrugged, trying to smile. Eve looked embarrassed – then stared over her mother's shoulder with such intensity every-one at the table turned.

At the door in from Reception stood a tall young man with major upper body development, a head of short snow-encrusted dreadlocks, near-black eyes in a wide brown face, and a shy, easy smile.

'Actually, I'm Spartacus,' Leo Ngatara said apologetically.

After the last Forestry Commission worker had stumbled out into the night, and Lachie and his pals pointed firmly in the direction of home, Shonagh locked the doors and set up a line of drinks along the scarred oak table below the scabby stuffed pike.

After his fine entrance – and how Kirsty would have enjoyed it, Shonagh thought – Leo had seemed subdued and cautious. It must be tough on him, meeting all these people who know each other so well. Kirsty had assured him Leo was *in*, had to be, and could fill them in on everything that had happened up till now.

So she took care to sit him beside her, and talk with him when no one else was. On the whole she was impressed: for all his build and power, he seemed easy-going and laid-back. Younger than Neil, less inward, more Kirsty's age.

Once she'd heard about the Samye Ling chalet, and worked out he and Kirsty must have spent three days there together while hiding out, she wondered just what had passed between them. She didn't believe he was just the simple country boy rugby-playing joiner he claimed to be.

In Kirsty's absence, it was Shonagh's role to run the meeting. She rapped her whisky glass on the table and called them all to order.

14

Jim MacIver put down the *Scotsman* and frowned. Not on account of its politics of late, far removed from its old liberalism, nor its metropolitan bias which rendered insignificant or merely amusing anything that happened North of Dundee or West of Milnathort. He frowned because violent murder was a sin, and it depressed him to be part of a species that went in for it.

Murder. With a knife, the report said. Cowards used guns, just squeeze the trigger and away you go. In Jim MacIver's thankfully limited experience, knife users were very different. They liked to see and feel what they were doing. The victim here was some kind of historian. He'd recently published an essay on the Stone of Destiny, apparently reported in this very paper. Why would somone violently murder a retired antiquarian?

Though it was the Sabbath, he picked up the phone and dialled his chief constable.

When Ellen Stobo came in from her walk, glowing from the cold, she found Jim still sitting in his chair with a newspaper on his lap, staring vacantly out the window at the hills. She focused on his wild crown of grey hair and the bald circle at its centre. My God, he really is not young, she thought. I must look old to him some-times. Yet when we sit together and talk, all that goes away and it's just him and me, and something feels alive and new again.

'What's up, Jim?'

He looked up at her. There's nothing like being looked at like that, with his pupils enlarging while she unbuttoned her coat. Thank God she'd stayed trim after retiring from the service.

'You're looking right bonnie, *a ghràidh*.'

When he used Gaelic like that, her knees wobbled, she felt the soft flush inside. Silly old fool, so far from home.

She bent over him and put her lips to the back of his neck, the weathered skin there.

'Silly old fool,' she murmured. His hand came up over his shoulder and found hers, and they stayed like that without speaking, gazing out the window at the hills in winter thawing.

At length he cleared his throat.

'Have you never been to Crieff?' he enquired.

A persistent man once he got going, Ellen noticed. She liked that about him, the way he became engaged. She didn't get his religious background – what the hell was 'free' about this Church of his, it sounded awful – but it didn't stop him engaging. He had a passion for absolute truth, was smart enough to know it wasn't to be found in this life, and stubborn enough to keep looking anyway.

So she stood by, watched and listened as he talked with the Crieff policemen. Like him she blinked at the description of the victim's last known visitors: a tall, lively well-built woman with deep red hair, supposedly some kind of journalist, along with a powerful Australian who was either very tanned or aboriginal. Both of their fingerprints were all over the study where the body had been found. Records were still looking for a match.

'It's not possible, is it Jim?' she asked as they left. 'It sounds so like Kirsty from last summer.'

'She's not the only lass wi the Burning Bush for a head of hair. I cannae see it.'

He nipped round to open the passenger door. She'd teased him about that but had learned to accept it. Don't let that country bumpkin act mislead you. There's a clear mind going on in there, and a good heart.

Kind, she thought. Of all the men I've wanted or enjoyed, when did I ever ask myself if they were kind? No wonder none lasted.

Yet kindness may outlast our thinning hair and fading senses. As the world grows dark, we're surely going to need it.

'She's out of her depth, isn't she?'

Jim nodded sombrely. They were back alone in his little police station, and he'd just had the word that one set of prints at the victim's house were identified as those of one Christine Tarbet a.k.a. Kirsty Fowler.

'You'll mind she changed her name by deed poll,' Jim said. 'Seems she got in a spot of trouble a few years back, forging painkiller prescriptions to help out a boyfriend. That's why they have her prints.'

'She's not named as a suspect?'

He shook his head. 'Peter Sidlaw was alive when they left, but they still want to talk to her. So do I, see what in the name she is up to.' He pulled some sheets from the old fax machine. 'Some people are born for mischief and high jinks,' he said. 'Our Kirsty being one. But murder, or going along with murder? Hell will freeze over first, and that hasn't happened last time I looked.'

She poured two drams from the bottle he kept in the desk. She was almost getting to like the stuff. Hard to imagine kissing, *really* kissing, a man who actually believed in hell. Not as a metaphor, but real and solid as Alberta, if somewhat hotter.

'The man with her doesn't sound like Neil Lindores.'

'Kirsty was aye game.'

She was still chuckling inwardly as he picked up his glass. *Game.*

If she's kept that car of hers, Jim thought, it's only a matter of time, though time is something she might not have much of.

He looked again at the faxed list of incoming calls Peter Sidlaw had received in the last weeks of his life. Most were local and accounted for. A few, from Edinburgh, Eskdalemuir, Dumfries – and Oslo. Just the one, but it had lasted forty-two minutes. Three weeks before his death. About the date that a man had left his motorbike and walked into the Rothiemurchus Forest with a Moon Runner ring to die: Colin Weir, last known address: Oslo.

It could just be coincidence. Oslo was not small. He put it to Ellen as she perched, frowning in concentration, on the side of his armchair.

'What does your second sight tell you, Jim?'

'Och, the second sight was on my mother's side,' he replied. 'It never came to me, only to my seventh sister.'

She glanced at him, his absolutely straight face, then softly punched him on the arm.

He grabbed her hand, held it as the fist relaxed. Her fingers interlaced with his for the first time since her arrival. Sometimes two skins, even if not in the first flush, are pleased to meet. Something relaxes within.

He slowly drew her hand to his mouth and kissed her fingers as she leaned down to him.

'Have you ever paid a visit to Norway, *a ghaoil*?' he asked.

'Oh James, I thought you'd never ask.'

He reached up to her. In a Highland police station, on a Sunday at that. Romance is not dead, it just lives cannily, with blinds drawn so passers-by cannot see in.

15

A late night for the former Macnabs was followed by another lengthy session when they regrouped next day. When Leo first broke the news of Peter Sidlaw's murder, the mood had darkened. This was not another summer poaching ploy; the world and themselves had become darker, wintry.

While Kirsty and Neil were on the way to Norway to find Inga Johanssen and her ring, the rest of them would concentrate on the Westminster stones. As the plans and possibilities evolved, the mood lifted. Their mission was to locate the three stones that had been in Andrew Jamieson's mason's yard that December night in 1950, break them open and see what was inside – what could go wrong with that?

After a quick pack and briefing of her assistant manager on Shonagh's part, they all left that small Highland town, anonymous to anyone apart from those who live there, for whom it is, quite rightly, the centre of the world.

Tricia, Eve and Jane drove back home, to Kirkintilloch and Cardross. Some people had to work, somebody had to go to school. Meanwhile 'the B Team' – as Trish had dubbed them – arrived by taxi at Inverness station and piled into the train South.

As the train crossed boggy moorland, Alasdair snapped open another can of buffet lager and announced he had no problem with returning the real Westminster stone – the fun would be in finding it. HRH was a decent chap, had played fair last summer. 'Respect is as respect does,' he murmured, and went back to abusing his body with metallic lager and little Indian *betis* that he'd picked up on his last Himalayan trip.

Shonagh swore that if *she* found the real Westminster Stone, it would remain in Scotland. 'It may be a fake, but it's *our* fake. We'll do a swap at the end and give them a copy, and then everyone will be happy.'

Murray said the stone was politically irrelevant, like any nationalist symbol, a distraction from the real struggle – but he'd enjoy broadcasting the discovery that the last seven hundred years of English kings had been crowned upon a witless fraud.

'Whit ye might call a concrete instance,' he commented as they sat trundling by Dalwhinnie. Alasdair said nothing, but stared longingly at the white slopes diminishing behind them, by way of filling the Jane-sized gap beside him.

How shameful, Leo thought, gazing out the window as they rattled over the Forth Bridge and the fall-out of Edinburgh began to glow in the distance. It's been a day since I thought of Kara. How could I?

'Here's where we change, Leo.' Shonagh's hand on his arm seemed sympathetic. It had been difficult getting to know this crowd, and she had been the most helpful. He felt the others were at best wary, at worst resentful. Something to do with this Neil bloke who, fair enough, was their mate.

What is she doing with him in Oslo right now, and why should I care?

The train ground into Waverley and there with handshakes and hugs (the former for Leo, the latter for Shonagh) the party split in two. Shonagh and Leo caught the train for Glasgow then Oban and thence to Islay, while Murray and Alasdair carried on overnight to London – more specifically, Westminster.

* * *

In a little room tucked away at the back of Highgrove, the equerry Jonathan Abernethy smoothed down his sleeve and coughed quietly once, twice, until Alasdair and Murray turned away from the window.

'Nice garden you got there, pal,' Murray commented.

'We like to think so. It is entirely organic.'

'Pity it ain't democratic.'

Alasdair broke in. 'Excuse my diminutive red friend. He's from Glasgow and still thinks socialism is a good idea.'

'And whit's wrong wi organized social justice?'

'It's a great idea,' Alasdair reorted. 'But so is faster than light travel. Unfortunately that doesn't work either.'

'Still happily bickering, I see,' the equerry commented. 'You two really ought to get married.'

'Na – the only reason we get on at all is we dinni see each other too often.'

A scrunch on the gravel, and they all turned to look down as a maroon and fawn car drove up.

'You can't beat Aston Martin,' Al said confidently. 'Best of British. Effortless cool.'

Two men got out. The one that they didn't already know was old but upright, and somehow joyous in the way he looked around, as though expecting to see interesting things everywhere. The other looked preoccupied, downcast.

'Gentlemen, your attention please. This is a serious matter.'

'What I dinni get, is why you don't break open the Stone yersel. Why get us?'

The equerry looked faintly embarrassed.

'Since the last coronation the, ah, instructions are that the Westminster stone is not to be examined any further.'

'Because you know what you'll find inside?'

'Because we don't know.'

Alasdair laughed. 'If there's a bit of paper inside from Andrew Jamieson saying the stone is one of his copies, it would be embarrassing if the news got out. So Mum's the word, eh?'

The equerry examined the plate of biscuits on his desk.

'You could say that. She would rather not know.'

'How very British,' Murray muttered.

'But HRH would?'

Abernethy inclined his head.

'It has to be done, but not by Highgrove. Are you willing?'

The two bickering friends, the wild colonial boy ('I'm a Tory anarchist libertarian with communist tendencies') and the committed activist ('I hae to believe we can make the world better than this') looked at each other.

'Absolutely, sir. Any chance of a discreet OBE ?'

'I do hope you're joking, Mr Sutherland.' He held out a brown envelope. 'Here's your documentation. It'll get you in and see you're left alone for a while. After that it's up to you.'

'And if we're caught, you'll deny any knowledge of us?'

The equerry perched on the side of his desk and unwrapped a chocolate biscuit. He scrutinized it critically then popped it in his mouth.

'Mint,' he said. 'My favourite. Good luck.'

As they stood outside the back door in the watery sunshine waiting for the car to take them into London, the old man from the maroon car walked briskly out of the stables towards them.

'Good morning, lads! Wonderful day!'

His accent was Scots. He wasn't just old, he was very old, but his eyes were sparks of blue light. His enthusiasm was catching, though Murray did his best to resist.

'It's no bad,' he admitted.

'Better than that, Mr Hamilton! Much better. It's the only one!'

'You know ma name.'

'Aye, and Mr Sutherland here. I just want to congratulate you on your high jinks of last summer – in difficult times, it cheered us up no end.' His leathery mask twitched, the tendons on his neck stood out among the muscular wasting of extreme age. 'Wish I'd thought of it first.' He held out his gnarled hand. 'Name's Alan.'

Alasdair shook that hand so enthusiastically it might just tear off. Murray had seldom seen him so impressed.

'Great to meet you, sir. How was the North Pole?'

'Cold, laddie, cold. Like the Himalaya but a lot flatter.'

He shook Murray's hand in turn, said, 'Well, good luck with your mission, lads!' and walked off into the garden, ancient head held high as it looked around, taking in the day. A hand came up, waved without looking back, then he was gone.

For once Murray was stuck for words. He stared after him, then at Alasdair.

'North Pole?'

Alasdair nodded.

'That man – he's got to be ninety plus – was a decorated RFC pilot in the Great War, travelled to the North Pole, became a GP then some kind of therapist. Friend of van der Post and HRH. Wrote some books too, I think. Bit of a hero of mine – before my father became a full-time alcoholic, he knew him. Name's Alan McGlashan. That's what I call a big life.'

Murray considered the shining space where the man had crossed the gravel. Very unusual for Al to mention anything about his dad.

He took his hands from his jeans, stretched and yawned in the sunshine, felt the light on his face again.

'You know, it *is* an awfy grand day,' he said. 'Let's go pinch something.'

Two days later, on a bitter grey afternoon, two Department of the Environment sub-contractors in new blue boilersuits, carrying bags of tools and equipment, went to the tradesman's entrance of Westminster Abbey and presented their authorization.

'Rope Access inspection?' the security man in black uniform queried. An ex-policeman, ex-bouncer, ex-husband, he was overly impressed by credentials he resented. 'We had some of you lot last month.'

'Aye, perhaps the whole establishment is coming doon.'

'It's a detailed photographic survey,' Al said hastily, holding up the Polaroid camera as the man went through their equipment. Harnesses, rope, helmets, couple of descendeurs, a rack of slings, carabiners, nuts and pitons. 'We've a list of the stonework to be inspected – most of it is in the roof and pillars. That's where the ropes come in.'

'Rather you than me, mate.'

'We mostly do this in the North Sea – rig inspection, looking for corrosion.'

'I expect it's well paid,' Security said gloomily.

'Not as well as it should be. Like yourself, eh? I mean, at any moment the IRA could break in and start throwing bombs.'

Security brightened up at the prospect. All he ever did was warn lost tourists away from places they shouldn't be. He didn't even get to carry arms.

'See those blokes over there?' He nodded at two young men in brown coats who looked like janitors as they leaned up against the main pillars in the nave, brooms in their hands as they gazed casually at the drift of visitors. 'They're the ones with the fire-power.'

Alasdair studied them, nodded. Of course they'd have professionals. Fortunately they'd be fixated on IRA bombs, suspicious packages, not a couple of stone inspectors.

'Better tell them who we are – I don't feel like getting shot today!'

The man laughed, walked towards the men in brown coats and left them to it.

Time spent on reconnaissance is never wasted. It was one of those maxims Alasdair Sutherland had picked up during his hush-hush training with the Territorial Army branch of the SAS. Though, as Murray and others had pointed out over the years, it would be a lot more hush-hush if he didn't drop so many heavy hints about it.

Toting cameras and bags of abseil gear – borrowed from one of those North Sea rig abseil inspection contracts that helped pay for Al's climbing expeditions – they checked out Poet's Corner and the obscure little door nearby, had a short detour up the steps into the Confessor's Chapel where the coronation throne stood, and hung around there, chatting as they looked about. Then they called the attendant and had themselves let into the upper inspection gallery doors.

They climbed narrow stairs so dim the head-torches came out. Smell of old stone and dust, faint odour of sanctity. Silent up there as they shuffled along the narrow passages. So old it might have been the inside of a mountain. Then unexpected little finds – a dried-out sparrow, a cigarette butt. In a little niche, something glinted dully. Murray picked it up and blew away the fine dust to find himself holding an unworn Queen Victoria penny, 1882.

Put it in his pocket. You never know, might be worth a few bob.*

Finally they found what they were looking for. The passage way opened into a little balcony, maybe three feet across, with a stone parapet. They stood looking down through empty space into the North transept. Faint echoing hush of voices from the insects below.

'Here?'

'Here.'

'The stone will hold? I want tae see ma wife and bairns again.'

Alasdair focused his head torch and looked closely at one of the little pillars of the parapet. It seemed sound, maybe a bit crumbly. Hanging out on the arch like that, there'd be a hell of a pull on it. Better to get inside for the belay.

Murray watched his old friend and irritant poke around the inner recesses. Now he was actually working, Al was not a clown but serious, focused, careful. Once a keen climber – the friendship between himself, Neil and Alasdair had been formed on the hills some twenty years earlier – and now an occasional one since the bairns had been born, Murray had entrusted his safety to Alasdair Sutherland many times through the years, and had never doubted his judgement.

* It turned out to be worth considerably more. Just how much, Murray won't say.

Pity about the politics, he thought, but I know he'll not leave me on the hill. A fool, but a sentimental one. He wouldn't sacrifice me to a principle, unlike some comrades I could name.

Would I? Have I? Have I sacrificed my marriage to my politics, like Trish says? These days we're living in the same house, but that's about it.

Up there, hemmed in by stone, up under the ceiling in the showplace of the British establishment, Murray Hamilton shivered and felt small, provincial and lost.

'Sound,' Alasdair announced. 'I've put in a friend and two nuts – you could abseil an elephant off that.'

He took out his flask and sandwiches and settled down in the niche, glanced at his watch.

'According to this, we're four hundred feet above sea level.'

Murray eased himself down opposite.

'You say you dinni function well below three thousand.'

'Let's draw a veil under that.'

Murray opened the box his daughter Eve had prepared. Cheese and ham with plenty pickle, and a couple of Tunnock's. Beneath them, her handwritten note. *Way to go, Dad.*

'All right, little 'un?' Alasdair asked. 'You look like life's a disappointment.'

'You think it ain't?'

Al grinned as he filched one of the Tunnock's, unwrapped the foil and bit in.

'I say, love it or leave it, matey.'

They settled down to wait.

Had there been anyone patrolling the low-lit interior of Westminster Abbey after midnight – and according to the notes Al and Murray had been given, there wouldn't be for another fifty-five minutes – he would have seen a red climbing rope silently lowered from the dimness of the roof until it touched the stone flags near the Confessor's Chapel. Had he had good hearing and an over-active imagination, he would have heard whispering from above as though ancient ghosts were arguing among themselves, before a bulky figure slid smoothly down, followed by a second, much smaller, one.

They looked around. Absolute silence reigned among the pews, the pillars, the old flags and regalia. Thinking of all that had gone on in here, centuries of ceremonies that advertised and concealed real power, for a minute they just stood there feeling small.

Al shouldered his pack and led the way up the stairs into the Confessor's Chapel. At the far end loomed the coronation throne. According to Kirsty's notes, once Edward I had realized the lump of sandstone he'd taken from Scone was a fake, he'd given instructions the wooden throne it was installed under should not be used by the king, only the priest celebrant. 'Draw your own conclusions,' she had written in the margin.

The throne was surrounded by spiked railings. No obvious gate in them. But the equerry had briefed them well, and Murray found the loose spike that lifted, then he pushed open that section of the railings. A slight squeak but nothing more. The railings were not alarmed.

But the Stone was. Had been, ever since the great heist of Christmas 1950. Al flashed his head torch and silently illuminated the four pressure pads, one under each corner of the Stone in its compartment under the seat of the throne.

The four pug dogs – or were they very pusillanimous lions? – around the corners of the dais glimmered dully as the torch beam moved until it settled on the alarm cable, hidden where they'd been told.

'Boltcutters.'

Murray knelt by the cable, positioned the open jaws around it then hesitated.

'This could be a set-up,' he whispered.

'How could you not trust anyone called Jonathan Abernethy?'

Murray hesitated. If they got caught, Trish would not be amused. Not much pleased her these days. 'It's no yer politics, Murray – jist that they matter more to you than we do.'

'Not true,' he whispered. 'It's no true.' Then he forced the handles of the boltcutter together and the cable parted.

The snap echoed through the chapel, floated out into the nave and echoed some more. They waited for the alarm bell.

Alasdair counted up to thirty elephants of silence then nodded. 'Always trust a man named after a biscuit.'

With Murray kneeling beside him, he reached into the recess under the throne seat and grasped the big iron ring set into the Stone. Murray gripped the other ring at the side where the repair line where the Stone had been broken clearly showed. They pulled.

A faint grinding, a little movement. They pulled again. The throne creaked but the Stone scarcely moved.

'Turn it so we can get at the broken bit.'

This time they both grasped the ring attached to Murray's end, and the Stone swivelled a little. Then a little more.

In a few minutes, sweating hard, they'd shifted it enough to have a go at it. They got out the chisels, the crowbar, the mallet.

'Goggles?'

'Goggles.'

They put on the protective goggles and leaned closer to the Stone. A couple of blows and the cement fragments that sealed the join broke away. A couple more blows and sandstone chips cracked off. Alasdair was able to get the tip of the chisel inserted.

'Hit that.'

'Ma pleasure.'

The ringing blow shrilled through the chapel. No stopping now. Murray whacked again and the chisel went right in as the corner of the Stone moved out.

'Wedges.'

Working fast – surely even someone patrolling outside must have heard that clang? – they heaved, twisted and wedged until the whole corner of the stone came away and Alasdair was holding the hefty chunk last pulled away by Ian Hamilton in the early hours of Christmas Day, 1950.

Some history there, for the first damage had been done by a

Suffragette bomb in the twenties. But no time to think on that, for there were the brass dowel rods from Andrew Jamieson and Billy Mackie's Clydeside repair job, and in the cavity alongside them was a yellowed tube of paper.

Murray fingered it out. The rubber band broke and the tube unrolled. They both knelt and held the paper in the twin beams of their head torches.

COPY No.1, Jan 51. A.J. fecit.

'That's clear enough.'

Then they had to look closer to read the smaller words written hastily beneath. *Where gypsies cross the line.*

'That's not.'

Then they heard the voices outside, then the clanking in the North entrance door as the lock's tumblers went over.

'Plan B, squaddie!'

They dropped everything and ran as agreed for the little door half-hidden by Poets' Corner. The old handle squeaked but turned. The door wouldn't open.

'Nivver trust a man named after a biscuit!'

But Alasdair gave the ancient timber a shoulder charge, and together they tumbled out into the cold, dead heart of London, Murray still holding the tube in his hand as he ran, like a baton to be passed on.

Jonathan Abernethy received the paper scroll with the air of a man being given 50p for his birthday by a well-meaning but senile aunt.

'I trust there was nothing to identify you among the equipment you abandoned?'

Alasdair shook his head.

'It's all A-OK, sir. But I'll need to invoice you for the gear. Money's a bit tight since the Pamirs trip.'

The equerry nodded as he studied the parchment.

'Not a problem.' He sighed then slid the paper into the inside pocket of his gorgeous suit. 'That clarifies the status of one stone. I'll pass this on. Are you making progress on the other two?'

'It's all tickety-boo, sir,' Al said confidently.

'*Where gypsies cross the line* – any idea what Andrew Jamieson meant by this?'

'It's obvious to me,' Murray muttered, tweaking fine dust from his short beard.

'And?'

'It's a *Daily Mail* editorial.'

The equerry nearly smiled.

'I could like you, stumpy. Certainly it's a clue, and I think we all know to what.' He looked at them both as they sat on the edge of the St Peter Park bandstand. 'I trust we are on the same side here?'

'Singing from the same star, sir!'

'Aye, we're aa swinging frae the same hymn sheet here.'

Jonathan Abernethy stood up, tall and elegant in his midnight blue wool Crombie.

'Have you two clowns any idea what my job is?'

'Aye, you're a full time lackey of the establishment.'

Abernethy dug his hand into his right coat pocket.

'I prefer to think of myself as a jackal of the establishment.' He held out a small brown paper bag. 'Take this,' he said. 'Keep in touch and there'll be more.'

He smiled again, then set off down the curving path towards Clarendon House. Murray opened the bag, looked in on two Empire biscuits.

'My favourite,' Alasdair cried, took one and immediately bit the cherry off the top.

'Not my taste,' Murray commented. 'Still, my daughter likes them weel enough,' and he stowed the bag carefully away in his old biker jacket. *Where gypsies cross the line.* Think on it.

* * *

Around the time the abseil ropes dropped from the ceiling of Westminster Abbey, the *SS Arcadia* left Newcastle for Norway. It had taken a flurry of phone calls, leave of absence, authorization letters, a long-unused passport finally located. Foreign money and thermal underwear. No condoms necessary (one having no eggs left in her basket, the other still wrestling with his Free Church conscience on the issue of extra-marital sex).

A small automatic, a solid Colt, or any sort of weapon to counter a man with a big knife? You must be kidding. Ellen lay on the top bunk of their cabin, listening to Jim's breathing below settle and thicken into a snore. Being properly equipped for this is about as likely as us having sex before marriage, and I've never looked to marry, especially not to a man I haven't gone round the block with a few times, and Jim – well, a man is his conscience and though I think it's stupid I can't force him and it wouldn't be right to.

Still, despite the snoring below and the wallowing all around as they headed into the North Sea, Ellen Stobo lay and smiled to herself as she flicked on the overhead reading light. At least something is happening. At least the kissing is so passionate and real. Who'd have thought it? Like being a teenager again, all that kissing and drawn-out desire, satisfaction achingly deferred.

She hastily picked up her book again. *Conversational Norwegian* can be relied on to damp down the fires.

16

A few drams on the Queen of the Isles

'That was lucky, Wullie.'

'That was lucky, eh, Bob.'

Pause. The two men considered the whisky bottle so deftly rescued from spilling.

'That was very lucky.'

Pause. Bob, with great conviction:

'Aye, we were very lucky there!'

When the two amiable drunks finally tumbled off the Oban train at Taynuilt, Shonagh and Leo were free to share their enjoyment in the cabaret that had unfolded in the seats across the aisle. The exchange became a theme, a talisman of the adventure they were to share. Whether being firmly ejected from a laird's house when their questioning became too persistent, or missing the Islay ferry by two minutes because the bus from Oban to Tarbet had been delayed by cattle on the road, they would look at each other and say firmly, 'We were very lucky there.'

Having missed the ferry and discovered there wasn't another until early next morning, there was nothing for it but to stay in Kinacraig overnight. The only vacant B&B had one room left.

'Twin bedded,' the lady with the mantelshelf bosom straining within her fawn cardigan said, glancing at Shonagh's ringless hand. 'What you do with them is up to you.'

Leo and Shonagh looked at each other.

'We'll take it,' she said firmly.

'Aye, we were very lucky there,' Shonagh said as they wandered along the Kintyre shore, shrugging into a chill Westerly.

'Yes, it could have been a double.' She looked up at him, unsure if he was joking. He laughed. 'Kirsty said you didn't fancy her. I think she was a bit put out.'

'Ach, she's a terrible woman.'

So that was negotiated, understood. He'd done that gracefully, she thought. Well, New Zealand had been the first country in the world to have female suffrage. He might be a rugby-playing country boy, but he was no redneck.

'And a real flash one,' Leo said.

Shonagh glanced at him. She had always liked and approved of Neil, had been delighted when he and Kirsty had finally got it together, and not a little dismayed, though unsurprised, when Kirsty had bolted after the Macnab summer ended. Now the two of them should be on their way to Oslo, which must be good. Yet Kirsty had sounded apologetic and nervous when she talked on the phone about the prospect of seeing Neil again, and Shonagh knew that Neil had been deeply hurt by her swift exit.

Not her affair. Still, she liked this one. Something buoyant and positive about him, for all his private sorrow.

'I'm sure she was,' she murmured, and had the pleasure of his blush. Right there, then.

They rounded a low rocky headland and looked down West Loch Tarbet at Islay, mist-wrapped like a pale shawl over its round-shouldered hills.

Her mother had come from the West side, a rickle of stones near Tormisdale, her father from Lewis. Much of Shonagh's adolescence had been on Islay, and it had been a difficult leaving. She went back seldom, even less once her parents gave up and moved to Glasgow. Round that time her mother had finally stopped asking when she was getting married; her father just looked at her wonderingly and shook his head. 'Nae grandchildren, then,' was his only comment.

She stood and stared across the Sound, aching.

'You're not ready to go home either?' Leo said at her side. She took his arm, squeezed and kept looking across the water, feeling the wind bring moisture to her eyes.

In those minutes, they became friends. They were lucky there.

Next morning the ferry left pre-dawn. Light in the sky behind, still dim up ahead as they sailed out of West Loch Tarbet. A good slap of wind kept them up on deck, huddled behind a bulkhead, each thinking scrambled eggs for breakfast had been a mistake.

Time for a history lesson to take the mind off the pitch and roll of MacBrayne's finest.

Purple knitted hat down over her ears, fleece jacket zipped up round her throat, Shonagh explained how the near-legendary Angus Og, founder of the MacDonald clan, had come down on Robert Bruce's side in the power struggles of the late 13th century. Angus Og's galley had left to take Bruce to safety, through these very waters, all the way round Islay and then to Ireland. For this act, Angus Og was attacked on his way to Mull – Shonagh's gloved hand indicated the northern horizon where rods of light poked down through cloud.

'He was imprisoned in Dunstaffnage Castle, North of Oban.' She pointed. 'That's across from Mull, behind those hills you canna see for the cloud. That's the Western Isles for you – rains for fourteen minutes every quarter of an hour.'

'What happens in the fifteenth minute?' Leo asked.

'They're the loveliest place in God's creation,' she replied. 'Unless it's the midgie season,' she added. 'In which case, it's hell on earth.'

She smiled then was silent, frowning across the choppy, platinum water.

'Anyway, Bruce rescued him from Dunstaffnage. Angus Og was more than a supporter – he was a near equal. Bruce was Norman-Scots, and Angus was Norse-Gael, but they were close. After his help at the battle of Bannockburn, Bruce awarded him Ardnamurchan, Glencoe, Lochaber, and a bunch of islands, including Islay.

People did that sort of thing then, awarding each other islands. That's when Angus Og became *Ri Innse Gall*.'

Leo Ngatara looked at her profile as she stared longingly across the Sound. She told history like his grandfather had, as if it had happened last week to people she knew well. Short, curly hair jostled by the wind. Strong swimmer's shoulders. A very sound companion.

'Come again?'

'*King of the Isles of the Strangers*,' she replied. 'Better known as "Lord of the Isles". It lasted for nearly two hundred years as an autonomous kingdom, with Islay as its headquarters. It was also the likeliest place to have sent the Crowning Stone for safe keeping while Bruce was fighting the English and his fellow countrymen.'

'Strewth, mate,' Leo laughed. 'That's real flash. So we're going to find the bonzer Scone?'

She elbowed him in the ribs.

'Don't give me yon. According to Kirsty, most likely the Destiny Stone was sent away again when the Isles Kingdom fell – to Skye, or back to the Mainland. No, we're still after the Westminster Stone.'

'How can we find it here when no one else has?'

'Because I have a cousin in Bowmore who came visiting round Christmas,' Shonagh replied. 'And he was after telling me about some recent excavations, and the stushie that they've raised, just like your Mr Sidlaw said. He's a bit of a blether is Donnie, but he doesna haiver. Look!' She pointed as they rounded the headland where a copper dome was picked out by a finger of light stabbing down from a break in the cloud. 'The Ardbeg distillery.'

'"Queen of the Isles"', Leo said, checking his Tourist Board brochure.

'Islay does have more distilleries per square mile than anywhere on earth,' Shonagh conceded.

'Well, we're lucky there,' Leo said, and together they stared over the rails as the island resolved into individual houses, a white car on the road, a man and dog walking on the low cliffs.

A new island, a new person – it's the same quickening of

the heart as fresh contact is made: foot stepping onto new ground, a glance exchanged between two people as they become friends.

It was Leo's first time in the West, and he couldn't have said exactly when or where it happened, but in the days that followed he moved in a subtly but distinctly other world.

The thin, angular man standing by a mud-streaked Land Rover when they came off the ferry was Shonagh's cousin. They embraced to their throaty, stretched-vowel language, and suddenly Shonagh made much more sense to Leo. She wasn't an exotic, she was at home.

'Leo – Donnie.'

Firm, bony handshake. Vivid blue eyes below tousled black hair, cheekbones like slanting arrows.

'*Ceud mille failte, Leo a ghràidh.*'

Shonagh elbowed her cousin.

'Behave yourself, Donald.'

There was a drive inland, glimpses of moorland mottled green and brown, camouflage colours, hiding their own beauty. Leo sat in the back, jolted and entranced, half-listening to the sound of Gaelic up front. Then there was coast, shoreline, a vast bay briefly sunlit. It looked like some of South Island back home, round Motueka.

He realized that again he hadn't thought about his daughter that day. That was supposed to be progress, but he felt a stab of loss. When Kara was not thought of, she was truly gone.

Then there were whitewashed houses along the shore, Port Ellen, and Donnie's house at the end, and a woman at the door, hair blowing in the wind.

'Yawright?'

It took him a moment to realize she was speaking Yorkshire, not Gaelic.

'Bonzer, mate.'

'Behave yourself, Leo.'

Like everyone here, Margie was windswept, casual, in the uniform of fleece jacket, sweater, jeans. Speech and movement seemed to have slowed, calmed, softened. The speed and patter of Glasgow Queen Street seemed impossibly distant.

Inside were children, scones and tea. Leo's room was small, with a window looking at a pier and the edge of a beach, and evening light decanting saffron and scarlet over the western horizon. No time to think and admire, because he was called out to have a first whisky put in his hand.

He sniffed cautiously and recoiled.

'Crikey,' he said. 'You drink this?'

In the first hour he was introduced to the peat reek of Ardbeg and Bowmore. For someone brought up on beer and wine with the odd vodka and Coke, whisky had been a shock when he'd first come to Scotland. He'd never really seen the point in it. But none had tasted like this.

'Voddy is for bairns,' Donnie said firmly, reaching down a different bottle from the row above the television. 'Whisky is for grown ups. We call this one Lagavullin. It's jist a wee bit heavier.'

Leo inhaled, felt his eyes tickle and sinuses squirm as a cloud of unknowing entered his forebrain. He drank, then cautiously put his glass down on the Westminster Abbey drinks mat.

'Jesus Christ Almighty.'

'Aye, it's Holy Spirit right enough.'

Leo Ngatara blinked a few times. It was like sifting molten peat through his teeth. He added a little more water and tried again. Same drubbing over his palate, like being bottom of the ruck at Wellington Park. Yet it was, in a strange way, a pleasure.

'I think he's getting the hang of it, Donnie.'

'Aye, there's four distilleries to go for the complete tour.'

'Leave the Laphroaig for another day,' Margie said firmly, dangling a happily screaming child by his heels. 'Let him work up to it.'

'Good idea,' Donnie said. 'We'll have a quiet night the night – there's a wee bit ceilidh for you the morn.'

131

'For me?' Shonagh said faintly.

'Aye, at Erskine's. You mind him?' Shonagh nodded. 'Dinna look so surprised – there's plenty folk here think well of you.'

'There's plenty folk didna.'

'Weel, they're maistly deid,' Donnie replied. 'And if they're not, it's time they were.' He turned his glass in his big weathered hand, frowning into the liquid's depths. '*Slainte mhath!* Welcome to Islay.'

Leo opened his eyes. He couldn't quite make the effort to raise his left arm to look at his watch. Why bother, anyway? The armchair was so comfortable, lapping round him with soft peaty brown warmth. Someone had placed a pint glass of water on the table. Thoughtless, painless, vacantly happy, he drank it.

Shonagh and Donnie were sitting cross-legged by the dying fire, heads close together, talking quietly in Gaelic. Shonagh was asking something of him. Donnie shook his head twice.

Leo recognized the word Finlaggan, and a phrase she said several times, sounded like *Ordoo Riovale Cathay*. Whenever she said it, Donnie seemed to withdraw a little. Still she persisted, undeterred, her big shoulders turned towards the fire.

Leo closed his eyes and sailed away to Tir na Og, the Isles of the Blessed.

He woke in his own bed. Opened his eyes cautiously. Identified a pint glass of water on the bedside table, reached out and drank it. No curtains, so he was looking out at the end of the pier, the beach, the sea grey and blue, fading out towards Newfoundland.

Knock on the door.

'You indecent, *m'eudail?*'

Shonagh looking chirpy in her usual outfit of jeans, boots and red fleece, bearing tea and Abernethy biscuit.

'So how are you this bonnie morning?'

He nibbled the crumbly biscuit, sipped the tea and considered.

'Sweet as,' he concluded. In truth, his head felt like a glass bell
– fragile, empty, and yet curiously clear.

Shonagh nodded. 'Stick to the whisky, drink plenty water, stay
away from beer and wine, and you'll survive. You might even learn
something to your advantage.'

The days that followed formed nothing as structured as a pattern.
They merely fell and splayed out like a deck of cards slithering to
the floor, and to Leo it seemed everyone on Islay simply played
them as they lay.

There was a deal of walking. In the days when they were young
and still ignorant of what life does, Leo and his wife had hiked a
lot in the Southern Alps, up on the high trails, flirting with the
snowline. And he had thrashed his body for numberless hours
over the hard training grounds of home and then the bogging
training grounds of the Borders.

So he reckoned himself leg-fit, but as hours passed and he staggered alongside a bobbing Shonagh across trackless wastes of
coarse grass, bog, peat cuttings and finally massive clumped
heather wet with rain then sparking in low sunlight, he had to
admit this was tough going. The uneven ground hard on the
ankles; his sodden boots so heavy; thighs aching from clambering
and lifting through mud, jumping one more oozing burn.

And when they came upon yet another silent inland lochan, or
scrambled the cliffs of The Oa with the western ocean loud below,
or walked the Rhinns from Bruichladdich to Portnahaven through
one afternoon of dark clouds, rain and brilliant glitter, Leo found
himself murmuring inwardly *sweet as*, *sweet as*, until the words
tailed off and there was no comparison left.

'I'd say we're looking for more than a stone here, *m'eudail*.'

A silence between them while Leo rested his legs in the lee of
the summit cairn on Guir Bheinn and considered the wilderness
of Jura across the narrow Sound.

'Are we going to find it?'

She looked at him, then over at the Paps opposite. She held out her hand, red-blotched, tilted it from side to side like a gull in the wind.

'Maybe. I suppose it seems to you all we're doing is wandering about the place, calling in on a few folk and spending the evenings getting pissed.'

'Well, yes. Though it's all good as gold, far as I'm concerned,' he added hastily.

'Groundwork, Leo. You can't hurry things here. Which isn't to say that folk are slow – not at all – they just pace themselves differently. I've been off the island a long time, and some people had problems with, you know, my sexuality and that. We have to put in the, ah, legwork.'

'So not hiring a car isn't just Scottish meanness?'

'Entirely not! We want to get somewhere – we walk, or someone offers a lift. It makes a difference. It's about connecting, not driving up to certain doors saying, "Excuse me, can you tell me where the Stone of Destiny is?" A knife isn't the only way to open a scallop.'

Leo thought of Adamson, the hunting knife in the holster, the catch in Kirsty's voice when she talked of the cold of it held to her jaw in Dumfries. One day there'd be a reckoning, with the knife taken out of the equation.

'What's the other way?'

'Sneak up when it's not slammed shut.' She laughed, warm and amused, and he thought it the most heartening sound he'd heard in a long time.

'Where did you learn that?'

'From a scallop diver, of course!' She packed her thermos into her day sack. 'Mind you, he may have been pulling my leg, because he did carry a very big knife in his belt.'

Leo stood up, stretched the stiffness from his damp legs. Mild sun on his face, the soft bog-myrtle wind, rain clouds clearing over Jura – he felt them all, especially the clearing.

'What I'm saying, Leo,' Shonagh said quietly, serious now, 'is when it's ripe, the fruit just falls. All you have to do is be in a position to catch it.'

Kara, dropping screaming-laughing from a tree, flush into his arms.

'I'll be there,' he said, and for the moment felt it true.

That evening and night – the third, the fourth? – brought a couple of large Bunnahabhain in a chilly breeze-block house in the place of that name, then a lift for a meal with a friendly farming couple near Ballygrant. Then they all went together, half a dozen now, to Bridgend where the talk was all in English, thence to a dance in a corrugated iron hall in Bowmore, where it wasn't.

The whisky went from peat dark to old gold to solid mahogany. It had become worryingly easy to drink. Around two in the morning, after many willows had been stripped, sergeants dashed and improbably gay Gordons and eightsomes unreeled, Leo stood holding the wall up with his back, a glass of Ardbeg in his right hand and a pint of water in his left. The stovies and cakes had been produced round midnight; now he felt a few late sandwiches and a mug of tea would put him just right.

With only a slight sway he excused himself from the Brummie on his right and the quiet-spoken German on his left – certainly not all the people on Islay were Gaelic, or even Scots, and they all seemed to be getting on with it – and set off for the tea urn.

'Ripeness,' he murmured inwardly. He passed behind Shonagh who was huddled in talk with a narrow-faced, shifty-looking, kilt-wearing man she'd been with much of the evening. She glanced round at him, slipped a quick reassuring wink.

'All right, *a ghràidh*?'

'Sublime,' he said and headed on his quest for tea and sandwiches. No worries.

Turning from the tea urn with the mug in his hand, looking over the wearying dancers, the faces shining or vacant or caught in the fire of the moment, he knew himself happy.

17

Late morning, Leo walked alone along the beach at Bridgend, watching sandpipers scuttering to align into the breeze.

He was thinking of his mother's toast-rack. One of those little silver-plated ones so common in his childhood, now just ornamental curios. This one had *A Present From Ayr* in curly writing along the base, and the toast would be stacked in it each morning, 'To stop it going soggy,' his mother explained.

He stopped walking and stood looking out, feet sinking slightly in wet sand. Where had that toast rack gone? What had happened to the order, the security, the certainty of that world embodied in his mother stacking toast in the rack as they all sat down to breakfast?

Gone. Mother, toast-rack, certainty, wife, child, all gone. There's absolutely nothing stays crisp in a soggy world. It seems they're dead right at Samye Ling, and yet they always seem so light-hearted. How is that?

'Hey, dreamer!'

Shonagh, waving and hurrying across the sand. He turned back to hear her news.

They got a lift to Ballygrant from two twitchers driving a rented Mondeo. A Laurel and Hardy double act: big bloke with a green woollie hat and new violet kagoule, his little mate in a new scarlet parka with a hood that enveloped his head, big binoculars and a camera bumping off his chest. Leo and Shonagh had seen them around the island earlier, trudging about looking lost and depressed. 'Bill and Ben the birdie men', she'd christened them, as though what they were looking for – some rare migrant warbler, apparently – was anything less daft than a Destiny Stone.

Neither Bill nor Ben were chatty, just asked where they were heading, muttered something about the weather being wrong, then let them off at the road junction.

Leo and Shonagh waved goodbye to the car and set off North across the undulating, trackless moor. The day was one of passing dark and light: showers, bright sun, rain, grey then blue soaring high over their heads again, as though the hours were being fast-forwarded.

As they stumbled on, Shonagh told him she'd made a break-through last night and finalized it this morning. The odd-looking chap in the kilt she'd been talking with was called Nigel Smith.

'I know, I know,' Shonagh laughed. 'But he's a MacDonald on his mother's side. I'd guess he doesn't like his father very much, because he's gone overboard on the Clan and Nation stuff, and speaks Gaelic with the oddest accent I've ever heard.'

Last night Nigel Smith had admitted to Shonagh he was of the *Ordugh Rioghail Cathachail Teampuill Ierusalem.*

'That sounds infectious,' Leo said.

'The Scottish Knights Templar,' Shonagh grinned. 'Aye, it's a bit of a fantasists' convention, but they've been keepers of various stones and regalia for an awful long while.'

They struggled over a watershed and there was an inland loch glinting like a stubby blade stretched away from them. No road, no wires, just one solitary cottage near the far end of the loch. Once the stronghold of the Lord of the Isles, it was one of the loneliest and most desolate places Leo had ever seen. *No permanence*, he thought as they stumbled across the moor and bog towards it. Get used to it.

As they got closer, Shonagh pointed out the two islands in the loch. The bigger one, *Eilean Mor*, once had a chapel, a Great Hall, guard houses, stores, wells, a jetty – all the signs of a centre of power. They stood at the shore, looking across at it: humps and lumps, two tottering gable ends, some low turf walls, marks of recent excavation.

'*Ní h-éibhneas gan Chlainn Domhnaill*,' she said softly. It sounded like wind blowing through long reeds. Leo looked at her enquiringly. Her face was sombre, her eyes distant. '*There is no joy without Clan Donald*,' she translated. 'It's from an old poem. It's what we do best, lament.'

Eilean Na Comhairle, 'Council Island', was tiny and just a rugby ball's punt from *Eilean Mor*. There was nothing standing there at all, though they could see the paler scars of some recent excavation.

'It's a crannog,' Shonagh said.

'Isn't that something you eat?'

'That's cranachan, *a ghlaoic*. Nigel Smith told me that when they began excavating here the other year, they discovered *Eilean Na Comhairle* is an artificial island. You get them all over Scotland. This was where the MacDonalds went to hold council.'

They stood on the low rocky shore, staring across at the islands. According to Nigel Smith, at different times two of the most precious Scottish stones had been kept here.

'Then the Lordship was dissolved and it's said a stone was moved away. Then some time in 1951 – after the Westminster heist – another stone arrived, and they hid it somewhere here, and that was fine until last year.'

'What happened then?'

'A systematic excavation funded by the Scottish Office – great for archaeologists and Islay, very bad for men hiding big stones. And here's the man himself,' she concluded, turning to watch the scraggy kilted figure who had emerged from the sole cottage. He seemed to be wearing half a pheasant on his head, set off by a bright blue kagoule over his kilt. He swung a heavy-looking sack as he walked.

'Nigel said he's going to show me something.'

'Hmm. Do you think it'll be very big?'

Shonagh laughed. 'I doubt it. But it took a photo Kirsty faxed me, of her with her ring, and an awful lot of Lagavullin and genealogy to convince him I could see it.'

Leo started to walk towards Nigel Smith but Shonagh stopped him with hand across his chest.

'Not for you, I'm afraid. They also serve who stand and get bitten by midgies. Anyway, I need some guarantee there'll be no funny stuff out there.'

'He looks funny enough to me,' Leo grumbled. 'The way he looks at you.'

'That'll be the glass eye. Fishing accident, poor laddie. Just wait here and keep watch.'

So Leo took out his binoculars and flask, sat by the shore on his small pack and watched Shonagh and her guide launch a tiny rowboat. With Smith at the oars, they made it across choppy water to the larger island.

There he watched them move about the humps and mounds, stop at a ruined gable wall. From the gesturing, she seemed to be getting a history lesson or guided tour. Leo sighed and took out his corned beef sandwiches, unscrewed the top of the little hip flask bought in Port Charlotte. How right the whisky tasted out there, by the murmuring water, surrounded by coarse grass and heather.

Then he started, blinked, and it wasn't on account of the Bowmore. He scrambled to his feet and stared across the water.

One moment Shonagh and Nigel had been standing by a low turf wall; the next they had vanished.

Nigel Smith crouched and pulled aside the big flat slab behind a low fence and the faded sign 'Keep Out – dig in progress'. Beneath it was a narrow hole, steps going down. Shonagh stared at it, then at his queer pale face. She couldn't decide which eye was the glass one, which made talking to him unbalancing, not knowing quite where to look to make contact.

'Down there?'

'It's an underwater passage out to the *Eilean Na Comhairle*. The excavation found the opening. They'll be back in summer to finish the job – that's why the Stone is going to be moved.'

Shonagh hunkered down and looked into the darkness. The hole didn't look well made or strong. What if it was flooded, or caved in? She began to sweat at the thought.

'You first,' Nigel said, handing her a torch. 'I'll be behind with the tools.'

'I'm not good at enclosed spaces,' she said faintly.

'"What does not kill me, makes me stronger."'

She did not consider quoting Nietzsche a good sign. Nigel's long thin hair whipped around his intense white face as he stared into her from one eye but she didn't know which.

'Good for you,' she said, and took the torch. 'Personally, what doesn't kill me makes me feel ill.'

Nevertheless, she took a first step down into the hole, then another. And another.

It was tight, only just wide enough for her shoulders. The walls seemed nothing more than packed earth as the slope steepened. This could not be right.

She looked back to see his scrawny body against the light at the entrance. He hadn't followed her. He hunched down, and she could see he was going to push the stone slab back over the entrance and leave her here.

Something dark left his hand, then the bang as his tool bag hit the floor, and Nigel Smith began to come down after her.

She turned and went on, half-crouched. Her torch light seemed to be swallowed by the earthy dark as the passage descended. Then the sides became stone, and solid rock overhead. They must be under the loch now. It was not a comforting thought.

She had worked hard on Nigel to get this far. Played on his insecurity and resentment he had never been allowed into the inner circle. The stone he insisted on calling the *Lia Fail* was going to be moved away before the excavation restarted in summer. A group of senior members of the *Ordugh Rioghail Cathachail* were coming from the Mainland to do it; it had been made clear he would not be among them.

Didn't he want to see it, just once? And know whether it was the True Stone or a copy? The others wouldn't tell him, surely he realized that? And then there was Kirsty, who had a Moon Runner ring, who was busy in Norway but had authorized her to find and open the damaged stone.

She'd worked on him all right. His one great moment. Touching the Stone. Opening it to see…

Curiosity, vanity, insecurity, whisky: a heady combination. And it had led her here, into this unstable underwater passage with a kilted one-eyed Nietzsche-quoting fanatic.

'The end,' she heard him whisper, much closer behind her than she'd realized. She jerked round, banged her head.

'For fuck's sake, Nige!' she said, because there are no swear words in the Gaelic; at least, no short ones.

'Sorry,' he said. 'It's said they left the *Lia Fail* in the wall near the end.'

She flashed her torch off into the darkness. Nothing but black there. She tried to picture the distance between the two islands. How much longer could this tunnel go on?

'So what's it look like?'

His right eye glittered in her torch light.

'I'm not sure,' he confessed. 'I think it's black meteorite, but it could be white marble. I'm sure we'll know it when we see it.'

Shonagh used some more Low Dutch then forced herself to shuffle on. The passage wall bulged, there was some debris on the floor as if there'd been a partial collapse. Sweating and shivering, she turned sideways, crouched and forced herself through the narrow gap remaining.

The floor started to slope up. It became earth again. They must be entering the *Eilean Na Comhairle*. Soon she'd see daylight again.

She didn't. Ahead was a heap of rubble, stones and peat, completely blocking the way. Not surprising, after five hundred years.

'This is the end,' she whispered.

'There is no end, only Endless Recurrence.'

'Sweet Christ, Nige, you give me the willies.'

But he didn't take offence, for his torch beam settled on an iron ring on a block set into the wall near the floor, and at the other end of the block was another ring, and near it was a dark crack line.

'The *Lia Fail*!' Nigel Smith gasped, and dropped to his kilted knees.

Which was bollocks, of course, the *Lia Fail* being the Irish Crowning Stone, which definitely existed and was still in Tara in Ireland into the 17th century, so it can scarcely have also been the original Stone of Scone. Not even the most mythic of stones can be in two places at once. Still, like 'Stone of Destiny', which she had learned from Kirsty came through a horrible mis-translation, courtesy of Walter Scott, *Lia Fail* sounded good, and what sounds good lasts much longer than what is true.

It certainly stuck with Nigel Smith, even once it had become clear this stone was not marble nor a meteorite fallen from the sky. It was a biggish lump of reddish sandstone, with a crudely-carved cross on one face. The Westminster Stone, then, or a copy of it.

Together they dragged the stone out of the wall and, panting, focused torches on it. Especially on the crack near the right-hand ring.

'It is sacrilege,' Nigel said. 'I can't take a hammer to this.'

'I can,' Shonagh said. 'I haven't come into this horrible pit just to look.' She spilled the contents of his tool bag onto the floor, selected a chisel and groped for the hammer. His hand closed on it first.

'No,' he said firmly.

'You promised,' Shonagh urged. 'As one of the *Ordugh Rioghail*.'

'I was fou.'

'A drunken promise is closest to our heart,' she retorted.

He blinked, but still held on to the hammer.

'Is that Nietzsche?'

'No, my granny. Look, the Stone has already been broken. All we do is open it, take a look inside, then mend it again.' Shonagh grasped the iron ring in frustration. 'For God's Sake, Nigel! No one will know.'

'I will,' he said, and looked sideways at her, the hammer bobbing in his hand.

Later, Shonagh often wondered what would have happened next, but the iron ring shifted in her hand. She looked down and saw the broken fragment had eased from the main block. Inside, a rod glinted dimly.

'Now we'll have to mend it, *m'eudail.*'

He put down the hammer.

Kneeling together in the dimness, they eased the broken fragment away. Two blackened rods, and between them nestled a tube of paper. As Nigel Smith grabbed it, the perished rubber band fell away. He shone his torch down and read, his long thin lips moving soundlessly. Then he sat back on his haunches, and silently handed the paper to Shonagh.

Her torchlight shook slightly as she read *Westminster Copy 2. W.M. fecit.*

She glanced at her companion. He was gazing blankly at the wall, a streak running freely from his left eye. How we need our cherished illusions, she thought. I may have done a wrong here.

Still she took care to read the smaller scrawl that followed. *Sit doon and ca' canny!*

While Nigel mixed stone powder and epoxy resin, Shonagh had a careful reread of the paper, making sure she missed nothing. The scrawl at the end seemed more joke than clue, just an old couthy saying. *Sit down and take it easy*. She shook her head, rolled up the paper and stuffed it inside her fleece jacket.

It seemed to take an age, putting the stone back together. With nothing to do but watch and wait, Shonagh felt her claustrophobia building. She forced herself to breath deep and slow, and tried not to see her torchlight as failing, her intent companion as cracked as the stone he worked on.

* * *

Leo had sat himself down in the lee of the cottage that had been converted into a display centre about Finlaggan and the excavation. After Shonagh and Nigel Smith had failed to reappear, he'd assured himself they hadn't dematerialized, which meant they must have gone into some well or underground chamber. The kind of place you might hide a big stone.

Fair dos. There was no way Smith could get away, so he couldn't be up to some stunt.

Leo poured tea from his flask and attacked again the awesome sandwiches Margie had stacked that morning. Good life, these jokers had. Kids and all. Hard not to look at them and remember.

He sat by the shore of Finlaggan Loch and remembered.

The more often he flicked through those images, the more removed and faded they got, like something being photocopied over and over. Now only in dreams did he meet Kara again, see her eyes looking into him, hear her voice fade, watch her thin hands working feebly on a jigsaw puzzle in the hospital in the last week of her short life. Leukaemia rips through a kid like a bush fire.

People talk about moving on. What a crock of shit. It's more about holding on, every day, while the things you most value are being torn from you. Repeat for as long as you live.

He swallowed cooling tea and was reaching for the hip flask when he heard voices. Bill and Ben the birdie men were ambling awkwardly down the slope towards the cottage.

'So your mate is still on the island?' the big one asked.

Leo thought of him as Bill. Big round head under the green knitted hat, like a tea cosy on its pot. His eyes weren't stupid.

Leo nodded, wishing them gone. The tense little one scanned *Eilean Mor* with his big new binoculars, then switched them over towards *Eilean Na Comhairle*.

'Can't see them,' he said. 'Must have gone under, like.'

His voice was scratchy, resentful. Leo, still sitting leant against the cottage wall, looked up at the two twitchers. The big one, Bill, peaked his hand over his eyes to stare into the light bouncing off the water, and then Leo had him. A face last seen under a baseball cap inside a 4x4 on a snowbound road.

Leo began to casually ease himself up.

'We'll just wait, then,' Bill said. 'Inside the cottage.'

The gun in his hand was big enough to blot out the world.

Two figures reappeared behind a mound on *Eilean Mor*. One waved towards the shore a couple of times, then they got into the tiny boat. Leo could see Nigel Smith's pheasant feathers stuck in his bunnet and read Shonagh's excitement in her gestures as she leaned towards her companion then looked back at the shore. He could see it all coming and there was nothing he could do. For a moment he was back in the children's hospice in the final days, helplessly watching the worst happen.

Life isn't meant to be like this, but it is.

'They haven't got anything in the boat!' Ben said. He stood at the cottage window with a short iron bar in his right hand.

'Get back from the window, mate,' Bill said calmly. 'Let them come to us.' He twitched his gun. 'You too, pal.'

Leo moved back against the display panels as Ben took up position behind the door. The boat reached the shore. He could hear excited voices. Bill was a few feet to his right, just out of reach, at ease, alert. If this had been a rugby match, Leo would have known just what to do, but even the most hardcore of rugby games didn't include guns.

So he waited, helpless. Heard the voices coming closer, Shonagh call his name, saw the gloating smile on Ben's face, the same as just before the 4x4 had rammed them. Only this time there'd be no let-off.

Shonagh pushed in the door, calling, 'Leo, it's a copy!' then stopped.

Nigel Smith was either brave or stupid. Ben's iron bar cracked down. Nigel screamed and fell to the floor clutching his broken arm. Shonagh crouched, her arms round him. Ben laughed like he'd done something clever as he stood over them. Bill stood calmly, watching Leo move back against the wall.

'So it's a copy,' he said.

'The Stone's all yours,' Shonagh hissed. 'If you want it, go and get it.'

'Not interested in copies, darling,' Bill said. 'There's only one Stone he's after. But I will have what you found inside.'

Silence, broken only by Nigel Smith's muffled sobs.

'You'll have the original paper or you'll have made a copy,' Bill remarked. Ben looked at him admiringly. 'So you can give it me, or I'll have my associate search you. Which may be quite intimate.'

Ben nodded, looked excited at this prospect. White-faced, Shonagh spat something Gaelic. Leo measured the distance. Too far. Once shooting started, it wouldn't stop.

'Give him it, Shonagh,' he said. 'You're much more important than some joker stone.'

Shonagh looked up at him, at Bill and Ben, then reached inside her jacket.

'Thanks for doing the legwork,' Bill said. 'Nice one.'

Ben smiled as he stepped away from the three on the floor. 'Trussed like turkeys, uncle Bill,' he announced. 'We gonna, like, finish up here?'

Bill looked out the window, then back at them. He checked his watch.

'No need. We'll make the afternoon boat.'

He stooped to pick up Leo's hip-flask, unscrewed the top, sniffed.

'You drink this?' he said incredulously. 'I'm a voddy man, myself.' He dropped the flask, watched the precious liquid glub onto the floor. The room filled with the reek of alcohol and peat.

'Amateurs,' he said.

As they went out the door, a thin, grating voice said, 'Boss will be pleased!'

'Boss will be fuckin delighted, Benny.'

Then the door closed and they were gone, leaving Leo in one corner, Shonagh and Nigel – who seemed unconconscious – in the other. Already the wire round the wrists was starting to burn; knees and ankles throbbed where they were bound.

'Bill and Benny,' Shonagh said into the silence. 'I must have the second sight after all.'

The daylight went. It became pitch dark, and very cold. The wires cut deeper. The room began to smell of pee. Nigel Smith learned that what did not kill him could hurt him very, very badly. Some seven hours later, round midnight, cousin Donnie arrived, with wire-cutters and two flasks, as instructed by his anonymous caller.

Sit doon and ca' canny indeed.

PART THREE

Been a long time getting here

18

How many, how ordinary, are the openings and closings in our lives! So thinks Inga Johanssen as she opens her eyes and wonders what sky her ceiling hides today.

Slight, upright, alone, she stands in black pyjamas, opens curtains and looks out on the whiter shade of pale that is Oslo in winter. She opens the bedroom door, opens bathroom then kitchen door. Before leaving she will close all internal doors (a small fetish perhaps, one she is trying to keep under control), then open and close the apartment door and out into the street.

Coming home from work – which is sometimes tedious, more often absorbing, for which she still gives thanks – she will click lights on then close the curtains. Pour a small schnapps and listen to the day's playbacks until time for bed. There she will open a book – biographies, of musicians mostly, though there's always a pile of crime thrillers, Ibsen or Tor Ulven to suit the mood – and enter a more vivid world.

The book, she has lately concluded, makes a more interesting (or perhaps just less demanding) bed companion than a lover. They do not twitch or snore, and one may close them at will. However, they do not keep the feet warm or press against one's back in the night. At length she will close the book, close her eyes, and only then reach to turn out the light.

As she prepares to leave for work on this particular morning, she is thinking how a whole life could be tracked in these openings and closings. One could imagine each moment as having a door into it, a door out. And in the little bright space between each opening and closing, a life is lived.

She is thinking all this, so quick does the inner stream flow when not frozen, in the time it takes to close the doors then shrug into her tan suede jacket, zip it up to her throat. Black cord hat with ear flaps, red scarf. She has a glance round – everything will be in exactly the same place when she gets back – then unbolts her door and steps out into the corridor. Her door handle, she feels it so clearly in that moment, her warm perishable hand on cool metal.

She turns her back on the corridor, still musing on the severances of our days, is about to pull the door to when a boot jams into the closing. A hand clamps over her mouth, another grips her neck and a force lifts her off her feet, bashes open the door with her forehead and throws her back inside.

The door slams closed behind and Inga's chosen, secluded life is over.

'What do you want? Money?'

He had done the scream-and-I'll-cut-your-face-like-salami part. They were in the sitting room, her lying on the sofa where she'd been thrown. Her neck felt twisted, her forehead throbbed from the door bang.

Her attacker was not a big man, even in the down jacket he was calmly unzipping, but she was small in this country of giants. He had tossed her across the room like an irritating book.

'Money?' The man looked offended. 'You think I'm some small-time mugger?'

His voice was flat and calm, accentless English. He seemed at ease, as if he did this every day. Perhaps he did. He peeled off his coat, then his blue suit jacket. Both neatly placed round the back of the chair, a man after her own terrified heart. Then he stood over her as she lay, and had a good look.

'You don't have to hurt me,' she said, her voice nearly steady. She may even have started to unzip her jacket. Surely no five minute rape could be as bad as the five years of emotional carnage it had taken for her marriage to be dismembered then salted away.

He took off his fur hat and placed it on the coffee table. His hair was shaved very short and left his head oval-smooth, like a brown egg.

'Not my type, sister. Not much on you.' He pulled up a chair next to the sofa. She wriggled upright, trying very hard not to admit the existence of the long pointed knife in his gloved hand.

I wish I'd done more, she thought. *Hidden less. Played more and better music. Not been such a sourpuss.*

The knife blade twitched like a conductor's baton, slicing time into tiny bits.

'Yes,' he said proudly, 'it *is* sharp. Top of the range. Look.' The knife blurred past her nose, thunked into her father's Thai teak table. A chunk went flying.

'Name's Adamson,' he said, examining the blade for notches. 'I want to buy something of yours, Miss Johanssen.'

She blinked at her name and did her best to un-cower.

'You have an unusual sales pitch.'

He nodded, then sat back in the chair. 'Good,' he remarked. 'You're quite tough for a scrawny little thing.'

To her shame, she nearly said Thank you. Instead she croaked 'Actually I am quite scared.'

'Who wouldn't be?' he agreed.

'So you know how it feels?'

Maybe she thought to try to form a relationship with Mr Adamson. The flat glare in his odd eyes put an end to that fantasy. They were not going to share life stories. The blade twitched and vanished into a tan shoulder holster. His hand went into his pocket and came out holding money. A lot.

'I'm not a thief,' he said. 'I'm willing to pay 20,000 krone for your Moon ring.'

'It is not with me.'

He leaned forward and looked into her eyes. It was like entering the North Sea in winter.

'I can see we're going to have fun,' he said.

*

He seemed to be in no hurry. He told her to phone the studio *in English* to say she had flu and wouldn't be coming in today. That she didn't want any visitors, not that many set foot on her little three-roomed private island. When she put down the phone, he made one quick flick and severed the line. Then they sat and looked at each other in the silent apartment, him with the big glinting blade turning restlessly in his gloved hand.

'I told you, my brother Colin stole my ring weeks ago.'

He grabbed her wrist so hard she felt the little bones crunch. He stared at her fingers, at the pale indentation where the ring had been.

'Tell me more,' he said. 'Look at me while you say it.' The liquid nitrogen of his eyes froze what passed for her soul.

She gave him the short version: Col's sudden appearance here a few months back, in search of sanctuary, a free bed, a less demanding dealer, a new start – the usual. It had gone on for years. But new was his interest in her Moon ring, only the remnant of her old street identity, her mother's I'm-off-to-my-new-life-in-Goa-be-groovy farewell present from years back.

'How long ago did he turn up?' Adamson demanded.

'Maybe a couple of months.'

He nodded. She saw his lips were full and pale and moist, like he'd smeared them with protection. You don't want to get cracked lips in winter here, even if you are a knife-wielding maniac.

But he wasn't a maniac. He was something she had never met before. The tiny unfrozen part of her was curious.

'I met your brother in a bar in Brussels nine weeks ago,' he said. 'He was in a talkative mood.'

'So he was high?'

'As a helium balloon. At first he bored me. Then he said something interesting. It's my job to listen out for such things, so I bought him some drinks and he became more talkative.'

He stopped there. In the pause that followed, some things began to make sense. When her mother had bequeathed the ring, she had become solemn and said it was one of a set and Inga was now its keeper. It had come down from her Scottish grand-father. She admitted she had no idea where the other rings were or what they were for, only that they were connected to a Crowning Stone.

Stoned, more like, Inga had thought. But apart from giving birth to her – a gift whose value she was beginning to question at this moment – the Moon ring was the only thing her mother had left her along with her name, so she hung on to it. Even when she left the street behind and the big hair, the dungarees, the strings and pipes and saucy swagger by which her extended family made their living, when all that went she kept the Moon ring, usually on her finger, where its pale green spark was her only adornment once the wedding ring had gone.

And Col had suddenly become interested in it. He even sug-gested that as Mum's son, the one who had been chosen to live with her and Falafel Fred in Goa, he ought to have it. She replied that she been the one who'd stayed to supervise Dad and be his front-girl for another five years and keep the money dropping into the hat.

Then he offered to buy it. She should have wondered at that, for Col didn't believe in money, any more than Mum or Dad had. Important things – dealers apart – were not done through money. Money was a drag, especially when you did not have it.

She caught him lifting it from her dressing table. There was a fight. It was not good. Things were done and said. He got a cut above his eye, she got some sore truths and her ring back. Then he left. He sobbed and he left.

When he came back a week later, he was different. Before, he had seemed obsessed. Now he seemed scared. Ashamed and scared. He kept putting his arm round her like she was fragile and precious.

Looking at Adamson, she began to understand why.

'I'm a patient man,' her captor said. 'I used the time to do my research about the rings. I found an article that confirmed the likely existence of a certain Stone, then secured a client for it. The potential fee made proceeding imperative. So I had to give Colin an ultimatum: either he got the ring from you, or I made him give me your address and came here myself. '

So her silly, charming, weak and sadly talentless half-brother might have convinced himself he was doing her a favour by stealing the ring – and getting whatever the agreed price was. He was not a thief, he just did not believe in possessions. Like her generous, careless and feckless father, he'd always been free with his own, would have given the sweat-soaked shirt off his back if she had asked, which of course she never did.

And then the fear would have started. What would happen once he'd given the ring to Adamson? What would happen if he didn't? What would happen if Adamson came looking for her?

'I suppose Col did what he always did when things became difficult. He ran away. I have not heard from him since.'

Adamson twirled the knife point on the Thai table. They both watched fascinated as it scoured out a hole. Then he looked up at her.

'He's weak, your brother,' he said thoughtfully.

'Yes,' she said. 'It is not his fault, just his nature. He is only my half-brother. I have quite a lot of them. Mum and Dad were…'

'Free spirits?' He inclined his head. 'Something of a free spirit myself.'

Do what thou wilt shall be the whole of the Law popped into her head – the blustery Aleister Crowley maxim her father liked to quote in justification for whatever he felt like doing at the time. She doubted if even Crowley had Mr Adamson in mind.

'But you're not a free spirit, Miss Johanssen, are you?'

'No. I think we just do what we must.'

'As it happens, I agree.'

Any dream she had of their building a captor–captee relationship and discussing the nature of Free Will went as he plucked the knife from the table and gripped her right wrist so hard she wondered if she'd ever play again.

'Some questions require answering,' he said. 'Do I believe you?

Do you really not understand the ring? Where is your brother now? Put your right hand flat on the table.'

They were coming to it now.

'Spread your fingers. Wider.'

She tried to not be there, like she did at the dentist's. He would not believe the truth when she told it. That is the worst nightmare, the one with no wake-up.

'In a moment I'm going to ask you some questions,' he said, 'and you are going to look into my eyes and answer them, and I am going to decide if I believe you. Is that clear?'

Her voice had seized up. She nodded.

'But first we're going to do some trust exercises.' A faint giggle forced up her throat. 'You are going to learn you can trust me to do exactly what I say. And I am going to learn to trust you will do exactly what I say.'

Perhaps she lost her soul for a moment. Then found a tiny distant furious corner of it.

'You enjoy terrorizing women?'

He seemed to find her amusing. 'I'm not fussy,' he said, twitching the hungry knife above her spread fingers. 'Men, women...'

'Animals?'

'Animals? You think I'm some kind of sadist?' He seemed genuinely outraged. 'In my spare time I like to study migrating birds.'

'Really?' she said. 'Where?'

'The Baltic, Shetland, Guatemala. The way skeins of birds gather and move across the sky, or settle onto water after a long migration, moves me deeply. And I am particularly interested in the accidentals, about which I am developing a theory. But what I really like, Inga – I think we're about to be on first name terms – isn't just scaring people or cutting them, though of course I enjoy that.'

'Do not keep me in suspense,' she croaked.

His moistened lips twitched.

'If you were a bird, I'd say you were a little Arctic tern.' He bent over her hand and circled the blade point a few inches above it. 'I really like to look into people's eyes and see them *give it up*.'

Then he got to work, doing what he liked best.

19

First he played the ticktack game with the point of his knife, flicking the tip down between her fingers, alternating spaces. The knife plunged faster and harder and jumped around more. Little chips of wood flew off the table. One touch of that jumping blade and a finger was gone.

At first it was so hard for her not to flinch as the knife thudded down. Then the blood and spirit abruptly went from her and it was possible to just watch, wait for his will. His eyes flicked up to hers and stayed there even as his knife kept drumming down.

'Good,' he said softly. 'Good girl, Inga.'

She had given it up. He had her. She was not so tough. Perhaps no one is. Then she felt a sharp burn down her middle finger.

'Oops,' he said. 'Sorry about that.'

They both stared at the blood welling up from the little slice taken off near her knuckle. Bright red it ran across the table, welled into the little pits the knife point had made.

'Where has your brother gone, Inga?'

She shook her head, unable to speak. Something complicated was happening inside as she watched her blood go out.

His free hand shot out, grabbed her jaw and made her look at him. The smell and feel of that leather marks her still. Eventually he nodded.

'Perhaps I believe he took your ring. *My* ring. So now we come to the more wide-ranging question: do you know where he might have gone? Do you, Inga? Keep looking at me.'

He released her jaw.

'No,' she croaked.

A long, life-ending pause. Her blood was flowing faster now.

'Perhaps you think you can protect him. I would guess you've done it before.'

'I have tried. It did not help.'

He nodded, almost sympathetically.

'We cannot help each other, can we?' He plucked the knife from the table, inspected the bloodied blade for damage. 'You do understand it is either you or him?' She nodded obediently. 'So tell me where he might be, or I will certainly kill you and it will not be quickly.' He wiped the blade across the back of her hand. 'A knife is much more precise than a gun, as well as the obvious advantage of being silent. Well?'

She made herself look into his eyes. He stared at her with hungry, impersonal interest, like a vivisectionist eyeing an unexplored subject.

'I try to help you,' she lied. 'Now please help me, I am starting to feel faint.'

He cleaned, bound and taped her finger. Did it very well, though the bandage slowly bloomed pink like rhododendron flowers as they spoke. She sat obediently on the sofa while he searched the flat, doing no more damage than he had to. He found her Norwegian passport, glanced at the photo inside then slipped it in his pocket. Neither of them commented on this. He didn't need to; she didn't want to. Her British passport lay in her sock drawer.

She told him where her address book was – he'd have found it anyway. He turned the pages, frowning.

'There's a lot of scored-out entries here,' he remarked.

'The people I used to know move around a lot. Especially Col.'

'But you don't?'

'Not any more.'

'You like Oslo?'

She swallowed, looked out the window. A light swirl of snow feathered the glass, white out of a white sky onto off-white streets. *Until very recently.*

'It will do for now,' is what she said.

He looked at her, then round the room, idly rapping the address book on his hand.

'You make decent espresso, little mouse?'

As she set up the coffee machine, awkward with one hand, he wandered round the sitting room. He stroked and tapped the necks of the instruments racked up on their stands. Bass, guitars electric and acoustic, mandolin, her fretless banjo, the Irish bazouki. She liked to keep them clean and tuned. Instruments are like people, they need to be played with regularly or they go dead on you.

He ran his fingers across the strings of the Martin, then the banjo, nodded approvingly.

'You can play these?'

'I chip in at the studio. I'm a trained sound engineer, but sometimes I produce, sometimes play.'

'I watched you go in and out yesterday.'

She shivered at the thought. A psychopath with self-control and method. He seemed unstoppable.

'I was in a band once myself,' he announced.

She fumbled with the coffee tin.

'What did you play?'

He glanced up, almost innocent in that moment.

'I was lead shouter in a punk band. *Anger Management*.'

'Was that your motivation or the name of the band?'

He almost chuckled.

'Both. We were not so good. Then I had a problem with the guitarist, so he couldn't play any more and things fell apart. You know how it is.'

'Yes,' she said. 'I remember.'

She found herself getting out the best visitor mugs, the dark stoneware ones from Harray, bought on an Orkney Folk Festival trip. Taken with her beloved while he still was that. Then they married – her choice, she knows, she knows, so keen to strike her parents dumb – and then gradually she ceased to be his only beloved, and then so many tears of rage, tears of grief. Nothing much had happened since but work, self-sufficiency and the odd yielding through pure loneliness. The last year had been not so bad. And then Col showed up. And now…

The espresso hissed and spat. Sometimes coffee smells like life itself. She shook her head, tried to clear away the weakness. Think, girl, think.

'Milk or sugar, Mr Adamson?'

He turned away from her Martin twelve-string, almost reluctantly.

'Neither,' he said. 'But a sweet biscuit would be good.'

They drank coffee, him on the interrogator's chair, her down on the sofa.

'Excellent shortbread,' he remarked. 'From Scotland?'

'Yes.'

'Colin brought it?'

She bowed her head meekly.

'Yes.'

He fanned through her address book.

'He's lived a number of places in Scotland. Edinburgh, Glasgow, Inverness, Tayvallich…'

'He's also lived in Spain, Switzerland, Belgium and Ireland. When he is not with my mum in Thailand or India. Buskers are like your migrating birds. They follow the weather and visitors, looking for the Golden Pitch.'

'Hmm. Ever find it?'

'After Mother left with Col, Father and I came to Norway. There were no other buskers, the people were friendly and well-off, the summer weather was great and everyone seemed fascinated by this cute smiling little girl playing bass and singing beside her dad. Money poured into the hat.'

He glanced at her.

'How much of the takings did you get?'

'Five per cent.'

'Huh.'

'I didn't need much more, just enough for ice creams and juice and the fairs,' she said defensively. 'People wanted to "rescue" me, but it wasn't like that. For a while it was mostly good.'

'Still, five per cent for the main attraction.'

'Yes, well.'

'But you don't do it any more.'

'It is not who I am.'

She could have gone on, talked about the life then and her leaving it and why, but he didn't need or deserve it. Instead she ate her shortbread and watched her bandage bloom.

'And the Golden Pitch?'

'Dad told everyone about it. He was like that. Guileless. Childlike, if you prefer. He wanted everyone to come and share. There was a whole scene. We still...'

Fortunately, he had lost interest. He bit into his shortbread, licked his lips. Maybe it was the sugar hit, but she was clear-headed again. And like a child she wanted to put off the nasty bit as long as possible.

'What do you do this for, Mr Adamson? If you don't mind my asking.'

He sighed like she was some stupid interviewer.

'Money, of course. Enough money in this one to let me retire, if I so choose.' He put his coffee cup down on the table, fastidiously avoiding her blood. 'A vocation,' he said. 'A man needs a calling in life, don't you think? Women too, I'm told. Mine is getting things for people, often from other people who don't want to give them up. It's... satisfying.'

'You should have been in the army.'

'I was.' He saw her surprise. 'Very broad church, the army, room for all sorts. I was in a specialized corner of it. Went to many odd places, got up to all manner of tricks.' For a moment he looked almost nostalgic. Then he shrugged. 'I left. Think I worried them, to be frank. A training officer pushed me too hard, so, well, he went to pieces. You might say.'

He laughed, drained his coffee. Back to business. His hand drifted back towards his shoulder holster.

'Can I say something, Mr Adamson?' He nodded briefly. 'I will tell you whatever I can to help you find Col, because I want to stay alive, and I will do anything for that.' She looked him in the eyes. It was so nearly true she hoped he wouldn't know the difference. 'I know my half brother. He's weak but he's not stupid. He is crafty enough to steal my ring, and crafty enough to see you'd come to me. Wherever he's gone, it won't be anywhere I can know or guess. You see?'

She put everything she had into that. His eyes were like mica now, flat and layered and shiny. Her finger throbbed and smarted and she felt sick as the adrenaline came on again.

'I have thought that,' he admitted. 'It's just a question of whether the weak part was stronger than the clever part. I mean, was he weak enough to contact you – explain, apologize? Hmm?'

'HE HAS NOT CONTACTED ME!' she screamed, then burst into tears.

She felt him studying her. His gloved hand grabbed her jaw, lifted her head to look at him through tears. No defences or dignity left, her eyes flowed hot and salty.

He stood up and shrugged on his suit jacket. Then his padded coat.

'You're not capable of lying any more,' he said. He pocketed her address book. 'I'm going now to look for your brother. If I find he's been in contact with you and you haven't told me, you'll lose your fingers one by one, then you'll lose a lot more before you die. You believe me?'

A conflagration lit behind his eyes. She sees it still in her worst dreams and wakes whimpering. Some days she sees it even when awake, and must grab her friend's arm to keep from falling.

'I believe you,' she said. 'How do I get in touch with you if he turns up?'

'Good girl, ' he said. 'I'll get in touch with you. I'll have some people make sure you don't run away.'

Just like that, he was going. Then he stopped at the door.

'Three things,' he said. 'You don't even think about telling the police. I have contacts here, and I'll know.' She shook her head. It hadn't even occurred to her.

'Second – do you understand the ring?'

She stared at him blankly.

'Never mind.'

He turned away, then turned back. It was deliberate. It seemed everything he did was deliberate.

'Third – what was the name of that guitarist? Gypsy guy who lost two fingers?'

'Django,' she said faintly. 'Django Reinhardt.'

'That's the fella. Good stuff, if you like that sort of thing. Wouldn't have been so clever if he'd lost three fingers, would he? Keep playing, Miss Johanssen.'

He left the sitting room. She heard him open the apartment door. She fell back on the sofa and shut her eyes. All the openings and closings of our lives, she thought.

The darkness changed behind her eyes. She looked and he was standing over her.

'Hope I never have to drink that stale coffee again,' he said. 'Get some fresh in for when I come back.'

'Yes,' she said feebly.

'Yes, sir.'

'Yes, sir.'

He chuckled as he set a brown fur hat on his head.

'Gave it up,' he said. 'They always do.'

Then he was gone. The apartment door closed and didn't open again. She lay waiting for the force that would let her move and do the things she had to.

He had been so very nearly right.

20

That shrilling sound was not in her head. Getting off the sofa was one of the bigger feats of her life. The bell was accompanied by sharp bangs on the door – impatient, anxious or angry, hard to say. Through the spy hole she saw a burly man with a weathered face, tweed jacket and wild white eyebrows. Beside him was a neat woman with short grey hair, and two of Oslo's finest cops. She had a quick think, then opened up.

'Are you all right, Miss?'

He spoke anxiously, in English. Scottish English. His eyes flicked from her bandaged hand to the severed phone line. *If you talk to the police, I will know.* Inga did not doubt it.

'There's been a burglary,' she said. 'Two men came in here and took some things. I got a slight cut.'

She turned to the policemen and said it again in Norwegian. Like policemen the world over – and she had long experience of them in her old trade – one took out a notebook and began asking questions, the simple insoluble ones, such as who she was and when and how. The woman asked if they wanted coffee and went to make it. She sounded American. She wasn't young, but quick and light and observant. Inga saw her pause over the two half-empty coffee cups.

The tubby Scotsman drifted casually round the room. He ran his fingers over the scarred table, sniffed the blood on his finger then looked on as she talked to the police, waiting for his turn.

While telling her tale she tried to work out who or what had brought them here. Had one of the neighbours heard something and summoned them? But her session with Mr Adamson had been quiet. No screaming, except inside. So what had brought a Scotsman – who was no civilian, for all his kindly-uncle act – to her door with two cops, and why was he looking at her in that detached yet sympathetic, almost sorrowful way?

She thought she had a pretty good idea. And then, looking down onto the street below at the tall thin man with a blue scarf, shuffling to keep his feet warm as he read advertisements in the shop window, she had another one.

She turned to the Scotsman who was waiting patiently, running a big weathered hand over the strings of her mandolin, letting the little trebles shimmer up through the sounding hole.

'Can you say whatever you have to say to me at the police station? I don't want to stay here.'

Then they were out of there, into the street and into a car, Inga Johanssen and her entourage, and there was nothing the startled man in the blue scarf could do about it. As their car went by, she glimpsed him entering the phone booth, fumbling for change.

Sitting pleasantly squashed up against Ellen in the back of the car as they sped through bizarrely clean, neat and prosperous streets, Jim MacIver pondered the lassie. Inga Johanssen was looking out of the window, face averted, collar up on her tan suede jacket. When she'd first opened the door, slight, white-faced, exhausted, for a moment he'd taken her for a boy, and nearly made an idiot of himself by asking if his mother was at home. New jeans, ribbed sweater, short flat hair the shade of coral sand at Achmelvich, eyes pale blue as the clear water there, small, tough and delicate – not his idea of a Scandinavian, which remained some big, full-blown Valkyrie.

He was old enough to not mind making an idiot of himself, but not in front of Ellen. Her hand tightened on his arm, she smiled at him and for a moment they might have been on holiday, exploring a new country, thinking about finding an interesting place for lunch and then going back to their hotel – separate rooms, of course, but for how long? – to resume the courtship of eyes and lips and hands.

Then Ellen nodded towards the slight hunched figure staring out at the streets, the bandage leaking blood, and Jim MacIver was back on the job again, trying to solve a suicide, a murder, the suspicious death of a retired stonemason, and the possible recovery of his country's Destiny.

Still, isn't it grand when your heart is not at your command?

* * *

In his hotel room the man who called himself Adamson hesitated, phone in one hand, today's passport in the other. Norway was not an easy country to operate in – for one thing, the police were quite well paid, with good pensions to look forward to, which is a nuisance. But low-life is low-life everywhere, and the ones he could buy here were at least thorough and persistent.

'Get the name of the British policeman,' he instructed. 'If possible, what he is doing here. What they are saying in the canteen. Any statement she makes. Do it now.'

He put down the phone, then the passport. Sat in the simple room's only chair, coat still on, and waited, and thought. He reached out a hand, dialled and cancelled his afternoon flight out of Oslo, booked himself provisionally on the next.

It couldn't be coincidence. What would bring a British policeman out of uniform to Inga Johanssen's door? Who was he?

She had been telling the truth about her brother, he had been sure of it. It had been in her eyes and shoulders, the surrender. But if that waif boy-girl had conned him, he'd have her pretty little heart out, pinked on the end of his blade, still beating.

He got up, walked over to the grimy little window and looked onto the slush-grey streets. She hadn't been arrested. So what news had the policeman brought? What would she tell him?

He lay on the bed and quickly, savagely, masturbated while waiting for the call back, picturing not Inga Johanssen's body but her expression as she *gave it up*.

* * *

In his working life, even in the largely tranquil Highland towns that had occupied his attention, Jim MacIver had often had to be the one to give bad news, the worst news. The more objective part of him divided the reactions into *Wet* or *Dry*. People either flooded with words and tears, or just nodded, stared silently, knowing it true. For them the tears and questions would come later.

Inga Johanssen was dry, very dry. One small, firm nod at the news, gently delivered, of Colin's death, as though something complex had been fitted into its inevitable place.

'Could he have been…?'

Interesting question, Jim noted. He didn't believe the burglary story for a moment. He'd have to approach this one cautiously.

'No, I'm afraid he did it himself. They think the drug came from Amsterdam, probably from one of the euthanasia clinics.'

She nodded, wrapped her fingers round the mug of coffee. Under the fluorescent light of the interview room, the faint band of paler skin on the ring finger was unmistakable.

'He had tried it a couple of times before,' she said. Her voice was pitched low, and her accent was unexpectedly English, with a faint Scandinavian wooden edge to it, like a narrow frame around a small seascape. 'It always seemed like a cry for help. Not that we really could.'

Jim thought of the body lying in a mound of leaves behind the ruined wall in the heart of Rothiemurchus Forest. Not the place to go to make a cry for help.

'And this time?' he prompted.

For the first time she looked away, squeezing above the bandaged finger.

'Forgiveness,' she muttered. It could have been a statement or a query. She frowned, as if another possibility had occurred to her. He'd give a lot to know what it was.

'We've been unable to contact any other relatives,' he said. 'Parents.'

'They move around,' she said. 'In different countries, usually with no postal address. Show people, you know.'

'And you are not?'

She flexed her wounded hand.

'I am not a show person.'

Steady buzz from the lighting, faint squeal of taxi brakes outside as Jim let the silence stretch. A thin trickle of powder snow drifted past the window, putting him in mind of his father carefully working his hair with the twin brushes. The old man had washed his hair with soap, thought shampoo was vanity. Had a great, proud head of hair to the end of his life, did Aonghas Dubh, plus a heck of a lot of dandruff, showering down on his shoulders.

All is vanity, vanity under the sun. Does it matter why one man killed himself, or even who murdered another and why? What do answers achieve? All just distractions from the oblivion – or judgement – that waits for us. Yet still, in the meantime, we want to know who did this and why.

He thought of Ellen, tactfully waiting for him in the cafeteria, and he smiled even as he reached into the little bag he'd brought with him all the way from Inverness.

'Your brother was wearing this when he died. I have formed a notion it is yours.'

The ring rocked on the table, glinting green, then was still. Inga's lips moved. A soft exhale, then silence.

'Yes,' she said, but made no move towards it.

'Do you know what it is?'

'Yes.' Then as he leaned forward she added, 'It is a ring my mother gave me when she left me.'

She's playing with me, he thought. After what I'm pretty sure has happened to her, and after just being told her brother is dead, this calm child is playing with me. Rarely was Jim MacIver baffled by human behaviour, except sometimes his own, but this time he was stumped. The lassie had wanted to come here, but she wasn't ready to talk openly.

Which was perhaps why he made a clumsy move.

'Tell me, lass – do you understand the ring?'

As soon as he'd said it, he knew his mistake. Twin flashbulbs of suspicion went off behind her eyes. Then some new resolve. She unzipped her jacket, shrugged out of it, twisted to place it over the back of her plastic chair. She looked out of the window where his father's dandruff was still falling on the shoulders of the cars.

'All right,' she said at last. 'I must tell you what I know. But I need to have a pee first – down the corridor?'

'Aye, in the cafeteria.'

She got to her feet, looked down at the ring. Shrugged.

'Want me to ask your girlfriend to join us?'

He damn near blushed. She looked down at him with a sudden, quite lovely smile.

'Be with you in two shakes,' she said.

Jim sat and waited. He looked at the snow falling then picked up the Rothiemurchus ring and examined again the scratches in the mount. Like the ones on his, they looked random, irregular, merely decorative or accidental.

But they were not the same as the ones on his own ring, securely locked in the safe back at his hotel. This had to be some kind of inscription.

Inga Johanssen rushed into the room, panting hard.

'It is your girlfriend! She's had some kind of attack – they've taken her to the medical room on the fourth floor!'

He was up and out the door. A moment later, so was she, pausing only to pick up her jacket. Her ring had gone with the policeman, he wasn't that careless, but that didn't matter now. At the end of the corridor where he had turned right to run up the stairs, she went left then slowed to stroll out of Reception with a nod of acknowledgement to the woman on the desk.

'*Takk*,' she said, and was gone, light and quick as a late leaf blown from a wintry branch.

21

Neil and Kirsty sat in the Jarlshof café in Oslo, neither saying very much. The overnight ferry had not been a success. Perhaps if it hadn't been for the boat, the pitch and roll, the bilious green cabin, they might have fallen on each other and let their bodies sort it out. The reunion had not gone as either of them had imagined (when they allowed themselves to) in the months since they had parted. Somehow their romance the summer before, which had seemed a breakthrough, one so alarming that she had taken flight, was now a cause of embarrassment.

This could take time, he thought. She's changed, I've changed. Last summer she helped me feel for the first time since Helen died. We'll find this Inga Johanssen and we'll find each other.

She glanced at him surreptitiously as he stared out of the window at the door across the street. He looks older, she admitted. Wish I hadn't slept with Leo. What's the right time to tell him? There isn't one. Now I've dragged him back in, we've got to see it through. He said he loved me. Six months ago it felt like I loved him. Isn't that what we're all after?

Neil leaned closer to the window pane as a taxi stopped. A slight, neat woman in jeans and tan suede jacket got out in a hurry. He glimpsed very pale hair, high cheekbones in a white face as she paid the driver and scurried to the door.

'*Ja*, that is her,' the waitress said. 'She is back early from the studio, I think.'

Kirsty reached across the table to grip Neil's hand, the first natural thing she'd done apart from throw up half the night.

'She's still alive!'

Neil watched the street door swing closed behind the small

hurrying woman with the vivid face, then looked back at Kirsty. He liked her, he really did, her wild red hair, glowing face, mouth ready to laugh or scorn. This rush of excitement, sense of a great game afoot again. It would be all right.

'You think she's got a Moon Runner ring?'

'Ailsa Traquair thought she did.'

'Did you think she was acting a bit weird?'

'I think she was just pissed.' Kirsty let go of his hand. 'Let's go get Inga.'

'Think first,' he said. 'How are we going to handle this?'

Kirsty pulled her are-you-kidding? face, the one he remembered from their first night in a country hotel when he'd briefly wondered aloud if this was a good idea before she'd crossed her arms and with that lovely woman's cross-armed gesture pulled her sweater off over her head and said *It is now*.

'I show her my ring and we take it from there.'

'What if she won't help or doesn't know anything?'

'You always see problems, don't you?'

'I try to be realistic.'

'Is that what you call it?'

'Aye, I do.'

'Hmm.'

'Hmm yourself.'

They glared at each other, then looked away, embarrassed.

'We'll have to get better at this,' she said.

'Sorry,' he replied. 'I'm a bit out of practice at you.'

'No worries,' she said and got to her feet. 'I vote we pay for this excellent coffee and cake, then go call on her. Adamson could turn up any time.'

Neil reached for his jacket. That pale, desperate face, glimpsed across the street as she paid the taxi. She had to be told.

A few minutes later, muffled in padded coats and hats, they pushed open the communal street door and went up the immaculately clean stair.

'No entry phone system,' he commented. 'I could like Norway.'

'Strikes me as more sensible than exciting.'

'Some kinds of excitement I can do without,' he murmured, following her up the first flight. A door banged and echoed above their heads, then a clatter of heels. A woman in embroidered high-heeled cowboy boots and mauve dungarees, tatty Afghan coat and a froth of blonde hair with purple threads came hurrying down, clutching a large bag in one hand and a fretless banjo in the other. She hesitated when she saw them, then gave a big beaming smile. Her face was painted, little blue stars on each cheek, a silver half moon on her neck.

'*Hei*, you are looking for Inga? Top floor on the right hands. I think she is just returning from the studio.'

'Thanks,' Kirsty said. 'We are old friends.'

'She has so many friends, Inga,' the clown replied in broadly accented Norwegian, continuing on down the stair in a cloud of patchouli. 'Knock loudly and wait – she is a little deaf, I think. *Ha det bra!*'

They hurried on up, smiling at the flamboyance.

'What is this – the Seventies?' Kirsty commented.

'She'll be one of the street buskers. The city used to be full of them in the summer. Not so common in winter.'

They found the door, read the neatly printed name, rang the bell and waited. Rang and knocked and waited.

Rang and knocked again. Then looked at each other.

'Try the other door.'

The stooping, elderly American in the next door flat shook his head.

'Inga seldom has so many visitors. I think she's just gone out again.'

'Fuck fuck fuck,' Kirsty hissed as they clattered down the stairs and out into the clown-empty street. 'Boots and big hair. She seemed much taller.'

'Now what?'

'At least we know what she's looking like now.'

Neil pictured again the brief flash of very bright eyes in the stairwell. Nothing remotely clownish about them.

'She's going into hiding,' he said. 'Adamson or someone must have frightened her. Did I mention Helen and I spent a summer here before we got married, made some musician friends in the old part of the city?'

'You know fine well you did not.'

'Well you ken noo,' Neil replied and standing on the pavement amid the swirling snow, he reached into his coat for his address book.

'Bugger bugger bugger!' Jim wheezed, bending over the table in the empty interview room.

'Strong language, dear heart,' Ellen murmured. 'Why is it you never swear in Gaelic?'

Jim MacIver blew out, breathed in again. He was built for comfort, not for speed. That panic-impelled rush up three flights of stairs, then running about shouting, then making for the cafeteria to see a familiar head calmly reading her notes on the Destiny Stone and in that instant grasping that she had become the point of his life, and that he had just been played for a fool by a slip of a lassie – well, it fair did for a man's heart.

'A curse in the Gaelic is very bad, and rather lengthy,' he replied.

'At least you have her ring,' Ellen said.

'It's no the ring I'm concerned about now. It's the lassie's life.'

Ellen glanced sideways at his serious face, red now with the chase, the thick white hair plumed. She squeezed his arm. You'll do, mister, she thought.

His informant said the man's name was James Naughton MacIver. With the Scottish Highland Constabulary. The Johanssen woman had said she'd been burgled – Adamson grinned at this – but had then disappeared. Simply walked out of the police station.

Adamson stopped smiling. 'Find her. I'll pay for four men, double the usual rates. Undamaged, yes?'

It seemed MacIver had come to Oslo following enquiries about the body of a man found in the woods in the Highlands. No prizes for guessing who that might be. So who has the ring now, he wondered? MacIver or Johanssen? Could be either, so go for both.

He gave his instructions, then called the airline to confirm his place on the evening flight to Glasgow, using his McCain identity. Not without a certain humour, Mr Adamson.

He needed to get a look at the coroner's report on Colin Weir, check the list of effects. The policeman will have to come home sometime. And more investigation in the Scone area was essential.

Simple. Clear. Interesting.

He went back to the window and watched the night come on in a rush. Felt good, felt in control.

* * *

To the very end of her strength she dragged herself, the heavy banjo weighing like a sheet-anchor as she drifted into the few old parts of the city hidden behind the wide bright arcades. Into the scattered little streets, the small squares where friends and family used to perform all those summers ago. When the crowd gathered and laughed and coins flowed from their hands into the guitar case, and Dad was still a hero and she was a child, and Mum was golden and even poor Colin…

The Golden Pitch. Right here.

She rang the buzzer, heard nothing. She dumped her leather duffel bag and thumped the door till her fist ached, then leaned her forehead on freezing painted wood, unable to go on. She slumped down onto the doorstep where she had once played. Her damaged hand throbbed and burned. The banjo clattered onto the pavement, the frozen strings clanged out of tune. Too much to think about, work out, endure, escape. Who were those people on the stairs? The Scotsman seemed nice and she had been ready to open to him when he had asked her if she understood the ring. Exactly Adamson's question. He must be in it too.

She had to get out of the city. It was no longer safe to be Inga

Johanssen. Time to leave and become someone she used to be. Get away, rest, hide, think.

She curled up tighter against the sub-zero air. A passer-by slowed, hesitated, moved on with a shake of the head. In the dark alley, the stars were so bright above. The photos that might explain it all were zipped into the secret pocket of her old performing dungarees. And somewhere in the distance, a chanting voice hoarsely singing 'Lonesome Blues', scuff of feet and slow thump of drum, the tap tap tap of a blind man's stick, slowing as it approached. Unable to move or even open her eyes as she sank, she felt the hand pass over her shoulder, hair, spreading into her face.

'*Star*. Fuck me sideways, *Star Weir*. You're colder than a landlord's heart.'

The scarred old Geordie voice that went back to when she was a child on the Golden Pitch made it possible to open her throat just enough.

'Need help, Blind Summit.'

She rose to the surface under weight. Heavy blankets, sour plum brandy in her mouth. Reached out and touched floor. Absolute dark, where? Panicked, then heard a snore, soft undulating up and down the scale, a minor Blues. No one snored like Blind Summit. It went with her father laughing, talking, smoking and playing with his fellow free spirits through the night, her falling asleep to those voices. Safe for now.

Star Weir – a copy, a fake, or simply an alternative version – let go and sank without trace.

22

A speck of dust no weightier than a thought must have touched calm water in the ice-fringed pool. Inga stood and watched the rings expand and ripple out as though the pool itself was shaping O! Shivering inside her Afghan coat, she felt the same exclamation widening through her. Oh, Colin. Oh.

'C'mon, princess,' Blind Summit grunted. 'Freezing me balls off here. Let's get a nice, warm pitch and give the people some Blues to feed their impoverished sensible souls.'

What started it, she wondered? What invisible speck set off those rings? Who can I ever trust to read my inscription?

She put her gloved hand round his arm as they set off through the park to the shopping centre. In her free hand she carried the fretless banjo and his little amp; mikes and leads, flask and biscuits were stuffed in her back pack. On his back the bass drum wobbled like a gigantic growth. Harmonica stand around his neck, guitar case in his gnarled right hand – these his wordly goods, his tools, the means by which he lived. These, and the tiny flat, and enough money for food and coffee and good – surprisingly good – wine at the end of the day, were what he had whittled his existence down to. A lifelong underachiever, or a freer man than most – the way one sees it says more about oneself than about him.

'You'll feel better when you're working, my love. *Better to play than lay by sighing.*'

'Yes, wise Master,' she murmured.

'Cheeky whelp. Have you no respect for the man who taught you your first diminished chords, wiped yer arse, showed you how to charm krone out of the sycamore trees, and generally imparted the subtle arts of the street entertainer when your father – fine musician, bless him, but scarcely a realist – was away with the blonde marijuana fairies?'

'None whatsoever,' she said cheerfully as she steered him through the swing doors into the warm arcade. 'And you confine your improper thoughts about my behind to your dreams.'

'Canny lass! Acknowledge no master – believe I taught you that.' He put out his hand, felt along the frame of the shop front, nodded. 'We take our stand here.'

'Is this your Golden Pitch, Summit?'

Blind Summit knelt to open his guitar case, took out the National, stroked the cold metal. He twirled his fingers, then cracked them one by one.

'The Golden Pitch is where you claim it, pet.'

He turned to her, fronds of grey moustache drooping down below his chins, magnificent and wrecked, frail and enduring. She had no idea how old he was, only that he was the one who had looked out for her as a child, who actually thought about what she might need. The others had merely praised and indulged her, calling it *freedom* because then they didn't have to bother their sweet stoned heads about her. As if calling a child *Star* was care and blessing enough. And for a while it had been.

'You see, darlin,' he said, serious now, 'to stand in front of people as we do and remain honest, you have to believe you are on the Golden Pitch, and make sure they believe it too. Then they feel special. Then they give. Everyone's a winner.'

She looked around the glass shop fronts, the video shop, electrical and white goods, outdoor gear, the over-sweet lotions and Mystic Healing place, the American-retrospective chrome cafe. The crowd drifted, looking for amusement and something to buy, having nothing much better to do, the children either held back or dragged along. The few old people, looking puzzled at the world they would soon be leaving, meekly kept out of the way.

Prosperous, stable, decent, bored and yearning Oslo. Her cut finger ached, she was a fugitive, an emotional dead loss, the former possessor of a ring whose meaning she didn't begin to grasp but for which her half-brother had died.

'The Golden Pitch it is,' she said firmly, and warmed up the banjo with a quick clawhammer *Squirrel Heads and Gravy*, began to smile at the passing faces, hop and bop and be colourful, starry, pull them in. She sent out the clattery, joyous notes, Blind Summit nuzzled in on the old National guitar, got the bass drum thumping, and they began to collect smiles and coins.

A fleeting, honest trade. As she played, behind her eyes those invisibly-created rings in the pool in the park kept enlarging, wider and wider through the neon-lit arcade, and she looked again on the gathering crowd as though each face were a receptacle, brief hosts of the being that moved through them, the pool in which its dust was registered and spread.

On the evening of the day Inga Johanssen walked out of the police station and forty minutes later Star Weir ran down her stairs with a bag, a fretless banjo and some photographs zipped into a secret pocket, Neil and Kirsty tracked down his old acquaintance Frets Bader in the university quarter.

Schnapps and Belgian chocolates were produced and welcomed, strong coffee drunk in the small, guitar-crowded living room. Helen was quietly mentioned, acknowledged, regretted. Briefly Neil saw her perched, calm, graceful and slightly bored, on the arm of the chair by the window. How she always seemed to be alighting temporarily, on her way to somewhere else!

But today was about finding the still-living, so he looked away and finally raised the purpose of their visit.

Inga Johanssen? Yes, Bader knew who she was. He had met her a couple of times when he'd been doing sessions at the studio. Quiet, serious woman. Good ears.

'You liked her *ears*?' Kirsty enquired. 'Nice lobes?'

'Discriminating,' Bader said severely. 'Some people have it.'

Some people have flair and charm, Kirsty thought, and you're not one of them. She didn't take to his professorial, ever so slightly patronizing and superior manner. Or maybe it was just her instinctive distrust of jazz guitarists. Too many notes and implausible chord shapes, too few smiles.

Still, for once she kept her opinions to herself, noted down the studio address.

Neil explained they had to find Inga, inform her of an inheritance. She'd left her flat looking like someone else. He described the cowboy boots, mauve dungarees, wild hair, the painted stars and moon, the banjo.

'Sounds like one of the street entertainers,' Bader commented. 'Not serious musicians. I do not know many of them. In summer they are many, but few stay here in winter. I would not know the person you describe.'

'Just because someone is a good musician doesn't mean they can't be an arse,' Kirsty commented as they left the flat. Neil didn't disagree. Helen had said much the same, but more gently.

Half an hour's walk later they announced themselves at the PlinkPlonk sound studio. Were told politely that Inga had phoned first to say she was ill, then later to say she had a family crisis and had to go away for a while. She hadn't said where. Other people had been asking for her, including a British policeman. Was there a problem?

'There may be if we don't find her first,' Neil said. The short, stocky sound engineer looked at him sceptically, then without comment turned back to soldering leads.

Neil described the person they met on the stairs. Did that description sound like anyone they knew? A street busker, perhaps? A name? An address?

The producer blinked once behind steel spectacles, the sound engineer hunched further over his soldering iron. They smelled the scorch of melted flux. They were told firmly a session would be starting soon, and they must leave, please.

* * *

'Could they have been less helpful?' Kirsty fumed as they headed for the city centre. 'Or are they just being Norwegian?'

'They don't know us,' Neil replied. 'Here it takes quite a long time.'

'Why shouldn't they trust us? I've an honest face!'

'Maybe you do,' Neil agreed. 'But does that make you truthful? Or entirely harmless?'

Light-headed with schnapps and hunger, they headed back through streets of crusty re-frozen slush towards the café near their hostel. As they went on they talked less, each thinking about the night that lay ahead.

* * *

That night, as the man currently calling himself McCain allowed himself one stiff inflight Bloody Mary and pondered his next moves – *Traquair MacIver Johanssen Dundas* – while he looked down on the soothing nothing of the North Sea, Jim MacIver and Ellen Stobo wandered hand in gloved hand from the restaurant back to their hotel.

She thought Jim seemed distant, or maybe just exhausted. Worried, certainly. He had decided that the best way to resolve this business would be to find the Crowning Stone.

'And the man with the knife?' Ellen asked. 'You've seen what he did to that poor Mr Sidlaw. And Inga Johanssen's table – those chips of wood, and the blood!'

'A dangerous man, no doubt,' Jim admitted. 'We're trying to get an ID. There are only so many in his trade. Then we'll know who we're after.'

'And then? You old fool, you're not even armed. What are you going to do if you find him – kung fu?'

As he picked up his room key at Reception, Jim straightened and chuckled.

'Swear at him in Gaelic,' he said. 'Bore him to death.'

She picked up her key. Another night of separate rooms? Life was too short. Maybe a drink would help soften this stubborn, kind man's conscience on the subject of extra-marital whatnots.

'Care for a late dram, Jim?'

He looked at her. She felt herself, her desires, motives, fears, her body – all seen – understood, accepted just as they were.

'Not tonight, *m'eudail*. Need my bed.'

But then he kissed her at the turn of the stair, so tenderly at first that she almost forgave him, and went to her own room shaking her head and humming 'Winter Wonderland'.

'I normally find this is the exciting part,' Kirsty remarked. She plumped up the pillows and sat up in bed, watching Neil dry himself from the shower. Not as tall— she blinked, killed the thought.

'You're nervous too?' he replied, wishing she wouldn't watch him. They didn't know each other that well. It had only been three times, however great and meaningful, six months ago. That summer had become myth, like all the summers before it.

This wasn't how he'd remembered or imagined it. The woman he'd thought on and tried not to think on all that time, was now sitting up in bed, full-breasted, coolly watching him naked.

The hostel room was warm, functional but not romantic, even once she'd found the right switches, the low lights that erased the first lines around her eyes. They were both tired, disorientated, uneasy, but there was only one bed and if they didn't do it tonight they'd have to admit something was not right, and then they'd have to look into why. For different reasons, neither wanted to do that.

He got into bed and sat up alongside her. They looked at each other, each wondering what the other saw. Nervous laughter and a sense of loss held in tight together, in where the ribs divide.

'Maybe for tonight we should just, you know, take our time.'

'You old romantic.'

'Not that old.'

She let that pass. The decade between them had at times been exciting – the gap across which the spark jumps. Sometimes it was just a gap.

'Derby and Joan night, then.'

'Two virgins.'

'Hmm.'

Her slightly bulbous eyes on him. His hand of its own accord moved across her shoulder, remembering that thick, soft, red-head's skin. His fingers passed over freckles, dragging his heart with them.

'Wish this was the first time,' he blurted, 'or the fiftieth. Not the fourth.'

'These young people, jumping into bed at the first opportunity,' she said, then wished she hadn't.

'I expect you've been——?'

'Been leading a quiet life,' she said. 'Hard not to in Dumfries. You?'

'I've been… resting.'

Her hand travelled down across his chest, belly, felt him tense there, then relax.

'Hope you've had a good rest, darlin.'

Together they slid towards the horizontal, and things began to come alive.

'You know what you said about just, you know, taking it slowly for tonight?'

'Aye.'

'Bollocks to that,' she breathed in his ear.

Inga Johanssen lay not sleeping, trying to think beyond Blind Summit's snore. A musical warthog, in full rut. Amazing anyone could be that loud and still sleep through it.

She could see now it was not really the ring that the terrifying man had wanted, but the marks on it. Same with that Scottish policeman. After talking on the phone with the woman at the museum in Edinburgh when Colin had begun to take an interest in the ring, she had taken close-up photos of the mount but never got round to doing anything with them. It was time she did, and found out what the feathery scratches meant.

No, better to trust nobody. Not without a lot of thought. Today's busking had been fun, the relief of being someone else. Such an honest trade, the street. I entertain, you drop money into my upturned silly hat. No dry ice, warm-up act, flash lighting or sound manipulations. Just living in the moment, free and natural, without plans.

She reached out her hand, felt the Star wig on the floor, dry and dead-feeling. Tomorrow she'd go to the train station and find a place where no one had ever known her as Inga Johanssen. Surely safer there – and quieter at night.

Blind Summit's snore hit a crescendo of 'No Sleep Blues', paused as he stopped breathing altogether, then crashed into another wordless verse.

'Neil, about Leo, that Kiwi rugby player who stays at Samye Ling that I picked up.'

A long pause as they lay together, sweating, sated, perhaps closer.

'You didn't?'

'I didn't know I'd be seeing you so soon.'

Her head heavy on his shoulder, cutting off circulation but it would be wrong to move. They lay silent for a while, sleepy-breathing, both wondering at the relief.

23

Early next morning a clownish woman with wild purple hair extensions strode in her embroidered cowboy boots and greasy old Afghan coat into the train station and bought a single ticket to Bergen. The short, pallid young man who had been drifting near the ticket office since dawn watched her, yawned and checked her height, shook his head and drank down more coffee.

Still, the banjo stuck in his head. Don't see many of those. Nor many buskers in winter going further North. Those types went South like birds, to Spain or somewhere.

He moodily finished his coffee, wishing he were going South. Saw two women, one of whom was small enough, approach the ticket queue. No, much too old.

The northbound train cranked up and eased away. If he found this woman, he'd spend the reward on a holiday in the sun. Get a tan, flash some money, get a girl who didn't mind about his teeth and his height. Now if he wore built up heels like those cowboy boots...

He stared after the dwindling train, squinted into the mono-chrome light.

In their trail round the shopping centres and arcades, Neil and Kirsty found the inevitable group of Bolivian pan pipers. They had just shrugged and shaken their heads when Neil had tried in English, Norwegian and very poor French, to describe the busker they were looking for. Kirsty mimed the banjo, the shaggy coat and wild hair, but elicited nothing more than a giggle and a stare.

'What's the collective for pan pipers?' she wondered as they moved on.

'A ubiquity?'

'Not bad.' She nudged him. 'I assume this bloke with the blank expression and the white gloves is a mime artist. Let's try him.'

The mime artist when questioned stayed in role. Shook his head, rotated several times and went back to polishing invisible windows. As they walked away, they heard laughter from the small crowd. Turned to find the man imitating Kirsty, her quick long-legged walk, swivelling eyes, full sardonic mouth. Then he did Neil staring at him, pissed off. More laughter.

'I hate these mirror people,' Neil muttered, then of course had his words and expression mouthed back to him. More laughter. Children giggled.

'Only one way to handle these piss-artists,' Kirsty said and began to walk straight at the man. Who inevitably had to back away. Kirsty followed him, grinning insanely. The mime artist faltered, looked nervous. Kirsty did his falter, his nervousness. The crowd laughed. Mime man tried an ingratiating grin. Kirsty did mime man doing ingratiating grin. Mime man turned and strode away in high dudgeon; Kirsty followed in high dudgeon. Then mime man wheeled round and stuck out his hand. Without hesitating, Kirsty wheeled and stuck out her hand into empty air and they marched in line down the arcade, wheeled and came back to applause.

Neil stood in the gathering crowd, smiling for the first time that day. Somewhere there was the thump of a drum, a whining slide guitar echoing down the brightly lit galleries. He found himself nodding, tapping his feet, mouth shaping on old Muddy Waters song 'Built For Comfort', then he signalled to Kirsty – now going round the crowd alongside mime man, holding out her hat as he did his, cleaning up by the look of it – and went to have a listen.

* * *

A blind Blues musician who really was blind. And good. At the song's end, Neil dropped a handful of coins in the guitar case.

'Thanks,' he said. 'Bit of Muddy Waters makes my day.'

He got an unexpectedly warm smile, flared teeth flashing above the pendulous grey moustache.

'The human juke box, me – just drop the coin right into the slot.'

'Do you do "Blind Willie McTell"?'

'You taking the piss, mate?'

'Not at all. It's a great song. Mind if I play harp?'

The moustache lowered, wobbled, then big scarred hands moved over the shining body of the National guitar.

'Not if we agree this pitch is mine.'

A couple of songs later ('Baby What You Want Me To Do' and the more obscure 'K.C. Moan', a jug band number that gave space for the harmonica and for Kirsty to harmonize 'Gonna love my baby like I never loved before'), the busker took a break. He lowered his burden drum and sat on it. Accepted the coffee Kirsty passed to him. They got chatting about this and that. He liked to play in winter, when there was less competition. And at night, which made no difference to him.

'Know a busking banjo player, pal?' Neil asked. 'Fretless one, I think.'

'Small woman,' Kirsty added. 'Lives here in Oslo. We're fans, looking for her.'

Blind Summit sniffed his coffee, thrust a pastry into his mouth.

'Hate fuckin banjos,' he growled.

The conversation seemed to die after that. A couple from the audience came up and talked with the musician. Ignored, Kirsty and Neil stood aside.

'Let's be going,' she said. 'Think we've offended him.'

'Maybe,' Neil replied. 'Let's just wait awhile.'

So they stood quietly off to the side. Heard the echoing click clack of metallic heels, saw two policemen coming down the arcade and wondered if the busker would get moved on. The policemen slowed; the taller one reached into his pocket and dropped a couple of notes into the case.

'The usual, Blind Summit,' he said, 'when ready, *ja*.'

'Always happy to feed the spiritual needs of the agents of state repression,' Willie said, baring his fangs. '"Statesboro Blues" it is. Ease me on my drum, man.'

As the policeman eased on the straps, Neil heard him say in Norwegian something about a banjo player, pretty girl, pity she wasn't here again today. Any idea where she is now? Blind Summit grunted, in Norwegian replied maybe he smelled too bad, the woman had to leave. He didn't know who she was or where she'd gone. Then he began.

Wake up mama, turn your lamp down low...

Endless repetition wears out feeling in most musicians; a few it strips down to the bones of their art. Blind Summit Robinson played for money and he played for himself. In the long reaches of the night I think of him from time to time in that bright temple to consumerism, ragged and magnificent in ancient gold-embroidered dressing gown, multiple bandannas and neckerchiefs, the grey droops of his smoke-stained moustache flapping stately like a heron's wings as he sang 'Mama died and left me restless, Papa died and left me wild'. And I see the tall fair policeman standing mouthing the words, feeding his soul on the song of an itinerant black man of the Mississippi Delta who had died long ago, Blind Willie McTell, and I wonder at our strangeness.

At the end of the song, Neil went forward and dropped more coins into the case, spoke quietly into the musician's ear.

'What did he say about Inga?'

'He said come back tomorrow.'

'Did he say why?'

'He said if we had another go at "K.C. Moan", maybe we'd learn to do it better.'

'I thought we were pretty good.'

'So did I. Nice to hear you sing again, by the way.'

'Good idea to bring the harmonica.'

'We needed an in, and I could scarcely hump my keyboard all the way here.'

'That would be a lot of humping,' she agreed. 'Best save your energy at your age. And?'

'And he asked me who recorded the song. I said The Memphis Jug Band. He said I probably wasn't a policeman or a homicidal maniac, but he needed to think about it.'

She took his hand as they went by the half-frozen pond in the park. Skin on skin as the sun came through with a little warmth. Maybe things were looking up.

'I said "Tell her we're Moon Runners and we hate Mr Adamson".'

'Subtle stuff, mister.'

Star Weir caught the train to Bergen but never arrived there, and the greyfaced woman waiting by the barriers gave up after the third Oslo train came in. Star had got off at Myrdal, lodged high in the throat of the Sognefjord glacier, then paced up and down the chill concourse, banjo and duffel bag slung across her back, shivering and checking the glances that came her way. She stared boldly back. In this outfit, being looked at was the point. Her Inga clothes were in her bag. She pined for them but it wasn't safe.

She remembered Myrdal. It had been when Mum and Dad were as together as they ever were, and she was starting to sing alongside them, and poor Colin whining flat and somehow charmless, did his best. They had worked the streets for a week one summer. In the evenings she had wandered off the brown earth paths above the village. Met a man there who looked at her funny but did nothing wrong. She'd been lucky that way, had Star, as if that persona had warded off all evil.

Remembering that man who'd stepped out from the trees, walked with her telling jokes, asking where she was going, and then the yearning look in his eyes when they travelled down her, she saw Adamson's face inside the cigarette kiosk. The scream stuck sideways in her throat like a bone, then she saw the man's eyes. Blue, indifferent, ordinary. Nearly the same odd oval head, but taller, less tanned.

She had to sit down, wait for the thumping in her head to stop. Rubbed her thumbs into the hollows in her temples, careful not to dislodge the wig. Afraid, in transit, lonely, she endured the wait until the train came in that would take her away to people who would hide her without question in a place where she had once been happy.

Mama died and left me restless, Papa died and left me wild...

Actually they left her lonely and wanting to be not like them. Still it's a haunting song, always held the crowd. People knew the feeling, handed small change to their children as though giving would ward off the truth of it.

She huddled deeper in her Afghan coat and hung on for her train.

'We're wasting our time here,' Jim MacIver announced, massaging his feet at the end of another day tramping round Oslo. 'Even her friends seem to know little about her.'

'And those who know aren't telling,' Ellen said, thinking of the people at the sound studio. 'Do you think she's still in the country?'

'She hasn't drawn out money or used a credit card yet. Passport's still sitting on the table in her flat.'

'There are ways.'

'Surely.' He sighed, put one stockinged foot on the bedroom floor then started on the other. 'If I hadn't been a damn fool and asked if she knew what the ring meant...'

'If wishes were fishes, men would swim free, James.'

'And women?'

'Women seldom wish for what they can't have.'

He glanced up at her, his bushy white eyebrows, such blue eyes. 'Is that so, Ellen?'

'Not really,' she admitted. 'It just sounded good.'

'Sorry to hear that.' He lowered his foot, picked up his tumbler of duty free Poit Dubh blended malt. 'Please sit by me a minute, lass.'

She sat beside him on his bed, feeling like a teenager in Edmonton, all those hours of Will we, won't we? His arm was firm around her waist as her head found the comfortable place where shoulder met neck. He smelled right. That was important. He was kind. It had taken half a lifetime of ill-advised forays for her to realize that was important too. When they kissed and touched, years dissolved. Desire is desire, at whatever age. May it never quit till they carry me out.

'Jim, I have to ask you. Have you never had sex outside of marriage? Since you and your wife...?'

He almost smiled as he put his glass carefully on the bedside table, then looked at her with such tenderness and regret her breath was caught like a moth in her throat.

'Of course I have,' he said.

'Oh. So why not—?'

'Because each was a mistake I regretted even as I was making it. *Mo ghoil*, I do not want to do that again, not with you.'

'Oh,' she said, and felt the little papery wings escape her throat.

'Being brought up in the ways of the True Faith – however sceptically – is not all whisky and roses,' he said. 'Please keep your head right there a while.'

'Does the Book not frown on pleasure?' she murmured.

'It does not frown on the joy you bring to me.'

24

There is a small town on the coast of Norway called Socke. It is the end of the line and of the road. The only way out beyond that is by sea, the route used by the 'Shetland Bus' during WW2, smuggling resistance fighters and servicemen on the run. It has the remains of a fishing industry, though the deep-sea boats don't sail from there now. Like many seaside towns, it changes completely in summer when the visitors arrive, and with them, dancing in attendance, the buskers. But in winter – and down in the toe of Socke the winter is deep and long and chill with precious little circulation – it's down to the hard core. Even the few exotics that cling on have to be tough and committed.

The train journey from Myrdal to Socke includes tunnels, galleries, bridges, improbable gradients as the line winds down the narrow-throated gorge towards the fjord. In the summer people come just to take that ride, to gasp and gape at trees, rock, water in motion and dizzying space.

But this was winter, the train was near-empty, and the woman huddled in the corner with the banjo sitting up on the seat next to her like a stick-figure companion, seemed indifferent to the spectacle outside, the snow so deep only the tips of trees still showed on the mountainside. Mostly she sat with the *Afterposten* held between her and the world. What else is a newspaper for?

She quick-read the news. Nothing much was happening in Norway, which made it a better place to be than many other parts of the world. She read the global bad news, tried to set that against the unknown mass of unreported good news, and to weigh one against the other. Then she gave up pretending this was a possible computation, and turned to check the music reviews. More Norwegian jazz recordings, some of them good, one a CD she'd worked on. She read reviews of a couple of biographies – Swedenborg and Nordahl Grieg – that aroused her interest, but she knew she'd never get around to reading them unless Adamson broke both her legs and left her immobile for six months. She doubted if she'd get off that lightly if he ever found out that one small, furious corner of her had not surrendered to him.

She put down the paper and frowned into the dizzying white drop outside the window. The Scottish policeman had come all the way from Scotland to ask about the inscription on her ring. *That* did not seem official police business. And the watchful American-sounding woman with him, what was that about? And that couple hurrying up the stairs to her flat, the noisy redhead and the thoughtful man who had met her eyes for a moment...

She must rest, think, recover. No going back to real life – if that is what it could be called, and some might disagree – till this was over, and it was not over yet.

She reached into her bag, pulled out her back-up address book, and began to look through it, searching through all the scored out names, places and numbers for the very few who might remain.

Looking more relaxed after a satisfactory night, Neil and Kirsty went to the shopping centre where they had played with the blind Blues musician, and wandered through heated glassy cloisters into the church of consumerism.

Neil shivered in the heat, let go of Kirsty's hand to point in the window of the TV shop where a number of shoppers had gathered before the multiple screens all showing versions of the same. That day's atrocity came from London courtesy of an IRA suitcase bomb in a bus.

'Blimey,' Kirsty said. 'It's almost enough to keep folk from their shopping. I need coffee.'

'Kirsty, folk have been killed there. You must feel strongly about it.'

'Just because it's London, not some far-off country I don't know? Some people feel strongly about football. Hey, look!'

She pointed, and through the glass wall of the atrium they saw a tattered, fabulous figure in embroidered dressing gown and moon boots, sporting multiple bandannas, waistcoats, scarves, pushing a laden wheelbarrow across the mosaic courtyard.

'Work!' Blind Summit said as they helped him unload the little amp and stand, the big drum, mike and connecting gear and stool. 'I've never taken a penny from the state in my life. Mind you, I've seldom given it much either, not wanting to encourage the buggers.'

'What do you do when you're not working?' Kirsty enquired, hoisting the drum onto his back.

'Play music, of course! With friends, when I can find them. Drink wine, make music, laugh and cry. It's not so complicated, life.' He nodded, sat down on the stool. 'Don't let anyone fool you into thinking it is. Guitar.'

Neil opened the case and put the gleaming National into his hands.

'Talking of friends,' Neil said.

'There is a green place far away,' Blind Summit said. 'Many hours from here by train, where in summer the musicians and street entertainers from all over Europe gather for our own festival. A blessed place where the audiences have leisure, taste and money, where the fair ladies are always enthusiastic, the sun shines by day and the moon by night pours down on our endeavours.'

'Are you always this long-winded?' Kirsty asked.

'It's me garrulous nature, pet. But this buskers' festival has long been dear to our mutual friend. Even when she quit the free life, she would always come back for that week in July. I think that may be where she has gone now, the end of the line.'

He tightened the butterfly nuts of his harmonica rack, sniffed the air with satisfaction.

'*Nuits d'Amor*, coffee and apricot pastries,' he observed. 'The smell of life itself. Kindly fetch me some.'

'This green place?' Neil said. 'What's its name?'

'Age does terrible things to memory. But if you and your friend put in an hour with me – my pals tell me she is a looker, which helps – and the hat fills up nicely, I may start to remember. Deal?'

'Deal,' Neil said, and went for the coffees and pastries.

The middle-aged woman with the flowing grey hair, long padded coat and marginal but persistent drug problem, was working too. She had a disability pension though it was hard to say what for, but extra money was handy and she'd always been inquisitive. She stood at the edge of the small crowd gathering around the blind musician, snagged from their shopping for a song. She had been closer the day before, close enough to hear the dark haired foreigner ask about a missing musician. Close enough to hear the name uttered by the tall redhead. That name was worth money. It had brought her back here today.

The instructions had come back through an intermediary. The couple. Stick with them. Especially the redhead. Good, easy money.

She sighed, for her feet were hurting her of late, and wished she'd brought a camping stool. With a nod from the tramp with the guitar, the redhead opened her mouth and began to sing 'I hate to see the evening sun go down', powerfully, full-throated, head up and big grin on her face.

The woman with the long grey hair sighed as she worked her way closer to the front. Music had never appealed to her. She was more passionate about football.

So while Neil delivered coffee and Kirsty gargled saline to help ease the tear in her throat, Blind Summit launched into the 'St Louis Blues' slide guitar break he had played ten thousand times before but never *this* time.

If I feel tomorrow like I feel today...

* * *

'You're great when you're meant to be performing,' Neil remarked as they entered the central train station. 'I still wonder what you do when the performance stops.'

'Christ almighty – not that again.'

The flash of irritation was – singing apart – the most sincere thing she'd come up with that day. Neil winced but said nothing and they stood side by side in the ticket counter queue, both feeling slightly scrambled from the night before. No doubt, they had a long way to go.

'Socke, please,' Neil said. 'Two singles.'

The woman behind them stepped out of the queue, her work done.

25

'So there I am lying on the side of the road in my undies, watching my old lady and her new girlfriend drive off with all my possessions. No guitar, no clothes, no shoes, no money, no van. Yeah, that was pretty funny.' Jugglin John tried to laugh but his jaw was screwed tight and his eyes glittered. Behind Neil and Kirsty, Zippo stirred on his mattress.

'Drag, man.'

Jugglin John reached for his clubs, let them run up and down his arm, across the shoulders, back down the other arm. He was not young. Deep drinking gouges below his eyes, scar across his squint nose, powerful upper body.

'Pretty devastating, yeah,' he said quietly. 'So who the fuck are you guys?'

Neil looked at Kirsty, Kirsty looked at Neil. In the corner the taciturn German known as Alf had put aside his saxophone and now sat forward in his chair, scraping his nails with a pocket knife. Even lanky Jan, master of mandolin, bazouki, horn and whistle, did not look so goofy as he leaned against the only door out of the little room.

'We're friends of Inga – Star,' Kirsty said.

'Kiss my arse,' Alf muttered. He took a quick, fierce toke, held it in, squinting at them, exhaled. 'When I was a child, my city was fire bombed – Americans by day, British by night. I saw a lot of madness, you know? I thought *fuck you all*.' He opened his eyes wide, stared unblinking. 'And I look at you, so bourgeois and plump, coming to our town and asking for one of us, lying that you know her, and again I think *fuck you*.'

Kirsty was rising, Neil grabbed her arm but she shook him off.

'Well fuck you too, mister! You're a shite sax player with one riff and a boring line in martyrdom. OK, I don't know Inga, but the same man wants to kill us and we're trying to stop him, and that's connection enough for me.' She stood tall, shaking, formidable. 'And don't you dare call me plump.'

Alf sneered but said nothing. Jan giggled at the door. Neil shook his head wearily. Jugglin John let his clubs run down his neck, one two three into his right hand. Then he put them carefully on the battered table, alongside the tuners, harmonicas, capos, ashtray of roaches, cigarette papers.

'So who *are* you?' Jugglin John asked. 'And who are these people following you about?'

Neil looked at Kirsty.

'I told you,' he said. 'You said I was being paranoid.'

A laugh of sorts from Alf.

'That doesn't mean they're not out to get you. This I have never forgotten.'

Kirsty slowly sat down beside Neil on the floor and took his arm.

'So,' Neil said, 'where do we go from here?'

* * *

The two men who had stepped out of the Merkdal train behind Neil and Kirsty both wore dark suits and ties under their quilted coats. They entered the Socke Hotel bar and took off their hats. Both had fair hair in neat crew cuts.

'Look like a couple of Mormons,' Kirsty commented.

'I don't believe they're preaching goodwill to all mankind. Nor are the three guys in the black van with painted out windows.'

Kirsty put down her cup, wishing she still smoked. At least it would keep her weight down. Plump! She'd so nearly told that Alf git about her uncle Ned who had flown with Bomber Command, but for once a modicum of self-control had kicked in.

'Frightened?' she asked.

'Quite.'

'Me too.' She reached across and gripped his hand. 'We can't turn back.'

He looked into her eyes.

'I'd say that's not an option.'

'So let's go do it right.'

They got to their feet, pulled on coats, gloves and hats against the frozen dark outside, then hand in hand and as casually as possible went out into the street for the entertainment that lay ahead.

The monthly music night was a small blaze in the long winter dark of Socke. The hard-core inhabitants ventured out, down to the harbour to hurry through the massive doors of the old Customs house. Even the fishermen sometimes came, and this evening there were more than usual and less sober. Hardened men, weathered faces, swollen red hands that would become arthritic.

The evening's performers sat on the front benches. Katz and Gerry Blooze, Jan, Dr Harpo, Fat Elsa and Zippo, they made up the old guard, the ones who hadn't gone South for winter. Call them old hippies, stunted survivors, idealists or under-achievers, this was the life they'd chosen. To their right sat the neat children from the small secondary school, fiddles poised. And in the middle, flanked by portly Cisco and tense Alf, a figure in faded blue dungarees tucked into embroidered cowboy boots, with wild fair hair and purple extensions falling down under a big black felt hat, sat nursing a fretless banjo with a bandaged finger.

Neil and Kirsty got into the two places kept for them alongside the musicians, a row behind the woman known as Star. The two men in black suits stood at the back, watching. No room for them to sit, but now they had found what they came for, there was no hurry. They had checked: no other exit. Just a little windowless room behind the stage, through an old iron-studded door. They could practically feel the money passing into their hands in a few days' time. They conferred, then called in the three bouncers hired from Oslo's waterfront. No point in them sitting outside in the van, drawing police attention.

A few uneasy glances from the audience when they came in. Something not right about those people.

Once they were all crammed in and the doors were shut, the music teacher got to her feet and welcomed everyone, then the children filed onto stage and the evening began.

Music and songs good, bad, indifferent, plucked, bowed or breathed, lit a brand against the dark outside. For a couple of hours no cars passed by the high snow banks, nothing stirred in the smothered trees. As Neil watched Inga Johanssen lean over her banjo, hat and hair obscuring her face as she played, he sensed the men arrayed waiting at the back of the hall, and he wondered as he had before at how hard it is to distinguish a refuge from a trap.

The evening finished with all players crowding on stage, playing 'Careless Love'. Neil and Kirsty were signalled to join them. She sang loud and free, glad to be on stage making music again, even in the face of what was to come. He snuck in under the radar with the harmonica, while watching the two non-Mormons ready their forces. Five in all. No sign of Adamson, that was the only plus.

He stared down at the big black hat, the averted face of the fretless banjo player, the woman who had brought them here. Three fingers rattled over her fretboard, light and fast and above all precise – the standard of a pro session player. The fourth finger was stiff with bandage. Alf too was staring at her with a kind of savage hunger. Not all old hippies are nice people. Some are desperate and hardened as the old Blues singers by their years on the road, their souls like leather. The kind of people who in the end were handed poisoned wine, and drank it down fast. *Night and day I weep and moan.*

At a nod from Cisco Holland, the barrel-chested accordionist, the players as one swooped into 'Pick a bale of cotton', and Blues became burlesque. Unable to follow, Neil happily handclapped and watched people doing what they loved best, and felt a sting of pride in his species. We can do this wonderful thing and it causes no harm. It's not even about money. This is glee. I'd forgotten about glee. Kirsty's right, I've been too serious too long.

Inga Johanssen was on her feet now, grinning and shuffling some private little dance. The pink tip of her tongue curled up over her neat upper lip as she concentrated on her fingers. She was being a backwoods banjo player, eyes rolling, cowboy boots weaving percussive patterns on the wooden stage as her hat bobbed. Her eyes glanced into his, as they had on the stair up to her flat, so pale blue and northern, and he saw her as two people in one, the self-contained, private woman and the pantomime musician, both looking through the same eyes. Was that a wink? Then she turned away, back into the safety of her friends, still playing and shuffling her dance. *O Lordy, pick a bale a day!*

One more sudden musical swerve – like a flock of starlings, Neil thought, turning themselves inside out and streaming off in a new direction – and they were into 'The Wild Side of Life'. Kirsty turned to him, eyes shining. 'Aren't they great!' She whooped and hollered, threw her head back, threw her arm round Alf's shoulders as he pumped his sax, and brought what might have been a grin to that beaten face. Neil had forgotten that, her capacity for pure enjoyment, her love of situations nearly flying out of control. *You gave up the only one who ever loved you! And went back to the wild side of life...*

Applause, the audience on their feet then making for the door, a slow, orderly moving mass of people. The children began to descend from the crowded stage. Behind them the accordion player and the banjo player in blue dungarees opened the door into the back room and disappeared inside. The remaining buskers hung around outside that door, chatting and putting their instruments away. They rather got in the way of the five men pushing urgently against the current of the departing audience, heading for the stage.

An old drum, accordions, the musicians and their instrument

cases, even the edge of the piano impeded the entrance into the back room. The old buskers themselves also got in the way until, at a nod from Dr Harpo, they parted and five adrenaline-pumped angry men hurried into the back room.

Apart from an old table with a big black hat and three metal banjo finger picks on it, the room was entirely empty. Then the heavy oak door was shut behind them and bolts slammed to.

Neil and Kirsty followed Jan's torch through the street that climbed out of town. Jan explained that the trapdoor and tunnel emerging on the far side of the harbour had been used for centuries for smuggling and later by the Shetland Bus. The men would be kept locked in the little room that had once doubled as the old jail, then tomorrow morning a call to the police would be made. But they must hurry, hurry.

Snow crumping under their boots, they hurried. Just time to notice stars splattered above their heads, feel the sub-zero air bite deep into lungs, icing over the sweat of the evening. Now Jan was leading them down a trail, half-dug into deep snow, banks glimpsed at shoulder height on either side, tops of silent, motionless trees.

Jan stopped in the forest, turned and shone the torch in their faces. Neil screened his eyes, looked around for the trap. Kirsty looked ahead where Jan's torch picked out a small brass troll face set in the snow bank.

'Knock once, pause, then once again, no more, go in,' Jan said. 'Have a nice night.'

Left alone, it was so dark they could scarcely see each other. Just the glimmer of snow and the faint yellow light above the knocker of the buried house. Kirsty took a deep breath then seized the troll knocker and banged once. Paused. Once more. She turned the handle and they went in.

A small, slight woman in jeans and tan suede jacket stood alone against the far wall. The rifle in her hand was steady as it pointed at Neil's chest.

'*Hei*. Shut the door. Bolt it.' Her voice was low but clear. Neil did as he was told, very slowly. The rifle swivelled towards Kirsty. 'You, tell me about Mr Adamson.'

'In Scotland I had his knife at my throat,' Kirsty said simply. 'I can't forget it. I think we both have something he wants.'

The very pale blue eyes blinked once. Two vertical lines framed the bridge of her nose.

'My friends say I should trust you. This is not something I do easily.'

A thump on the door. Pause, then another. Inga Johanssen carefully stood the rifle against the wall. She swung a green leather duffel bag across her shoulder then stooped to pick up her banjo.

'Here is transport,' she said. 'We leave now.'

As Cisco Holland, stout and calm, a pony-tailed chain-smoking Buddha, drove his old van through the night, Neil, Inga and Kirsty spread out on the back benches. Dim yellow interior light on the faces, bittersweet chocolate and coffee thickening in the mouth as they talked, the mutter of foreign radio from up front: journeys made in haste by night, never to be forgotten.

Not wanting Inga to feel outnumbered, Neil and Kirsty had eased away from each other. Kirsty told her tale, starting with Billy Mackie's story, concluding with how after Adamson's visit the dying stone mason insisted she took on his Moon Ring.

Inga listened, her face still, concentrated. Without comment she popped out her lenses and put on little glasses with round red rims while Kirsty told her about the real stone and Neil watched the two women, one so reserved, the other fizzing.

'So it is this original Crowning Stone that Mr Adamson wants?'

'Yes, he's been hired to get it.'

'Who by?'

Kirsty shrugged. 'Some collector. Maybe some ultra-nationalist tax exile with more money than morality. The Stone is extraordinary.'

Inga looked down at her hands. Neil looked at them too. Small, white and very capable as they'd flown over the banjo strings. A dark stain had spread through the bandage.

'If we can find it, we could give it to him,' she said. 'Or sell it to him. Then he might go away.'

'You can't be serious.'

Inga stared at Kirsty.

'I am nearly always serious,' she said. 'Are you not a serious person?'

'My outlook is girls just want to have fun.'

'Not this girl.'

Kirsty thumped the bench beside her, leaned forward.

'That bastard helped kill my friend Billy Mackie. He did for Peter Sidlaw, a sweet man who never harmed anyone. He treated me like a piece of meat. He terrorized you. And you say give him the Stone?'

'It is only a stone. It means little to me.'

Kirsty stared at her like she came from a different species.

'You said your brother is dead because of him – does that mean little to you?'

Fire and ice, Neil thought. Except as he looked at Inga's face, it wasn't coldness he saw there.

'It's a bit academic,' he said hastily. 'Given we don't have the Stone. If this policeman has your ring, Inga, we only have Kirsty's inscription, and STAFR is not enough to find the Stone.'

Inga Johanssen glanced at him, then looked steadily at Kirsty, stroked her bandaged finger, as though comforting a wounded creature.

'You will not presume to talk of my half-brother again,' she said. Her anger was swift and silent as a punch in the dark. Even Kirsty recoiled, was about to speak but Neil nudged her arm. As she turned to glare at him, Inga reached inside her tan jacket.

'But you are wrong. We have more than one inscription,' she said, and as the van crossed into Sweden by a snow-lined backroad, she showed them the photos.

* * *

A near-penniless man is driving through the night on a road that never ends, though he certainly will. That's life. But we don't know where and we don't know when, for this road is one long travelling round a bend.

The traveller is the aggregate of the road, Cisco Holland muses as he double-declutches the decrepit gearbox. The Swedish border was an hour back, crossed without incident. Just another six hours to go.

He blinks his eyes, focuses briefly on the VW insignia on the wheel, then back to long range vision. It's an eye exercise on long drives, and a useful outlook in general, he reckons. Focus on the close to, or else *sub specie aeternitatis*, meaning the very long time before you were born and the very long time after you're gone. In the brief meantime – though Lord knows this night seems long – we are driving down this road with our eyes wide open.

Et mentem mortalia tangunt. The tag, donated by his father the Latin teacher, dangles in his mind where some might have a St Christopher and others a nodding dog. 'And mortal things touch my mind.'

Cisco picks another pre-made roll-up from his tin, sparks it alight then drops his big hand onto the coffee flask. He glances in the mirror – all quiet now in the back. The three are curled like dimly lit worms in their sleeping bags. The redhead with the big voice lies face down, fully stretched, one arm thrown out. Her hand nearly but not quite touches the man lying on his side, half-curled, with a small dark look in his face. And Star, well Star lies a little apart from them, twisted on her back with only her face glimmering in the pod of the bag, distant and calm.

Cisco drags deeply then slowly exhales, remembering her mother.

He drives, his closest companion the big box accordion strapped into the seat next to him. As the night wears on, he moves onto bigger roads, the cleared highways, then the jewelled carriageway. He smiles in the dark, thinking now not so much of Gudrun in her prime (he once imagined he might be Star's father and now, somewhat to his regret, is pretty sure he isn't) as of the cats' eyes of his childhood. Being driven by his parents through the night, struggling to stay awake in the back seat, watching the green-white flashes appear and disappear, that's when he'd first got it. Those eyes come alive and glow only in the moment, are dark before and after our passing, and wee Billy Holland aged eight swathed in musty travelling rugs got the message, that we are a travelling light and we spark in the moment we're in.

And they think they're being driven to safety, he thinks. Sleep on, children. Sleep well. Mortal things touch my mind.

26

Neil and Inga sat at the window of Cisco's cousin's apartment, looking down over Stockholm. A bright blue day, sun bouncing off the snowy roofs, water dripping from the eaves. A sense of easing up, getting somewhere. Maybe they were through the worst.

He glanced at Inga, thinking she did not look well. Paler than pale, her cheekbones now had a sweat on them and she kept gripping her bandaged finger. She had told them about what she called her 'interview' with Adamson, and Neil marvelled at her toughness. Her voice had remained low and calm, her eyes distant. He wondered at the cost of such self-control.

During the night and again this morning, there'd been arguments about going to the police. Inga was dead against, certain Adamson would know and be true to his threat. He was that kind of man. On the other hand, who else would deal with him?

Kirsty took the line: find the Stone, give it to the National Museum, then Adamson will move on. 'Our best chance,' she'd insisted, 'think about it.' Then she'd gone off to make some phone calls, find out how things had been going with the B Team back in Scotland. Cisco was still crashed out on the settee, covered in an old travelling rug, accordion upright beside him like a headstone.

As Inga stretched out to pick up her coffee, her rust-brown sweater rode up her arm. Neil stared at the thin wrist, blue vein, pulse beating. He imagined her natural heart rate was that of a small bird. As she drank, he noticed a dark line on the inside of her arm. It started at the wrist, leading back up her arm from the freshly-bandaged finger.

'Inga,' he began, then Kirsty whooped into the room, throwing her coat over the accordion.

'Result!' she said. 'Two results! Al and Murray got into the Westminster Stone, and Shonagh and Leo found another in Islay.'

'And?'

'And neither of them is the original fake! They're just copies of the fake, like Billy Mackie said.'

'Hope this isn't too confusing,' Neil said to Inga, taking his gaze from her arm.

She shook her head. 'I am accustomed to fakes and copies,' she said. She nodded at the sleeping Cisco. 'He isn't one of them. He's the real thing, one of the original hard-core buskers.'

They all contemplated the sleeping walrus, the indecipherable tattoo that ran faded all down the bare arm across his chest.

'Well, anyway,' Kirsty said. 'We've got two clues where the real fake Stone of Scone may be.' She took out her notebook and waited for their attention. 'Your starter for ten,' she murmured. '"Where gypsies cross the line". And your second "Sit doon and ca' canny".'

'Take it easy,' Neil translated for Inga. 'I don't get it.'

'Nor do I,' Kirsty said. 'Nor do the B Team. Maybe when we get home it will make more sense. Keep thinking, it will come.'

They sat and argued about what to do next. Finally Cisco woke, stretched, drank coffee, picked up his accordion and headed for the nearest heated public space.

'That's the way to live,' Kirsty commented in the emptiness after his departure. 'Be free, owing nothing, open to new adventure every day.'

Inga looked at her, made no comment.

'Looks like its own sort of treadmill,' Neil said. 'Go out and play the same songs every day, earn some money, get stoned at night. From where I'm sitting, it's a life, but no more free than any other.'

'Where you're sitting sounds like an excuse for not going out and getting a life.'

'You don't have to sit where I'm sitting.'

'Why would I want to?'

A pause as Neil and Kirsty looked at each other across the smoked glass coffee table. Then he turned and looked at Inga, chin propped on her hands as she studied them.

'What do you reckon?'

Her smile hovered then vanished like a white hummingbird.

'Cisco is a good man,' she said evenly. 'Yet it is not clever to imitate the life of someone you admire. We must find our own, not a copy. In our world, I think this is not easy.'

They sat in silence for a while, Neil and Kirsty both wondering with which of them Inga had been agreeing.

'I like to come with you to Scotland,' she announced. 'I want to find this Stone, it is the only way to be safe. Also I think Oslo is too dangerous.'

Kirsty nodded. 'You'll be safer with us. We'll take the photos of your ring's inscription to Ailsa Traquair in Edinburgh, see if we can get it translated. Also I want to see some people' – she glanced at Neil – 'about the Westminster Stone. They may also be able to help us with Mr Adamson.'

'Not the police?'

'Not the police, Inga.'

'I have been wondering how Mr Adamson knew about the inscription when neither I nor my brother did,' Inga said. She hesitated. 'Also I am wondering how he found me. Not so long ago I talked again with Ailsa Traquair on the telephone, and I thought she sounded too interested in me.'

A long pause. Neil looked at Kirsty.

'You said she was very nervous when you turned up.'

'Well, yes.'

'She's the acknowledged expert on fellowship rings?'

'Where would Adamson have gone after Sidlaw?'

'Bloody hell.'

'Fuck me sideways.'

They looked at each other, both feeling stupid. A little puff of laughter from the end of the table, then Inga Johanssen spread her hands onto the two photographs of her ring's inscription.

'I think we can make advantage from this knowledge.'

Kirsty's taxi to the airport pulled away. Neil and Inga waved and went back inside to wait for their taxi to the emergency out-patients. The blood poisoning trail was dark on the inside of her arm from wounded finger to armpit. She was sweating as she sank back into the sofa, her cheekbones glistened, her flat hair gleamed like magnesium and she seemed exhausted.

'I'll come with you,' Neil said. 'Once you get the antibiotics it's just a matter of waiting.'

'Thank you,' she said quietly, then keeled over sideways.

Star light, star bright, you got the loving that I like all right
Turn this crazy bird around, shouldn't have got on this flight
tonight

Humming, Kirsty pulled down the plastic flap over the few lights below then sank back into her seat. Ate the peanuts, drank the Bloody Mary and tried to catch up with her life of late. First too little, then too much.

One cannot have too much. Adventure, flight by night, affairs of the heart – this is what I was made for. Give me excess of it.

And yet, looking back at Neil standing by Inga – what a prim little madam! – as they'd waved goodbye, she'd felt a downward lurch of the heart, that pang which is hard to figure but is never wrong. *Shouldn't have got on this flight tonight.*

She crunched ice between her teeth, felt the chill ache in her jaw. Then in its passing she had an image of Leo in his chalet at Samye Ling, the chalet where they'd done the bonnie deed. (These Buddhists take the hump over desire and suffering. Really they should get used to it.) She saw him standing in the doorway, looking out into the dark. He'd be listening to the river run down through the night, with Orion the Hunter mid-leap across the northern sky.

Neil is looking for home, she thought, that's what he wants. Young Leo is in his sanctuary now but he is still on the hunt, handsome dreadlocked boy.

Different person, different stage of life. And me, now?

Some salty peanuts, then more juice. All life is in the alternation, in desire and counter-desire.

Goodbye baby, baby goodbye, shouldn't have got on this flight tonight.

The sound that woke him was not in his throat nor in his head. Wordless vowels, despairing, harsh as twanging catgut. *Aaiee!*

Terror absolute, resigned horror complete. That twanging cry again. *Aaiee!*

He was on his feet, through into her room. Her shape was twisted in winding sheet, duvet on the floor, eyes open and unseeing as she cried out again.

She shrieked as he grabbed her. Hot and damp and shaking, her head against his chest. 'It's all right, Ingy, it's all right.'

'He is cutting out my heart!'

'It's all right, I've got you. It wasn't real. This is real.'

'I'm frightened of dying so.' Her eyes wide, the black pupils enormous.

'He's not here. I'm real. Inga, this is real. Say it to me.'

'This is real?' Her eyes came back to him. 'Neil.'

This is real. So much heat in her.

He spent the rest of the night on the leather armchair in her room, watching her sleep fitfully in the pool of the bedside light. The thick scent of new leather, acrid sweat of her terror lingering, smoky jasmine from her white-blonde hair when he'd held her hard on his chest – how they possess him now.

This rose of watching, he thinks blurrily, blooming and dropping its petals.

27

No phone call, no warning given.

'It's all right, she is expecting me,' Kirsty lied to the museum receptionist easy as breathing. She hadn't been a lawyer in an earlier life for nothing.

Along the corridor, hesitated at the second door. Deep breath. No reason why Adamson should be here. One knock and in.

Thought Ailsa Traquair was going to keel over her desk.

'I've brought a copy of the inscription from the Oslo ring. We hoped you might help transcribe it.'

Ailsa's white hands made aspens seem rigid as she took the paper.

Kirsty waited, drinking strong coffee as Ailsa Traquair leant hungrily over the page, free hand already reaching for her dictionary. Kirsty tried to look eager, as though she does not already know what the runes will say.

Annat.

Suitably cryptic, with maybe a hint of the Annaty burn, not far from Dunsinnan Hill. That should keep Adamson busy, and take the heat off our po-faced miss back in Stockholm. With the inscription in his possession, Adamson will have no need of her or the ring.

Back out in the corridor, Kirsty waited until she heard the click of the phone inside the room, the little beeps of dialling, the low, frightened voice. She nodded and padded away. Now to meet Shonagh and young Leo, drive down to Samye Ling. It'll be great to have the car back and be independent again.

She was much too pleased with herself to think more about that car.

* * *

'Cisco Holland is a true Romany,' Inga said as she fed the photo of her ring's inscription into the fax machine. 'A gypsy without home, but at home everywhere. This is not so common.'

Neil looked away from the view of the street below. No thugs, no goons, no sadists with knives. A mild, pleasant, secure morning in orderly Stockholm. None of us will die today. This is real.

'What did you call him?'

'A Romany. That is what they say here. Why?'

'"Where gypsies cross the line",' Neil replied. 'Romanies. Is there an atlas here?'

'Over there, second shelf.' Inga stared down at the fax machine, her head a white tennis ball, bobbing. 'I hope my aunt can deal with this. If it's in Old Norn or Scottish Gaelic, she will have to consult. It may take a while.'

Neil nodded as he took down the big atlas. Crossing the line. Romany. He found the Scotland page and ran his finger down the roads streaming South out of Edinburgh. Found the A701, then the familiar junction, the bridge and the river. Saw again Kirsty waiting to pick him up in the last light, leaning cool and triumphant against her car, snow settling on the bonnet pulled down over uncontrollable red hair. The relief, the anger, the lurch of the heart at seeing her again.

Crossing the Lyne indeed.

Normally she preferred to drive rather than be driven, but the Maori warrior looked so pleased and right at the wheel of her green Wolseley which he'd picked up from the ferry car park. So Kirsty got in the front passenger seat, slung her bag behind and nearly hit Shonagh sitting quietly there.

'Grand to see you too, *a ghràidh*,' Shonagh murmured.

Grand it was to be driven at decent speed through the thawing Borders, snowdrops bending under dripping trees, flash of yellow from crocuses, breeze punching blue holes through a sky that had been lowered like a dustbin lid over the country for months. Good to catch up on the Islay adventure – a pang she had not been there – and to tell the story of Oslo, the buskers, the escape from Socke, the night drive to Stockholm, and the strange little creature that was Inga Johanssen. Naturally she didn't dwell long on Neil.

It was good too to drive under the welcoming arch into Samye Ling, see the little coloured prayer flags ripple and snap jauntily against blue sky. Good to walk down the familiar line of chalets, not quite meeting Leo's eye as they passed the door to his bedroom. She dropped her bag on the floor and felt as near to home as she ever wanted to.

'Yes, I was married. To Helen.'

'And you truly loved her?'

Neil turned from the window and looked at Inga as she lay resting on the couch, rug up to her squared-off stubborn little chin. He was getting used to her voice, so nearly colloquial. The Scandinavian edge didn't sound so flat now, he was getting a feel of the nuances in it. It was subtly foreign, but then so is anyone else. Which is the interest.

'I did.'

'So why did it end?'

'She took ill and died next to me on a flight back from North America.'

Inga opened her mouth. Closed it again.

'I am too inquisitive.'

He shrugged. 'Talking doesn't make it worse or better. She's still not here, and never will be.'

In a while he would go to pick up a Chinese take-away, but for now there was nothing to do but wait for the antibiotics to do their work. In the meantime they were just talking, letting the afternoon pass and words take them where they would.

'And then?' Inga asked.

'And then?' He looked down at his hands, spread and brought them together as though cupping something unseen. 'After six months I was greeting – crying – only at weekends. Friends like Alasdair and Murray and Tricia were very good to me. After two years I cried only at anniversaries – her birthday, my birthday, Christmas, wedding day, death day.' His hands parted and let the invisible drop. 'People who are not there any more gradually get left behind. That's partly what we cry about.'

'Yes, I think so.'

She looked at him. He looked at her. They'd return to that one later.

'And then?' she prompted.

'Then last summer I had an adventure in the Highlands with my friends – Al and Murray, Jane and Trish, that crowd. In the course of it we met Kirsty.'

'And?'

He picked up her banjo, flicked the strings. He put it down gently. Not his instrument.

'Later I'll ask you personal questions and you'll have to answer. You do know that? Price of admission, Inga.'

She flexed her wounded hand.

'If it helps pass time.' She took a deep breath, let it out. 'I sometimes think our life is like being in a dentist's waiting room. We pass time trying not to think about the bad thing ahead. Reading magazines, watching TV, playing and flirting a bit, while we wait for the inevitable. Sorry to be pessimistic,' she added.

Not far off his own outlook in darker moments. It had irritated Kirsty. In comparison with this woman, he was the cheery optimist. It was an unfamiliar role.

'Nevertheless,' he said, 'I did love Helen. "Flirt a bit" is glib – though God knows we do.'

'And Kirsty?' she persisted.

He diddled his fingers on the banjo strings. And Kirsty?

'She thawed me out.'

'And then?'

'Blimey, Ingy. We had three nights of bliss, the love word was used. When the adventure ended, she took fright and ran.'

She considered this.

'My mother called herself a free spirit too. And I suppose she was, in her mind.'

'You are not?'

'I am the most unfree and loyal person you are ever likely to meet.'

Her blue-green glacier eyes on his, and for a minute he seems to look into the heart of her.

Inga Johanssen shrugged then propped herself up on cushions.

'Anyway, with Kirsty – is it love again, if you don't mind my asking?'

'No,' he said softly. 'I don't mind you asking. I don't know. It's all a bit… odd.'

'There I agree with you.'

He glanced at her, then fiddled with the banjo strings. Such a humorous, joyous, raucous instrument, and she had played it well, doing her funny-silly hillbilly shuffle.

'I'll go and get our Chinese,' he said.

'Yes.'

He picked up his jacket, hat, scarf.

'You'll be all right here?'

'Peachy,' she said. 'Peachy keen. Sorry about last night,' she added abruptly. 'Waking you like that.'

Startled, he looked at her. Looped his scarf around his neck.

'My privilege,' he said, and left.

She lay looking at the ceiling, the spotless ugly chandelier. This is real, she thought. This is real.

'"Annat",' Adamson repeated. 'Are you sure?'

'That's what the runes said,' Ailsa Traquair replied. 'No doubt about that.'

Standing at the window of his room in the empty upper corridor of the old George Square Hotel, Adamson dragged his attention away from the ants below. Something about the way she had said that. One must attend to the nuance of servants.

'Where is there doubt?' he said.

A silence at the other end of the line. He heard her sigh.

'The runes didn't feel right. Wrong period, wrong calligraphy, not like the ones on the other ring. And there was no extra single letter. Of course, it could just be the way she'd transcribed them.'

When Adamson finally put down the phone, he stood for a long time looking down at his feet. Hummed a line from Anger Management's only demo 'Up Against The Wall'. Had anything been quite as sweet since? Perhaps he had underestimated the redhead. Inga Johanssen he would settle later.

He looked down at the street below, watched the tops of all the little heads as they went about their tiny lives. He flexed his hands and smiled. He could already smell her fear, her contrition, her despair as she gave it up too late.

Yes, time to reel in Christine Fowler.

PART FOUR

Gonna be a long time gone

28

Life, that gorilla, thought Leo. It steps out from behind a bush looking scary, then offers you a banana. What it doesn't tell you – because, after all, Life does not really talk to us – is that there is another gorilla right behind you, and it wants that banana too.

Later he would wonder whether one of his more alert ancestors had been looking out for him. He had woken suddenly in the dark in the little spare room in the chalet, thinking about Life and gorillas and what Kirsty had not said about lover man Neil in Norway. He saw again the way she had jumped down from the town bus and crossed the road towards himself and Shonagh in the car, head high, so eager and bold.

Ah, she was a doozy and no mistake. And likely not destined for him.

What with that and maybe a bit of his ancestor prodding with his *okinula* stick from the Shining World, he could not lie there. So he got dressed, made tea, and with a torch padded up the track through the chill, damp hour before dawn, around the corner and in the back of the meditation hall. A sense of presence on the other side of the wall, of many people breathing there, being silently present, witnessing.

Not for him, but he wouldn't knock it. He climbed the backstairs careful not to spill, put mug and torch up on the joist and swung up after them.

To the end of his days every morning Grandfather Ihaaka climbed up to a cleft in the rock way above the creek that bordered the farm. 'My place of reckoning' would be the nearest translation. Leo didn't know what Granddad did there, but always when he came back down his eyes were full and glowing. Over the last while that space under the eaves in Samye Ling had become his own place of reckoning, where he could just sit, breathe and let be.

So he was sitting there in the near-dark, drinking tea at the dormer window he had spent the last days framing up, when he saw sidelights come slowly through the entrance arch. No sound, the vehicle must have been coasting.

It stopped at the edge of the drive. There was just enough faint first light to give it shape. A boxy 4x4. He put down his mug and quietly pushed the window open.

Someone got out. A torch came on, the sidelights cut. A second torch. The yellow-white lights criss-crossed, stabbed about, and he glimpsed a face last seen in the driveway of a snowbound country hotel with gun in hand. The two lights moved slowly down the drive that wound the long way down towards the chalets and the river. He saw no more because he was swinging down out of the place of reckoning with torch in left hand and a hammer in his right.

He took a short-cut through to where the 4x4 was parked. After a quick moment's work there, he cut across the courtyard, past the side of the studios, through the vegetable garden and came out at the far side of the chalet. It was not quite dark, and with eyes adjusted and knowing the way, he did it torchless. Whiff of sandalwood as he silently opened the door, then glanced back.

The two torches came round the far end of the row of chalets. Their beams passed over Kirsty's car, hesitated, then made their way towards the chalet nearest to it. So they didn't know which one. There was still a chance.

He had never made jokes about how long women take to get dressed. Rather it seemed to him when it really counts they adjust quicker, as his mother had to widowhood. While Kirsty and Shonagh scurried about, he locked the door and stood behind it, hammer in hand, briefly entertaining some notion of being the hero, boffing the bad guys while the women escaped and he got shot.

Through the side window he saw lights coming on at the first and second chalets. Sound of voices. Then torch beams stabbed his way and he ducked back.

'Out the rear window,' he hissed.

For once, no wisecrack reply, just the window quietly opening. Shonagh climbed on a chair, leaned, then wriggled out. Faint gleam of Kirsty's exultant face as she looked his way, then she was more elegantly gone, and a moment later he postponed heroism in favour of flight and followed.

They met up down the slope by the river, among the leafless trees. 'What now?'

A splintering crash from up the slope as they forced the chalet door. Torchlight at the back window. He'd left it open, stupid stupid boy. A beam swivelled their way, settled on Shonagh's head-scarf dangling on a hawthorn above them.

'Split up,' Leo whispered. 'Meet at the car in five minutes.' Then he crashed off through the saplings, drawing the torches after him.

Down in the dip near the river he paused to look back. One light was coming his way. A glimpse of another, heading away, a faint shout. A crack that might have been a breaking branch or a shot.

Games with pals in the hills of childhood, be useful now. In the near-dark he scrabbled in dirt and picked up a rock. Hoping there was nothing much between himself and the river, he hurled the stone as far as he could.

The splash was loud in the pre-dawn and the torch obediently flinched towards it. Then he was off, moving silently as possible through birch saplings, heading for the barn. Slipped in the back door and stood in the gloom. The monastery's five cows shifted but stayed silent. He smelled their reek, heard one pant heavily, sorrowfully it seemed. On some mornings he'd reverted to country boy and taken them out to pasture, letting Malik sleep in for once, so they were used to his presence.

He padded up the length of the barn, cautiously slid back the big door and looked out. A torch was moving steadily back down the main track, heading for Kirsty's car. Someone was using his brain.

Leo gripped the big door, pulled it back along the runners then with all his strength heaved it shut again. The crash echoed, the startled cows complained. The torch hesitated then turned his way, and he was off again.

He ran diagonally across the pasture, then jinked left and crawled back along the drainage ditch. Raised his head and saw the torch. Then it was turned off. Not good. The opposition would be able to see better now, and daylight was coming in, shortening the odds.

He left the ditch and sprinted across the open ground towards the main block. In the front door, along the corridors, past the workshops, into the kitchen. The figure bent over the stove straightened up.

'Shit, you gave me a fright!' Chulia squeaked. Leo saw himself as she did, muddy and scraped, panting with torch in one hand and hammer in the other. 'What's going on?'

'Life,' he whispered. 'Don't worry about it.'

Then finger to lips he was out the side door. Past the teaching workshops where he had never got round to learning Tibetan. The try line that was Kirsty's car was only a hundred metres away, and if he prayed for anything in this life since his daughter died it was that his two mates would be waiting by it.

He came round the corner and saw Kirsty standing in the gap between the sheds with her hands raised.

'OK,' he heard her say. 'You got me.'

Then the big bloke they called Bill stepped into the open, gun in hand. Fair play to her, she saw Leo standing behind him but her resigned expression never changed.

'I'll come with you,' she said. 'No need to use that.'

Bill was the length of a cricket pitch away. Leo threw the hammer hard as he could.

Two shots cracked into the air as Bill went down. He hit the ground making whimpering sounds, clutching his back. The gun bounced from his hand into the dirt. Leo grabbed it then they were running for the car.

Kirsty bundled in behind the wheel. No Shonagh.

A shout from behind. Shonagh was sprinting towards them, but Ben followed twenty yards behind, iron bar pumping like a baton in his hand. Monks in saffron robes had emerged from the dining room, wondering what the noise was. They were witness to extreme anger, pain and fear, one man groaning on the ground – the full samsara, the tormented world of illusion. It was a teaching more forceful than Lama Choeden, the Retreat Master, at his most severe.

As Shonagh ran towards them, Leo saw it all in adrenaline-slowed motion. Saw the baffled faces, her despair, feral Ben savagely grinning as he gained on her. Leo hesitated with the gun in his hand, then Lama Choeden quietly stuck out his staff. Ben tripped, crashed into the dirt. Then Shonagh was in the back of the car and they were roaring off up the drive, slewing under the Peace Arch and out of there.

'Well aimed, young Leo,' Kirsty said, her eyes over-bright, full on him. 'But you might have gone for his head.'

'Too small a target,' he said. She braked violently before the double bends into the bridge. Still on hyper-clarity he saw the rhododendrons gasp back as they passed.

Shonagh was twisted round, looking out the back window.

'Don't worry, they'll be a while yet,' Leo said, and dug the 4x4's rotary arm from his pocket, tossed it out the open window then looked across at Kirsty. 'Where we heading, boss?'

'"Where gypsies cross the line",' Kirsty replied. 'It's got to be Romanno Bridge. You can put that nasty gun-thing away.'

Weaving up the B709 as it flirted with the White Esk through the heart of lonesome Ettrickdale in wintry first light, one might say they had a date with destiny. Which, however uncertain, beats having no further destiny at all.

29

Her life story, should she ever choose to tell it, could as well be entitled 'The Girl Who Ran Away from the Circus'.

If you met Inga Johanssen now, say you were the person sitting across from her on the morning train, you would not think it likely. No face paint, swirly scarves, bright-coloured hair or comic hat. In her sober new jeans, black rollneck sweater and tan jacket, clean short hair, downcast eyes half-hidden behind spectacles as she reads *New Scientist*, you would, she hopes, see no hint she spent the first sixteen years of her life entertaining on the street. Only a certain intensity in her, as though she were reining in something through force of will, might make you look twice. Then look again.

Which street? The Street they called it, and rightly, for it could be any street anywhere in the world that her extended family made their own when they trundled into town on horse and cart with their baggy pants, striped waistcoats, assorted hats, scarves, feathers and chokers, moustaches trailing, juggling instruments, clubs and burning torches, wobbling frantically – it looks like someone could fall any moment and very occasionally someone does – on the tightrope of their living.

Among her many 'uncles' (by which she now understands to mean her mother's lovers) was Magic Sam, and he was a master of the Tragic Fall.

Magic Sam wobbled, flailed, the tightrope kicked free and he crunched down onto the cobbles. Lay there whimpering as the concerned braver spectators approached, bent over him...

He rolled to his feet, plucked one burning torch then another from under his jacket, and leapt back onto the rope, juggling fire, eyes rolling, taking time to orchestrate applause and point to her, his charming ukulele-playing protégée in oversize dungarees, hair down to her skinny behind, in full silver face-paint taking round the bowler hat for tribute.

She saw most of Europe by the age of eleven, or at least the streets and parks, camp sites and arcades they made their own. She knew the faces gathered round, those many races, eyes, clothes, languages, coinages gathering in the lining of caps, guitar and accordion cases. When the audience forms, its hope is always the same: that they may experience the miraculous, the song that moves the heart, the truthful illusion.

Her falls, it seems, are always real and always hurt. So she is careful.

From all the cards of memory she could pluck one and show it to you, near-stranger sitting across from her on the train to Zeebrugge, pretending not to be studying her over your magazine. She was once a keen student of eyes and their glances. She knows how they flick from what her hands and voice do, to hips and breast, just checking. She knows how to meet them, and how to look past and beyond so you know you never can reach her. Yet perhaps she likes your hands, your self-doubt and absence of judgement as you glance at her. Though you can joke, she senses you are serious, unlike your lover.

She could pick one card and show you. She is eleven, still child-skinny in faded dungarees as she stands barefoot on warm grass in a licensed park – Geneva? Frankfurt? Barcelona or Trondheim? – playing bass and harmonizing 'Rank Stranger' with her dad to her right with his long black ringlets, winking at the ladies, grinning for the grannies and rolling his eyes for the kids.

The fat, warm bass strings are fluid under her fingers. She is hitting fresh harmony notes just right, and he glances at her as if astonished he has produced such a wonder, and as he turns back to his crowd in the strong light she sees for the first time there is grey in his long hair, deep lines set around his eyes and mouth.

As she goes round with the hat, she stares at children her own age while they stare back at her. They go to schools and learn things, live in one place, have a regular park to play in. Their lives have shape and direction. She sees in their eyes curiosity and wonder, and know they want to be her, in the circus.

She wants to be them. She has always known this.

Her father's charm, his spontaneity, his innocence are all real, that's why they work so well on so many crowds, so many ever younger women. He needs her now Gudrun and Col have gone, to be his friend, to harmonize, to draw the crowd and go round with the hat. To see him home when he takes too many drugs, to make him smile in his brief, devastating sorrows. And she will do it for another five years through the interchangeable streets, parks, arcades of Europe, but already she is plotting to leave the circus.

She left one autumn morning in Barcelona. Woke in her pup tent the day after her eighteenth birthday and knew it was time. The Fudge Mobile was silent as she slipped a note under the door to say she had been accepted for a Sound Recording course in Oslo. *PS Don't smoke too much and eat the greens! Love and all – Inga.*

Then she slipped out of the camp site with pack on back and dew-damp tent under her arm, walked to the big road and stuck out her thumb. In Paris she sold the Gibson ukulele and set of whistles for food, new jeans, proper lace-up leather shoes and a smart zip-up tan suede jacket, very bourgeois, the first of many. In Stockholm a friend cut and washed the dye from her hair in exchange for her multi-coloured dungarees. Only the Moon Ring, Mum's parting present, remained from her former self.

By the time she stepped down from the train in the neat, rational, orderly streets of Oslo, she had ceased to be Star Weir, former child prodigy of the street. In her new uniform, she was already calling herself by her mother's name to better blend in. Taking a short cut through the Astra Park, she saw a crowd had gathered round a busker. She stood at the back and watched. It was Swiss Frank the puppeteer, hands twitching the lines as he bent above his creation Job the Busker. Job rolled his eyes, tuned then strummed his guitar, flirted with the audience, was absurdly pleased with himself, then heartbroken when a little girl turned away.

He was good, Frank, melancholy and in his way something of a genius. He lived and travelled in a converted hearse, alone with his puppets. He was family, he was circus. Him and Dad had been pals, and he was not one of her uncles, his inclinations being otherwise.

The crowd were spellbound, laughing, touched. Small children were given money to drop in the stovepipe hat. A teenage girl stared and yearned. Inga identified not with Swiss Frank but with Job the Busker, jerked by wires.

She dropped some notes in the hat then walked quickly away. Puppets make her sad. They are not different enough from ourselves. Frank had glanced but not recognized her. That made her feet light as she passed out the park gates. She had left the circus.

Real life began then. Discipline, training, regular work, then she jumped into a regular marriage – shocked Mum and Dad there! – and in due time a regular divorce. Then she led her solitary, passionate inner life and not such a bad one until poor half-mad Col ran away with her ring and then the man with eyes like flaking mica came calling.

She glances up at you, who meet her eyes. She feels your instinctive approval, that you actually get her, and she smiles a little. Your redhead lover waiting in Skye is everything Inga is not, truly of the circus, the street, the travelling show.

You put aside your *Rolling Stone*. She turns another page of *New Scientist*. You lean forward.

'So we've established you're straight,' you say, alluding to an embarrassing mutual reflex last night after you held her through another nightmare. 'When did you get married?'

'I don't discuss my heart with strangers,' she says and turns another page, tangled up in Super String Theory.

'But we're not strangers now, are we?'

As Inga Johanssen, who was once Star Weir and must accept that sparky variant still lodges within, slowly puts the magazine aside she knows that the heart, that silent-flying owl, cries only when it is hunting. And as she starts to tell you about her life, she has to acknowledge that hunt it must, if it is ever to be fed.

30

The day put on light as Kirsty forced the old Wolseley through Ettrickdale. In that empty valley a solitary farmhouse or forester's cottage huddled like a wounded hare in its dreich scrape, then nothing for miles on end. This was once bandit country, she mused, covered in trees and shrub, with secret byways the reiver horsemen took. A spot of rape, pillage, rustling and kidnapping, then ride home again through the dawn, keeping an ear and eye open for revenge hot-trod following behind.

She glanced at Leo, his broad face, curved lips near-smiling, brown hands cautiously examining Bill's gun. *This one was never made for the monastery. It was scary back there, but going out that window my God I felt alive.*

In the back seat Shonagh was humming as she watched the hills go by. *I've heard them lilting at the ewe-milking.* Laments, laments, is it all the Gaeltachd can do now?

She studied the set of Kirsty's shoulders, the pale skin of her neck where that unmanageable fiery hair parted. There had once been a time of drunken confessions, confidences, intimacies that had so nearly crossed the line, but the world had moved on. *The flowers of the forest are all wede awa.* I am surrounded by friends, Shonagh thought, so why this doomy feeling, this dirge for Flodden fields?

'How's it going in the back there, *a ghràidh*?'

'I was wondering if Leo would have used that gun.'

'I was kind of wondering that too.'

There was a long pause. Shonagh watched the strapping boy's shoulders tense, but he said nothing as he put the gun in the glove compartment. She was thankful that, for once, Kirsty didn't press the point.

They breakfasted in a café in Innerleithen, the bleak end of the Borders behind them, prospect of finding the real Westminster Stone ahead. Flushed, exhilarated, still jittery, they ate and talked quickly. Finally finding the Stone would be one for Billy Mackie, the solution to a long-standing mystery, and a great story. Then they could concentrate on finding the true Destiny Stone.

'Shouldn't we phone the others?' Shonagh said as they left the café and walked down the village street to the car. Kirsty shook her head.

'Let's do this one on our own, then celebrate together.'

Leo was silent in the back as they followed the broad, soil-brown Tweed up the valley on the narrow, twisting, tree-lined road. That moment when Kirsty had raised her hands in surrender and Bill stepped out with a gun. Quicker than thinking, he'd thrown the hammer, knowing it would hit. As for using the gun himself? It was not a question he wanted to ever have to resolve. Either way was bad news.

By a bridge over the Lyne Water, a B road was signed 'Romanno Bridge', and as Kirsty swung onto it Leo stopped looking behind. Though it surely would take Bill and Ben a while to extricate themselves, and they could have no idea where their quarry had gone, it was still good to be off the main road.

It was Shonagh who insisted they hid the car short of Romanno Bridge. Up ahead was the Moffat road, no point taking the very outside chance Bill and Ben might drive up it on the way to Edinburgh. So Kirsty parked up a track behind a sagging corrugated iron barn, and in the end that made all the difference. The three of them walked up the empty road on a still, falcon-grey, end-of-winter noon, into Romanno Bridge.

What they saw was scarcely a village, just a row of buildings on their right leading up to a crossroads, with a scattering of houses

to the left and in the trees behind. The pub sign on the red sandstone building creaked as they passed. Somewhere a dog barked
then thought better of it. Another ghost village – the few houses
looked prosperous enough, but no one was about. Everyone must
work in the city, or in the out-of-town shopping centre. And on
the left was the new bridge over the fast-running Lyne and before
it the hump-backed old red sandstone bridge that gave the place
its name.

'Mighty big name for a mighty small town,' Leo commented as
they walked towards the old bridge.

'It's here because the two roads come together,' Kirsty said
slightly defensively.

Shonagh put her hand on the sandstone parapet. 'It might be
disappointing, *m'eudail*, but then again you and me are here for
no better reason than our parents coming together.'

'Fair play,' Leo admitted. 'If what we're looking for isn't here, I
don't know where it is.'

'Hell's claymores,' Kirsty said. 'Not at this time in the
morning.'

A car came down the main road, slowed a little as it went over
the new bridge, then drove on. A grubby workman's canvas shelter
stood in the car park at the far side of the old bridge, next to a
yellow van with 'Highway Maintenance Contractor' stencilled in
bright red letters on its side. Of the workmen there was no sign,
only a faint murmur of a crackly radio playing *Stuck in the
middle with you* for the nostalgically-minded.

Now where might one sit doun and ca canny?

'If in doubt, try the pub,' Kirsty said.

The little bar was empty except for an old collie dozing on a
linoleum floor. It opened one eye as they came in, saw nothing
remarkable and closed it again. Kirsty pinged the small brass bell.
A door opened and a teenager hosting a lot of black eyeliner,
white face and black lips shuffled in behind the bar.

'Whit ye wantin?'

'We're looking to meet a friend here. He said we'd find him in a place where we could sit doon and ca canny.'

'Can sit here if ye want.'

'Thanks, but is there anywhere else he might have meant?'

The Goth raised her eyes from the prison floor for a moment and surveyed them gloomily.

'I'm telling you, there's nuthin nowhere here.' She sighed, tucked a hank of jet-black hair behind her ear. 'Since I was wee, the only thing that's ever happened was the new brig and a phone box that doesni work.'

'What about the workmen over there?' Shonagh asked.

'They're fixing the auld seat.'

Leo looked out the window at the canvas shelter a hundred yards away.

'Any idea when it was made, this seat?'

A shrug. 'They cry it the coronation seat.'

'I bloody bet they do!' Kirsty whooped, and they left in a hurry.

There was nothing in the yellow Highway Maintenance van but a pack of cheroots on the dashboard and an old sweater trailing over the back of the passenger seat. David Bowie's 'Quicksand' was oozing tinnily from inside the canvas shelter, along with a low scraping sound. Leo wished he had not left the gun behind. He looked at Kirsty and gestured down the road towards the car but she shook her head, pulled back the shelter's flap and stepped inside.

'Spare a cup of tea, guv?'

'Afraid not, old girl – but I can offer you a seat on the ancient throne of Scotland,' Alasdair Sutherland said. He sat on a camping stool, grinning up at them. 'Wondered when you'd get here.'

Murray put down his chisel and hunkered back from a slab of red sandstone cemented into a stone bench.

'Aye, sit doon and ca canny, queenie,' he said, pushing his sleeves back up.

*

Two evenings earlier in downtown Kirkintilloch Murray and Alasdair had been bickering fitfully, while Eve was trying to do her homework in the corner, preparing for life in the real world.

'Kings, I canni be doing wi them. I'd as well see all crowning stones returned to the quarries of history.'

'Along with the Communist cause? We're at the end of history now, matey!'

'So business rules the world. Look around ye! It's fuckin appalling, no?'

Alasdair shrugged and reached for another slice of Tricia's gingerbread. No way anyone could improve on that.

'Be philosophical, matey – don't think about it.'

Murray stared at him. Alasdair looked up innocently as he licked sweet crumbs off calloused fingertips, the prints erased by years of rock climbing. Murray could never decide whether his old friend and sparring partner was a stupid man pretending to be smart, or a smart man pretending to be stupid.

'Anyway, youth, we'll never find the Stone until we get a half-nelson on these clues. "Where gypsies cross the line". Maybe you could do some political analysis on that one.'

'Maybe you could—'

'Romanno Bridge,' Eve had said quietly, not bothering to look up. 'The waters of Peeblesdale include the Whiteadder, the Blackadder, the Eddleston Burn, the Ettrick Water and Lyne Water.'

'So we came down here yesterday, and found this old public seat,' Alasdair said. 'It had a shell of wood round it, but inside we could see stone.' He gestured in the corner, where some timbers were neatly stacked. The biggest one bore a brass plaque inscribed 'Sit doon and ca canny'. 'This is a one-goat village, but still we could scarcely start pulling apart the seat in public.'

'So we went hame and found some stencils,' Murray added. 'Did the sprayjob, picked up my tools, and got this old shelter from a pal who used tae use it at Faslane.'

'Very nice too,' Kirsty said.

In the dim light inside the shelter, she knelt in front of the low red sandstone block, ran her hand over the rough red cross incised on top. Checked the old break in the corner that had been repaired by the young apprentice Billy Mackie in a stonemason's yard one freezing night in December 1950. She touched the soft, rough stone, closed her eyes for a moment, let her lips move. Mission accomplished, pal.

'Okey-dokey,' she said and stood back. 'How much longer before it's chipped free?'

'Fifteen, twenty minutes,' Murray said.

'No mobile signal here – I'm going to the pub to use its pay phone,' she said. 'See you back here.'

She pushed out of the canvas flap and emerged blinking into the light. Alasdair followed her out.

'Bit of a thirst, old girl,' he said, and together they hurried over the old bridge towards the pub.

Alasdair sat at the counter happily getting on the right side of a pint of lager and shooting the breeze with the collie and the Goth lass. Neither were very responsive, but the lager was clean in his throat and it was soothing in the bar, one of those places where life has taken a cigarette break and is still smoking away elsewhere. He could hear the murmur of Kirsty's voice from the phone booth as she checked in with Abernethy the equerry chappie.

Yes, they'd found the coronation stone of the kings of England since Edward I took it from Scone. That's what he called a ploy. Now what comes next?

Kirsty emerged from the booth and beckoned him over to the door.

'So they're dead chuffed with us?' he asked.

'Yes, yes,' she said, but frowned. 'I've arranged delivery. But just at the end, Abernethy said something about checking my car. I'd been telling him about Bill and Ben and Adamson, how they keep finding me, and he said maybe there's a tracer on it. Do you think that's possible? Would you recognize one?'

Al stared at her.

'We did surveillance in my SAS TA training. Yeah, I'd recognize most bugs.'

He grabbed his pint and drained it, nodded to the collie and the cute Goth chick and then they were out the door. Eileen MacArthur slumped against the counter, the dog closed its eyes and dreamed of sheep. Truly, nothing ever happens around here.

They hurried down the minor road, edgy and alarmed. Glancing all around and seeing nothing but the workman's shelter, they went up the track to the Wolseley parked behind a barn.

'Got a torch?'

'Sure.'

While Kirsty paced up and down, biting her nails and thinking *Shit shit shit*, Alasdair poked and flashed and prodded under the car. He started at the front end and worked back. Focused and absorbed, he checked steadily, remembering how this went. Tapped on the sump, listened. He heard a distant van, tensed, then the sound died.

'See anything?'

'You need a good clean under here.'

Finally he used the screwdriver to scrape away more dried mud under the rear wheel arch, flinched his eyes away from the falling grains then looked again.

He came out from underneath with a small curved box on the flat of his palm. With two semicircular dents on one end, it looked like a large black beetle.

'That's it?'

'Afraid so, old girl.'

'No aerial thingy?'

'Metal car body acts as one.'

'Oh, right. And it's working now?'

He nodded. 'Good piece of kit. Fair range.'

'We'd best smash it.'

He withdrew his hand.

'Na, we can do better than that. *Enemy weapon is best weapon.*'

'I suppose you picked up that pearl in the TA?

He shook his head.

'Na – *Biggles Flies East*. We'd best have a confab.'

Together they hurried back up the track and onto the road, looking around more warily now. She checked her watch. Over three hours since they'd fled Samye Ling. How injured were Bill and Ben? That hammer had hit hard, but the thud had been muffled by Ben's thick coat. How long would it take them to get another rotor arm?

'How's lover boy, then?'

'He's not my lover boy.'

'I meant Neil.'

'Ah. Well he—'

Alasdair had grabbed her arm.

'Down!' They crouched by a low dyke that ran along the minor road.

'Follow me.'

So for once she did as instructed, followed Alasdair Sutherland on a rapid crouch, over the dyke then quick wriggle under a couple of fences. Panting and muddy-kneed, she caught up with him in a ragged clump of willows hanging over the Lyne. Crouched, she parted the dead undergrowth and looked upstream to Romanno Bridge.

Behind the workman's shelter now sat a white van. Exhaust plume rose into the cold air. The rear doors were open. As they watched, two figures came out of the shelter. No missing the short dreadlocks around that bowed head. Nor that he was moving slowly, awkwardly, dragging one leg, and his arms were tied behind his back.

Behind him was little Ben. He too was moving awkwardly, but still prodded Leo into the back of the van with his iron bar. A minute later he emerged, closed the doors and quickly limped back to the shelter.

'Back to the car for the gun?'

Al shook his head. 'No time. Look.'

Big Bill's bowed back shuffled out of the shelter, then Murray, face-on. Between them they were dragging a low red block, while Ben stood watching the road.

'They're going to take Murray and Leo with them.'

Alasdair nodded. 'Hostages. Good practice.'

'They'll meet up with Adamson.'

Al looked her in the eyes, serious now. 'I expect so.'

Now they were lifting the stone into the back of the van, shepherded by Ben.

'I got us into this,' Kirsty said. She grabbed the bug from Al. 'You phone the equerry, he'll know what to do.'

Then she was out of the willows and running towards the white van. It was the bravest and possibly stupidest thing Al had ever seen her do. Bill had already spotted her and then it was too late to do anything but watch her feign surprise then resistance, be dragged inside along with Shonagh, and the doors closed behind them and the white van headed North on the Edinburgh road.

31

As the van turned hard left, Kirsty was rolled across the floor and banged her head on the edge of the so-called Stone of Destiny.

'Ow,' she said quietly. She felt a warm trickling, then a tickle down her cheek. She grunted to Shonagh, who rolled towards her.

'All happy-clappy in the back there?' Bill called cheerfully.

'Grand, thanks,' Kirsty replied. She caught Shonagh's eye and nodded towards her jacket pocket.

'There'll be prayers when the boss meets you again.'

'Aye, he'll be fuckin delighted,' Ben cackled. 'Says we can have the leftovers.'

'And then there's the dyke,' Bill said.

'She'll be a hoot when she toots!'

Shonagh shook her head wearily. Kirsty leaned in and whispered in her ear, then shuffled round so Shonagh's bound hands were closer to her jacket pocket. Felt fingers scrabble and grip.

'Have those brave lads woken up yet, Benny?'

Ben twisted round to look at Murray and Leo lying curled where they'd been thrown.

'They're not so lively.'

'You gave Tonga quite a thump on his brown noggin.'

'I did that!'

'Wait till I get the hammer on him, see how he likes it.'

Giggling, Ben looked forward again. Shonagh prised the metal bug from Kirsty's jacket and pushed it under a tool bag. The van slowed, lurched, stopped at some lights. Left turn, then a right soon after.

Murray opened his eyes, looked vacantly at Kirsty then closed them again. There was a dark stain down the side of his head. Leo lay motionless on his side, mouth slightly open, breathing heavily.

The van was on a dirt road now, climbing. It slowed, lurched and bounced. Baddinsgill, Kirsty thought. We've been through West Linton and now we're on that track to Baddinsgill Reservoir, South side of the Pentlands. Nothing up there but a ruined bothy. Good place to wait. Good place to make some people disappear.

Wish I'd had more good sex, more songs, more laughs, been more straight with friends. Wish I'd told Dad what an arse he is. Wish I'd truly loved someone, even myself.

The van lurched one more time then stopped.

Hands tied behind their backs with electric cable, they sat propped up against the walls inside the bothy, boys on one side, girls on the other, light rain falling on their faces through the non-existent roof. Every so often Murray opened his eyes but Kirsty thought he was scarcely there. Leo's chin was down on his chest as he twitched. Shonagh looked at Kirsty who looked back at Shonagh. Slight shake of the head. Roughly: *we're not done yet.* Bill and Ben stood at the empty window, looking down the valley, smoking, waiting.

The Westminster Stone had been left in the van parked outside. So had the tracer bug. Kirsty had time to think of many things, among them that Adamson must have first bugged her car back in Dumfries, before the funeral. That was how the 4x4 had found her and Leo, then tried to run them off the road. That's how they'd known about Samye Ling. When Leo had gone to Islay, and she had been in Norway, the car had sat unused in a car park by the terminal. The moment it was moved, when Leo had gone to pick her up in Edinburgh, they had known.

So is this how it ends, sitting against a damp wall in light rain, needing a pee and much too late trying to make sense of everything that has led you here? Yes, it probably is.

Still, better thinking about anything other than what Adamson would do when he arrived. She hoped it would be quick but that wasn't likely. He would first want to know the real inscription on Inga's ring. She could picture the runes clearly, could probably draw them if push came to shove, as it certainly would. Then she would be disposable. They would all be.

She glanced at Shonagh beside her. She was staring at Billy's back, humming something Kirsty couldn't quite catch. Billy put his gun on the window ledge, said something to Ben and they both laughed. Sitting next to Murray, Leo's head came up, he looked around wonderingly. For a moment he looked at her. She mouthed something of an apology. He shook his head, almost smiled. Bill turned to check on them and Leo's head fell forward again.

'Would you two like money?' she said. 'A lot of money?'

'We all like money, darlin,' Bill said. 'School fees and that. Girl's right into fashion and the boy's after a new top of the range mountain bike. No pension in our line of work.'

Kirsty tried to get her head round this hard luck tale.

'Got the child support fuckers after me,' Ben offered. Smirked. 'A few kids about the place, like.'

'Don't approve of that, Benny boy,' Bill said. 'A child is for life, not just for birthdays. Anyhow, about this money?'

'The people we're getting the Stone for are connected. Very well connected. They'd pay big time if you gave it to them instead of Adamson.'

Bill looked at Ben then checked out the window at the empty road. Sighed regretfully.

'Only two problems in your suggestion, lady. First up, it's not that stone in the van the boss is really after, though he's ready to pay for it. It's you. Second, if I cross Mr Adamson I'll never sleep easy enough to enjoy my retirement.'

'I'm no feart of him,' Ben muttered.

'That's because you're thick, cousin Benny. You see, darlin, it's like Mr A is the contractor, and we're just sub-contractors here. We don't like country and we don't like mud. I just want to be done here, get paid, and be back in my neighbourhood. Bit of enforcement, bit of protection, run a few hoors – nothing fancy, no drugs. Just a quiet life, see the kids do well and get to the university.'

'Drugs!' Ben said. 'Loadsa money there, man!'

'Loads of Yardies and dead bodies.'

'You big feartie! Live fast, die young, leave a beautiful corpse.'

'Bit late for that, Benny boy.'

'Ach ya big … *bourgeois*.'

Bill laughed quietly, then winced and clutched his back. Scowled at the unconscious Leo.

'He'll no throw anything again once I'm done with him.' He glanced at his watch. 'So, no deal, sister. You can bring it up with the boss when he gets here. Shouldn't be long now.'

Then they all waited some more.

She raised her head. There was a smell of pee from someone, she hoped it wasn't herself. Hard to be sure, all damp with the rain. There it was again, the faint engine sound that had brought her back. Bill and Ben had heard it too. They were stirring at the broken window, craning their heads out.

Murray's head was back against the opposite wall, his mouth open and eyes closed, the blood clotted down the side of his head. For some reason, haste or carelessness, his hands had been bound in front rather than behind his back. The electrical flex round her wrists was tight, unyielding and hurt like hell. Her fingers were white, completely numb.

Beyond Murray, Kirsty could see through the non-existent door down the valley. Saw the dull gleam of the burn, and bits of the track, and in the distance a hint of buildings at West Linton through the misty drizzle. And on that track a dark blue car was moving, slowly heading their way.

'Here comes the man!' Bill said. He flicked his cigarette out the window and leaned out.

'Aye, there'll be fireworks now!' Ben left the window, casually kicked Leo as he passed then stood in the doorway, the little short-nosed gun in his right hand pointing at the ground. Leo groaned and slumped forward onto his knees, opposite Bill. Kirsty wondered again just how much damage that iron bar had done.

The sound of the motor got louder. Suddenly much too loud, and from above. Bill leaned out the empty window, craning his thick neck to look up. Benny ran to the doorway, and past him Kirsty could see the blue car had stopped half a mile off. The sound was deafening now.

'Chopper!' Ben yelled. 'What the fuck—'

Ben raised his gun at the sky, Bill turned from the window signalling *No no no!* over the din as Leo pushed off from the wall and launched himself into the biggest hit of his rugby-playing life. Crunch as Bill's head hit stone while Murray looped his arms over Ben's head and pulled bound hands back hard on the throat, but Ben was turning in towards Murray, and Kirsty was still paralyzed as he got the gun round, Murray frantically trying to turn further behind Ben but he got stuck in the corner and the gun came round to Murray's side. The shot was just louder than the motor roar, then the second bang and Murray went down, then three shots crashed through the back window from Colonel Mitchell, and Benjamin Cochran's short, wretched life ended.

The blue car reversed down the track, swivelled and was gone.

A man was dead, another probably dying, and nothing was funny any more. For the rest of her life Kirsty would see the stubby grey gun come round to find Murray's side, the shot and then another, and her friend falling while she herself did not move. The perplexed look on his face, as if to the end he couldn't credit the way things are. And once in a while Shonagh would hear someone sing 'The Flowers of the Forest' and have to excuse herself before she threw up, seeing again bits fly out of Ben.

Alasdair gripped Murray's shoulder as the stretcher went to the chopper.

'Hey, you're way too old to die young, squaddie,' he said, but Murray was going.

Two soldiers – SAS, Kirsty guessed – rolled Bill onto a stretcher, carried it to the hatch and pushed him in. The big head lolled, the dark jowls now grey. He did not look a well man. For a moment she thought about the son waiting for his new bike, the daughter wanting to keep up with her pals.

Colonel Mitchell grunted and got up from squatting beside Benny's body. He looked straight at Kirsty.

'Anything you want to add? Some useful remark about state fascists?'

She shook her head. The two soldiers carried Ben out. His skinny white arms flopped down from the stretcher. She glimpsed a blurred tattoo on his wrist as it trailed on the grass.

Colonel Mitchell looked down at the stained earth, contemplated bits of grey matter then scuffed dirt over them with his shoe. Outside, Shonagh was throwing up.

'We'll prioritize your friend,' the equerry said, then waved the chopper away. 'We'll pick up the man in the car sooner or later.'

'Sooner would be good,' Leo muttered.

Blank, exhausted, feeling nothing but nausea, Kirsty followed Abernethy to the white van. He looked different in combat gear, alert, at home. He threw open the rear doors and together they looked at the real Westminster Stone, its two iron rings glinting dully, a faint depression on the top, the rough cross.

'I hope your boss can sit authentically now,' Kirsty said. 'I doubt I ever will.' She turned away to put her arms around Shonagh, and they held each other up until Leo stumbled over to join them, and they stood there swaying as the rain drew damp curtains down across the Pentland Hills, while somewhere up above them Murray Hamilton was ceasing to be anything but memory.

32

Green, he wonders, why is it always green? Not the bright green of trees or grass but the pallid green of sour apples. And the yellow is never quite sunshine, more watery sick. Already Leo hates the waiting room in the Northern General, the cheerful smiley faces stuck on the walls, next to the notice warning they will be prosecuted for assaulting or abusing the staff, and on the opposite wall the STD and vaccination posters telling them how to look after themselves and protect their children.

Back home, he spent a lot of time in such waiting rooms.

When they went through to Intensive to see Murray after his first emergency op, Leo stood between Kirsty and Shonagh. He took in the papery hospital gown hitched up one bare arm, the needles and the tubes coming from arm and side, the drip and the not-quite-transparent mask over Murray's face, the big tube rammed down his throat.

He made it to the sink, just, spewed till his sight went.

To say it brought it all back would be putting it kindly. He got out of that room, found a quiet corner, sat and cried his guts out. Now he just sits, empty.

'It's my fault. Is it my fault? It's my fault.' Kirsty grips his arm, white and shocked, all her bounce gone. 'I got us into this. Stupid, useless woman.'

Dry-eyed and empty now, he sits with her as she curses herself, accuses herself, defends herself. In her more coherent moments she tells him how she'd been a lawyer here in Edinburgh, defending luckless no-goods like Benny. Leo feels marginally stronger because she needs him to be as he hears about the boyfriend, the pub band she'd sung for, the recreational drugs and the forged prescription pads she'd got from one of her clients. How the boyfriend's needs had got out of hand, likewise her need for him, how it had accelerated like a merry-go-round till she'd crashed out of law, just missed a jail sentence, changed her name and went to the Highlands.

She grips his hand, staring into his face, her bulbous hazel eyes flecked with red, snot dripping from her nose – not a pretty sight, but real raw human. Then again he is no pin-up boy, red-eyed and breath bitter with sick.

'I thought it was a game,' she blurts. 'But this is real and I think Murray is going to die.'

He puts his arms around her. What more can he do? What less? Shonagh comes out of Intensive and stands looking down at them for a bit. She nods like something makes sense then pulls Kirsty up and takes her off to the Ladies.

Leo sits on, looking at the cheery posters, hating them. Alasdair slumps down wearily after making another phone call, looks down at his beaten-up climber's hands.

'Murray didn't have to do that, did he? I mean, we had it covered.'

'Yes, but we didn't know that.'

'So he had to do it?'

'He thought so.'

Al looks at him gravely.

'Bound hands against a gun?' He shakes his head, looks down at his hands again. 'I wouldn't have had the guts.'

'Nor me.'

A pause. Al studies his hands some more.

'You knew he was going to?'

'He kinda signalled.'

'So you had to go for the big lad.'

It is not really a question. Leo just nods. He wonders how much damage he's done to big Billy, and whether he cares at all. There was a time he'd been a happy, untested boy, his only scars the skin-deep kind from joyous contact sports. Going back to those days is not an option. He has no idea at all where he will go from here.

Kirsty and Shonagh come back in and head for Intensive. A nurse tries to stop them, asking if they are family.

'Aye, we're family,' Shonagh says so fiercely the nurse lets them by. Leo knows he cannot go back in there. Can't face the tubes and drips and mask and ventilator again. He bows his head and waits.

'You did good, youth,' Alasdair mutters, but Leo cannot find it in him to reply.

Some time in the night, Murray's wife Tricia arrives. Apparently she'd been at a conference when they'd contacted her, had taken hours getting back, the train broke down twice. Leo has met her only once before, that night at the Atholl hotel, and he reckoned her down to earth, direct, resilient. She could have been a Kiwi.

He has never seen a face drawn as tight, like she's had some kind of drastic face-lift. Her cheek bones are taut as bows, eyes like flint headed arrows. The daughter, Eve, stands behind her. Tricia's eyes flick over them all, then at the Intensive Care sign. Kirsty is on her feet, makes to put her arms round Tricia.

'Don't you fuckin touch me! This is your fault, getting him intae yer daft games.' Tricia pushes past Kirsty and through the swing doors. They close with a sigh.

No one speaks. Kirsty sways, looking at them, at the door where Tricia and Eve have gone. Leo thinks she is going to faint. She looks utterly lost and hopeless. For a moment, as she falters, he seems to glimpse the effort of will it takes to be her.

Then she takes a deep breath, pushes open the door and goes into Intensive Care.

Raised voices, a crack, then Kirsty walks back out. She looks at them all with one side of her face red, then keeps on walking. Leo hears her footfall echo down the corridors then the outer door bangs. He looks to Shonagh, is about to follow when she shakes her head, gets up and hurries after Kirsty.

Alasdair's hand tightens on his arm.

'Let her go for now,' he says. 'Women do that stuff better. Ask my wife Jane.'

'She needs—'

'You did well, Leo,' Alasdair says quietly. It is the first time he has used Leo's name directly. 'Now you do nothing for a while. I've got to get in touch with someone.'

He goes off. Leo slides sideways on the old bench, rests his eyes from the sour green walls and the cheerful, lying posters telling us we can protect our children.

Commotion in the night, people in white coming and going fast through the swing doors. Murray has started bleeding internally again. Even Tricia is kept out.

'His guts are mangled from the first shot,' Alasdair mutters. 'The second smashed his pelvis. Even if he pulls through, he'll not be the same.'

No terrible jokes from him now, just dark seriousness and resolve. Leo just nods, unable to speak.

For something has finally got through to him. Maybe it has been building all those weeks at Samye Ling. Maybe he has been picking up whispers of it in his space under the eaves above the meditation hall.

Sleep-starved, half-concussed, he looks round the room now rancid with sweat, sorrow and fear. He takes in the people he has come to think of as friends: Alasdair still frowning at his hands as if the answer lies there; Tricia in urgent conversation with a nurse, Eve quietly at her side; Shonagh and Kirsty close in the corner. He looks at them and finally sees it is not that some people are incautious, stupid or simply unlucky, while the rest of us will be all right. None of us will be all right. Mountains, sunsets, good times, bad times, mates, children – nothing endures. Nothing. No exceptions.

He reckons he comes from a pretty decent country, well away from the world's problems and with few of its own. Always a positive outlook. No worries, mate. Little wonder it has taken him nearly thirty years to see the truth.

He thinks of Murray, bleeding away in the next room. Then pictures flicker through his head of his child living and the one image of his child dead, and for the first time he sees how one leads to the other, not because of an obscene fuck-up or cruel joke, but because that's how life is.

So Leo Ngatara sits quietly in the waiting room at four in the morning, no longer quite as young, smelling like a front-row's jockstrap, having his mind blown by the bleeding obvious.

Late afternoon the next day, everyone's feeling a bit fresher after a few hours kip in some hostel in subterranean Edinburgh. Seems Murray has got through the night. They've stopped the internal bleeding, poured more blood into him. Leo still has a cruncher where the dead boy cracked him with his bar. They've done the head scans and nothing too fatal there. No worries, yeah? He'd been knocked out before, by the boot of one of his own forwards, and knows it might be a while before the world gets back to normal. Not that it ever will, of course. He's got the message.

He hears footsteps clacking down the corridor. Alasdair looks up like he's expecting this, the door opens and Leo sees a tallish worn-looking guy in a dark jacket enter and, half a yard behind him, someone with short near-white blonde hair Leo takes for a boy till he gets a second look and her wide, vivid eyes take a first sweep over him.

Interesting to see how it goes. Alasdair is on his feet, hand out. Guy grabs it, claps him on the shoulder then hurries on to Kirsty and they hang on like they each think the other is going to fall. The little white-blonde lady stays back. Tweed jacket guy is holding Kirsty's shoulders, looking into her eyes and talking quietly, urgently, like they're the only people there. You might think they were brother and sister as much as lovers, the way they hold each other.

Tricia and Eve come out of Intensive. Neil – for of course Leo knows it must be him – lets go of Kirsty, embraces Tricia. Eve looks like she's seen her Saviour, cries 'Uncle Neil!', grabs his arm as the three of them hurry through the swing doors to see Murray.

Pale as Kendal Mint cake, the woman watches them go, fiddling with the zip of her tan jacket – which, collar up and all, she looks pretty cute in if you like that boy-girl sort – then goes over to Kirsty. The two of them sit down, start talking urgently but do not touch.

All that remains is for Leo, formerly Mr No-Worries, to go over and be introduced. She nods, holds out her hand. Her grip is a little skeletal but strong. The chunky ring on her finger presses cold into his bruised knuckle.

'I am Inga Johanssen,' she says. Her voice is clear, just a little raspy. 'You are Kirsty's friend.'

Their eyes meet above the handshake. Hers are very steady, paler than the horizon on South Island.

'I hope so,' he replies.

In that moment they begin to get each other.

33

In the wind-shadow behind the scrub willow fence, the snowdrops bent their heavy-headed, sterile whiteness. Jim MacIver grunted as he straightened to look to the crocus shoots for relief. Purple glints in the slit of one, yellow in another.

Patience, he thought. In God's good time.

'Hey, Greenfinger!'

Ellen stood in the door – how right she looked there, so alive and womanly in that strange poncho-thing that had raised eyebrows round the village – waving him in.

'Phone call! Your chief constable.'

Jim wiped cold earth from his hands, left Nature to it and hurried in. Her arm briefly around his waist. How could he have lived so many years without this?

'It's about the family that used to own Dunsinnan Hall. Oh, and he seems very curious about me.'

'So am I, my beloved. So am I.'

She snorted, slipped away, back to the table where their researches lay spread. Even as he wrapped his earth-stained fingers around the phone and prepared to speak, he looked at her averted, listening head and knew things could not go on like this.

'Jim, a fine morning.'

'It is what the Lord has chosen to send,' he conceded.

'Be that as it may. I have managed to contact the man you wish to speak with. He says he will be in touch very shortly.'

As the voice buzzed on in one ear, outlining hopes and anxieties – this investigation needed to show some progress or the less official aspects of it would have to be dropped – inside his other ear

Jim MacIver heard the quiet voice he trusted beyond all others murmur *You know the solution.*

Since first looking down at his old friend, so diminished as he lay inert in the hospital bed, Neil has brooded on Murray's last lunge at Ben, trying to fathom it.

It seemed Murray did not know Al had gone to call for assistance, nor about the tracer bug Kirsty had left in the van. It had been impossible to tell him – in the van he'd been unconscious; in the bothy there'd been no opportunity to talk. He went for Ben believing this was their only chance.

So it was heroic, desperate, but also misguided and unnecessary. Had he waited half a minute longer, the equerry and Mitchell and the two back-up soldiers would have sorted it out. Maybe Bill and Ben would have had the sense to surrender and no one would have died. Maybe.

Perhaps Murray's struggle with hands tied against a man with a gun was his final protest against the way things are. In terms of outcome, he was part-successful and part-doomed, and he probably would have settled for that.

Perhaps Murray sensed he could die then and there, perhaps he almost wanted to. For now Neil was forced to admit what they had all been denying, that for some time Murray's despair had run unvoiced and deep. The Cold War was over, only one side held the field. There was no good cause left, only single issues, and he had never been content with single issues.

And it seemed Murray had been losing more than a cause. In the last while he had been losing everything that made his world hold firm. Eve had been calmly – frighteningly calmly – candid about it when she took Neil to the crowded pub across the road from the hospital and made her godfather buy her fresh orange juice. Her mum had given up on her dad some time back. She'd been 'seeing' someone from her work. Eve didn't think they had actually, you know, done it. And now, whatever happened to Dad, they never would, because Mum would feel too guilty.

253

She wouldn't leave him now, so maybe all this was good.

Wearily Neil put his arm around Eve, the nearest he had to a child of his own. Perhaps he had always taken too rosy a view of things. He had always assumed that whatever difficulties they'd been having, Tricia and Murray were solid. He had thought all their friendships were solid, but now he didn't see how Kirsty and Trish could ever be close again, and he had doubts about Kirsty and himself. He kept seeing a freckled forearm flopped down off the hospital bed, the needles stuck in it. How small Murray was once all his struggle had gone. He had little round ears with no lobes.

'I'm sorry, Uncle Neil,' Eve said. 'I had to tell someone.'

She ran one finger lightly round the rim of her glass as together they looked at the ignorant, happy carry-on all around them. As tears blurred his eyes, under her finger the glass began to sing one long, unyielding note.

Next day they gathered again, in a booth in the old café across from the hospital. Only Tricia was absent. She'd looked at them incredulously then turned back to contemplating her unconscious husband and the rest of her life.

They were jammed into the booth, shoulder to shoulder, with coffee and Tunnock's all round. Kirsty accepted Neil's makings and rolled herself a cigarette, lit up. She drew deep, found you cannot fill a void with smoke, then put it aside.

'I am so sorry,' she said. 'I got you all into this.'

'Blethers, *a ghràidh*. We got ourselves into it.'

'At my suggestion. In the name of our friendship.'

'In the name of our friendship, yes. And you ask us to regret that?'

Kirsty looked around the table at them: Neil, Eve, Alasdair, Leo, Shonagh. Inga, sitting sideways-on, stared steadily back at her then nodded. Kirsty looked down at her hands and blinked. Swallowed.

'So we – well, HRH – have the Westminster Stone. That part is done. We found the real fake.'

'Very post-modern and not a bad result—'

'Tell that to my dad,' Eve said quietly.

Neil closed his eyes. It had been another careless, unthinking quip. Eve gripped his arm.

'But he wanted to,' she said. 'Dad was aye for daft games and lost causes.'

Kirsty studied her defunct roll-up. Lit it again, took a drag, pulled a face and put it back on the battered tin ashtray to go out again.

'So what do we do now, guys?'

'We solve the clues, find the Destiny Stone, complete the mission!' Al said. 'It's the only way to get Adamson off our backs. Then we do right by Murray and Trish. Yeah?'

'Yes,' from Neil.

'Aye to that,' said Shonagh.

'*Ja.*'

Kirsty looked to Eve who nodded. She took a deep breath.

'Thank you,' she said. 'Thank you all so much.'

'I have had my ring runes translated,' Inga announced quietly. She looked round the booth. 'It did not need much translating, for the runes say NES, and this word you know. It is like in Inverness.'

'That's all?' Kirsty said.

'There is the rune for P on the other side of the mount.'

'An abbreviation? Someone's initial?'

'Maybe it's part of a word, along with Kirsty's U,' Shonagh suggested.

'Or the whole thing is an anagram. Or each ring is.'

'We'll need the third ring to work it out,' Neil said. 'Any idea where it might be, Kirsty?'

'Not a clue.'

A long scratchy pause, like there used to be at the end of a record, the music over but the apparatus still running.

'I hate anagrams and riddles,' Alasdair said. 'Why couldn't they just have put an OS map reference number on the rings, maybe played with the eastings or northings? That's how we did it on our field exercises.'

'Yup,' Kirsty said. 'Shame they didn't have OS maps in the twelfth century. So we have NES, a river mouth, and there are dozens of them in Scotland, and STAFR, which could be a staff or an office or pretty much anything at all.' She shrugged and sat back from the table, stared out the window at the Edinburgh rain. 'I thought we could do this,' she said quietly. 'I thought it would work out somehow, like it did last time.'

I see us still, sitting round that scarred formica in a café that had not yet been made over, back in the days when the only world was the grubby actual one, with nothing virtual or ironic in the little red tin ashtray on each table, and coffee came from a big catering tin and tasted of nothing much, and the city and the century we inhabited were old and battered and somehow stalled as we ourselves were that morning when we sat there, facing the fact that life wasn't going to work out as we wanted. Now only the rain, the small rain of Edinburgh with a hint of grey sleet in its slanty falling, remains the same.

Alasdair drove Tricia and Eve back home to Kirkintilloch in Murray's old painter and decorator van, still bearing the 'Highways Maintenance Contractor' stencilling that had seemed so witty at the time.

It was a long and mostly silent drive. There was little that could safely be said. Murray was stabilized for the time being, was about to be moved to a less urgent ward before the next operations on his pelvis. The new worry was his damaged liver. But Eve needed to go to school, Tricia to sort out things at home and work and get some sleep before going back to the hospital. Both were unresponsive to Alasdair's ramblings, so after a while he gave up and had himself a think.

They had to press on. Otherwise it was all completely pointless. Which he suspected it was anyway, but a mission is a mission, a route is a route, and that's the game we play. Mostly he found a few simple slogans got him through life. When they didn't he felt horribly lost for a moment, then acted on instinct.

So on the motorway with squeaking wipers, peering through the murk, he thought one more time about STAFR and NES. On account of twenty years of climbing, Alasdair Sutherland was well acquainted with the roots of Scottish hill and place names. He was musing about *Nes* or *Ness*. River mouth or confluence of waters. As in Inverness, Blackness, Stromness. The old Welsh equivalent was *Aber*, as in Aberdeen, Abernethy, Aberystwith. Of course sometimes *Nes* became *Age*, as in Stannage, Dunnage, Dunstaffnage...

He blinked, his foot hesitated on the loose accelerator pedal. Eve glanced at him but he said nothing. He just kept on driving, now not minding the rain, not tired at all.

'Makes sense!' Neil exulted. They were back in the café over the road from the hospital. The mood had changed since Al's excited phone call. 'The Lords of Lorne who held Dunstaffnage were Bruce supporters, so the Stone could have gone there after Scone.'

'Doesn't fit,' Kirsty said. 'These runes might indicate Dunstaffnage, but that doesn't square with what Andrew Jamieson said, about it having been "sent back hame".'

'It's got to be worth a look. At least we can find a local historian or archaeologist and see if they've any suggestions.'

Kirsty sighed.

'I still think it's in or near Dunsinnan, but there's little point in us looking there. There have been a dozen or more excavations, and either someone found and moved it, or it was never found at all. No reason we should do any better, there or Dunstaffnage.'

'Every reason,' Neil said. 'We're the good guys!'

'Since when? We just do what we want, like everyone else, even Adamson.'

My God, he thought, she looks weary.

'I agree with Kirsty,' Inga said. 'But we are misled when we think we do what we want. Mostly we do what we must.'

'You hum that, I'll play it,' Neil said. 'So who is coming to Dunstaffnage to have a poke and speir around?'

'Not me,' Kirsty said. 'Murray has another op tomorrow. I have to stay around.'

'Leo?'

'Headaches,' he said. 'Reckon I'm still concussed.'

Shonagh stood up.

'Neil and Inga should go,' she said. 'Nothing is going to keep Al away, so meet up with him there.'

'Fine,' Kirsty said. 'Take my car.'

And so it fell.

34

Jim MacIver made coffee for himself and, with a broadminded shrug, a decaf for his beloved, and together they sat down at his kitchen table to read the typed pages that had arrived in the post that morning. For a while there was only the chill, cleansing wind of late winter shaking the died-back garden outside, and the shuffle of paper as, with a glance at her, he turned to the next sheet.

One bright, chilly February forenoon in 1802, keen to get outside after a week of great rains, two lads followed the swollen Kennaty burn to the lower slopes of Dunsinnan Hill. Jackie Laidlaw was a strongly-built fourteen-year-old, destined to take over from his father as Laird Dundas' orraman or general labourer to the estate. His companion's name is lost. To be utterly forgotten is, after all, the destiny of most of us!

Be that as it may, that morning Jackie Laidlaw and his young friend spotted a great landslip further up Dunsinnan Hill. They scrambled over the avalanche of turf and stones, and near the top of the slip came on a dark hole that had opened up.

The boys crawled into the cave, the bolder Jackie in front, not caring that he'd get a row from his mother for his muddied britches. A few feet in, mud gave way to level stone and the roof lifted. When they cautiously stood up and ran hands over the sides in the dimness, they discovered the stone was masoned. They realized this was not a natural cave, it was a small chamber.

They knew, as did their elders, that the Dunsinnan Hill was haunted. For generations, once a year lights had been seen at night where no lights could be. The terrible King Macbeth still roamed the hill, mourning his sacked castle. A sleepless lady – some said she was both sleepless and headless, though Jackie thought that a great nonsense – was said to walk the summit around and around all through All Hallows.

Moving across the chamber, the companion was hit in the back of his knees by something cold and hard. He fell backwards with a scream followed by a groan. Jackie Laidlaw started and banged his head off the ceiling, fell to his knees and crawled to his friend lying on the ground. He too hit something cold and hard.

He felt along the top, the sides. A great block of stone, very smooth but with carved ripples down the sides. His pal had tripped back over it and was now groaning on the floor.

'Pull yersel tegither, ya big feartie. Help us find the treasure.'

But they found no treasure in that dim chamber. Just the muckle stone and a couple of metal rods with round bits at the top. A quick scrape and even they couldn't pretend it was gold or silver.

Nothing there to get excited about. They left the rods, guiltily crawled out of the narrow entrance and went home with muddy knees. A week later, after yet more rains, the hillside slipped again and the entrance hole was lost.

There it would have ended, and young Jack Laidlaw's life left unrecorded as his forebears, with only the bare details on the lichened headstone in the old kirkyard by Moot Hill at Scone. But one night years later, Big Jackie was celebrating the birth of his latest child in the Meikle Inn, and the pouring rain outside put him in mind of a forenoon when he was still young and free, and he blurted out his tale to the landlord: the hidden chamber, the big carved stone, the metal rods.

The landlord blinked, listened, asked a few questions and gave Laidlaw another dram on the house. Then he left his wife in charge and hurried through the rain to Dunsinnan Hall.

*

The Laird's hurried excavation was of low archaeological standard. He put four Irish labourers on the job with pick axes, bores and shovels. On the third day of prodding around the area Laidlaw thought he remembered, the ground gave way beneath their feet and they all fell into an underground chamber. By a minor miracle, none were injured.

And there it sat, the *lapis fatalis*, the Fateful Stone, the true Stone of Destiny – a large, rectangular, ornately carved marble block with the metal hoops attached to the sides for carrying poles. Beside it lay two round plaques or targes. Dundas picked one up and examined it by the light of a flickering oil lamp. All around the curved rim was a wrought inscription in a language he could not read.

His letter appeared in *The Times* in January 1819, and the following day in the *Scotsman* and the *Herald*. It reported the discovery in Dunsinnan Hill of a chamber containing a big carved stone resting on four metal legs, and of 'the strong belief entertained in this part of the country that it was only a representation of Jacob's Pillow that Edward took to Westminster.' It also informed the public of the two round inscribed plaques, and of how they had been translated from the Gaelic by 'a gentleman', who had rendered it as reading *'Under your protective shadow lies the kingdom until angels carry you back to Bethel.'*

The letter concluded 'the curious stone has been shipped to London for the inspection of the scientific amateur'. But it was never recorded as having arrived. Ten days later another letter appeared, saying the original find had been a hoax, just a New Year joke. The stone they found, if indeed they found one at all, has never been seen since.

*

At the bottom of the last sheet there was a note in elegant cursive handwriting.

Forgive my prose style – as a solicitor I am not accustomed to flights of fancy! Thomas Dundas was my great-great-great-grandfather, and this was the family story that came down to me. I do not know how much credence to attach to it. I was the principle source for much of the material relating to the 1819 find, recently published by my sadly-deceased friend Peter Sidlaw. There are, however, further elements which I am bound by a client to keep confidential, these to be released only to one who can produce such a ring as I under-stand from our mutual friend is at the heart of your investi-gations. Under these conditions, perhaps we should arrange to meet. Yrs, R.T. Dundas (former Writer to the Signet)

Ellen Stobo drained the last of her decaf. Only so much excite-ment a woman could take.

'What do you think, *m'eudail*?'

She considered.

'It fits with Peter Sidlaw's article. The family name is right, and the part about the two letters to the newspapers is true enough. The Dundas family sold the big house two generations back, but this man might still know something.'

Jim nodded. He was not pleased the chief constable had hinted to Dundas about the Rothiemurchus ring. Perhaps it had been necessary to get his co-operation.

If nothing turned up soon, he'd have to hand over the enquiry and go back to being popular PC Plod on his wee patch, and how long would Ellen stay then?

'I think the time has come to spend a chilly day or two in Auld Reekie, *a ghràidh*.'

'Ah James, how you can sell to me.'

Her hand on his, still warm, still needing, still feeling.

*

Neil's flat was silent and coldly musty. The coffee cup he'd abandoned on his way out the door to catch the bus to meet Kirsty at Romanno Bridge was exactly where he'd left it on the mantelpiece, no more empty or full. The newspaper still lay open on the table, shoes were still muddy in the hall. It's what happens when you live alone – leave the house and nothing changes, except the fine smirr of dust collecting on the mirror.

It must happen all the time, he thought, dust like invisible indoor snowing.

He used his key and went into the office rooms. His desk was covered with his stand-in's work. He glanced at some new copy, took in the handwritten corrections: a woman's writing, assured. She seemed on top of the commissions he'd left behind: the workwear catalogue, the S&N Hotels, the smokeless coal ads.

At a glance he could see she had the zip, the conviction he'd lost. The only writing that had aroused his interest this last while had been his on-the-side account of last summer's adventures.

He scribbled a note for his partner George. *Finished soon. We need to talk about the business. Go well – N.*

'This is your business, Neil?'

Inga was standing silently in the doorway. He wondered how long she had been there.

'The unglamourous end of advertising,' he said apologetically. 'I keep meaning to get out. I'm tired of using words to sell things.'

She gestured towards the photo above his desk.

'That is her?'

'Yes.'

Helen laughing in sunshine, nothing special, just a moment in a life.

'What is she pointing at?'

'I've never stopped wondering.'

Her hand dropped lightly on his arm but she said nothing. He opened the lower desk drawer, felt inside and brought out a fat folder.

'Here,' he said. 'Some reading material for the trip.'

She took the file, took in the cover scrawl '*John Macnab revisited*', glanced inside.

'Is this what I think it is?'

He shrugged, closed the drawer.

'Let you see the crowd you've got yourself into.'

She looked up then, like a solitary little heron startled at its work.

'Am I? You all seem to have known each other for ever.'

'Shonagh approves you, so you're in. Also Al reckons you're a cool chick.'

'Is that what he said?'

'Afraid so.'

'Well I never,' she said. 'Social acceptance, all the way from the late Sixties.' Still, she did not seem displeased. She stood frowning thoughtfully, shifting from foot to foot in her cherry red boots, weighing the manuscript in her hand. 'What about Kirsty? What does she say?'

'You are very different,' he conceded.

She laughed, seemed genuinely amused. White teeth in a neat mouth that he'd learned loved eating cake but seldom allowed itself to. Passionate or prim? Her kisses would be one or the other, no in between, for some lucky person. He looked down and closed the drawer.

'Let a thousand flowers bloom?'

'Something like that.'

He took a last glance at Helen as he always did before leaving the room, then they were off. All the way down the road she lingered in his head, smiling, pointing at something he would never know.

35

Sitting in the lobby of the Arts Club, Edinburgh, re-reading Dundas' account of the rediscovery of the Stone in Dunsinnan Hill, Jim MacIver shook his head, to clear it rather than express disbelief. He was beyond incredulity now, had been ever since he stared down at the ring on the man's hand among dead leaves in Rothiemurchus Forest.

The second letter to the newspapers stated the first had been a hoax. Which was true? What is a man to believe?

The porter passed with a look that made Jim glance at his brogues to see they weren't muddied. He always felt like a peasant in Edinburgh, with heather coming out of his ears instead of merely hairs (what was it with those hairs?). He felt in his trouser pockets for his ring – since Sidlaw's murder it seemed unwise to walk around wearing it. The Rothiemurchus one from the finger of Colin Weir was in the safe at his hotel. Ellen would be research-ing at Register House to clarify the ownership of Dunsinnan Hall then and now.

Under the porter's watchful eye, Jim folded away the Dundas manuscript and had another look at Peter Sidlaw's article, the one that had got him killed. The detail of the inscription on the plaques being in Gaelic interested him, for there was an old word meaning 'protective shadow', *sgonnsa*, and it was pronounced 'skoon'. As in Scone.

It could be just coincidence.

'Here comes Mr Dundas now, sir,' the porter said, sounding deeply surprised.

Jim glanced through the window and watched as up the sunlit

steps sauntered a slim, elderly man in a perfectly cut three piece green tweed suit, removing his dark green trilby as he reached the top step to reveal beautiful long white hair brushed smoothly back on his head. One elegant hand passed over those sunken, shining temples, then Mr R.T. Dundas, former Writer to the Signet, stepped through the door into the subdued splendours of the Edinburgh Arts Club.

In their secluded corner in the main smoking room, Dundas finished carefully examining the ring, paying particular attention to the scratches around the mount.

'Am I to understand this is yours?'

'It was my father's.'

'But there is another? From your investigation?'

Jim nodded. 'I do not carry evidence around with me.'

'Quite rightly,' the retired lawyer murmured. 'I am most delighted to make your acquaintance, Sergeant MacIver.' As he handed the ring back to Jim MacIver, his pale face fell into a warm, human smile, though his eyes, or something around those eyes, remained sorrowful.

Robert Dundas, three times great grandson of the Laird who had organized the 1819 Dunsinnan dig, raised his sherry schooner, tapped it gently against Jim's tumbler of Bowmore (how many years old, for the Lord's sake? The smell of the malt was detonating forgotten pleasure centres located in the upper reaches of the MacIver nose).

'Your continued good health,' he murmured.

'Slainte,' Jim replied. 'And to your client, of course.'

Again that quick, resigned smile.

'Thank you.'

They drank, then put their glasses down and considered each other. Of a writer to the Signet, Jim reminded himself, one might expect a high degree of probity and discretion – also omissions and half-truths, if necessary. For all his gentle manner, the man seemed ill at ease, or perhaps just excited.

'In light of your ring – what a pity you did not bring the other – I am prepared to show you the lesser-known postscript to our family story. I shall leave you here for five minutes while you read it.'

What is not generally known is that two days after his letter appeared in *The Times*, Laird Dundas had received an urgent note all the way from Skye, sealed with red wax stamped by a crescent ring. 'Imperative we hide the Stone. Do not, repeat not, ship South. The Kingdom depends on the protective shadow. Will explain on arrival. Yrs MacDonald, gent.'

It was not the first flustered communication he had received since publishing his letter, but certainly the oddest.

Dundas poured a dram and walked out into the walled statuary garden. Here in the folly his family nicknamed 'Little Delphi', littered with ivy-encrusted copies of Roman sarcophagi, funeral styles, Egyptian artefacts and armless – in one case, headless – Minoan statues, he felt safe, at ease with the whisky in one hand, the letter in the other. Through the trees and drizzle, he could see the flank of Dunsinnan Hill. In the yard to the left, the Stone lay crated in the stables, ready to be shipped South. The London Society of Antiquities was expecting it. Perhaps they would be able to make sense of the hieroglyphs and patterns inscribed along its edges. As for the plaques lying on his desk, they were pretty, curious things that his housekeeper had cleaned up nicely. He would keep them, perhaps crossed above the mantelpiece for the edification of visitors.

Still, it would do no harm for the London Society to wait a day or so. He rang for old Laidlaw and gave his instructions.

Four days later, Calum Morrison MacDonald, gent, came up the drive of Dunsinnan Hall astride a lame pony. He himself was tall, thin and faded like a wraith, grey whiskered and his fine clothes worn threadbare. Even the great swinging kilt was faded grey. He beat on the front door with a bronze-topped stick until the housekeeper opened up, took one look at this outlandish figure and told him firmly to take himself off. No Jacobites here, if you please. This is a respectable Whig household.

Laird Dundas, who had been watching the arrival with some amusement, crossed the hall and welcomed his visitor. They shook hands and went into the study, with orders not to be disturbed.

Despite the housekeeper's best efforts – her ear pressed to the keyhole – no one knows what was said between the Whig laird and the impoverished, landless Jacobite who stayed for a whole week and finally left looking much better fed, as did his pony.

A solemn letter was written to *The Times*, apologizing for this childish hoax, a traditional Scottish Hogmanay prank. And the Destiny Stone vanished from the stables, never to be seen again in the region of Dunsinnan, or anywhere else.

Jim MacIver drained the last of his Bowmore with appreciation and regret, put the pages aside as his host returned.

'So Calum Morrison MacDonald was a Moon Runner?'

The retired lawyer looked sorrowfully at him.

'You are from Lewis yourself?'

'Aye. But my maternal grandfather and his people were Skye men of Sleat. My ring came from him, through my father Aonghas Dubh.'

Thomas Dundas rested his pale, talcum-dusted hand lightly on Jim's tweed jacket sleeve and smiled.

'Calum MacDonald was the last of his line. My belief is you have the ring he wore that day. He was a direct descendant of Angus Og, close friend and supporter of Robert Bruce.'

The ring lay between them on the little mahogany table. Caught in the sun, it seemed bigger and brighter, and a breathless feeling came over Jim MacIver. With Angus Og, founding father of the MacDonald clan, they had just stepped back into the great peat bog where myth and history ooze together.

'These Moon Runner rings,' Jim said. 'How do they help find the Destiny Stone?'

Dundas gently removed his hand and folded it into the other. He looked, Jim thought, like a grey setter in his refined gentleness, fine high cheekbones, the melancholy.

'I was hoping you might know.'

'Another drink,' Jim MacIver said firmly. 'My shout, I insist. Unless you have an appointment?'

The retired lawyer smiled. In that warm smile lay utter loneliness, long accepted.

'I have no appointments.'

Over his second Bowmore, thick as a black house with peat-reek, Jim learned of the legend – the likelihood – that in the early 14th century the true Crowning Stone had been moved from its first hiding place. With opposing armies moving across the country, and Edward I still on the prowl, it wasn't safe in Dunsinnan Hill. It had to be moved beyond Edward's power. The story was put about that it was hidden in Skye.

'May I ask where it really went?'

Again, that warm, lonely smile.

Dundas nodded to the glass secure in Jim's fist.

'Probably the same place as that whisky.'

'Islay?' Jim took a long drink, let sensation soar through his mouth, nose, head. 'Crikey.'

'And then with the fall of the Lord of the Isles, I surmise it was returned to its original hiding place in Dunsinnan. Which was where my family found it by accident several hundred years later. Once the letter had appeared in the papers, Calum Morrison MacDonald came to explain what the Stone was and why it had to be hidden again.'

Jim sat back in his chair and considered. He looked at the ring, his ring, sparking in the sunlight, then at the retired lawyer opposite. There were many questions left, but only one that mattered.

'So where do you think it is now?'

Dundas regarded him levelly.

'I am not a Moon Runner,' he replied. 'Nor was my forebear Thomas Dundas. He merely bought the estate, which has, I regret to say, subsequently passed out of our family. He knew nothing of the Stone beyond rumours. So Calum Morrison took it into his care, as was his right, and it may well have been he who had rings made with new inscriptions to indicate the Stone's new home. There is another detail, so unsubstantiated I did not include it in my account...'

He paused. From the dining room came the low hum and clatter of money encountering influence over lunch. Jim MacIver waited, not pushing. It was, he claimed, his only talent. Robert Dundas shifted uneasily in his armchair.

'We know the Stone left Dunsinnan House on a moonlit night in January 1819 in a cart going West, accompanied by Calum Morrison MacDonald. It was never seen again. There are stories it is hidden still in Skye, in some archetypal cave behind a water-fall.'

'Are there any caves behind waterfalls not crammed with lost treasures?'

'I have not heard of one.'

Jim nodded resignedly. He drained his glass and put the ring back in his pocket. Dundas coughed, reached into an inside pocket.

'However, Mr MacIver, my client has authorized me, if I thought you an honest man, to ask you to meet at this place, where she might be able to show you something of considerable interest.'

Jim glanced at the postcard he'd been handed. A high-walled irregular castle built onto a rocky pedestal, surrounded by wood-land, sea to the front and back.

'Yon's Dunstaffnage, over the bridge from Connel. In the West.'

'Just so. You must bring the other ring to show you have the right to full disclosure. It seems the third ring is lost forever.'

'How will your client know when I'm there?'

Robert Dundas rose in one elegant movement, smoothed soft shining hair back over his temples then deftly fitted his hat.

'Because I myself will accompany you.'

36

Late morning the following day Alasdair Sutherland rumbled up the Loch Lomond road in Murray's painter and decorator van, left foot bopping on the floor to Little Feat's 'Willing' on the cassette player, fingers rapping on the wheel, all systems go, enjoying the onrush of winding road, trees and water. Inactive, he became moody, restless, and as near to depressed as he could be. When he wasn't climbing or fishing, adventuring or generally *doing*, he drank too much. Jane said so, and he knew it. Didn't want to go the way of his father.

Coming to the fork at the Tarbet Hotel, he surprised himself by impulsively slewing left at the last minute. Oh well, let's find out what that's about.

On that short, exhilarating crossing to the next loch system (*tarbet* equals 'place where boats are hauled over', thus several of them in Scotland), he thought on his dear Jane and the pleasures of last night's catching up. Once this little jaunt was done, they'd both go over to Edinburgh to see Murray, check on how the wee fella was doing.

He frowned, rounding the top end of Loch Long. Truth be told, hospitals gave him the willies, as did physical infirmity. He had invested totally in his body. When it faltered, he wanted out, no messing, no decline. Seeing Murray lying there, all bust up and half-gone, well...

He truly hoped to die before he grew old. With forty behind him, he was now old enough to know better what that meant, and still he wished it. Another twenty-five years, he half-thought. Some more mountains, more trips, try and make some money and see Jane right – the fact that Jane's salary from nursing was their only steady income was one he preferred to overlook – then it's off for the ultimate nap.

Anyhow, life without Jane was not worth contemplating, so he'd be sure to pop his clogs first.

So with these half-formed inner ramblings accompanying the lift and swirl of Lowell George's bourbon-sweet guitar, Alasdair Sutherland came to the top of Rest and Be Thankful. He stood at the edge of the lay-by there and looked back down the glen where the cloud shadows passed above the remains of the old twisting single-track road, the way folk used to come. And was he thankful to be standing, still alive and surrounded by the hills he had known and sweated on for twenty years? You bloody bet he was.

An hour or so ahead of Alasdair, Neil and Inga kink through Crianlarich, under the railway bridge and accelerate North in Kirsty's green Wolseley. On impulse – because the afternoon is fine by March standards, his companion apparently enjoying herself, and there is no point in arriving early at Dunstaffnage – he takes the right fork after Tyndrum instead of heading directly for Connel.

It's been fifteen years since he last burned thigh muscles up the long dour slab of Ben Dorain on the right. He finds himself telling Inga about a trip with Alasdair and Murray, must have been a decade back, when they got off the train at Rannoch Station and yomped into the wilderness, still arguing happily about whatever great issue of the day. Climbed Meall Buidhe in the summer gloaming, lay down on its lee slope in bivvy bags with only a hip flask, chocolate and talk to see them through the short, pale night.

The whole next day they had spent crossing the wearisome slopes above Glen Lyon with nothing human in sight. Afternoon and Murray caught brown trout in Loch an Daimh, cooked them quick over a fire coaxed from heather and lochside driftwood. High up there, with enough breeze to keep the midgies honest, blue smoke fading into bluer sky, they shared food then talk then silence.

'We almost never left,' he confesses. 'All our partners were back home – Helen was still alive, before we got married – and they meant the world, but for those days it was just the three of us, and life was simple and right.'

She glances at him, his long face lit by memory, the black hair flecked with grey above his ears, no sorrow just pleasure as he tells it. She once made her own trips into the summer mountains, most especially up to that *saeter* owned by Conrad's family, sleeping with him in the hay loft amid the nose tickling mustiness, living in his arms at night and by day the music they teased from mandolin and fiddle.

'I remember,' she says. 'It can be very good.'

'Then the rain came later above Loch Lyon, and we spent a rough night on the col of Beinn Mhanach over there.' He points out beyond Ben Dorain's khaki slopes, out to where the heads and shoulders of hills slump together like vast slumbering squaddies. 'Next morning we squelched, not saying very much, over the saddle and down into Bridge of Orchy where we'd left the car at the train station. Man, I've never been so pleased to get into dry clothes and a café fry-up.'

It's been too long, she thinks. Too long since I've ventured out there.

'Yes,' he murmurs, looking at her expression. 'Too long.'

As they enter Bridge of Orchy and take the B road West, she begins to improvise an a cappella Blues-style song, just to see where it might go.

'*Hit the loch with a hammer*
Get waves then you get rust'

She hears his giggle. Good to see him laugh as he carries it on.

'*I say we do what we want to*
You say we just do what we must'

So he'd remembered her heartfelt remark. She looks out of the window at the strange abandoned country.

'Okey-dokey,' she says. 'A refrain to round off the verse, then we're halfway to a new song.'

Thus occupied, they follow the shallow, peat-brown Orchy down to Dalmally and what lies beyond.

Alone in the back seat of Robert Dundas' 1971 Mercedes Coupé, Jim MacIver shivered with apprehension as they drove into the Pass of Brander where the walls of Cruachan and Beinn Ghlas squeeze Loch Awe into a dark trap. His father had told him stories of the battle here, where the MacDougalls of Lorne, waiting to ambush Bruce's forces coming through the Pass, had been themselves trapped from above, broken and fled to Dunstaffnage, which they then lost. That was in 1308, and his father had told it as living history.

Looking at the heads up front, he shifted uneasily, for the place frankly gave him the heebie-jeebies. He was glad he had let Ellen persuade him on the matter of firearms, and made that call to the chief constable. It weighed heavily, uncomfortably in his tweed jacket. By agreement he had his own Runner ring in his pocket, Ellen had the one from the dead man in Rothiemurchus Forest.

A life spent in anxiety is a life wasted. But listening to the murmur of conversation between his beloved and Robert Dundas – they seemed to be discussing Scots Law – he had a feeling something was coming to an end, just like the great Awe. This morning Ellen had talked of home, how the thaw would soon be coming to her lands and the horses would need to be let out and fences mended around what she called the cabin – though the photo she carried showed a two storey house built of massive logs, cooried in among trees, and in the background the first slopes of the Rockies rising across the creek.

Yes, the winter was coming to an end, and she'd be going. And this investigation, the chief constable had made clear, was running out of time. The man called Adamson, prime suspect for the Sidlaw killing, had disappeared after some kind of kerfuffle in the

Pentland Hills. Losing Inga Johanssen in Oslo had made Jim look incompetent. With DUN and NES his only clues, the whereabouts of the True Stone remained unknown.

The third ring, was that what Dundas' client had to show him? And would that be enough to find the Crowning Stone?

In his pocket, Angus Og's ring was hot and damp with sweat as the car slid free of Brander, kinked through Taynult and headed for Connel Bridge and the headland guarded by Dunstaffnage. Jim MacIver intently studied the back of Ellen's neck, the tan glimpsed below her hairline as she leaned forward. We're nearly there, he thought. *Thig peileir dian à gunna Ghaoil.* A vehement bullet will come from the gun of Love.

Who knows what impulse made Alasdair not turn right at Inveraray as he'd intended. Maybe he wasn't ready to turn away from the westering sun spreading butter-yellow all down Loch Fyne, or maybe it was something else. Strange trip this, all these odd thoughts and feelings. Must be a bit upset.

Lochgilphead, then. He had arranged to meet Neil and the Norwegian bird at Dunstaffnage, late afternoon. Be a bit late now. Time Neil had a mobile, everyone was getting them these days. He'd have been happier without his – a man can be too easy to get hold of – but Jane insisted. Anyway, no worries, they'd meet there sooner or later. He had his tent, stove and sleeping bag in the back, and a full tank of petrol. He was a free man.

At Cairnbaan hamlet he looked on the lush low-lying green lands around Crinan canal, thought *Kingdom of Lorne*, and knew then what had brought him here, on the long way round to Dunstaffnage.

He parked by the sign. No one else around. Good. This should be a private moment.

The sun was low over his left shoulder as he quickly climbed the hill. A wee knoll, really, a mere few hundred feet of rock outcrop, but still one of the most significant sites in the formation of Scotland. He loved that stuff, knowing the history. One of the few good things his father had given him, along with self-belief. With luck the old man's self-sabotage had died with him.

The faint path rose, wound through a narrow gap – natural? – in the rock, then across the small rising enclosure and with the land fallen away flat on all sides, the Moine Mhor, 'the Great Moss', stretching away to the North, Jura and Colonsay floating under bloated low sun to the West, he stepped onto the summit of Dunadd Hill.

He removed his right boot, then the sock. He took a deep breath and fitted his bare foot into the imprint in the living rock, stood tall and stared out. The Scotti had come from Ireland to land boats on these shores and make their kingdom. Then they beat up the Picts till one of their own, Kenneth McAlpin, was crowned King of all Scotland on the Stone we're all after. And a long time later their descendants went back and colonized Northern Ireland, beat up the natives there. Man, you got to laugh. Pity those guys with their suitcase bombs don't.

When Murray gets out, he thought, I'll take the wee fella here, carry him up if necessary, and crown him King of Dal Riata, King of Scotland. Of course he's a republican and probably wouldn't want it, but I'll tell him it's a small country and he's got to be related.

Alasdair stood there for a long time, feeling numbness creep upwards through his shin. God knows I'm not that smart, he thought, having never hammered at the gates of the university. In my life I hammer – delicately – into ice and frozen turf. That's my way.

He stood a while longer with the sweat chilling on his skin. Wee Murray's politics make most folk feel guilty they don't care like he does, but not me. He has his thing, I have mine. It's all bosh anyhow, everything but standing high and looking over the planet, feeling yourself alive, is bosh. Shame it made my pal so pissed off so much of the time.

Then into his head abseiled a memory of Murray poaching the mid pool on the Alt na Harrie the summer before. Dawn, mist rising from the clear deep brown water, trees dark on the skyline of the crag above, and the wee fella furling and unfurling his Spey cast in the early blue light then sending that line out to kiss into the shadow by the big rock, and for once he had looked totally at ease, with no quarrel with anything, at one with the world and his place in it.

Alasdair moved off the rock slab, hastily pulled sock and boot onto white numb foot. This one's for you, old son.

Back in the car he stuffed emergency rations into his maw, checked the watch. He'd lost a fair bit of time with that palaver, and would be late for the rendezvous at Dunstaffnage, not that it would make much difference.

When Alasdair Sutherland got it wrong, he did so as he did everything else, completely and without reservation.

'It must have known a few adventures, this car.'

Neil nods, pulls down on the wheel as they come into the right hand bend. Feels the drag, hears the tyres squeal though they're not going fast. The car lurches, straightens.

'Loads of style, but a pig to drive,' he says. For a moment he sees Kirsty, intent, squinting into the light, sparring with him as they drove down from Tomintoul to Braemar that summer. Strong, proud hands, head, mouth. Remembers her rare tears, down at the midnight river. And the time when they sang together at the Atholl, after the salmon was poached and the voices, the company, life itself all felt right. His fingertips buzz with remembrance of her soft, freckled skin, the unexpected seriousness of her passion the three times they made love. The fourth time, that night in Oslo, might have been 'Hello Again' or 'Goodbye'. Either way, it had been different from the others.

He glances across at Inga Johanssen, her slim upper body leaning forward as she rummages in the glove compartment for sweets, and he seems to see her truly for the first time. He senses what it might be to be her. To be Baked Alaska in reverse – cold on the outside and heat within.

'This is not so legal, *ja?*'

She is holding a large gun of a dull, flat grey that seems to drain light from the air. The long brown butt protrudes below her fist.

'Careful!'

He slews to a stop, looks around. They are somewhere on the moors above Taynuilt, no one else on the empty winter road but still his skin crawls.

'Do not worry,' she says calmly. 'The safety catch is on.' Her thumb brushes the little burr. She turns it over, checks the maker's name, weighs it in her hand. Clicks out the long magazine, nods, slots it home.

'It will be from the fight at Samye Ling,' Neil says. 'Apparently our Maori warrior got it from one of Adamson's pals. Kirsty must have forgotten about it.'

Inga raises her eyebrows.

'You think so? It is a useful weapon. Single shot or – like this – it is machine pistol, carries twenty rounds. You just press and keep on pressing till your troubles go away, our instructor used to say.' She looks down at the gun, shakes her head. 'It is the kind of stupid thing men say. Not so accurate.'

'You've used one of these?'

She looks at him, amused.

'On the range, *ja*. Not often.' She seems to take pity on him. 'I like hitting targets, I enjoy sports for one. I try archery but I am not strong enough. So I join the gun club. No strength required except mental.'

'Are you good?'

'Good?' She frowns, seems to give this serious consideration. 'I must try to be.'

'I mean good at target shooting.'

She laughs, her whole face brightening.

'I know,' she says. As she stuffs the Beretta into the green leather duffel bag she carries everywhere, she adds, 'Music and shooting I am good at. People – not so very good.'

'You're not doing so badly,' Neil says.

'Really?'

He looks at her.

'Really,' he says, then puts the Wolseley into gear and hits the road to the West again. You get the beat, he thinks, then you lose it, then you get it again.

'This is not the first thing I remember,' Inga says. She gazes out the car window at the shifting, watery light of the West. 'But it is the first time I *come to myself*. I am running around a back garden, wearing green corduroy. It is bright and sunny but nothing special, and suddenly I stop because for the first time I see myself. I know I am here, in this place, wearing green. Me, here.' She is silent. He waits, feeling himself with her. 'So I start running around, turning and twirling, to see if I can lose it, but when I stop I am still here, the world is still round me. I cannot lose it or myself. I have never forgotten this feeling, it has never changed even in unhappiest times. You understand?'

Neil has put his hand on hers, the second entirely natural thing he has done with her. The back of her hand is small and warm, the bandage rough.

'I get you.'

Her hand has flinched and now relaxes. He sees the side of her mouth twitch.

'Perhaps,' she says quietly, and reaches for her old friend the Blues.

As she strums the banjo, neither of them says anything for a while. They come to the junction by Connel Bridge, that grey box-girder over a white-flecked tide-race, and turn South towards the ancient stronghold of Dunstaffnage. She sings

I got one foot on the platform
And one foot on the train

37

The champagne-coloured Merc Coupé slowed at the barrier, then with a twitch of Dundas' hands it bumped onto a dirt track, through the trees then back onto the driveway running up the Dunstaffnage promontory.

'What a magnificent car,' Jim heard Ellen say.

'It was my father's one indulgence. He was an advocate too, like his father.'

'So I guess it was inevitable what you became.'

Dundas nodded briefly. He didn't seem happy about it.

'And your mother?'

From behind, Jim saw the shoulders tense.

'She is still sharp as a coulter blade.'

Water to the right, Loch Etive. A glimpse of water to the left, the Firth of Lorn. Such a strategic position, commanding the seaward access into Loch Awe and the heart of Scotland. No wonder the Dal Riadic kings made a stronghold here. According to Ellen's research, St Columba's relics were brought here from Iona, maybe along with his travelling altar stone, hundreds of years before the kingship moved to Scone. Now perhaps the Stone had come back here.

A scrunch on the gravel, the car stopped under the castle. It was big, dark, irregular, perched high on living rock. Strange phrase, Jim thought as he got out, 'living rock'. Surely it's just dead.

They stood there on the empty gravel. The sun had fallen into cloud, a chill wind oozed through bare branches, the light was starting to sink into the ground.

'Historic Scotland,' Dundas said, pulling off his driving gloves. 'Closed to the public this afternoon.'

Jim looked to Ellen, got a slight shrug of the shoulders.

'And your client?'

'She's within. The castle is HS but the gatehouse inside the walls stayed in our family. I didn't mention? Look!'

He pointed up where three windows rose above the battlements. A light was on, faintly.

'She will have seen our arrival. Follow me.'

He turned, and hurried across the gravel and led them up a stone stair. At the top it turned into a round-headed doorway set in a recess. The huge metal-studded door was closed. The lawyer knocked the side of his fist on it three times.

'The stairway is quite new,' Dundas said quickly, his feet jittering on the stone. 'Eighteenth century. There used to be a drawbridge.'

'Interesting,' Ellen said. She was studying the wall above the doorway. One tiny window, a few slits. 'This was a serious castle.'

'Completely humourless,' Dundas agreed, but his mind didn't seem on his words. 'Ah!'

Thud of bolts, then the door opened. A stooped middle-aged man with wild black hair and thick black horn rim glasses stood blinking at them.

'James MacIver?'

'The same. This is my friend, Ellen Stobo.'

'The Canadian. Welcome to the old world. I'm MacIntyre.'

'Thank you,' Ellen said drily.

There was a pause. No handshakes offered.

'Come on in,' the man said. 'Her ladyship is waiting up in the gatehouse. Lead on, Mr Dundas.'

He let them pass then closed and bolted the door. They went through into an enclosed courtyard: some half-ruined interior walls, a complete battlement above, a raised rectangular structure that Jim guessed to be the well. And off to the side stood a three storey house, sombre and shabby. MacIntyre lifted the latch and opened the unpainted old door.

'Come on in,' he said.

They filed into the dimness. MacIntyre flicked on the light and closed the door. When he turned round, there was a gun in his hand.

Jim and Ellen looked to each other, then to Robert Dundas. He was studying his polished brown shoes.

'So much for her ladyship,' Ellen murmured.

'Oh, I can oblige there,' Adamson said. His free hand flicked inside his jacket. 'Meet her ladyship.'

The knife, longer and sharper than any knife has a right to be, glimmered then disappeared back into its holster. The gun remained.

'I must warn you, she has a wicked temper and a very sharp tongue.' The man who called himself Adamson straightened up, pulled off his glasses and the black wig, dropped them on the kitchen table.

'Dundas, please remove the implement our haggis hunter carries inside his jacket. Thank you.' He took the gun, glanced at it then dropped it casually in his pocket. 'You mustn't blame Mr Dundas,' he said easily. 'I made him an offer he couldn't possibly refuse if he wants to keep his reputation and his saintly mother alive. Now we will go upstairs in the following order: lawyer, Miss Canada, PC Plod. Yes?'

And so it was, up a narrow stair, in that order. After passing dim portraits and a set of crossed pistols mounted on the wall, the stair opened into a sparsely furnished sitting room. Jim and Ellen stood by some old display cabinets. Dundas hesitated by the window looking down on the gravel.

'I'm terribly sorry,' he said, looking at them for the first time. 'I really had no choice. My mother, the family reputation, my reputation...' He spread his manicured hands. 'So sorry.'

'Mr Dundas. Come here. Now, out into the passageway.'

Adamson stood in the doorway where he could still see Jim and Ellen, gun trained on them. Dundas went past him and out of sight.

'Yes,' Adamson said. 'That'll do.'

One shot, a muffled squeal then a thump. The gun was back on them before Jim had taken his second step.

'Right,' Adamson said. 'Now we get down to it.'

Jim's Runner ring rattled on the display cabinet glass. Below it were old pistols, some rusting skean dhu daggers, a claymore. Useful weapons in their time, Jim thought dismally. *Their time is past and so is mine.*

'And the other one.'

'I don't have it.'

'You were the Rothiemurchus investigating officer. You confirmed to our deceased friend you had it. You were told to bring both.' He stared at Jim, his eyes starting to light up. 'You've seen what happened to the historian and Dundas. Know I am serious. It will be fourteen hours till anyone comes, and if you don't tell me where the ring is, every one of those hours will be given over to her ladyship.' His left hand drew the long blade, gun in the other hand. 'And there will be time for your friend here. I almost hope,' he said reflectively, 'that you will say no.'

Jim looked down, as if thinking about the offer. The cabinet had a small padlock. *Break the glass, snatch the skean dhu. Hopeless of course. He'd have to kill me. He doesn't want to kill me, yet. So...*

'I have it,' Ellen said. 'Here.' She stepped forward.

'Lay it on the case, then back away.'

She did so, silently cursing. *He was a pro, probably army trained. This would not be easy, but she was trained too.*

'Excellent. Back onto those chairs. Sit on your hands.'

Never taking his eyes off them, Adamson reached for Jim's ring, turned it to the electric light.

'Very good. Mr Dundas, please read and translate.'

Robert Dundas stepped into the sitting room, a tiny smirk on his cultured lips. He took both rings and went over to the high window. There he took out a notebook and a magnifying glass. Ellen and Jim sat on their hands, incapable of speech.

ANDREW GREIG

'I'm afraid he has a weakness for the theatrical,' Adamson said. 'Like many of his persuasion. So what do the runes say?'

Dundas looked up from his notebook.

'Just a minute,' he said. 'One is Norse, the other Gaelic.'

Adamson caught the baffled look that passed between Jim and Ellen.

'You didn't know?'

'I thought they were just scratches,' Jim said. 'My father too.'

Adamson laughed. It seemed to give him pleasure.

'Some Fellowship, these Moon Runners. Couldn't even read your own runes.'

Robert Dundas stepped away from the window.

'The main inscriptions read DUN on Mr MacIver's ring, and NES on the one from Norway. The latter is often rendered as NAGE.'

'You haven't got the third ring,' Ellen said. 'That could be anywhere.'

'True,' Adamson conceded. 'But I do have the inscription, through a helpful friend at the Museum of Antiquities. Christine Fowler was given her ring by William Mackie.'

'Kirsty?' Jim said faintly. 'Kirsty Fowler?'

'You know her?'

'A bittie.'

'Interesting. Her ring read STAFR. So altogether, my friends, we have *Dunstaffnage*. Nothing there I hadn't guessed already. And the auxiliary letters?'

'We have T, P, U.'

'What do they mean?'

'I cannot even hazard a guess,' Dundas said. He smoothed his silky hair back across his temples. 'They could be a name, a place, a shorthand prayer or curse. It's not my area. I suggest you consult Miss Traquair, for I can't help you any more.' He fitted his trilby, picked up the rings. 'I must go now if I'm to get back to Edinburgh tonight. You said I could keep these.'

'Yes, indeed,' Adamson said. 'You cannot help me any more.'

He shot him in the heart. The lawyer folded onto the floor, his

285

knees up at first then slumping over. Adamson glanced then shot again.

A last wheezing exhale, then silence. Adamson stooped for the rings, put them in his pocket.

'Look at it this way,' he said. 'He got to die twice. The first time was more convincing.'

What form of life is this? Jim thought. And then he heard an engine, tyres on gravel, stopping outside.

Adamson crossed to the side of the window and looked down.

'This just gets better,' he said.

Standing on the gravel, Neil stretched and groaned. A long day's drive. The castle looked massive, sitting high on its rock, dark against the failing light. It also looked deserted and closed. Still, a rather swish old car sat on the drive, a faint warmth and smell of oil rising from the bonnet. No sign of Murray's van. The agreement had been: the castle, late afternoon. Default: the village pub.

Inga looped her duffel bag across her shoulder, turned up her collar and began to walk around the base of the castle. Her pale hand rested on the rough agglomerate, wondering. Spooky place, this headland, all the bare trees and the dark evergreens, the ruined chapel down the walk. To think this country's Crowning Stone could be hidden here.

It wasn't her country, but it seemed to mean a lot to her friend. 'It's not so much my country, more that I am its,' he had said as they crossed Rannoch Moor. 'Independence is a mirage, but I believe in this.' Strange place, to inspire such belonging. Alasdair, Shonagh, even Murray, they had it too. How different it must be to have this feeling. To be part of. Maybe not a weakness but an inspiration.

Well, well, she thought, stroking the rough overhanging rock, damp now with first dew. Who would have thought it?

*

Twenty yards behind her, Neil slowly circled the castle. No sign of weakness anywhere. Murmur of water through the trees where Lorne's galleys would have pulled up. The Stone too would have come by water, maybe from Iona, no distance at all across the Sound of Mull. Something real was waiting here. He could sense it all around him.

Inga was waiting at the foot of a stone staircase.

'Back to the village?'

'Aye, Al is probably in the pub.'

But still they stood there, looking around.

'I suppose that is the curator's car.'

'I suppose so.'

'There is no hurry. Let us just look from the top of the stairs. We should see water from there.'

And so they went up the stairs to where the little sign said 'Closed'. The sea glinted faintly through the trees. Neil pointed out the dark humps of Mull, Ben More silhouetted against the fading light. Then North towards Morvern and Cruachan. He told her 'Cruachan' was the battle cry of clan Campbell. Imagine running into battle shouting not the name of a king or a faith or a leader, but the name of a mountain.

They heard bolts drawn behind the door, then it slowly opened. Neil stepped forward, about to explain they were just looking around and would come back tomorrow.

'Miss Johanssen, welcome to my humble abode. Bring your new friend in with you.'

38

Neil went up the winding stair, past the crossed pistols. He glanced back. Inga swayed, looked as though she might collapse. Adamson, gun in one hand, gave her behind a slap with the other.

'Giddyup there. You – into the room.'

They stood in the sitting room. A settee, couple of chairs, a dusty display case. A bad smell, something darkly gleaming on the floor. As they turned to face Adamson, Neil instinctively took Inga's hand.

'Sweet,' Adamson observed. 'I was hoping you might be able to help me find a rather valuable Stone. For your sake, I hope you can. Tell you what – help me find it and you can keep all your fingers. Your friend might even keep his toes and other appendages. What d'you say?'

'Yes,' Inga managed. Her voice sounded strange to her, dry, foreign, ruined.

'Good. Very good.' He rattled two rings down on the display counter, picked up one between gloved fingers. 'You may recognize this one. It came from your brother's hand. Sit over there, on the chairs.' In the motion of sitting, Inga let her shoulder bag slip to the floor behind her feet. 'Now sit on your hands, children, and listen to the master. We have three inscriptions – yes, all three – and they indicate this place, Dunstaffnage. You must have guessed this, to come here?'

They nodded obediently.

'But there is no Stone waiting in the courtyard with a sign saying "Collect twenty million dollars".' He looked up at them, eyes ablaze. 'Yes, that much. I have a very wealthy and slightly mad client, a Scottish enthusiast you might say, who has outbid all the others. And I am of a mind to retire.' He gestured around the room, knife in one hand, a glittering pointer. 'All this becomes rather sordid, this killing and pursuing and persuading. It doesn't please me as it used to.'

'Bird watching,' Inga said. 'You want to investigate bird migration.'

Adamason beamed.

'Very good,' he said. 'You remembered. Yes, I will turn my talents to ornithology.'

And he thinks his client is mad, Neil thought.

The man was on a high, Inga could see that, she'd seen it in musicians coming off stage, still flying, looking for some more action. A time when mistakes get made. He might recover at any time. She back-heeled her bag half under the settee and kept her gaze on Adamson's face.

'In addition to Dunstaffnage, the rings have three more letters. P, T, U. I am hoping, Miss Johanssen, that as a Runner you may shed some light on what this might mean.'

He's like my sadistic old Latin teacher, Inga thought, except he has a knife instead of a chalk duster.

'I need to see the inscriptions in full, in good light,' she said. 'Where possible, the original runes on the rings, as well as the translations.'

He glared at her suspiciously.

'Why the originals?'

'Because it may be the exact positioning of the runes, plus the extra letter, has some meaning. My mother – she was a Runner – said something about the markings being like a compass.'

Neil blinked. She kept things to herself, this one.

Adamson considered.

'So you'll require?'

'Good light, a magnifying glass, a compass,' she said without hesitation. 'Also a plan of the castle and its grounds, and an Ordinance Survey map. Oh, and some tracing paper and an HB pencil.'

'And you think you can find the Stone?'

'I hope so,' she said. 'I want to live to play the banjo better.'

He stared at her. With difficulty she met his eyes, kept hers from dropping towards the bag behind her feet.

'Well, well,' he said softly. 'Find it, and I might throw in your boyfriend too.' He reached behind him, flipped open a small black case, felt around inside. He tossed her a pair of handcuffs, light and hard. 'Clip his wrist to that radiator. Now come with me, lady. We'll try and find what you need.'

Neil stood helplessly cuffed to the radiator pipe while Adamson had Inga search through an old desk in the corner. She found a guidebook with the castle plan. Adamson took a magnifying glass from his pocket, wiped it before handing it to her. He produced an OS map from his briefcase. She found a pencil.

'Compass and tracing paper,' Adamson said. 'Kitchens and hall. You wait here, Sunny Jim.'

Inga went out, down the stairs with Adamson behind her, knife hanging casually in his hand. Once they'd gone, Neil pulled at full stretch, tried to get a foot to her green leather bag. Half under the settee, it was just out of reach. Redemption lay slumped over, its drawstring loose. The radiator would not budge even a fraction. No way to pull that handcuff off. A stick, then? He waved his one free hand but there was nothing. No convenient broom handle or fishing rod. Life doesn't work like that, he should know by now.

I can hear the whistle, but I can't see the train.

He waited. Thought. Tried not to think. Waited, sick at heart, trying to keep his mind and feet off the sticky stinking darkness congealing on the wooden floor right next to a big old cupboard.

By the time Alasdair arrived at the barrier to the Dunstaffnage promontory, it was too dim for him to spot the dirt track that went round it. He shrugged, got out of the van and sniffed the different air of the West. Thought of the pub in the village, sitting there with the first of many lagers, waiting for Neil and Inga.

No, Jane had the right of it. The bevvy was becoming a problem. Take a recce first, then the drinks.

He sauntered up the road through the trees in the dimness, whistling quietly. 'Annie Laurie' it was.

Past the creepy chapel, ruined and half-hidden in the woods, around a curve and there it was. Real fuck-off castle, man. All dark, blank walls with slits. He crossed the grass, automatically put his hand to the rock base, checking it for holds. Some good bouldering on rough agglomerate. Above that was dressed stone, sheer of course, maybe a hundred feet to the top, but should be holds there if you knew how.

He came around the corner and saw two cars, one familiar. Blimey, they must be here already. Gone for a walk. Or maybe inside, though the place looked shut up. Best check. As he came to the stone stair that seemed to lead up to the way in, something blinked at the top of his vision. He walked back onto the grass and looked up. A row of rounded dormer windows stood above the battlements, and a faulty light was blinking on and off. There was even a silhouetted figure at the window, waving.

Being a friendly chap, he waved back. More waving. The light blinked on, off, on, off, on, off. Then a pause and three longer blinks. Then the three short ones again.

He was up that stone stairway at a run, pushed on the door. Solid. Quietly he turned the big ring handle and tried again. Locked or bolted. He looked up and experienced that clearing in the head and body that came rarely for him but when it did it made life worth living.

The corner, had to be. Back down the steps, put his right hand up on one sheer side of the wall, then got his body and other hand to the other face. Gonna have to lay-back this, all the way up. In the near-dark, sight unseen. In my best trainers.

Piece of duff, man.

* * *

'I think you're playing for time, missie,' Adamson said. He put his coffee mug on the glass-topped display case and glared down at her head bent over the map.

'Not playing,' she muttered. She placed the two rings at the upper corners, pulled down the third inscription and pretended to be examining it in detail. She steadied the tracing paper, drew a few lines through from the map. Took a compass bearing back to Dunadd Hill, as though all this mumbo-jumbo could achieve anything.

Because he was right, of course. She was playing for time. Her bag was still half-under the settee. Neil had not been able to get to it.

'Feel faint,' she said. 'Got to sit down.'

Clasping the notebook, she sat. Think. P, T, U. TUP. PUT.

'You've got two minutes to come up with something.'

That Latin teacher used to pull out his watch and count down. Sad little sadist...

She couldn't conceal her twitch of excitement. Adamson was onto it.

'You've got something?'

'Toss me that Guide.'

She caught it, opened, checked the castle plan as she felt with her foot.

'Not so hard or complicated, in the end,' she said. 'My mum and dad disapproved of formal schooling, but I rebelled and got myself what education I could.'

Adamson whacked the side of the display cabinet with his knife. A chunk flew off and fell into the sticky stuff at Neil's feet.

'Give it,' he said. 'No more games. Give it up.'

She stared back at him, kept her eyes up as she hooked her right foot round the strap.

'It's Latin,' she said. 'Do we have a deal?'

'The deal is I pass her ladyship through your friend's privates if you don't give it up in a count of five. Five. Four.' He took a couple of steps away from the cabinet, towards Neil, the blade starting its hungry shimmy. 'Three. Two.'

'P, U, T. *Puteus*, Latin. A well. The Stone is in the well.'

His long oval head tilted. Considered.

'Yes,' he smiled. 'Top marks. So now—'

'Put it down, pal.'

A shake went through Adamson, the knife stilled. He turned slowly to face the doorway where Alasdair Sutherland stood with a brass-handled duelling pistol, snatched off the stairwell, levelled at his chest. Then Adamson laughed.

'That's an antique, my friend,' he said. The knife came alive again. 'It's not even loaded.'

'This is,' Inga said behind him, and her hand came up from her bag with the long-handled gun, and she pressed and kept pressing till all her troubles were over.

39

Dunstaffnage Castle did not open to the public next morning. It did not even open to the baffled curator, turned away by two men without uniforms. He looked at the array of cars on the drive, at the two vans with grim-looking men emerging from one, then at the helicopter.

'Why not take the day off,' the young man in the very nice suit advised. 'Business as usual tomorrow.'

Once the curator had been escorted away, shaking his head at what he might tell them in the village, Abernethy turned away and hurried back up the stone stairway with Colonel Mitchell.

With an angle-grinder, they cut away the iron grill over the well. The two bodies had already left the premises, then the special cleaners went in and got to work. Jim MacIver, now released with Ellen from the upper tower room, was questioned, given firm instructions as to exactly how things went from here on in. He nodded, stony-faced.

The Naval diver abseiled down the well with a long pole, a camera and a powerful torch.

Food was brought, bacon rolls and coffee for those who could not leave, which included everyone still living. Inga shuddered at the dripping ketchup roll, took the coffee and stared at the grass. Nothing green there, nor blue up in the sky, only Adamson skewing round as the bullets ripped into him, the arm with the knife flying up in some monstrous salute, and in his eyes the gates of hell opening to her.

'Did what you had to, young 'un,' Alasdair said. 'He'd have

killed all of us and enjoyed it.' He bit into his bacon roll, suddenly starving, wishing he was allowed to phone Jane. 'Glad it wasn't me had to do it. Can't squash a fly these days.'

Nothing she could say to that. She silently watched Neil, deep in talk with the Scottish policeman she'd run away from in Oslo. After the killing Neil had held her tight for ages, which had helped. But this time he could not say 'It's not real'. When he finally let her go, she hadn't been able to look at him. Didn't want anyone to look at her.

The Canadian woman they had freed from the tower room came over and sat on the bench next to Inga. She put an arm around her and for a long time they said nothing, just watched the abseil rope tightening and slackening over the parapet of the well.

'I had to do it, once or twice, in the line of duty,' Ellen Stobo said quietly. 'Even when you know it's right, it's not right. Things are never the same after.'

'I thought I was one of the good people!' Inga cried. Ellen looked around the chilly courtyard where busy men were undoing what had been done, at the well where the lost might yet be found.

'At least now there is an after for things not to be the same in,' she said quietly, to herself as much as to the young woman quietly sobbing into her shoulder.

The sealed pouch lay on the curator's desk, still dripping slime. No carved stone down in the well, the diver reported, only this, lying in a big empty recess. Might have been a stone there once.

Abernethy cleared the room of assistants, leaving Colonel Mitchell, Inga, Jim and Ellen, Neil and Alasdair.

'Here we go,' he said, and cut open the bag.

Two metal rods with flattened discs on the end. Writing curled round the rims, not English or Latin.

'I'll give you a bad translation,' Ellen said, checking her notes. '"*Under your protective shadow lies the kingdom until angels carry you back to Bethel.*" The Destiny Stone casts the protective shadow, the kingdom is Scotland, and Bethel is an entirely spurious reference to Jacob's Pillow. These sconces were found along with the Stone in Dunsinnan Hill in 1819.'

'Blimey,' Alasdair murmured, put out his hand to touch them but Mitchell smacked it away.

'It seems the Stone has been moved yet again. Any suggestions where or when?'

It seemed no one had any. Abernethy reached inside the packet again and pulled out a little sculpture of a young man's chest and head, tilted it to the light and read out the inscription on its base.

'Delphi.'

Abernethy frowned. 'This is just some cheap little knock-off. It's not even stone. Any ideas what this means?'

'We've been taken for a ride,' Colonel Mitchell said.

'The Stone has been moved to Delphi?' Alasdair suggested innocently.

Ellen Stobo glanced at Jim who seemed deep in thought or prayer. She quietly nudged till she had his attention, then nodded. Neither of them said anything.

Neil stood beside Inga. When the firing had stopped she had not screamed or sobbed or fainted. He had felt only relief as Adamson shook apart then dropped. The cost, the aftershocks, came after. Now she finally looked up at him. He took her hand, her hand took his, their complicity sealed.

While the equerry told them all how things went from here, Neil gazed wonderingly at her, then out of the window to where the round-shouldered island hills were being stained red by the low sun. *This slop of quickening clay, how beautiful it is, how easily spilled.*

He had to tell Kirsty the dark adventure was over.

That afternoon, as the vans began to leave and the pilot sat patiently in the helicopter, Jim MacIver beckoned to Neil and Alasdair. They left Inga with Ellen and followed him down through the woods to the shores of Loch Etive. He removed his tweed bunnet and let the cool wind lift his wispy hair, as though he could think better that way.

He looked at the mountains of Mull while his mind went further West across the Minch. He thought on Skye, on Lewis, on Angus Og the *Ri Innse Gall*, and he tried to weigh his sense of what was right against what the Law required.

'I want to be meeting with you all in Edinburgh,' he announced. 'Especially Kirsty. There will be an enquiry, but they're minded to cover this up on grounds of national security, which I'm thinking is good news for your young friend.'

Neil nodded. He could see the complete abandonment of due process was deeply disturbing to their old adversary and friend. For himself, he could not forget Inga's face, the light in her eyes as she brought the machine pistol up, pressed and kept pressing till Adamson dropped in pieces on the floor. This was the same person who had calmly said, 'I am the most loyal person you're likely to meet.' The same quality made both true.

Kirsty seemed lightweight in comparison, an untethered balloon, bouncing merrily around the walls and ceilings of life's party.

'Good stuff!' Alasdair enthused. 'We'll go to the Café Royal – well, except for Murray, but I'll smuggle in a couple of cans for him – and yarn about all this till pigs fly home.'

Jim stared at him.

'By Crikey, you're an eejit, Mr Sutherland,' he said. 'And thank the Lord for that, for who else would climb those walls to pull an ornamental pistol on a madman?'

'All I could think of,' Al apologized. 'The bampot was about to deprive Neil of his goolies, the pistol was on the wall, so I grabbed it. Hey, I felt like a highwayman! Adam Ant!'

'You and Murray,' Neil said quietly. 'If you weren't both mad, we wouldn't still be here.'

They stood there for a while, silent by the small waves, breathing in, breathing out, being still here.

'A meeting,' Jim said firmly. 'We need to talk of the place called Little Delphi.'

He pulled on his bunnet and stomped off back to the castle.

40

Alasdair drove Tricia one more time from the hospital back home to Kirkintilloch. Murray had had his third operation and had been scanned, as Tricia said, more often than the public loos in Buchanan Street. His liver and colon both had permanent damage, his pelvis would probably never knit properly. He would function but not as before.

'I'll no be surprised if he starts a nationwide campaign for universal wheelchair access,' Trish said.

'The day Murray stops fighting the world is the day to start worrying,' Al replied.

'He's rejoined the Labour Party. Says there's going to be an election soon and things can only get better.'

Alasdair shrugged. 'Better, worse? Two monks once stopped me on the trail below Temboche Monastery in Upper Nepal. First one said he saw death in my eyes. The second told me that just to be here, we must have been promoted.'

A loud cracking sound came from the back. Tricia's hands flew out, she went white.

'Whit the hell is that?'

Alasdair reached one hand back over the seat, lifted a small cardboard box and put it in her lap.

'Open it.'

A large and warty toad eyed her back.

'Whit the fuck, Al?'

'I found it at the bottom of Dunadd. Thought you and Murray could do with it by your garden pond. You know, like they say in the song?'

'Song?' she enquired, glanced at her watch. Should be back in time to get the bairns' lunch. Get Mum in for wee Jamie, make sure Eve wraps up well for the trip.

'*You, who are on the road, must have a toad that you can live by*,' he sang.

Tricia covered her face with her hands, groaning.

'You deserve to die,' she said.

'I will, but not so soon. Nor will you. Nor will Murray. We'll have to settle for that, old girl.'

The blameless toad looked up at her and creaked uneasily. Jamie will love it, she thought. She closed the box, sat for a while silently watching home approach.

'Thanks,' she said at last.

Cold wind through dry branch at the foot of Dunsinnan Hill. Late afternoon sun with a hint of warmth in it begins to level over Scone as Kirsty and Neil climb. That old track down below was where the Stone had been taken to its first hiding place in the scene from Peter Sidlaw's forgotten novel. It seems that now it had come home, just as Andrew Jamieson had confided to his apprentice. In a few hours they will know for sure, but for now it is time to resolve other business.

'So you're not getting a thank-you session with Himself?'

'Not bloody likely. With all the stuff that's gone down and had to be covered up, his people are keeping him well away.'

'Shame. I always wanted a chance to turn down my OBE.'

Kirsty laughs quietly.

'Me too.' They keep on climbing the rough, steep path, choosing the next steps carefully. 'We were always just useful idiots, Neil. They got their real fake Westminster Stone back. Abernethy says they may return the fake fake to Scotland, to please the natives. I said "So long and thanks for all the macaroons."'

They puff onto the summit of Dunsinnan, taking in the humps, dips and wrinkles there. Many strange things under their feet, old strongholds, hiding places, bungled excavations.

Neil stares at the low hills of Fife on the South-East horizon. A body should always have something to yearn for.

'You see yourself ever going back to live there?'

'I've always wanted to end my days in the place I tried to grow up,' he acknowledges. 'Ideally a long time from now, in the East Neuk, somewhere on the low coast between Kaiplie and Crail.'

'I'd like to breathe my last by the shores of an unknown ocean.'

They stand a while, listening to what has been said.

'That's it, isn't it?'

She ducks her head and takes a deep breath.

'Yes.'

They turn to look each other in the face. Affection, friendship, now truly fond.

'Still love you but.'

'Me too, babes.'

Neil has a last look back to where he came from, where the darkness is silting up the valleys but light remains on the tops. Kirsty stares off West where the brief post-sunset light is flooding. Somewhere out there is a seat in the window of the world.

Then they link arms and bump back down Dunsinnan Hill.

'I suppose she's got her own strange charm.'

'In time you'll enjoy standing on muddy touchlines in the rain.'

They make the rest of the descent in silence until they reach the lay-by where the daffodils blow ragged.

'Hey, you reckon it will turn out to be the real thing?'

He looks across the roof of her car at her, drums his hands on the metal.

'Let's go find out.'

Shonagh walks down the institutional corridor – what do they do with all the air they remove from these places? – and enters Ailsa Traquair's office. She takes in the clean dustiness, the reference books, the order and the passion behind it. Sees the pallor of the long-faced thin woman behind the desk, her dark eyes slightly moist as they move over her, quivering like a ship's compass mounted on oil. Sees the flush come to those pale cheeks as they size each other up.

'You caused my friends a lot of problems,' Shonagh says. 'But Kirsty said I should come see you, and bring these.' She puts the sconces down on the desk, sees Ailsa Traquair's whole body come alive as she leans over them. Feels the mind begin to fly. What it is to care passionately. 'I hoped you can make up for it by taking discreet care of these.'

'I am so sorry. I was completely terrified of him. I want to help now. Anything at all.'

Shonagh looks at the pleading, fervent face framed by long black hair. She's straight from El Greco. Beautiful. Hasn't anyone noticed?

'Well, you can buy me lunch for a start.'

In a while they leave the Museum of Antiquities and go to the little African restaurant where they eat fiery okra stew and drink bottled Italian beer. And there Shonagh becomes funnier than she has known herself to be, finds how much she enjoys coaxing a smile onto that rapt face, and Ailsa discovers her life is not arid and pointless but interesting, entertaining and unexpectedly open-ended. And they both feel how good it would be to be looking, close up, into eyes that are not one's own in the bathroom mirror each morning.

As she lightly clasps Ailsa's elbow on the way out, crossing the road, Shonagh thinks *Càirdeas snog a' dùsgadh*. The beginning of a beautiful friendship. Maybe Kirsty knew fine what she was doing, sending me.

Well ensconced in the warm lobby of the Scone Hotel, Jim MacIver poured his beloved tea then looked at her gravely across the table. It had to be now, before the night's shenanigans.

'Ellen, there is something I need to say to you.'

She stopped with a buttered scone halfway to her mouth, then slowly returned it to her plate.

'Go on.'

'It's quite important, so please listen carefully. I don't think I can say it again. This is difficult...'

'You're making me worried.'

'But it has to be said. In all fairness to both of us.'

'Yes?'

He spread his big hands helplessly, looked down at them, wondering what the lines of his life meant, where they led. They led to this.

'Ellen, I have to say this. I have no choice. Or maybe I mean I have.' He looked up at her gravely. 'I'm not too old to learn to ride across the river into the trees and up into the Rockie mountains. I mean to say, for goodness sake, *a ghràidh*, please take me home and marry me.'

'You... You...' He looked back at her, chin propped on his fists, grinning. 'You deserve to be horsewhipped, Jim MacIver.'

'Can I take that as a yes?'

She picked up the buttered scone, then decided to add jam. Never too late to rock and roll.

'Can you promise me passionate sex from time to time, and holding each other when we take a lie-down in the afternoons?'

'I hear it's a broadminded country, and of late I am feeling pretty frisky. I'll even bring you tea and scones afterwards.'

She looked back at him.

'I warn you, James, I will never become a Free Presbyterian.'

He shrugged. 'I would not interfere with your private conscience. But you might do well to take some language lessons. That way you will understand my pillow talk.'

She munched into her scone. He drank his tea.

'Also,' he added thoughtfully, 'you would not be wanting to meet your Maker without a word of the Gaelic.'

In opposite directions, Leo and Inga walked slowly around the mound of Moot Hill. At the close of the day, it seemed right to come to see where it had all started, in the humped grounds of the now-vanished abbey. At the far side of the hillock, they met face to face. More accurately, her face at the height of his chest.

'I do have some people I miss,' Inga said, looking up. 'People that knew me when I was young. I don't see them often enough.'

He nodded, feeling the pang.

'New mates are good too,' he said. 'I'm not ready to go home. If it is still home.'

'Here is not my home, but these people care about it so much it makes me curious. Neil says independence is a slogan, not an option – do you think that is true?'

He looked down at her white, determined face. Hesitated then felt he had to say it.

'The old life has been kicked into touch, right? Best we can do is catch the new one and run with it.'

She put her hand on his sleeve, the first time she'd touched him since they'd been introduced. He could see she wasn't much of a one for touching, except when it mattered.

'Shonagh said about your daughter. I'm so sorry.' He nodded silently. She removed her hand, zipped her jacket up to her throat and shivered. 'Let's go read some minimalist novels on the tomb-stones over there. Then we'll get some hot tea and meet up with the others.'

As they walked towards the old graveyard, Leo said, 'So we're part of this bunch now.'

'What a strange thought, being part of something.'

'Could be worse.'

'Remind me exactly how.'

Leo stopped by the first funerary slab, its inscription high-lighted in grey-green lichen, and pointed down.

It was midnight before the last lights went out in Dunsinnan Hall. Then some very chilled people stirred under the pine trees, crossed the open ground and assembled outside the walled private garden once nicknamed 'Little Delphi' by the Dundas family. The current owners had come from the South of England. No reason to think they had a clue what was within.

The wall was high and topped with spikes but the moon tore free of the clouds and after his free ascent of the corner of Dunstaffnage castle, for Alasdair Sutherland this was almost disappointingly easy.

He disappeared over the top. They heard the thump as he jumped down. They stood waiting: Neil and Kirsty, Leo, Inga, Shonagh, Jim MacIver in his muffler and greatcoat, Ellen in her big Canadian down jacket. Tricia and Eve, moonlight shadows carved deep in their faces. Neil glanced round at his friends. How much older we look in this light.

'Why did you not tell Abernethy?' Kirsty muttered to Jim. 'You being the Law and that.'

'They made a desert of the Gaeltachd and now they want our Destiny Stone? I'd rather go and live in Canada.'

'But you are. Congratulations, by the way.'

'Thank you,' Ellen whispered. 'I hope you'll visit us there.'

'I've always wanted to ski the Rockies. Leo?'

'Good as, girl.'

A rope ladder came looping over the wall.

'Moon Runners first,' Neil said. 'Inga.'

She smiled at him, flash of teeth in the moonlight, pools of shadow in her eyes, then put her feet to the rungs.

Inside Little Delphi, ivy, rhododendron, fuchsia and hawthorn had run wild. With eyes adjusted, as the moon sailed through clouds like spilt milk, they moved watchfully through the ornamental garden. An Apollonian head glared down from its pillar. A row of sarcophagi like pale bathtubs. Neil found Leo pulling ivy away from a funeral stile and together they hunkered down to run eyes and fingers over the formalized grief, the living saying goodbye to the departed. *Et in Arcadia ego.*

They looked at each other.

'OK, mate?' Leo whispered.

'OK with me. You?'

'Good as.'

They let the ivy drape fall and moved on. Heads, busts, fake plinths lay half-sunk, lichen-encrusted. The antique statue of Ossian felt like some composite, maybe fibreglass mixed with stone dust. A small ring of Neolithic standing stones enclosed an Abyssinian winged lion. A miniature Sphinx crouched under a fuchsia bush. A copy of Cleopatra's Needle tilted into the arms of a beech tree, next to a standing stone with Celtic knots on one side, horsemen on the other.

'The battle of the seven kings,' Al whispered to Tricia. 'When Kenneth MacAlpin took over the Pictish kingdoms. Glad you came, lass?'

'I'm only here because Murray insisted.'

'Since when did you do what the red dwarf wanted?'

She looked at him, moons glinting in the damp corners of her eyes.

'Things have changed, Al.'

He looked down, obscurely ashamed.

'I'll be around, Trish. Get him back on his feet, like.'

'I know. Ta.'

At the end of the garden furthest from the big house, Eve stood by an ivy-smothered Greek temple. Neil saw his goddaughter's hands flitter like albino bats in the moonlight as she silently, frantically, waved.

Gently pull back the ivy, scrape off the moss, and look on the Destiny Stone.

It's big, a deal bigger than any Westminster Stone. Celtic knots swirl their double helix code down the blackened edges. Pictish salmon, wolf, stag, plus some beast that never was, are locked in chase all down the back. The top has a depression, maybe once a shallow baptismal font or simply a comfortable place to park one's arse. On one side, when the moon rides away from the cloud-tatters it faintly outlines a rampant bull, head twisted back, accepting the knife. On the other, Norse galleys in formation. The front – if it is the front – is a dense screen of carved foliage and waterhorses.

For a long time, no one speaks. They look, peer, touch, taking it in. Kirsty opens her mouth then changes her mind. They look at each other. In a kitsch garden where periods and cultures are mangled together, this is the real thing. And where better to hide it than among so many fakes, simulations and copies?

'Finders first,' Shonagh says at last. 'On you go, Evie.'

Eve in her duffel coat and the beret Neil gave her for Christmas, sits on the Stone. She will never forget those faces turned her way, the Stone so cold and hard beneath her as she accepts the honour and responsibility pouring down on her like the moonlight.

'Sherbet Fountain,' she whispers to herself.

It was a mongrel Stone we left there, many different races, styles and cultures inscribed together on it. Which was appropriate, if not necessarily tasteful, because we remain what we always were, a right mixter-maxter. A mongrel people. A strained but still-holding communality.

After all taking a turn on the Stone, except for Jim MacIver who stood watching without comment, quietly turning the ring on his finger, we pulled the ivy over it again, climbed back over the wall and melted into the night.

After all, no Stone, however symbolically loaded, can lastingly redeem our lives, any more than falling in love does. But the dark adventure to find and comprehend it, then knowing it really does exist and where to find it again, that just might.

So we left it there, without regret. Hand it over and most likely such a potent symbol would never be seen again. Or it would be just another thing we pay to queue for, and so it would become an imitation of itself. As it is, the Folly Garden is open to the public one weekend a year, and you yourself may push unobserved through the kitsch, part the ivy and sit on the Stone, rest the flat of your hands on its strange, hard lines, and sit up a little straighter, a little more awake.

Opening

Spring, and one fat blackbird whistles on the ledge. From our garden shed an albino blackbird whistles whitely back. Or did she start it, and he merely echoed her desire? Who knows. I seldom wake that early.

Inga sits cross-legged on the kitchen doorstep drinking coffee strong and black, banjo propped against her knee. She waves, I wave back.

Call and response, response and call, who can pronounce on the order of it all? We speak back the world after a brief delay, and the length of that lapse is exactly the distance we stand without the garden we are standing in.

Magic and loss, let them weigh the same with us as she takes up the banjo and airs an evolving Blues that is not so unhappy after all.

> *I can hear the whistle*
> *But I can't see the train*
> *Deep inside my heart*
> *Burns an inverted flame*
> *Been a long time getting here*
> *Gonna be a long time gone*

ACKNOWLEDGEMENTS

* *The Search for the Stone of Destiny* by the late Pat Gerber (Canongate) remains a broad-ranging, useful introduction to most aspects of the tangled histories of 'the Stone of Destiny'. She was a lovely, helpful person whose enthusiasm helped get me started on this novel.

'Where is the Real Stone?' by the late A.C. McKerracher (the *Scots Magazine*, Dec. 1984) is a detailed, clear-eyed and persuasive thesis on 'Columba's Pillow', which got me going and suggested a possible path through the forest of myths, lies, fakes, deceptions and wishful thinking that has grown up around, and helps to hide, the Stone. I went to talk with him twice about his research and my own take on it. He was open, hospitable and scrupulous. I liked him very much. He did not live in Crieff.

My thanks to Professor William Gillies of the Dept of Celtic & Scottish Studies at Edinburgh University, for seeing me right with the Gaelic. Also to Lesley Glaister and Sandy Greig for their helpful readings.

Many elements in this story are true. Among others are Edward I making off with the Stone of Scone, his furious response on believing he had been duped, the 1950 removal of the Stone from Westminster Abbey and the making of a (disputed) number of copies, the Scottish Templars and the church at Dull, the excavation of the crannog of Eilean Na Comhairle on Islay. Others – such as the continued existence of the ancient, ornamental

* Some of the characters in *Romanno Bridge* appeared in my earlier book *The Return of John McNab*.

Dalriadic Crowning Stone – are highly possible. A few are improbable, though I hope this does not include the emotional lives of the people whom I have accompanied in these pages. I hope there are no impossible things here, not even Adamson.